"Mike Baron writes like the bastard offspring of James Crumley and Rex Miller, in prose so hardboiled you'll break a tooth." —Jeff Mariotte is the former editor-in-chief of IDW Comics, and author of horror novels and thrillers including *7 Sykos*, *Missing White Girl*, and *River Runs Red*.

"Mike Baron is like Quentin Tarantino on paper." —Kevin J. Anderson is the *New York Times* best selling author of the Dune series as well as his own space-spanning series such as The Saga of Shadows and The Saga of Seven Suns.

"Mike Baron writes like he's thirty minutes ahead of us every step of the way. He's sending pop culture references and political perspective to us wrapped in bone-cracking action tales paced at ballistic speed. His people are real which makes the mayhem real. He bends prose to his will and makes you love every page. There is no one else writing with a voice as wild and different and strong as this samurai word-smith. His newest creation, Josh Pratt, pushes him even further out on the ragged edge of genre action fiction. Josh joins the Baron pantheon of entirely unique, fully-realized characters that touch something in he reader's heart and mind but continually offer surprise. This is not the Same Old Thing. Oh, the crazy-crazy, frenetic punch-ups are all here. Trust me on that. But so is Baron's gift to make us laugh, snort and question our own reality." —Chuck Dixon is the award-winning writer of *Clinton Cash: the Graphic Novel*, and a prolific comic writer notable for long runs on *Batman* and *The Punisher*.

"Biker hits you like a knuckleduster to the teeth. The prose is tough, tight, and totally entertaining. Josh Pratt is my kind of private eye—Biker tough, always relentless, and the instincts of a killer." —Paul Bishop, author of *Lie Catchers*.

"They say a tiger can't change its stripes, and with Mike Baron's character Josh, that's partially true. Josh has been hardened by life on the street, as well as behind bars. But he's got a new mission now. And when a courageous, struggling comics writer and artist begins receiving death threats, Josh seems like the only man to whom she can turn. Is she more than the crime-wise Josh has bargained for? There's certainly more to this red-headed comics bohemian, than initially meets Josh's eye. If you loved Jimmy from *Things To Do In Denver When You're Dead*, or Keaton from *The Usual Suspects*, you will instantly find Josh both enjoyable, and compelling. This is a terrific ride of a story that pulls no punches." —Brad Togersen, Hugo, Nebula, and John W. Campbell nominated writer.

BIKER

BIKER

MIKE BARON

Distributed in 2016 by Open Road Distribution
180 Maiden Lane
New York, NY 10038
www.openroadmedia.com

BIKER

CHAPTER 1

David Lowry sat on Josh Pratt's leather sofa with his arms on his knees, his disconsolate posture at odds with his chartreuse and magenta Hawaiian shirt. "Those dogs would never leave my yard. Never. We have the invisible fence! Louise is going crazy."

David and Louise Lowry were Pratt's new neighbors across the street. They had built their four-thousand-square-foot mansion three years after Pratt had moved into his modest ranch house. Now Pratt was surrounded by McMansions and his home was considered an eyesore. The remains of a '68 Camaro resting on cinderblocks in Pratt's front yard did little to dispel this impression. He'd refused to sign the petition for a neighborhood association but they'd formed one anyway and now he was in deep shit because he seldom mowed his lawn.

Lowry had showed up at Pratt's door at nine on a warm Thursday evening frantic and disheveled. Pratt thought, oh no, he's come to bitch about the lawn.

Instead he said, "You're a private investigator, right?"

Smelling money, Pratt nodded and held the door open. His private investigator career was stalled. He was thinking about going back to repo.

"You want a drink?" Pratt went to his liquor cabinet and pulled out a bottle of Jack Daniel's Black and two tumblers. He looked at himself in the mirror. He looked like a cage fighter. His skull had one eighth-inch buzz. His left eyebrow resembled a railroad track from prison fights. Inked biceps bulged from a sleeveless gray sweatshirt. Pale blue eyes looked back from a crackle finish, a delta of lines that made him look older than his thirty-four years.

Pratt got ice from the refrigerator and poured a couple fingers into each tumbler. He set one glass down on the scarred coffee table next to an S&S engine resting on an asbestos pad like a hot dish. Lowry grabbed the tumbler in both hands like a man seizing a life preserver and drank. Pratt sat opposite in an overstuffed chair he'd salvaged from Student Moving Week.

The fact was that for the six months he'd had his investigator's license his only work had consisted of delivering summonses for attorney Daniel Bloom.

"When did you first notice they were missing?"

"Around five. We searched everywhere. Do you have any idea what could have happened to them?"

Pratt rubbed the bridge of his nose. Pratt had introduced himself when Lowry first moved in, and Lowry, a University fund raiser, had been noticeably cool, like he'd opened his refrigerator and found a rat. Pratt had invited him over for a beer. Pratt had seen the faint sheen of disgust and a hint of fright in Lowry's eyes as he mumbled something to the effect that yeah that would be swell, one of these days. *What the fuck was this blue-inked biker doing in his neighborhood?*

And six weeks later here we are.

Pratt had a terrible thought. "I have an idea."

"What is it?"

"There are gangs on the south side who cruise neighborhoods for small dogs they use as 'bait' to train their pit bulls." Pratt didn't mention the old white Ford panel van he'd seen earlier. It had just looked wrong. He'd meant to write down the license but it sped away before he could get a look.

"In Wisconsin?!" Lowry asked, incredulous.

"I'm afraid so."

Lowry's face morphed into a mask of horror. "Oh, no no no! Not George and Gracie!"

Pratt had seen this before. You ripped the veil aside and life was full of maggots.

"Do you have a photo?"

"Are you online? Give me your e-mail address and I'll send them as soon as I get home."

Pratt didn't have a card. He took out one of Daniel Bloom's and wrote his e-mail address on the back. "That's a friend of mine on the front, you need a good criminal attorney."

Lowry stared. "Why would I need a criminal attorney?"

"I'm just sayin."

Lowry tucked the card in his breast pocket. He was sweating heavily and had a Nixonesque shadow on his jaw. He was in his late forties, an aging athlete gone to seed. Pratt could see Lowry's pink skull through a bad comb-over whenever he leaned forward. "I'd like to hire you to find George and Gracie. Can I do that? Do you search for missing dogs?"

"I get two hundred a day plus expenses. I report every Monday morning. If anything important turns up I'll phone you."

"Do you need a check? I forgot to bring my checkbook."

Yes! Pratt exulted. He needed a new roof. The septic tank was backing up. He was spinning his wheels, working on the basket-case Harley, waiting for something to happen. There had to be more to life than handing out summonses, raising hell on Saturday night and going to church on Sunday. God must have had a higher purpose when he sprung Pratt from prison and got him his license.

"Don't worry about it, Dave. We're neighbors. Send me those pictures and tell me what they were wearing, the color of their collars and what tags."

Lowry seemed almost pathetically grateful. He grabbed Pratt's hand in both of his. "Thank you. Louise will be so pleased to learn you're on this. She's been hysterical all evening."

Lowry and Pratt rose together. At the door, Lowry said, "When can you start?"

Pratt looked at his watch. It was nine-thirty. "I'll start right now."

CHAPTER 2

Pratt had once been Defense Minister for the Bedouins, an outlaw gang out of Milwaukee. It had been seven years since he'd been sentenced to prison for assault, possession of a controlled substance, possession of illegal firearms with intent to distribute and conspiracy to commit murder. He would still be there had it not been for Chaplain Frank Dorgan and attorney Daniel Bloom, who got his conviction overturned and helped him get an investigator's license with the complicity of a flexible judge.

Pratt put on a vest and leather gloves, went through the kitchen door into the garage and pushed the garage door button. The vinyl door retracted in a series of clanks, revealing a maroon Road King with a Screamin' Eagle kit, bobbed fenders and drag-style bars. He wheeled the bike out onto the gravel drive and got on. He reached into his tank bag and pushed the garage door remote. It was a clear, warm evening in July.

Pratt rode to the Anchor Inn at Schenk's Corners, a biker bar in the heart of Madison's blue-collar East Side. Across the street was a uniform store and a check-cashing place.

Pratt backed his Road King to the curb and set the stand. Eight choppers were lined up like heavy metal soldiers in front of the Anchor. Signs on the wall said "MOTORCYCLE PARKING ONLY." Seven of the choppers had ape-hangers, high bars that stretched you out like a drag chute. It was a shotgun bar—bar on the left, booths on the right, pool tables and restrooms in back. Pratt heard Bob Seger through the open door along with curse words breaking the surface of white noise like leaping dolphins.

It was ten-thirty and the Aztec Skulls were in town. The Inn was their favorite Madison bar. They had chased out all the other clubs. Even the C.C. Riders avoided the Inn when the Skulls were in town. Pratt touched the gold cross around his neck.

Lord please don't let me hurt anyone.

A familiar rush flushed outward from his belly. Pratt cycled air until he had things under control and pushed through the sea of bodies clustered around the open door. The bar was jammed. No one noticed Pratt. In his black leather vest, black boots, diamond earring and burred skull he looked like half the bikers in the bar. He scanned the crowd for familiar faces.

A haze of cigarette smoke hung at head level. To the cops it wasn't worth the hassle enforcing the smoking ordinance. Pratt glanced out the door as Madison PD cruised by in a plain-Jane Crown Vic. Pratt fitted himself sideways into the crowd like a nickel in a slot, working his way to the end of the bar. He caught the eye of the twenty-something waitress in Daisy Dukes with a butterfly tat on her shoulder. He ordered a Fighting Finches Maibock. Did that make him a faggot? So be it. He watched while the waitress worked the taps, drawing Bud after Bud for the Skulls. He counted six patches including two Skulls playing pool in the back.

The prez held court at the deep end of the bar surrounded by three bros, enough hair, muscle and leather to build a yurt. The rest of the crowd was East Side blue collars coming off the late shift at Oscar Mayer, a couple of well-tanned cougars in a booth and a handful of neighborhood drunks. The noise level was slightly less than a Boeing 747 taking off. The Skulls projected a two-foot force field in all directions.

Somebody bumped the juke. Bob Seger skipped a beat and a scuffle broke out. Two drunks fighting over who hit the juke. The head

Skull looked at the combatants with disdain. He was six three, 'roided out in wife-beater and leather vest with a broad Aztec face and Zappa mustache.

The drunks formed a scrum and penetrated the Skulls' force field, bumping into Zappa himself. The prez turned and without batting an eyelash slammed his bottle butt-first on top of a head. The other Skulls joined in and in an instant the two drunks were on the floor defending themselves against a fusillade of kicks from every side. The crowd moved back to give them room.

As quickly as it began it ended, like a summer squall that roars up out of nowhere and blows itself out. The prez turned away in disgust. "More beer down here!" he bellowed. Bottles of Bud slid down the bar. The Skulls preferred their Bud in a bottle because it made a better weapon.

Pratt slowly began to make his way toward the back of the bar. A boot extended from one of the booths. "Yo Josh." Pratt traced the boot to a familiar face. Brian Andrews owned Cap City Choppers, where Pratt had had his ride modified. Andrews had a shaved skull and mutton chops and was sitting with a pale-faced girl in a halter top with dirty blond hair down her back. Opposite was a biker and another woman whom Pratt didn't know. The biker's greased-up pomp and her bouffant were dyed an identical mahogany with caramel streaks.

"My man, my man," Andrews said, exchanging a slap dap with Pratt. "Scoot over, kitten. Make room for the man."

Pratt slid in. Andrews introduced the other couple as Forrest and Amelia, up from the Quad Cities on their way to the Ho-Chunk Casino, in Baraboo. An Altoid tin served as an ashtray, overflowing with a half dozen American Spirit butts. A lit cig dangled from Forrest's lip.

"You know what they say," Forrest growled. "You can lose a ho' chunk of change at that casino!" His laughter turned into coughing. Amelia smacked him on the back of his black leather jacket with the flat of her hand.

"Cough it out, baby. Cough it out."

"How's that chopper coming?" Pratt said.

Andrews was building a chopper with a custom frame and two Yamaha 650 engines in tandem. The bike had dual chain drives, one on each side of the rear wheel. The front fork jutted forth at an impossible angle. The front suspension was made out of a leaf spring from a '59 Chevy. It had a turning radius of a quarter mile.

"Takin' her to Sturgis next week. Wish me luck."

Pratt bopped fists. "You got it."

Andrews never missed the annual Sturgis Rally. He met his first two wives there. Pratt had been to Sturgis four times before he went to prison. Even from inside the walls, cons followed the annual rally closely on the Internet. The official Sturgis website listed fines for breaking such city ordinances as Indecent Exposure, Disorderly Conduct, Dog Running at Large and Pratt's favorite, Atrocious Assault.

Pratt nodded toward the rear. "What's goin' on?"

"Those motherfuckers are into dog fights."

"Dog fights?" Pratt said. "Really?"

"They should be shot," Amelia said.

"The head honcho was showing off pictures of pit bulls. Doing lines on the counter."

Pratt excused himself. "Catch you later."

He worked his way to the end of the bar where the Skulls clustered. A snork cut the air. A Skull was snorting meth off the mahogany bar with a cut-up soda straw. The bartenders looked the other way. The head Skull held a snapshot of a pit bull and showed it around. The pit had a scar slicing through one eye like a canyon.

"That's Money!" he said. "Money in the bank. He got jaguar in his blood, man."

"Nice Staffy," Pratt said.

The Skull turned toward him with pinpoint pupils. "What choo say?"

"Nice-looking Staffy."

"The fuck business is it of chours?"

Pratt held the leader's angry gaze. "None. I just know a good Staffy when I see one. I'd bet on that dog."

The leader stared at him with such fury Pratt steeled himself for attack. The prez was like some of the pits Pratt had worked with in the joint. You didn't know if they would bite you or lick your hand. Like a switch was thrown, the Skull's face morphed from anger to bonhomie as he grinned snarkily. "What's choor name, motherfucker?"

"Josh Pratt. What's yours?"

"Manny Robles. These scumbags are Dog Breath, Taco and Deuce. Make room for Josh Pratt. Choo know what, Josh? Choo *can* bet on that dog! What are you drinkin'?"

Pratt quickly drained his glass. "Bud."

Taco, who had the Harley logo tattooed on his forehead, looked at him with undisguised malice.

"Hey Annie honey!" Robles yelled, making a circular motion with his hand. "'Nother round!" He handed the photo of the pit bull to Pratt. "Sir Money his own bad self. He's fighting Chucho's Machine Gun, eighteen and oh." Robles watched Pratt closely for his reaction.

"Really. I would like to see that."

"Ride with us you'll see it." Robles held his hand up for a dap.

"How do we know this guy ain't a cop?" Taco said.

"Good question. Here's one way to find out." Robles reached inside his vest and removed a glass vial filled with white powder, took off the lid, shook a lump out on the smeared bar top and put the jar away. Robles flipped out a balisong knife with a flashy reverse maneuver and wrangled the powder into a line. Taco grabbed a straw from the bar and used his boot knife to cut off a three-inch segment, which he handed to Pratt.

"Hoover that," he said.

CHAPTER 3

"What is it?" Pratt said.

"What the fuck do you care?" Taco said. His swarthy skin was pockmarked like the moon. "You want to ride with the Aztec Skulls you do the line."

"'Cause I like cocaine but I don't like meth," Pratt said.

Robles put a hand on his shoulder. "Well choo in luck 'cause that there's straight from Hugo Chavez' house stash."

Pratt had done his share of coke and knew what to expect. He'd come to dread the howling void it left when it wore off, the countless wasted nights lying awake sweating, listening to his pulse. He hadn't done coke in years. One line. It would be fun for the first twenty minutes, not so much riding a bike at night.

Pratt took the straw, leaned over the bar and snorted half the line. He put the straw in his other nostril and did the other half. A surge of electricity jolted his nervous system. Instantly everything seemed brighter and sharper. Strength and reflexes grew exponentially. The boom of the juke's bass popped his soles like a suspension bridge. The waitress sashayed their way holding a tin tray containing five Buds and five shots.

Robles laid out lines for the boys.

Taco grabbed his shot, tossed it back and slammed the glass on the bar glaring at Pratt, daring him to do the same.

Fuck, Pratt thought. He took a shot and slammed it home. He got in Taco's face, so close he could connect the blackheads like constellations. "Still think I'm a cop?"

"I don't know, homes. Maybe you wearin' a wire."

Pratt could smell Taco's rank animal scent. "It ain't enough you see me snortin' blow, now you want to do a pat-down? You'd get off on that, wouldn't you?" Robles, Dog Breath and Deuce laughed. Taco showed his teeth. Pratt pulled his shirt out of his pants to reveal a six-pack with nothing on it but ink.

Robles put his hand on Pratt's shoulder. "It's cool, bro. It's cool. Taco's been up for three days. He won't sleep until he mangles some motherfucker."

"Hey Taco man," Dog Breath said. He was a young, powerfully built Hispanic with a goatee. "You get in another fight here they gonna eighty-six us. Chill, dude."

"Let's ride," Robles said. "Tell them fuckers."

Deuce went back to the pool tables and cued the brothers. People pulled away from the gang as they headed for the door like Poison taking the stage. Outside they climbed on their bikes.

Robles was parked next to Pratt. Robles rose up and came down on the kick starter three times before the engine roared to life with a shriek that made trash dance on the sidewalk.

Robles turned toward Pratt. "HEADIN' FOR THE ILLINOIS BORDER. JUST HANG WITH US!" Robles faced front and screwed two wax earplugs into his ears. Pratt reached in his tank bag and did the same.

Pratt gave him the thumbs-up, feeling the liquor in his belly, a bright sharp glaze in his head. He could handle it. Nothing to it. Muscle memory. By the time they got to the dog fight the coke would have run its course, leaving him jangly and wanting more. Robles in the lead, they pulled out one by one and headed up Williamson toward the State Capitol. Taco waited until Pratt pulled in line behind Deuce before leaving the curb.

They cut over to East Washington, where they picked up a Dane County Sheriff's cruiser that followed them around the Square, out West Washington to the Beltline. Pratt felt the atavistic satisfaction of being part of the pack. Nobody fucked with the pack. It must be like how a wolf felt. Or a jackal. They turned south on Highway 14. The county mountie followed them all the way to the county line. In his rearview Pratt saw the big HPO get out of his car with a Smokey hat and stand there watching until they were out of sight.

At Brooklyn they turned off the highway onto a county road.

The bikers headed south through heavily forested hills, the din of their engines careening off the trees and rolling over the fields. Robles set an 80-mile-per-hour pace. The Aztec Skulls clustered in tight formation like fighter planes. Pratt always thought he had too much imagination to ride. He could easily envision the aftermath of a clash at speed. He'd seen it happen. Twisted bikes, smashed bodies. No one wearing helmets. Brains like spilled oatmeal.

Stay cool, Josh. Don't freak yourself out. Light touch on the bars and keep your eyes down the road. Fucking Taco was right on his taillight. If Pratt had to brake there'd be a collision. The convoy entered a thickly wooded area, trees coming right up to the ditch. The deer was the most lethal animal in North America. It caused 235 fatalities a year. It leaped in front of traffic in every state, but particularly in Wisconsin. Pratt nervously eyed the tree line. Any deer stupid enough to ignore their rolling thunder deserved to die. Pratt did not want to join them. They were clustered so tightly together that if one went down they all would.

Pratt laid off the throttle. Taco pulled up alongside and shouted, "Twist it, homes! We ain't fallin' behind!" Taco opened his throttle and shot forward, his bare-bones 102-inch chopper exploding with torque and sound, 130-decibel Bronx cheer. Pratt struggled to keep up but at least he was now the tail and didn't have to worry about being back-ended by some cokehead.

They roared through a tunnel of trees, leaves and twigs jumping in their wake. They entered a timeless space where nothing existed but the infinite road and the sensation of speed. No thought, no self, only the droning groove of the engine through seat and handlebars into the bones and the wind whipping past. It brought back memories of countless nights running with the Bedouins. *My pappy said, "Son you're gonna drive me to drinkin' if you don't stop drivin' that hot rod Lincoln."* Pratt couldn't get it out of his head. The night smelled rich with loam and pine. Moonlight dappled the road. The forest dropped away and they were once again in farmland, clusters of lights like tiny freighters on the rolling prairie. Somewhere south of Janesville the smooth blacktop changed abruptly to tattered asphalt as they crossed into Illinois.

The convoy turned off onto winding gravel. Pratt caught a glimpse of the street sign: Jorgensen Road. A farm up ahead. Robles slowed down. The bikes clustered at the gate. There was a dude with a sawed-off. He was Mexican, had a shaved skull the shape of a howitzer shell and wore a ground-length duster. Robles hung inside the gate while the others roared into the farmyard. Pratt pulled up. The dude with the shotgun eyeballed him with thinly veiled disgust.

"Who's this?" he grunted.

"He's with me," Robles said.

Howitzer waved them through. There were a dozen-plus bikes parked on the hard-packed earth outside the barn, plus a half dozen pick-ups and an old Ford van. Fifty yards away and up three steps was the two-story wood-frame farmhouse, lush planters hanging incongruously from the veranda. The sound of a locomotive emanated from inside the brightly lit barn before breaking down into its components. Men shouted and dogs snarled. It was the opposite of music. The keening yowl of a dog in pain cut like a knife.

Pratt pulled in next to Taco, reached in his tank bag and tossed a coffee can lid on the ground. He kicked the stand out onto the lid. He followed the Skulls into the barn where three dozen men, most in leather and colors, surrounded a fighting ring that was a fifteen-foot square enclosed by a four-foot wood fence. The floor of the ring was covered with straw, much of it stained black from blood. Outside the ring, men tended their dogs, thick-shouldered scarred pit bulls who'd known neither love nor tenderness. A panting, downed dog lay on the straw. Its owner entered through a gate, grabbed the gasping animal by the scruff of its neck and dragged it out of the barn whimpering in terror.

Seconds later there was a gunshot.

Pratt looked around and wished he hadn't. A man beat a dog with a heavy leather strap. "You! Worthless! Piece! Of! Shit!" The dog lay on its back, an arc of yellow piss hitting its belly in terror. Pratt forced himself to look away.

It was just dumb luck. Lowry hadn't known about Pratt's biker past. The fund raiser had serendipitously called on the one private investigator in town who knew what had happened and where to go. Luck. That's all it was. Pratt would keep telling himself that in the days to come.

Pratt had never liked dogfights, and the Bedouins never had a thing to do with them. But a lot of bikers did.

Pratt loved dogs. He'd loved Barkley most of all. He remembered the day when Duane, his father, brought home the squirming ball of fur and handed it to him. "Here. Don't say I never gave you nothin'." It had been Pratt's tenth birthday.

The pup had chewed its way through their rented trailer, chewing one of Duane's good cowboy boots. Duane came home shit-faced, saw the boot and went after Barkley with a .357.

"No Duane!" Josh shouted, grasping the dog and leaping out into the trailer park, where he hid in the equipment shed all night until his father passed out and it was safe to sneak back into the house. Duane was still passed out when Josh got up the next morning and took the 7:00 bus for school after stashing Barkley with a friend.

Pratt missed Barkley more than Duane.

About half the crowd was Latino, the rest redneck trash like him. No women. A man built like a Sherman tank, arms blue with ink, dragged his snarling "Staffy" into the ring. As if they could rub the stink off what they did by calling their pit bulls Staffordshire Terriers. A freak in Oshkosh B'Gosh coveralls, skin scarlet with rosacea and 'roids, followed restraining a lunging beast, its fur streaked with blood where teeth had gouged furrows in its flesh.

Pratt had seen enough. He looked around. Money was changing hands. All eyes were on the ring. The Skulls snorted ice and tossed back Jell-O shots from a Coleman cooler. Pratt edged out the door. Nobody gave a shit.

The yard was lit from a pair of flood lamps mounted high on the barn. The air was cooler outside. The soundtrack of hell emanated from within. The old Ford van was parked sixty feet away in shadow, off by itself. As Pratt approached he heard whimpering and scratching from within.

The rear doors contained no windows and were not locked. Pratt opened the doors with a nerve-wrenching shriek. A raw animal stench, part shit, part fear, nearly knocked him down. The back of the van contained three rows of cages on each side in which small dogs and cats had been imprisoned without water or bedding. The floor was covered with tools. One cage held a Yorkie with a sequined collar. Another held a marmalade cat. Two schnauzers yapped at him in desperation.

"George and Gracie I presume," Pratt said reaching for the cages. He eased them out and set them on the ground.

"HEY ASSWIPE," penetrated Pratt's head like a particle beam. "WHAT THE FUCK DO YOU THINK YOU'RE DOING?"

CHAPTER 4

The coke had left Pratt jittery. He rode that jitter and the frisson of fear and excitement he got from the Voice. A familiar fury amped up his nervous system, a willingness to engage, an I-don't-give-a-fuck ethos. His mind worked strikes, take-downs, submissions. Ignoring the Voice, Pratt scanned the floor and spied an ax handle.

"HEY MOTHERFUCKER I'M TALKING TO YOU," the Voice blasted. Pratt slammed the van doors shut, shoving the caged schnauzers behind him with his foot. He held the ax handle by his left leg and looked at the Voice.

A skinhead the size of a Kodiak bear wearing a black leather vest that highlighted his massive biceps and pecs strode toward Pratt in steel-toed boots. An unreadable message in blue Gothic script splayed across his chest. The tat on his left arm showed a rattlesnake winding through a skull. The tats on his right arm were so thick they looked like a screen. He had a metal stud in the center of his chin over a Billy goatee that looked like a woman's pussy hair. A patch on his vest identified him as a Mastodon out of the Quad Cities. The Mastodon's homeboys boiled out of the barn joined by most of the house, high on ice and Jell-O shots.

Heart going *boom boom boom* Pratt held his right hand up like a traffic cop. "Stop!" he commanded.

The Mastodon stopped, an expression of utter disbelief on his concave face.

"I'm a private investigator. All I want are these two dogs. Let me have them and I'm out of here."

How was he going to get them out of there? Bungee them to the back of his bike?

"You ain't a cop?" The Mastodon was incredulous.

"I'm a private investigator. All I want are the dogs."

"I DON'T THINK SO MOTHERFUCKER." The Mastodon advanced, eyes blazing with incendiary rage and joy.

"Kick his *ass*, Barnett!" someone called.

"Beat *down!*"

Cell phone cameras appeared.

Mumbling obscenities Barnett came at Pratt like a linebacker.

Bending like a sprinter Pratt ran straight at the big man, swerving and ducking at the last minute as he whacked Barnett's left knee with the ax handle with the satisfying smack of Barry Bonds knocking one out of the park. Barnett sank like the Twin Towers. Two Mastodons calved like icebergs from the crowd, one swinging a chain, the other gripping a Bowie knife the size of Rhode Island. Pratt stepped backwards onto Barnett's head, grinding it into the dirt.

Thank you, God, they don't have guns.

That could change in an instant. Pratt had heard a gun. He'd thought about bringing one. He wished he had one. The Mastodons split, the one on Pratt's right grinning as he swung the chain in a figure eight. They planned to catch Pratt between them. Pratt danced backward to the van, flung the door open and grabbed a two-pound steel wrench. The chain guy rushed and lashed out, bringing the heavy chain down in a vertical arc meant to bash Pratt's skull. Pratt juked to the right and threw the wrench ass over teakettle with as much spin as his thick wrist could deliver.

The chain guy's mouth went oval an instant before the wrench struck him in the middle of his forehead with the jawed end. The chain guy staggered back two steps and sat heavily on his ass.

"*Uf*-da!" someone said. "That's gotta smart."

"Yo Barnett."

Barnett sat up clutching his knee. "Shit!" he spat. "What's the matter with you assholes? Fuck him up!"

The other Mastodon danced forward, knife moving in a tight little pattern. The freak was between Pratt and the van so Pratt did something he'd seen in a *Punisher* comic book. He scooped up a handful of pea gravel and hurled it in the knife man's face. The dude instinctively threw up his hands. Pratt rushed in with a kick to the nuts that lifted the hapless Mastodon off his feet. He fell to the ground howling and curled up like a shrimp.

"*Hay*-zeus," someone reverently intoned.

An anaconda-like arm snaked around Pratt's neck. He grabbed hold of the elbow with both hands to work a little breathing room but by then a couple more Mastodons had moved in to deliver kidney-rupturing body blows. Pratt kicked up and caught someone in the jaw.

An instant later he was driven to the ground by the sheer force of blows. Now it was his turn to curl like a shrimp as bikers went to work with steel-toed boots. Pratt couldn't see daylight. He tried to shield his head and gut as blows rained down like a meteor shower. Bone-deep pain churned through his ribs. Pratt had a very high pain threshold. He was near red line. A wooden bat bounced off his ribs with soul-stopping force and he began to wonder if he was going to make it out of there alive. A slick nausea ballooned from his broken nose and worked its way to his stomach.

All for two dogs.

The smack-in-the-face report of a shotgun instantly sucked the air out of the yard. Heads swiveled. "Back away from him. Get back or I'll blow your fuckin' heads off," a woman said. Pratt incongruously registered her sexy contralto and wondered if her looks matched her voice. Gradually, grudgingly, the bikers backed off. One last kick to the kidney from Taco who held the bat.

I'll be pissing blood for a week, Pratt thought.

Slowly, painfully, he got to his feet. Cracked rib. Jolts of pain radiated through his thorax like starving cats released form a cage. Loose jaw and lumps and abrasions up and down both sides. He turned toward the shooter. She stood atop the three stone steps leading to the farmhouse holding a pump-action Remington in parade position. His first impression: That body. Latino voluptuous. *Huh! Good God!*

"He's a fuckin' *cop*, Cass!" Barnett said, hanging onto a brother.

"I'm a private investigator," Pratt said. "All I want is the dogs."

A rumble of discontent rolled through the barnyard. The night was young. There were dogs which hadn't fought. Some bitched about the interruption. Others bitched that the fucking Skulls had brought an outsider.

"Hey," Cass said, setting the shotgun on its butt. "Hey! You know what? Y'all been here all day, fightin' your dogs, pissin' in my yard and suckin' down my hard cider. It's one thirty in the morning. Why don't y'all get out of here? That's it! Show's over! Nice seeing y'all!"

"You're getting' paid," someone rumbled.

"Yeah, until I say when. Well it's that time of night, gentlemen! Pack up your pit bulls and go home."

More grumbling. Some of the boys were looking at the woman with ill-concealed lust, figuring their odds against the shotgun. Might be worth it A tawny-haired beauty of five six in ass-hugging jeans and Luchese boots wearing a flannel shirt tied off across her taut belly. Wide mouth and fearless green eyes. A scar along her chin line only made her more interesting. While bikers bitched Pratt edged his way out of the crowd toward the steps leading to the farmhouse.

Damn, he wished he'd brought a gun.

Too late for that. She'd likely saved his life. He had to stand by her. He turned at the base of the steps and faced the yard. Most of the bikers had gone back to their original clusters and with much grumbling were loading dogs into pick-ups.

"You know bitch, we might not come back," someone said.

Cass half-lifted the scatter gun. "I reckon I can live with that heartbreak."

"Yo, bitch," said an Aztec warrior. "Maybe we come back when you ain't expecting. You ever think of that?"

Cass put the scatter gun on target. "Bring it on, Salazar."

The Aztec shrugged and walked to his hardtail.

Motorcycles cleared their throats, a mechanical cacophony that rose and rose until the ground shook and every bird had fled. They heard it in Chicago. One by one the bikes roared out of the yard up the dirt road, leaving a cloud of dust that hung in the air like the aftermath of some disaster. One by one the pick-ups followed until the last set of taillights disappeared in the cloud of dust and the last straight pipe coughed a mile up the road.

Pratt turned and looked at the woman.

"Thanks."

"Can you walk? Come on up and have some coffee."

CHAPTER 5

Pratt followed the woman up the stone path, up three wood steps and into the old farmhouse. She walked with an unself-conscious metronomic sexiness. Stoked by exhaustion, adrenaline and post-coke jitters, Pratt was glad he'd worn a cup. He had a hard-on like a Saturn booster. A stitch in his side screaming with every step couldn't put a dent in it.

Every time he saw a woman he'd like to fuck he got a hollow, hammering sensation in his chest. Possibility and failure. This one had an ass like a ripe peach. Pratt knew guys who'd let the genie out of the bottle. He was afraid what his own genie might do, if he ever let it loose. He said a silent prayer.

He didn't care that the babe was hosting dogfights. He didn't care if she was a murderer. He just wanted to fuck her.

The woman opened the screen door and Pratt followed. It slammed shut behind him. She walked past a staircase through a living room outfitted in fifties shag into a lit kitchen with a well-grooved hardwood floor. The round kitchen table was made of oak with four oak chairs. There was a pot of coffee on the stove.

She set the shotgun down in the corner, turned and offered her hand. "Cass Rubio."

She had a firm, warm grip. She smelled of jasmine and a touch of something tart. "Josh Pratt. This your farm?"

"I'm a renter. Have a seat. Would you like some day-old doughnuts?"

"Yeah sure, why not."

Cass set a white bakery box on the table. "You sit while I get the first-aid kit. You looked dinged-up pretty good."

"I think I got a cracked rib."

"Poor baby." Cass entered a bath off the kitchen and returned with a white metal box marked with a red cross. She set it on the table and opened it. She used a cotton swab dipped in rubbing alcohol to mop up the cuts and abrasions on his face. She applied a jumbo Band Aid that covered half his forehead. Her fingers were cool to the touch and each time she touched him she sent a jolt of electricity straight to his groin. He shifted and adjusted to hide his erection. Of course it was all fantasy. A genuine looker like this wouldn't tumble for a grimy ex-con.

"Take off your shirt."

Pratt peeled off the vest and shirt. She stared at the dragon tattoo winding around his torso. "You'd make a nice mural for a Chinese restaurant." She touched the crude cross on his bicep. "This doesn't fit."

"The price was right."

She touched his ribs and he winced. "You could play the xylophone on these. This must be the rib, huh?"

She poked again and he flinched, gasping. Her scent was pure sex, something she got at Walmart named after a celebrity.

"I don't have enough bandage to do it right so I'm going to have to use duct tape."

Pratt nodded. Cass opened a kitchen drawer and took out a spool of gray tape. She wrapped it around his ribs and over the shoulder so that he felt he was encased in high-flex body armor.

"How's that?" she asked when she'd finished.

Pratt shifted. "Great. I can barely move."

"You should see a doctor. I only had one year's nurse's training."

She brought him a mug of coffee and plunked whole milk in a carton on the table. They sipped coffee and ate day-old doughnuts.

"Are you really a private detective?"

"Yes. My neighbor hired me to find his schnauzers. I got lucky because I know a little bit about cycle gangs."

"You got lucky all right."

Pratt grinned. "You saved my life."

"Doubt it. They're nasty but they're not killers."

They sipped coffee in silence.

"Do you find people?"

"Sometimes."

"Reason I ask, I have a friend, a very close friend who's Crohn's. Sixteen years ago she gave birth to a boy. When the boy was two his father stole him and she hasn't seen him since. Is that the kind of thing you do?"

"Yeah. I'll give you my card, she can call me." He pulled one of Bloom's business cards from his wallet and wrote his phone number and email address on the back.

Cass looked at the card, shrugged, put it on the table.

"I want you to meet her. We're kinda short on time here because she's married to this big-shot builder who has no idea of her past. He's on a business trip right now but he'll be back Monday. I wonder if it would be possible for you to meet with her this weekend. Money is not a problem."

Pratt shrugged and winced. "I guess. I've got to get those dogs back. I'm on a motorcycle."

"I've got a Ram. I'll help you return the dogs if you'll meet with my friend."

"Does she know you're doing this?"

"Yes she does. She asked me to find someone. Pure luck you showed up here tonight." She gazed at him frankly with those deep green eyes. Pratt went a little vertigo. He remembered the dog pissing itself in terror.

"Mind if I ask you a question?" he said.

"Shoot."

"You seem like a nice lady. How come you're allowing dogfights in your barn? You know who those people are?"

Cass exposed Chiclet teeth. "I know those people better than you think. I needed the money. I'm through now. It's over. Seeing what happened tonight I've made up my mind."

"What do you do when you're not running dogfights?"

She leaned back and crossed her legs. The bottom of a rose tattoo extended beneath the cuff of her jean. "I sell fireworks."

"Really?"

"You know. Black Cats, Roman Candles, Whistling Buzz Bombs. I run a string of five stands from here to South Dakota beginning in mid-June. You see that big fireworks sign out by the interstate just north of Janesville? That's mine. I used to work as a magician's assistant but he died in one of his escapes."

"So you got stands out now."

"Yup. I make my rounds on Monday."

There was a hint of a smile at the edge of her mouth. Was she jerking him around? He had no way of telling. He was clueless about women. His girlfriends had all been either drug addicts or insane. Cass gave off good vibrations but she was setting off warning bells too. Dogfights were a problem.

Pratt loved dogs. Always had. He'd participated in the Puppies Behind Bars program, raising service dogs for disabled veterans. Ever since his old man had brought home that squirming mutt when he was ten years old. Of course a couple years later ol' Duane got mean drunk one night and drove Barkley across town and dumped him in a strange neighborhood. A couple years later he did the same thing to Pratt.

"You worked for a magician? Where was that?"

"Little carnival called Deming and Gold's International Cavalcade of Stars, out of Oakton, Florida. They went bankrupt a while back. Gave the elephant to the Milwaukee Zoo."

"Where you from, Cass?"

"What are you, investigating?"

"I can't place the accent. You're not from around here."

"I was born in Florida, lived all over the south. What about you? I don't see a wedding ring."

Pratt laughed. That was never in the picture.

"No girlfriends?"

"Nope."

"No significant others? Pets? Dogs? Cats? Boa constrictors?"

"Nope."

Cass pulled a pack of Marlboros from a drawer in the table and lit it with a Zippo. She blew a smoke ring at Pratt. "I had a bad experience with dogs once."

Pratt didn't know what to say. She wanted something. He wasn't clear what. He wanted something too but hadn't a clue how to get it. He hadn't slept in twenty-two hours and was seeing spots at the rim of his vision.

"You seem like an interesting guy."

Pratt shrugged. "I don't know about that."

"Do you like me, do you like what you see?" Cass said.

Pratt nodded.

Cass stood, arching her back and taking a long draw on the cig. "No place going anywhere tonight. Come on upstairs with me."

"I could sleep on the sofa."

She looked down her chin at him. "Do I have to spell it out for you?"

CHAPTER 6

"Son," Duane once told him. "Every now and then you're going to come across a setup that seems too good to be true. Take it. Women really are crazy."

If there's one thing Duane knew it was how to talk women into bed. He had no idea how to keep them or forge a relationship based on love and respect, and he duly passed that void onto his son. Duane lived by two mottoes: any woman could be had, and he who strikes first wins.

Pratt followed Cass up the Mayan stair, a mule following a carrot. She led him to a bedroom beneath the eaves with two windows looking out on the front yard. A faux Tiffany lamp on a night table cast a warm glow. The room had a hardwood floor with a couple of scatter rugs. A framed Monet print hung on the wall next to a black and white photograph of a group of bikers, men and women, in front of Devil's Tower.

Cass stopped just inside the door and turned around, pressing herself into Pratt. His hands automatically cupped her ass and they swayed into a deep soul kiss that left him gasping like a gaffed fish. She put her hand between his legs and flashed a wicked grin. "What's this?"

Pratt blushed crimson. "A cup."

Cass appraised him with a hint of respect. "Give me a minute."

Pratt couldn't believe his luck. He'd never been good with women. His longest relationship had lasted three months. She'd left him because he was a "thug loser."

Thank you, Jesus, he thought. Was that appropriate?

Pratt took off his shoes and socks. The door to the bathroom opened. Cass walked toward him nude. She turned around displaying a Harley tramp stamp on her ass: a unicorn. A garland of tattooed roses circled her left breast. Another rose on her neck.

"Take 'em off," she commanded, yanking off his jeans like a magician pulling the tablecloth out from under a place setting. His ribs strobed white hot. She peeled off his cup and supporter and tossed it in the corner.

Cass leaned over him and shut off the lamp. The glow from the yard lights was more than sufficient to illuminate her perfectly toned body and satin skin that tasted of cloves.

"Just lie there," she growled, straddling him. "Let me do all the work." He grasped her hips. Her high, small breasts brushed his gold crucifix. As she lowered herself onto him pain intensified his pleasure, like a single drop of black in a bucket of white paint. Cass pinned his wrists with her hands and moaned while she stared into his eyes. She reached behind her to cup his balls in one hand.

Afterwards they lay side by side staring at the ceiling fan. Cass lit a cigarette and blew rings into the downdraft, where they whipped to mist. Pratt wondered what he'd got himself into. He didn't believe in love at first sight. He wasn't sure he believed in love at all, except for God's, and that had come only lately.

Pratt dozed off for a couple hours, popped out of it at the crack of dawn.

Still tired, there was no way Pratt could sleep. Too much too quickly. Too many things to digest. Were the Mastodons coming after him? How soon should he phone Lowry? Was this the beginning of a relationship or two ships passing in the night? Did he want a relationship? He was used to being alone.

Cass' hand drifted across his stomach. "That's a wild tat. Who did it?"

"Kasamura Oda. Twenty-eight hours non-stop and two bottles of Scotch."

"I'm too wired to sleep."

"Me too."

"Let's go get some breakfast and then we'll drop your dogs off."

"Oh shit." Pratt swung his legs off the bed and pulled on his skivvies and trousers. He moved as fast as the bandages and pain allowed. Crabbed down the stairs, banged out the front door and stiff-walked to where he'd left the two schnauzers in their cages. One was up and looking at him with a piteous expression, big brown eyes pleading, *Where's my breakfast? Where are my people?* The other was asleep. Stacking the cages, Pratt took them into the barn and released them in a horse stall.

"Hang on, fellas."

He found a metal pail, filled it from a ground faucet and put it in with the dogs, which drank head to head like magnetic Scotties.

Going back to the house was harder than leaving. It was all uphill. Pratt hung onto the plumbing tube railing, then the wood banisters on the porch. He climbed the steep stairway hanging onto the rope banister like an ancient penitent approaching a mountain monastery. Pratt showered. Thinking about the night gave him a hard-on. He wasn't about to let this one slip away, not if he could help it. He had no clue how to proceed.

All his life he'd believed there was a secret book outlining proper behavior under any and all circumstances and everybody had a copy but him.

Should I go for another round? What if she's not in the mood? Will I make a fool of myself, lower myself in her eyes? Where's my lifeline? Somebody give me a clue.

Cass was downstairs cleaning up in the kitchen when Pratt came down the stairs hanging on to the rope banister. She wore those same damned jeans, a Sturgis T-shirt over no bra, her auburn hair tied in a ponytail sprouting from the back of her Brewers' hat. She carried a fat black leather Harley wallet with a chain around her belt.

The shotgun was nowhere in sight. Cass led the way out the door, down the steps, down the path, down three more steps to the barnyard where Pratt's bike remained as he had left it.

Thank you Jesus no one fucked up my bike.

Cass went to a separate two-car garage, backed out a black Dodge Ram right up to the stone retaining wall surrounding the house. She opened the gate, pulled out a slab of plywood and laid it between truck and lawn.

"You can ride your bike around back and load it into the truck here."

Pratt did as she said. Pain prevented him from exerting the necessary pressure to bungee the bike in place. All he could do was sit on the bike and use his weight while Cass yanked on the nylon belts, cinching them tight.

They put George and Gracie in the back of the truck and drove to a Cracker Barrel on the Interstate. They sat opposite each other in a booth and ordered Denver omelets. Pratt downed three Tylenols.

"How are the ribs?" Cass asked over a cup of coffee.

"I've had worse."

"Okay, Tarzan."

"I used to ride with the Bedouins."

"What happened?"

"I got busted. Did four years at Waupun. I came to Jesus while I was in prison and straightened out my life. I have a good lawyer who got my record expunged and helped me get an investigator's license." Pratt left out Judge Harvey Bannister, a Bloom crony and the subject of an ethics investigation.

"Are you one of those Jesus freaks?" A wrinkle of concern climbed Cass' forehead.

"What do you think?"

Cass smiled slowly. "If you are, you're the craziest Jesus freak I ever met. Wasn't Jesus supposed to be a pacifist?"

"No, that was Ghandi. Jesus kicked ass when he had to."

The waitress brought their breakfast. It was eight by the time they finished, late enough to call Lowry.

The fund raiser answered on the first ring. "Dave Lowry."

"Dave, this is your neighbor, Josh Pratt. I found your dogs."

"You what? That's great, Josh! Great! Honey! Josh found the dogs!"

Shrieks and jubilation. Pratt promised to be there in an hour. He grabbed the check when it came and paid it with his MasterCard. As they headed to Madison, George and Gracie with their snouts in the wind, Pratt's cell phone rang. He looked at the little window.

"Hello, Danny," he said, greeting his friend and mentor. "What's up?"

"Got a job for you. Can you stop by this morning?"

"How about eleven?"

"See you then." The lawyer hung up.

They rode in silence. Cass turned the radio on to a blues station out of Chicago.

"There's something I should tell you," she said.

Uh-oh. Here it comes.

"This guy who stole Ginger's son, the boy's father. Moon's a killer."

"How do you know?"

"I knew him. If you go back sixteen years and look at the papers you'll find a couple of unsolved murders. One in Beloit. Another I know about. Guys who cheated Moon or pissed him off. We used to hang with the War Bonnets, Ginger and me."

"That's a bad bunch. But it's been sixteen years. This Moon may not even be alive. The boy may not be alive. I might not be able to find him. Sixteen years is a long time."

"I understand."

"How well did you know him?"

"Better than I know you. I was his old lady for about a month, until he met Ginger. I was just a stupid teen."

"Tell me about him."

"I'd rather you heard it from Ginger."

"Fair enough."

Traffic was light and they made Madison in plenty of time. Pratt directed Cass clockwise around the Beltline to the far West Side, where they took County Trunk MB to Ptarmigan Road, a meandering blacktop that wandered southwest to northeast through forest, much of it reclaimed for million-dollar homes.

Pratt had bought his place eight years ago for $210,000 cash, money he'd received in a settlement resulting from a motorcycle accident. An old woman in a Buick had T-boned him at an intersection. Fortunately she was driving very slowly.

When Pratt moved in he had no neighbors. Since then a developer had bought up broad swaths and terra-formed the land into Whispering Oaks. They passed several bodacious mansions under construction.

Pratt pointed to a pale yellow ranch style set back from the road behind a scruffy lawn, the dry-mounted Camaro, double attached garage and satellite dish. "That's my place. But turn into Dave's place. It's right across the street."

Across the street, the Lowry residence gleamed atop its perfectly manicured lawn, square columns framing the arched zebrawood double front door. Vertical windows gazed down the lawn at the road and the eyesore across the street. Cass turned in and drove up the velvet blacktop. George and Gracie stood in the bed with their little white paws on the gunwales, barking and wagging their stumpy tails. Each bark was a pitchfork behind Pratt's eyes.

Dave and Louise Lowry poured from the front door down the broad flagstone steps to the pick-up, where each hoisted a schnauzer and cradled it to their bosoms. Gracie was so excited she pissed down the front of George's shirt. He didn't notice.

"Josh, that was outstanding work. Outstanding. Would you like to come inside?"

"No thank you, sir. I've got to get going. This is Cass, by the way."

Holding the dog against his chest Dave wiped his hand on his pants and shook Cass' hand. Cass introduced herself to Louise.

"Well let me pay you at least."

"Don't worry about it," Pratt said. "I'll bill you later."

"No. I insist. Please. Both of you step inside a minute."

Shrugging, Pratt and Cass followed the Lowrys into their foyer, fifteen feet to the exposed beams from which descended a wagon wheel chandelier. The décor was New England roadhouse with exposed wood, wood floors, a stone fireplace glimpsed through an archway, expensive modern art rugs, leather books with gold-lettered spines. Old Masters in gilt frames.

Lowry set the dog down and walked into a little office off the kitchen. He sat at an antique roll-up desk, wrote out a check in a big green checkbook, put it in an envelope and handed it to Pratt.

"By the way. we're having a little party next Friday. Hope you can make it. I'll send you an invite."

"Thank you, sir," Pratt said, sticking the envelope in his hip pocket.

It wasn't until they got in the truck that Pratt looked at the check. Five thousand dollars. Not bad for a night's work.

CHAPTER 7

They drove downtown.

Cass waited in the truck while Pratt sprinted up the stairs to Danny Bloom's office in the Kipgard Building on King Street just off the Capitol Square. The building was a two-story 1950s office block with two suites on each floor. Danny's suite faced the parking lot and an old residential neighborhood just off the isthmus.

Perry Winkham had been Dan's receptionist since Dan helped him win acquittal in a prostitution case. Unfortunately, two days after the acquittal while Perry was celebrating with some pals at the old Rod's Club, he wandered into traffic plastered, got hit by Two Guys and a Truck and ended up in a wheelchair.

"Nick Danger, everybody!" Perry sang as Pratt entered the foyer. "Nick Danger! Go right in, Nick. He's waiting for you."

It was unprofessional but Perry kept his job. Pratt figured Bloom had a weak spot for losers. *Just look at me.*

Pratt passed a disconsolate gangly black teen in a letter jacket and Air Jordans sitting next to his mother, a plump matron in a tired green dress. Bloom specialized in drug cases. Pratt walked down the short hall, conference room on one side, bathroom on the other, and entered Bloom's office without knocking. Bloom had his Skechers up on the desk, his pear-shaped body tilted back in a mesh office chair, speaking to the air.

"You're joking," Bloom said in a high-pitched voice that was surprisingly effective with juries. He held back. He never screeched. He approached the jury and spoke to them intimately, never raising his voice.

Two years ago Bloom had a small-time criminal case in Grant County. Pratt was there on another case but stayed to watch the arguments. The judge was a piss-poor dolt with no equal in his inability to grasp legal concepts, but who, for some inexplicable reason, thought he was smart.

The DA gave his usual dreary argument for conviction, then Bloom stepped up. He smiled, the jury smiled back. He relaxed, so did they. They were one, Bloom and the jury, like he was sitting with them. Bloom started talking about how his poor client was being railroaded, called his client a "miserable wretch." The DA objected. "Judge, he can't call his client a miserable wretch!" (reinforcing the term for the jury). The judge said, "Mr. Bloom, don't call your client a miserable wretch."

Now everybody knew the poor guy was a miserable wretch. Bloom continued, "As I was saying, look what they are doing to this miserable wretch. . ." Again the DA objected. Again the judge admonished Bloom and added, "Don't call him a miserable wretch ever again in this court!" The judge was shouting at Bloom in open court. The jury loved this to death, loved Bloom, and felt mighty sorry for the miserable railroaded wretch.

Bloom stopped. Not a sound for at least a minute. He looked at the judge. He looked at the DA and at the wretch. He looked at the jury. He walked to the back of the courtroom, stood with his back to the judge for a full minute. Silence yawned. Everybody thought, What the hell? Bloom walked back to the podium, looked at the jury and said, "Judges come and judges go. DAs come and DAs go. But justice lasts forever. All I ask, my friends, is justice for this miserable wretch."

The man was acquitted in twenty minutes.

Feet up, Bloom fenced with his invisible opponent. "That's an insult, Bobby. I can't tell my client that. If you can't do any better than that, I'll see you in court."

He listened, winking at Pratt and holding up a finger.

"You do that, Bobby. Pound a little sense into your client. Good. See you there."

The Skechers hit the plush cocoa shag. "Listen. The three Goldberg brothers, Norman, Himan and Max, invent the first automobile air conditioner. July 17th, 1945. You can look it up. Detroit—a hellhole. Ninety-seven degrees in the shade.

"The brothers walk into Henry Ford's office and sweet-talk his secretary into telling Henry that they got the most exciting innovation since the wheel.

"Henry invites 'em in. They insist he come out to the parking lot. They tell him to get into the car, which is about 103, turn on the air conditioner and cool the car off immediately.

"Old man Ford gets very excited and invites them back to the office. Three million he offers. The brothers refuse. They'll settle for two million but they want the label 'Goldberg Air Conditioner' on the dash. No way Ford, a notorious Jew hater, is going to put the Goldbergs' name on two million Ford cars.

"They haggle back and forth for two hours and finally agree on three million dollars and just their first names. Which is why all Ford air conditioners say Norm, Hi, & Max."

Bloom tilted back with a big grin on his puss. Pratt stared at him.

"Ahhh! Why do I bother? You're a *schmendrick!*"

Bloom riffled through a stack of papers and withdrew a manila envelope, which he opened. He slid out a photograph and tossed it in front of Pratt. Bloom had a pear-shaped head, a halo of hair surrounding a monadnock skull, round, rimless glasses reflecting the light. He looked like Gyro Gearloose.

"Ever see one of those?" he piped.

Pratt picked up the photograph, a black and white glossy of a Ducati, frame and body sheathed in slick bodywork. Beneath the bold logo it read "Desmosedici" in small letters.

"The Ducati V-4."

"Exactomundo, my friend. They retail for seventy-five thousand bucks. Two days ago, hijackers jacked an England semi north of Baraboo and made off with four of these things. They were headed for a dealer in the Twin Cities. Trans-Continental asked me if there were any chance they could be recovered. Naturally I turned to you."

"How soon do you want me on this?"

"Yesterday."

Pratt set the photo down. "That might be a problem, Danny. I'm meeting a potential client this afternoon and I sort of made a commitment."

"You're meeting me first."

"I know but I promised. Let me talk to her first and I'll get back to you."

Bloom drew a hand through a few strands of hair. "Want to go smoke a joint and get lunch?"

"Can't, Danny. Got someone waiting. I'll get back to you this afternoon."

"A dame I'll bet."

Pratt stood. "Danny, you're too sharp."

"Yeah yeah, let me know how it goes."

Outside Cass leaned against the truck. She and Pratt got in the truck and took the causeway to the Beltline. A dozen triangular sails ghosted across the smooth blue surface of Lake Monona. Cass drove east and took the Interstate toward Chicago.

"I just spoke to Ginger. She's expecting us."

"Okay."

"That your lawyer friend, Bloom?" she said.

"Yeah."

"Some pretty sketchy people going in and out of there."

"Dan's a criminal attorney. One of the best in the state. He specializes in drug cases."

"Jews make good lawyers."

Pratt looked at her. "We're all equal before the Lord."

"That's just a fact, Josh. Jews are good in law, medicine and show biz."

"Where'd you learn that?"

"That's just a fact. Just go look at their names."

The Interstate was moderately busy with traffic flowing north and south. Pratt watched farmland pass, wondering what to say or if he should even bother. "He got me out of prison for no other reason than he liked me."

"Josh, I'm sorry if I offended you. He's a prince, far as I'm concerned."

Cass turned west north of Beloit on State Highway 213. Soon they were in coulee country, winding green valleys, rolling farmland and forest. Signs advertised Renk Seed. Waist-high corn waved in the breeze. They passed a gated community of enormous houses called Glen Haven.

"That's one of Nathan's projects. That's Ginger's husband."

They turned onto Makepeace Road, a winding blacktop through woods marked here and there with gated entrances. They came to a gated entrance of wrought iron between brick pillars, mailbox inset in one pillar, com panel in the other. The gates were closed.

Cass pushed the call button. Long seconds ticked by before someone answered.

"Who is it?" A woman's voice, flat, impersonal.

"It's Cass, Ginger. I brought the investigator."

"Just a minute."

The gate clicked open and swung inward, parting in the middle.

CHAPTER 8

Trees arched over the winding blacktop creating a green filter, sunlight dappling the road. The trees thinned, and they emerged in a clearing in front of an overgrown wood lodge with a shake roof and vertical redwood boards. Vines climbed the stone façade on either side of the log portico. The driveway looped under the portico circling a ten-foot-pond with a fountain in the center spewing water straight up. Gently rounded bushes grew against the wall like green sentries. Flowers burst in profusion surrounding the turn-around. Two baskets overflowing with marigolds, pansies and hollyhocks hung over the main entrance.

Cass parked under the log roof and got out. Pratt heard birds twittering, insects chirping, the susurrus of the breeze through the forest. He inhaled deeply the smell of pine.

The smell of money.

A woman opened the front door and Pratt's first impression was of a gamin, Audrey Hepburn or Leslie Caron. A slight, feminine figure with a long ivory neck, short pageboy hair and a Mona Lisa smile.

"Cass," she said.

Cass stepped forward and enfolded the smaller woman in a crushing embrace. When Cass released Ginger, Pratt saw that she was holding a cane.

"Come in," the woman said smiling, revealing something of her true age. Pratt shut the door behind him.

"Ginger, this is Josh Pratt."

Ginger's grip was surprisingly firm. "Cass has told me a great deal about you, Josh. Please, let's go to the porch. I have iced tea."

Pratt wondered what Cass had said considering they'd known each other less than twenty-four hours.

Ginger wore a blue terry cloth robe snugged around her waspish waist. She led them down a short hallway lined with photographs of the family: husband, Ginger, two grown-up step-kids. Horse trophies in a cabinet. Ginger led them onto a broad screened-in porch overlooking a deck and swimming pool, the green canopy of the forest. "Please sit." Ginger made as if to pour iced tea from a glass pitcher. Cass took the pitcher from her. Ginger's feet rested on a cougar skin.

"You sit," Cass said.

Ginger eased herself into a leather glider, carefully setting her cane over the armrest. Pratt sat opposite a low glass coffee table on a bamboo sofa with embroidered cushions.

"Cass tells me you want me to find your son."

"Yes that's right, Mr. Pratt. You know I don't have long and I would like to see him before I go."

"She's full of shit," Cass said, handing Pratt a glass of iced tea. "She'll be around to kick our bones."

"I have to warn you that sixteen years is an awful long time. Chances are you'll be wasting your money. And please call me Josh."

"I have to try." She reached for a zippered leather binder and removed some snapshots. The first one, in faded color, showed an extremely young Ginger looking lovingly at a newborn baby."

"Where's the father?" Pratt asked.

"He was in jail when this photo was taken. He also had a thing about having his picture taken but I do have this." She handed him a faded black and white showing four bikers outside an old farmhouse making obscene gestures toward the camera.

"Moon's the one with the shaved skull."

A muscular figure with a bony head, aviator shades, tribal tats circling his upper arms and a Fu Manchu. He wore a wife beater, jeans and black boots with silver buckles. The others all had facial hair. They all had tats.

"That was taken at a farm he used to rent. Moon cooked meth for a living. He was very good at it. He may still be at it if he's still alive."

"What does your gut tell you?" Pratt said.

"He's alive. Moon is harder to kill than a government program. He's a kung fu master. He trained at the Shaolin Temple in China."

"Really."

"I know that sounds silly, Josh, but it's not. He went to China. He was gone for six months. If you Google Shaolin Temple you'll find their home page. Anybody can train there." She toed the rug. "He's a Sioux Indian. Do you see this cougar skin? Moon killed it with a bow and arrow. I keep it to remind myself what he was like."

"Tell Josh about the abduction," Cass said.

Ginger looked inward. Sadness set in around her eyes. "I told him I didn't want to see him anymore. The same day the police raided his lab. There was a shoot-out and a War Bonnet died. Moon was convinced I'd fingered him. This fucking bitch he was banging may have told him. Eric was three months old. I thought Moon was gone forever. He's obsessed with revenge. He always told me that and God knows I saw enough proof of it. I only went outside for a minute, to take a look at the garden. I left Eric sleeping in his crib and when I came back he was gone. I saw a truck beating it down the street. It was too far away to see the license.

"I phoned the cops right away . . ." She stared at her lap. A sob broke the surface of her lips. Cass sat on the armrest and put an arm around her.

"Come on, babe. Tell it all. Pratt's gonna make it right."

Pratt wished she hadn't said that.

Ginger pulled a tissue from a robe pocket and honked. "That was sixteen years ago. I have not heard one word from or about Eric since. The police did everything they could. They put out a nationwide bulletin. *America's Most Wanted* did a segment. Nothing. It's what Moon does. He claimed to have 'second sight,' whatever that is. And sometimes, it seemed as if he knew what was going to happen before it happened. Used to freak the shit out of everybody, but it was probably just his spooky personality and the power of suggestion. Moon can be very persuasive. He's not stupid."

"I'll need everything you've got on this guy—pictures, correspondence, whatever. I'll need you to make me a list of his known associates and hidey holes."

Ginger reached for the black valise. "I've been keeping that list for years."

"Why didn't you try to find him before?"

Ginger threw her hands in the air with a half sob, half laugh. "I don't know what else I could have done! I hired a private detective. All he did was take my money. I was insane with grief and worry. I even went to club hangouts to find him. I was nearly raped several times. The police warned me to stop looking. So I stopped. What else was I supposed to do? Nathan knows nothing of this. I'm going to have to tell him."

"Nathan is your husband?" Pratt said.

"Yes. Nathan Munz. He's a developer. We've been very happy together. He treats me like a queen. He knows I have a sketchy past and he accepts me the way I am. I've got two wonderful step-kids. I should be happy." She laughed/sobbed.

"I get two hundred a day plus expenses. I report every Monday."

"Cass," Ginger gestured toward the patio doors. "Would you bring me my checkbook from the kitchen alcove?"

Cass went inside.

"How bad is it?" Pratt said.

"Right now it's not too bad. It comes and goes. I have good days and I have bad days. The trouble is it affects everything else. Today is kind of a middle day. Listen. I have to tell you something. It's something that Moon told me."

She paused, as if gathering herself. "When Moon was seven years old he went to the county fair with his father. Moon wandered off by himself. While he was walking, another boy snuck up behind him and jabbed a pin in his ass. Moon turned around. The boy was with two friends, sauntering with exaggerated innocence, fully cognizant of what he'd done. Moon followed him for the rest of the day. Found out where he lived. And then he waited. He waited for eight years, when they both were in high school. He waited for that boy after school. Every day that boy took the same shortcut home through the woods. Moon waited with a baseball bat and when the boy came, Moon sprang from hiding and broke the boy's knees. He placed the bat on the boy's throat and told him who he was. Then he stood on the bat until the boy was dead. Moon told me this and I believe him. That was his first murder.

"He said if I ever told anyone he'd kill me."

Cass returned with the checkbook and a glass, handed the checkbook to Ginger, walked to the far end of the patio to smoke a cigarette. Cass pulled the black valise onto her lap and used it as a desk.

"I'm writing you a check for ten thousand dollars. Let me know when you need more."

"Ginger, that's not necessary."

"I think it is. Cass speaks very highly of you, and I trust her instincts." She tore the check out and handed it over. "Find my little boy."

CHAPTER 9

Cass and Pratt returned to Cass' farm with Ginger's file. Once inside they fell onto the old sofa in the living room and tore each other's clothes off. This is the life, Pratt thought, fucking her doggie style on the sofa. Cass was by far the best-looking woman he'd ever scored and he had no intention of letting her get away. Until she grew tired of him, as she inevitably would.

"Son, don't expect it to work out 'cause either she's gonna dump you or you're gonna dump her. That's just the way it is."

But life had proved Duane wrong on a number of points so there was hope.

Pratt swallowed three ibuprofen, bungeed the file to the back of his bike and promised to call. Cass ran down the steps for a final embrace that stitched pain like a machine gun up his side and roused his dick.

"What's so funny?" Cass said, smiling.

"You are."

"Can you ride, baby?" Cass said, hanging on to him.

"I can always ride. A cement mixer could run over me and I'd still ride. I'll call you."

"You'd better."

He got on his bike and cranked.

Pratt needed his computer. The computer had revolutionized investigations. Everyone and everything was up on the Internet somewhere. Half the prison population was on Facebook. Thank God Chaplain Frank Dorgan had convinced Pratt to take a computer class in prison. He had even learned how to type.

Pratt rode the back roads. He saw several deer, one of which watched him curiously as he motored by.

Dear Lord, he prayed, *please help me find that good woman's son and grant her some peace.*

It was seven by the time Pratt pulled into his driveway and used the remote in his tank bag to open the garage door. One half the double-car garage housed his stealth Honda, a gray four door. The other half was devoted to bikes, including the basket-case chopper whose engine rested on the living room table. Old tin Harley and Indian signs hung on the wall. There was a workbench laden with tools, a motorcycle lift, an air compressor and a ten-speed Trek.

He got off the bike and collected his mail from the roadside box. Bills, *The Horse,* various come-ons. He sat at his computer in the spare bedroom he used as an office. He Googled War Bonnets. The Wikipedia entry said:

> *The War Bonnets Motorcycle Club is an outlaw motorcycle gang and organized crime syndicate. The club is headquartered in Sioux Falls, South Dakota, and was originally formed in 1969 by Native American Vietnam veterans who were refused entry to the Hells Angels because of their race. Law enforcement officials estimate there are approximately 100 to 200 full patched (official) members.*
>
> *It has its main presence in the Upper Midwest.*

Several reports in the *Des Moines Register* about War Bonnet meth activity. Pratt Googled Eugene Moon. Nothing. He conducted a LexisN search with the same result. He Googled the Shaolin Temple and found their web page. They were indeed accepting Western students.

Last time Pratt went to Sturgis the Hells Angels had the nitrous concession. The Sons of Baal had the marijuana concession. And the War Bonnets had the meth concession. Bike Week began on Monday. Pratt had mixed feelings about Sturgis. There were good memories and bad. Over time, the good had become tainted with the bad. He hadn't been to Sturgis since before he went to prison.

Pratt was stuck. So he did something he never would have done in his previous life. He called a cop. He called MPD Detective Heinz Calloway. Calloway was on the Gang Task Force. His specialty was outlaw motorcycle gangs. Go figure.

"Calloway," the detective answered on the second ring.

"Heinz, it's your favorite biker. I'll buy you lunch if I can pick your brain."

"What about?"

"A missing person case involving the War Bonnets."

Beat.

"The War Bonnets. Ain't heard that name in years. Well it just so happens lunch is open tomorrow. You can meet me on the Union Terrace at one."

Pratt worked on the basket case engine in his living room, fitting the new S&S pistons by hand while *American Idol* played in the background. He turned the television off at ten, washed his hands and face and knelt by his bed as he had every night since his release.

Except last night.

"My Lord, I want so many things I'm ashamed. This is just a general all-purpose prayer to let you know you are in my thoughts, I'm trying like hell to love my neighbor, and please have mercy on that good woman Ginger Munz. Amen."

He waited a minute.

"And please let Cass and me turn out well."

CHAPTER 10

In the morning Pratt flexed his ribs. Not bad. He had to run. He'd been putting it off and putting it off. After a breakfast of cold fruit and a banana, he put on his sweats, running shoes and Brewers tank top and clipped his iPod to his belt. He went out to his driveway to stretch. George and Gracie yapped savagely at him from the top of Lowry's drive.

"Yap, you thankless bastiches," Pratt said, feeling the pain in his ribs crackle throughout his body like static discharge. He took off down the road in long, easy strides listening to The Shazam at top volume. Every step brought a jolt flashing strobe-like through his body. The pain lessened as he ran. Or maybe he became used to it. It wasn't severe enough to keep him from running. He was used to pain.

Run it off.

He passed a mini-mansion rising a quarter mile down the road. A mile further on, ground was broken for a strip mall. Civilization on the march. It wouldn't be long before it was solid megalopolis from Chicago to Milwaukee to Madison.

He gave it two miles before turning around, the pain a familiar throbbing presence. An old friend. The trip back was slower. He stripped the duct tape off in the shower, put on fresh jeans and a Badger T-shirt that covered the dragon. A few crude jailhouse tats peeked out from under the sleeves. He'd been meaning to have them lasered but never seemed to find the time. They might prove useful.

He spent an hour cruising the web, stopping at his favorite sites, chatting with friends he'd never met.

At twelve-thirty Pratt saddled up, locked the joint and headed into town. He found a motorcycle parking place directly across from the Student Union and backed in between two plastic-sheathed crotch rockets. Frat boys loved to cruise in shorts and flip-flops. First responders scraped them up off the pavement with spatulas. The Union was chock-a-block with students, faculty and downtown workers looking for shade on the broad terrace overlooking Lake Mendota.

Pratt went up the broad steps past the Socialist Workers Party, Vegan Sisterhood, Committee to Eradicate Capitalism and the Freedom From Religion Society. In the crowded lobby students and businessmen lined up for a scoop of Babcock Hall ice cream. He walked through the Stithskeller and the Rathskeller, studious moles with their noses in laptops, Germanic heraldry on the wall, out the double doors to the patio where a hundred people lounged at round green tables beneath the shade of a towering oak. Two toddlers played precariously on Paul Bunyan's chair while their mothers laughed and talked.

Calloway raised a hand from a table beneath the oak. Pratt put the valise on the table and sat. "How'd you get this table, Heinz?"

"Got lucky. Now you want to feed me before you ask what you're gonna ask? My stomach thinks my mouth has died and gone to hell."

"What are you having?"

"I'll take a cheeseburger with a side of kraut and a Capitol lager."

Pratt went down the steps to the outside grill where four students did a steady business in charcoal-grilled meats and drinks. He stood in line. A girl with a diamond nose stud took his order. He returned to the table with a platter containing their food.

Calloway waited while Pratt sat and folded his hands. "Thank you Jesus for this food we are about to eat."

"Amen."

Calloway grabbed the burger in both hands. "Give a man a minute." He wore a white short-sleeved dress shirt, a red tie with a gold pig tack and pants so sharp you could cut cheese in the crease. He chowed down with gusto. No drop of ketchup landed on his shirt.

Heinz Calloway was a six foot five black man with a drifting eye. It wasn't lazy. Nothing about Calloway was lazy. The eye looked disconcertingly to the sky while the other eye pinned you. Calloway used the eye to masterly effect during interrogations. As a youth he'd briefly joined the Jitterbugs, an all-black Milwaukee based MC. The initiation involved smoking a bowl of crack at one hundred miles per hour. Calloway got out before he committed a felony and enlisted in the Army, where he'd trained as a military policeman.

He had a PhD in criminology and rode a Victory.

Pratt dug into his cheeseburger. He finished half before coming up for air. While Calloway ate Pratt filled him in on the job. "I figure my best bet is to find Moon."

Calloway pushed the tray away and took out a spiral pad. "Eugene Moon," he said while he wrote. "The War Bonnets are so fucking crazy even the Hells Angels give them a wide berth. Keyser Soze crazy. They had a feud going with the Sons of Baal in Pueblo. Sons of Baal vowed to kill the local War Bonnet prez' family. Wife and two kids. So he killed them himself before the SOB could find them. Strangled the wife and drowned the kids in the bathtub. Then he went to war on the SOB and killed three of them before he was gunned down in a House of Pancakes parking lot. I'll try to dig that up and send it to you."

"Eugene Moon?"

Calloway shrugged, eye on the sky. "That was a long time ago. Rotsa ruck, as they say. I'll run it through the NCIC. Gimme a call tomorrow."

"Sturgis starts on Monday. The War Bonnets have the meth franchise at the Buffalo Chip."

"I would rather crawl a mile through broken glass than spend a night at the Buffalo Chip," Calloway said. "You might check with the hospital where the boy was born. Some of them take fingerprints of newborns."

"Is that legal?"

Calloway shrugged. "Who knows? Sixteen years is a long time. Good luck with that. You going to church?"

"Yeah."

"What church?"

"Resurrection Life. It's out near New Glarus."

Calloway held his hand out. They did the soul clasp. "Stay strong with Christ, brother."

Calloway heaved himself to his feet. Putting the spiral pad in a hip pocket, he headed toward the visitor's parking lot along the lakefront.

Pratt found a pay phone in the Union, which he preferred to his cell phone for sound quality. Included in the papers Ginger had given him was Eric's birth certificate at Our Lady of the Redeemer Hospital in Beloit. He bounced from administrator to administrator before landing with a woman in Records.

"Excuse me, what is your interest?" the woman said.

Pratt explained.

"Well there's a problem. The hospital moved in 1998 and the old building was demolished. A lot of records were lost."

"Didn't you put the records on a computer?"

"They should have, but I'm not finding anything. They could be in there but who knows under what program or heading? I'm sorry Mr. Pratt. We don't have the time to conduct an exhaustive search. We have our hands full just keeping up with the flow of patients."

Pratt thanked the woman and hung up. He stopped at the bank on the way home, deposited his two checks and took out two thousand dollars in hundred-dollar bills. When he got home he phoned Ginger. She sounded weak.

"Hello?"

"Ginger, Josh Pratt. Sorry to bother you."

"No bother. What can I do for you?"

"You said Moon was an Indian."

"He claimed to be part Lakota, and he did have an Indian cast to his features. The dark hair and complexion. He used to scare the bejeezus out of grown men with his crazy Sioux witch doctor act."

"Did he mention what tribe? Any relatives?"

"No. He never said. All I know it was in South Dakota somewhere."

"Thank you."

Pratt was feverish with excitement. It was almost as if Jesus had given him this assignment to pull him out of his funk and point him in the right direction. To find a little boy stolen sixteen years ago. It was a hell of a lot more satisfying than finding a couple of schnauzers or even the Ducatis. Pratt's own father had abandoned him at a Bosselman's truck stop one frigid December evening in Nebraska when he was sixteen, the year Eric was born.

It was one-thirty in the evening and they were on the move, running from angry women, bill collectors and the police. Omaha. Duane had been running his roofing scam, duping little old ladies out of their life's savings in exchange for little to no work on their roofs. They lived out of Duane's old F-150. Duane got drunk, got in a fight with a bouncer at the Dew Drop Inn, got his face smashed in and his ass thrown out the door. Pratt watched it all from a booth in the deepest part of the bar, trying to withdraw in upon himself, trying to be invisible.

Pratt followed Duane out the door, helped him up from the trash-strewn gutter. As Pratt seized his father's arm and lifted, Duane looked up with an expression of hatred and disgust. An icicle pierced Pratt's heart. His father was no good.

"You!" Duane spat, shoving Pratt away and regaining his feet. "Why the fuck did I bring you along? Remind me."

A couple late-night tokers watched from the front of the building. Pratt wished he could pull in upon himself and disappear like a singularity.

Duane stumbled for the truck. He'd narrowly avoided arrest that day when he saw the OPD car pulling into the trailer park where he rented space.

Time to blow this town.

Pratt barely made it around and into the passenger seat before Duane goosed the engine. The old Ford sounded like Pratt felt. It sounded like it was about to tear itself apart. Duane paused once to snort meth off his thumb and then they were outta there, endless

Interstate 80 where the plains stretched to infinity on either side of the road. At night, with truck stops and towns appearing as gleaming jewel cluster mother ships against an onyx sky, it was easy to believe they were a spaceship traveling through an infinite void.

Pratt turned on the radio, found a country station. Duane lit a Marlboro and swatted his son's hand away. "I don't want to hear that sad-ass country shit! I want some fuckin' rock and roll!"

Duane twisted the dials, the truck describing a serpentine pattern in his uncertain grip. Pratt was sure they were going to roll over into the ditch. An outraged semi blasted them with air horns as Duane barely avoided a head-on, swerving back into his own lane at the last minute.

"Hand me that peppermint schnapps in the glove box," Duane said.

Pratt stared at him fearfully.

"Do it, you little piss-ant! What the fuck are you good for?"

Pratt opened the glove compartment. A stack of maps spilled out on his knees. He reached in, found the slick glass container and handed it to his father, who snatched it up greedily, clamped the cap in his teeth and unscrewed it one-handed.

Duane found an oldies station playing the Rolling Stones. "Factory Girl."

"Yeah, I know that bitch," Duane snarled, tipping the schnapps back. Pratt hoped they would get busted. He'd seen Duane drive drunk before but never like this. His old man appeared naked in the moonlight, a drunkard, a coward, a liar and even though Duane had attempted to beat the nascent belief in a superior being out of him, Pratt offered up a prayer right then and there that they somehow survive the night.

Drunkard or not, Duane was Pratt's old man and he loved him.

The signs said GAS, FOOD, LODGING, next exit. Bosselman's reared its logo fifty feet above the pike. Duane took the exit abruptly, cutting across two lanes of traffic like a madman, outraged truckers laying on the horns. For a second on the curve the old truck lost traction and began to hang its tail out but Duane turned into the curve and regained control.

"I gotta take a shit," Duane said. "Might be awhile." He reached in his pocket and removed his turquoise and silver money clip. He peeled off a twenty and handed it to Pratt.

"They got video games, get something to eat."

Despite the late hour the truck stop was hopping. Pratt could see truckers in ball caps through the windows of the café. Duane pulled up at one of the self-serve pumps. "Go on. I'll come lookin' for ya when I'm ready to go."

Pratt got out of the truck and started for the truck stop.

"Wait a minute," Duane said, taking off his cheap digital wristwatch and handing it to Pratt. "Twenty minutes! Don't forget."

Pratt rolled toward the truck stop, the twenty burning a hole in his pocket. It was the most money he'd had in his hands in years, possibly ever. It hadn't occurred to him that ol' Duane was ditching him like he'd ditched women, jobs and friends.

So when Pratt suddenly realized a half hour had gone by, he looked for his father. He looked in the men's room and the café. He looked in the store and the parking lot. He ran frantically around the Bosselman's until a trucker the size of a polar bear held out a telephone-pole arm. His gut loomed over a belt buckle the size of a dinner plate. He wore an "I'm Irish Kiss Me" T-shirt.

"Hey kid, you all right?"

Pratt stopped, gasping. He burst into tears.

Even today the memory drew a cloak of crimson shame over him like a burka. He'd acted like a little pussy bawling his eyes out to a stranger. He hadn't seen it coming. His father never loved him.

Pratt didn't like to go there but it was always in the back of his mind. Chaplain Dorgan told him there comes a point in every man's life when he learns to stop blaming his parents and take responsibility.

Back online. There were five main tribes of the Lakota: Oglala, Hunkpapa, Sans Arc, Brule and Blackfoot. Each had its own website plus there was a United Lakota website. Moon was a common Indian name but there were no Eugenes.

His cell phone sang "Sweet Home Alabama."

"Pratt."

"Hey, man," Cass said huskily. "What are you doing?"

"Nothing. Want to come over?"

"I was thinking about bringing you some dinner. You like Thai?"

"Yeah sure. That would be great."

"Okay, lover. See you in about twenty minutes."

The things he did for pussy. Pratt hated Thai.

CHAPTER 11

Cass burrowed into Pratt's armpit, her hair splayed across his chest. The radio was turned down pumping out jazz so blue you could smoke it.

"Can I ask you something?" Pratt said.

"Go ahead."

"What are you doing with those dogfights? You seem like a warm person to me. I just don't get it."

Cass sighed and turned over, moving away so she could look at him. She reached for her vodka tonic on the bed stand. She'd brought both vodka and tonic. "Don't judge me, Pratt. I like you and you like me. Isn't that enough?"

"Dogs used to lick Lazarus' sores. They are holy to the Lord, just like you and me."

"I knew this Jesus crap was going to rear its ugly head."

"I haven't exactly been preaching the gospel to you have I? There are lots of things I could say. 'The Lord is good to all, Compassionate to every creature.' Psalm 145:9."

"I knew it!" Cass snarled, sitting up and grabbing her drink and pack of American Spirits. She got up naked and stalked out of the bedroom. A moment later he heard the back door slam.

"Way to go, Pratt," he said, looking around for his jeans. He did not want Cass to go. On the other hand, her behavior reminded him of past relationships that hadn't ended well. None of them did.

"And God said, let us make man in our image," Pratt muttered under his breath. "Male and female created he them."

He pulled on his jeans and followed Cass out to the rear deck, where she stood furiously smoking a cigarette staring at the trees, arms crossed over her breasts. Guiltily he glanced around to make sure none of the neighbors was watching. He had no neighbors, yet. A yellow bulb over the back door kept the mosquitoes at bay.

He went up to her and put his arms around her from behind. "Come on, baby. I promise not to preach." *Why am I apologizing?*

"I had an old man once," she said taking a long draw on the cig. "He used to quote scripture while he beat me."

"I'm not like that."

Gradually she began to soften.

"I have a temper." She turned and put her arms around his neck, cig dangling. "Let's go back inside. Just don't quote scripture to me."

"I won't," he said. Her anger was like a summer storm. It flashed and thundered and then it was gone. *Lord, how am I going to bring this woman to you if I'm forbidden to speak your word?*

Maybe he shouldn't try. Maybe he should just enjoy it while it lasts, like his old man said.

Cass went into the bedroom, found his old plaid robe and put it on. She made a beeline for the kitchen. She opened the liquor cabinet and reached for her vodka. "Want one?"

"Couple fingers of that Irish Mist."

They went back outside with their drinks and sat on the glider, his arm around her.

"Are you part Indian?"

Cass shifted around, pulled his arm tight. "I'm half Cheyenne. My old man, Nathan Breedlove. He lived up to his name too. I have a half dozen half brothers and sisters."

"Tell me about Moon."

She stiffened like plaster of Paris. Pratt waited. Not another storm, please.

"I met him at the Ho-Chunk Casino. I was a blackjack dealer. He sat at my table. He stood out from the geriatric crowd like a red Popsicle. He love-bombed me and I fell for it. He tried to get me involved in some scam to rob the casino and I lost my job. We're both lucky they didn't charge us."

"Tell me about the man, his personality, what he likes and hates."

"Moon is scary. He's the type of guy walks into a room and every other man feels his scrotum tighten. There's just something about him, some craziness in his eyes that warns you off. Moon's ready to take it to the mat over the most trivial shit. Some dude—a fucking Mongol—owed him like two hundred bucks and kept shining him on. So Moon waited for the guy outside a bar and when the dude came out Moon clocked him with a baseball bat. Dude woke up wired to the wall in a storage locker. Moon released a wolverine into the locker, shut the door and left. They found the guy's body a week later because of the smell. The wolverine had chewed its way out through the floor."

"A wolverine," Pratt said.

"Moon's a trapper."

"Where would he find one?"

"Northern Minnesota. He's smart. The way he talks you'd think he went to Harvard."

"How tall?"

"Six feet, one hundred ninety pounds. I've seen him bench-press four hundred pounds. He's got tribal tats around his left bicep, a portrait of Crazy Horse on his right. He's got a lightning tat here." She touched Pratt's neck.

"Eye color?"

"Brown eyes. He had beautiful hair but he kept his skull shaved. Always carries a Bowie knife."

"What type of man is he? Do you think he has any fatherly feelings toward Eric?"

"Moon doesn't love anyone or anything but himself. I don't know. Maybe he's changed. They say fatherhood can do that to a man. Not from what I've seen. What about your old man? Didn't you tell me he left you at a truck stop?"

A helix of shame and fury wrapped itself around Pratt's spine. *Duane.* He didn't want to think about Duane. Not now. Not ever.

"Yeah, Duane was a piece of work. What about Moon? Did he say where he was from? Hometown? Did he mention any family?"

"No. He was as mysterious as the fucking Sphinx."

They sat in silence looking at the stars through the trees. After a while Pratt stirred. "Come on. Let's try to get some sleep."

They went back inside and went to bed. Pratt lay on his back for a long time staring at the ceiling.

"Pratt. You awake?"

"What's up, babe?"

"Please be careful. I'm afraid you won't come back."

"This is your idea."

"I'm sorry I thought of it."

CHAPTER 12

Hold up your hand and make the peace sign. What do you see? A V-twin engine. The most natural engine configuration in the world, especially when put into a two-wheeled chassis. The angle of the V matches the angle of the front down frame perfectly. The crankshaft turns the belt. The rider sits on top. It is a match made in heaven, which is why God rides a Harley.

Madison to Sturgis was eighteen hours. Pratt had done it twice on a hardtail. He was no longer the young speed- and pussy-crazed fool. Two nine-hour days on a bike were enough. He went online to check the action at the Sturgis home page and some chat rooms. Every hotel and camping hook-up had been reserved for months, some for years. There wasn't a bed to be had within a hundred miles of Sturgis.

That left the Buffalo Chip. It consisted of ten acres of rolling prairie built around a huge stage, people flopped wherever there was space. The shows and the drug market made the Chip the venue of choice for those on the down low. Smart travelers brought motor homes with their own bathrooms, some with garages in back for their bikes.

The Chip's lavatories were beyond heinous—a hundred thousand drunk-ass bikers shooting, snorting, smoking and shitting made them so. Some bikers had sex in the lavatories. There was a special patch for that.

Cass watched Pratt prep his bike. "Will you call me when you get there?"

"Sure." Pratt put a tire gauge to the front tire. Thirty-five pounds. The back tire needed air. The bike looked like a pack horse about to head into the mountains. The pillion was piled high with pup tent, sleeping bag and waterproof duffel for extra clothes. Pratt had fitted a jumbo tank bag to the tank—sacrilege—and filled it with personal effects. A half windshield was bolted to the handlebars.

Cass watched until Pratt gave her a hug and a shove toward the door. "I'll call you tonight."

Once she was gone Pratt went into the basement with its oxblood shag rug, giant flat-screen television, stack of DVDs and door to the utility room. Pratt looked down at a fallen tower of DVDs. Jean-Claude Van Damme, for the love of Pete. Pratt pulled out his keychain and unlocked the deadbolt to the utility room. Inside was a Centurion gun safe, six feet tall. Pratt swiftly dialed the combination and opened the safe.

To carry or not to carry, that was the question.

A pump-action twelve-gauge Remington, a Chinese SKS, a Ruger 9, a John Wayne commemorative .45 and a Python five-shot .38. He took out the .38 and hefted it. Wheel guns were elegantly simple. They never jammed. It only held five cartridges but he wasn't anticipating gang war.

Lord, do I need this gun?

Leave the gun, Jesus said.

Pratt put it back and shut the safe.

Pratt phoned Louise Lowry and asked if she would take in his mail. "Anything I can do, just ask," she said.

After a final check Pratt hit the road. He headed north on 12/18 toward Baraboo. From there it was a couple of miles to the interstate. A handful of other bikers trickled onto the road. Some passed, giving him the sign. Once on the interstate there were more bikers, convoys of them. Pratt saw license plates from every state in the east plus Puerto Rico. Bike Week didn't even begin until tomorrow. He saw convoys of helmetless hard-asses, riders and old ladies trailing braided leather streamers, older prosperous couples on Gold Wings trailing matching trailers with teddy bears bungeed to the sissy bars, the Fast and the Furious on Yamaha Yzs, Honda RRs, Ducatis and GSs with their butts in the air wearing full-face helmets.

A home-made trike the size of a Rolls-Royce rumbled by with a V-8 engine. The driver wore antique aviator goggles and a leather helmet with his beard in the wind like a character from a Jules Verne novel.

Pratt shook his head. He didn't see the point of the land yachts. They took up as much space as a car and couldn't bank into a turn.

He made camp at the Sioux Falls KOA, a wooded site along the Sioux River, chock-a-block with true believers. Pratt set up his pup tent, rode his bike into town and had supper at an Arby's. The restaurant was filled with bikers heading west. He phoned Cass from his booth.

"Hi, babe. How you doing?"

"I'm fine," she said. "I'm holed up in my bedroom with a shotgun filled with double ought buck in case those fucking *maricons* come back." Her words sounded slurred.

"If you see those guys call the police. Don't mess around."

"Forget it, baby. I don't need no fuckin' cops. I thought I saw someone eyeing the place this afternoon but maybe it's just nerves. I wish I had some big fucking dogs for protection."

"Well listen. I just called to tell you I'm fine and I miss you. I'll hit Sturgis tomorrow afternoon and I'll phone you then."

"Yeah. Oh I miss you too, baby. I wish I had y'all here to keep me company instead of this old shotgun."

"Don't shoot yourself. Talk to you tomorrow."

Pratt nodded to several booths of bikers on his way out, got on the bike and returned to the campground. Fireflies twinkled in the humid Midwest evening. Mosquitoes strafed his ears. He smacked on some Deet and sat on a bench for a while listening to the carousing, music and wild bursts of laughter, an occasional whiff of marijuana. Bikes popped and roared long into the night. Pratt screwed wax ear stopples into his ears and fell asleep.

He got up early and pulled out the plugs, filling his ears with the roar of other early-rising campers. The mood was festive and friendly. Bikers greeted each other as if they'd known one another forever.

Pratt broke camp and put an hour under his butt before stopping for breakfast at a service plaza outside Mitchell. At the Missouri he headed north to get off the interstate. He headed west on 14. Thousands of other bikers had the same idea. The trickle of bikes had formed into mighty streams all rushing toward Sturgis. A dozen bikers swooped by on Valks with swords mounted on their backs. By the time they all passed, Pratt figured out they were the Nordic Raiders out of St. Paul.

County mounties crouched in the median. From time to time Pratt passed some hapless jerks by the side of the road next to their inert bike as a Sheriff's deputy looked up their licenses in air-conditioned comfort. The South Dakota Highway Patrol's Dodge Chargers had a sinister quality as if the devil had designed them to strike fear into travelers.

The sun seared in a cloudless sky. Towns were few and far between, interspersed with fields of corn, alfalfa and soybeans. Grain elevators stood lonely sentinel at every town. Pratt pulled over at a roadside—a gravel lot and a picnic table already filled with resting bikers. The fifty-gallon trash receptacle overflowed with discarded fast-food wrappers and paraphernalia.

Pratt took off his leather jacket and stripped down to a turquoise tank top. He put the goggles back on and roared west, feeling the wind suck the moisture from his skin like a *chupacabra*. Insects smacked a Billy Cobham solo against the windshield. Every gas station and fast-food joint between Pierre and Sturgis was a mini-con filled with laughing, red-faced, bearded and tattooed bikers, their old ladies and bikes. Pratt flashed the biker salute a million times.

As he got closer to Sturgis the highway became more congested until it was virtually wall-to-wall bikers punctuated by the occasional motor home, terrified parents gripping the wheel, eyes straight ahead, thrilled kids hanging out the windows exchanging hand signals with the bikers. A biker slowly cruised up to the open rear window of a Lincoln and high-fived a delighted five-year-old.

A hundred and fifty miles from Sturgis the highway opened briefly and the big bikes rolled westward at seventy miles per hour with mere feet between them. Pratt hung a hundred feet behind a contingent of Minneapolis Raptors rolling in tandem, fat with bulging saddle bags and old ladies. Pratt glanced in his rearview.

Something red winked a hundred feet back, juking and jiving with incredible speed, weaving in and out between slower bikes like a mechanical needle. Pratt couldn't take his eyes off it, navigating on autopilot. He flicked his eyes back and forth between the road and the rearview.

It was upon him. It was past, leaving behind a weird howling croon as the helmeted rider hoiked the bars and went into a wheelie at well over a hundred miles an hour. Jaw on the tank, Pratt watched the lunatic shoot through traffic, finally throwing down the front wheel and accelerating up the shoulder like a missile.

Only one bike in the world made that sound or moved that fast.

A Ducati Desmosedici.

CHAPTER 13

Thirty miles out traffic came to a halt, bikers lined up four abreast across both lanes as overwhelmed state troopers attempted to keep order and keep the line moving. All the rushing rivers of chrome, rubber and steel converged in the shallow pond of Sturgis.

The sun beat down. Heat from three hundred thousand internal combustion engines rose up. The world shimmered in the heat. The highway was a solid mass of machines and humanity rumbling and buzzing like a frenzy of flies. Pratt shut his engine off and walked the bike forward, grateful he'd laid in a six-pack of bottled Gatorade. It took him two hours to cover the eight miles to the entrance to the Buffalo Chip, which lay east of town near Bear Butte.

The line waiting to get into the Chip stretched for two miles along the shoulder. Pratt worked his way toward the back of the line in inches, fighting other bikes and pedestrians the whole way. Good-natured grumbling.

"Yo, Gut Wrench!" The voice of a rudely woken bear split the buzz.

Incredulous, Pratt looked at the line of bikes waiting to get in.

"Over here, Numb Nutz!"

Pratt couldn't believe it. Man Mountain Maier, former War Counselor to the Bedouins at the head of a group of six. Pratt hadn't seen him since before his conviction. He pulled up next to Man Mountain and kicked out the stand. They exchanged the soul clasp.

"Shit, man, it's good to see ya!" Man Mountain rumbled. "How long you been out?"

"Got out in '07, Mountain."

"You wanna ride with us? Save you some time."

"I don't want to cut in line."

"Forget that shit! Every club here has been cuttin' in members! Hey, make room for my man Gut Wrench!"

Man Mountain threw out the kickstand, got off and introduced Pratt to the rest of the club as "Gut Wrench." Man Mountain was only five six but was bulked up like the Hulk. With his white Santa Claus beard he looked like your worst nightmare of a troll. The other Bedouins were younger and not as hell-bent. After the big bust that sent Pratt to prison the Bedouins all but disbanded, only to reform years later with a more sober and mature outlook. Man Mountain was the only charter member left.

A pumped kid with zigzags cut in his hair solemnly clasped Pratt's hand. "Man, you're a fuckin' legend. Fuckin' Gut Wrench. C'mere, man. I been hearing about you all my life." The kid gathered Pratt in a crushing embrace. "Rock on, dude."

Pratt was mortified by his nickname and had done all he could to forget it. Nobody asked him why he was there. It was just a given. It took three hours to buy their tickets and work their way to their campsite through the heat, dust, dogs, bikes and children continuously cutting in front of them. They wound behind the immense stage that contained luxury accommodations for the guests. The rest of the Chip contained no accommodations save for the notorious concrete pillbox lavatories radiating stench like air fresheners in reverse, and lines of porta-potties, a recent addition to handle the overflow.

A red-hot iron pressed against every inch of exposed flesh.

The Chip smelled of suntan lotion, beer and barbecue.

Choking dust hung in the air.

Tens of thousands of people partied too hard to notice.

The Bedouins had staked out a place at the West End Camp in the southwest corner far from the stage, right up against the barbed wire marking a farm. Pratt set his pup tent at the end of the line next to the fence. Some Bedouins had no tents and planned to sleep under the stars. Great if it didn't rain. If it rained, as it did about one quarter of the time, the Chip turned into Andersonville.

As Pratt stood atop a grassy knoll surveying the acres and acres of biker encampments, he thought, *I'm too fucking old for this.* There was only one thing left to do. He pulled out his cell phone and called Cass. Got a message.

"Hey babe, I'm at the Chip. It's hot and crowded. Talk to you later."

There. Done. Should he have told her he loved her? He'd only known her three days! He wished he had that book, the one with all the rules.

It was already seven and some country duo was twangin' away on the big stage. Edgar Winter was the headliner. Pratt got on his bike and rode the half mile to the front of the stage and the vast semi-circle of concessions at the back of the field. He ate a brat and drank a beer and settled down to watch the show.

Down in front several hundred bikes were parked tighter than a Harley showroom facing the stage. Pratt sat on the ground midway back amid biker families on blankets. Some had brought folding chairs and portable tents. Caravans of people moved to and from the drink concessions holding plastic cups of beer. As the sun sank behind the hills the crowd grew until there were several thousand people camped out in front of the stage.

The acoustic had packed up and left the stage to a smattering of applause. A man in jeans, white shirt and suit vest came out with a wireless mike. "HELLO BIKERS!"

A roar of white noise rose from the crowd accompanied by the shriek of unmuffled engines.

"We're gonna ask you to turn those engines off so we can get this show on the road."

"WHO THE FUCK ARE YOU?" a bull moose bellowed.

"I'm Bob Jacobs, your master of ceremonies! BOB JACOBS! BOB-JACOBS.COM! Now I'd like you all to give a big, Buffalo Chip welcome to the man who, more than any other, made 'chopper' a household word: Peter Fonda."

Peter Fonda came out to huge applause followed by a husky biker wheeling a chopper with an extended fork. Fonda wore snakeskin boots, a Nudie shirt with mother-of-pearl buttons, a ten-gallon hat and aviator shades. He waved to the crowd and said, "I'm here to give away the Make-A-Wish Foundation's raffle chopper."

Thirty feet behind Pratt three Hells Angels carried a heavy nitrous cylinder, which they set up on a promontory and began filling balloons. Five bucks a pop. It had been a Chip tradition for over twenty years. The cops tended to overlook this mild crime. Indeed, there were no police in the Chip unless they were undercover and cycle gangs were notoriously difficult to infiltrate.

Fonda joked with the crowd, opened the envelope and read the winning name. A man whooped and cartwheeled onto the stage. Arm in arm with Peter Fonda he posed for photographs.

Fonda concluded and handed the mike to BOBJACOBS.COM. Bob Jacobs introduced Gretchen Wilson. Standing O.

Pratt remained where he was, of interest to nobody but interested in everything. You couldn't deal crank like nitrous. Chip security would tell the cops. The Chip's owners did not want drug busts or ODs to become part of the Chip Experience.

The crank dealing went on in the shadows, a lot of it in the big semi-circle facing the stage. Pratt got up, wandered through the crowd to the drink vendor at one end of the semi-circle and bought a Pepsi in a jumbo cup. He went behind the booths and walked the semi-circle in shadow, glancing between the booths sipping his Pepsi. The human zoo never failed to fascinate.

Black bikers had become a common feature in recent years. Dykes on Bikes had also increased their numbers. Pratt walked the circuit checking out babes and colors. Gretchen Wilson ended her set to another standing O. BOBJACOBS.COM reminded the crowd about the Red Cross tent accepting blood donations. Pratt wondered if they did any drug testing—before or after.

A rippling blast of alto sax erupted from the stage. Edgar Winter. Pratt turned toward the stage and got shoved aside by a burly mass of muscle and body odor emerging from between two booths. A shove like that would normally ignite an ass-whupping but Pratt wasn't thinking about that. His eyes were glued to the patch on the back of the man's black leather vest.

Pratt followed the War Bonnet into the crowd.

CHAPTER 14

The War Bonnet twitched across camp right through people's camp-fires. One dude yelled, "Hey asshole!" The War Bonnet stopped and turned slowly like a Ouija board planchette. He had a face like a mako shark. Dead eyes. The dude shriveled. The War Bonnet made a beeline through campgrounds across roads heading southwest, the direction of the Bedouins' camp.

Pratt hustled to keep up. He went around camps rather than give the pissed-off campers a second chance at manliness and had to cover more ground. His whacked-out ribs rang every time he juked. A goon on a KTM motocross jumped the path in front of Pratt cackling like a hyena. The bike slammed into a gorse bush with a horrendous grinding sound and a scream of pain. A Geico caveman chased his old lady in a drunken rage. A naked bearded giant, dead ringer for Goya's *Saturn Devouring His Son*, capered with a weather-balloon-sized dollop of nitrous from which he inhaled, dancing madly in the moonlight.

A lady biker rode by on a Bourget wearing nothing but jeans. Pratt thought he was having an acid flashback.

Pratt followed the War Bonnet, worried that he might lose him in the black leather sea. The Bonnet's once white and red patch was so

grimy it was almost illegible. Now he was out of sight. Pratt stepped
it up, jogging. He circled a campfire off the end of a bike-toting land
cruiser, a motor home with an attached garage.

"HEY MOTHERFUCKER!" roared a familiar voice. Pratt couldn't
believe his ears. He looked ahead and kept jogging, his ribs preventing
him from breaking into a flat-out sprint.

The voice pounded up behind him, breathy and menacing. "Hey
asswipe, I'm talking to you."

Pratt glanced over his shoulder as Mastodon President Barnett
limped at him full-tilt boogie with a tire iron. Déjà vu all over again.
Pratt's heart leaped into overdrive. The lumbering giant was right on
his ass. Instinctively Pratt lashed out with a side kick, catching Barnett
in the breadbasket and setting him on his rump. The impact sent an
atomic fireball up Pratt's side. He gasped involuntarily.

"*Whooo!*" a spectator cried.

Chain Mastodon and Knife Mastodon lumbered toward him like a
bad sequel, red eyes testifying to a long hard haul followed by serious
partying. And now it was ass-kickin' time, as it was every evening. The
stitch in Pratt's side slowed him down just enough to catch the end of
Chain's chain on his shoulder, sending a numbwave down his arm.
Pratt faced the Mastodons on a dirt path with alder on either side, less
than twenty feet from a campground. He glanced down looking for a
weapon and spotted a used condom.

Knife Mastodon came in low, slicing upwards. Pratt back-stepped,
barely missing the blade, tripping over an exposed root, falling on his
ass. Chain came in whipping a figure eight, whomping at Pratt's legs.
Pratt withdrew a nanosecond ahead of the chain and scrambled to his
feet, his back against a cottonwood. He looked around for a weapon.
All he had was a buck knife.

Whack! The chain peeled bark off the tree where Pratt's head had
been. He ducked under, planted his crown in Chain's groin and took
him down wrestler style. Pratt crawled up the guy's crotch and head-
butted Chain in the nose, imparting a nausea-inducing blow-back,
blood rushing to his head. He saw stars and flashing blade. Pratt rolled
to one side as the Bowie knife came down, cutting a slash in his jeans
and ending up in Chain Mastodon's thigh.

"AROOOOO!" the Mastodon bawled. Figures danced around the perimeter, filming with their BlackBerries. One dude had a Bonaroo video cam.

Great, Pratt thought.

Barnett used his tire iron to push Chain Mastodon out of the way. Bikers came running. Hot damn. This was better than Edgar Winter.

"That skinny dude's quicker than a cougar," said a bystander.

"Yeah, but three Mastodons . . ."

Pratt scooped up the discarded chain as Barnett charged, tire iron held over one shoulder like a golf club. Pratt whipped. The chain clanged off the iron and hit Pratt in the head. He whirled it overhead like heli rotors and cracked it at Barnett's tire iron hand. Two more Mastodons came running. Pratt stood in a circle of ice-crazed bikers wanting to kill him. They bared their teeth and sprayed spittle. Pratt hadn't been in such a life-threatening situation since his first week in prison.

I wish I'd brought a gun! he thought.

Barnett came in high. Knife Mastodon came in low. Pratt kicked Knife Mastodon in the nuts, threw up an arm and caught the tire iron on his elbow, igniting a thermonuclear explosion that turned his vision white and neutralized every muscle in his body. He couldn't seem to catch his breath.

Pratt went down.

The inchoate roar of some massive carnivore filled the hollow, a sound so deep and primeval it made the hairs on Pratt's neck stand. It came from up the trail behind the Mastodons. Before Knife Mastodon could turn his massive body, the flat of a Scottish Claymore smashed down on the top of his head, collapsing him like a sledgehammer hitting an empty beer can.

The four remaining Mastodons swiveled to face a lump of humanity wearing denim coveralls over an oak-barrel belly, beard to gut, a Viking helmet with two bull's horns, holding a two-handed sword with a three-foot blade.

The Nordic Raider used his sword like Pete Sampras, knocking Mastodons out of the way, parrying steel with steel and smacking steel on flesh. He flicked his Claymore around like a baton, elegant loops ending with the clash of metal on metal. He scooped the blade from Knife Mastodon's hand. He worked his way back to Pratt, where they stood back to back facing all comers.

"Thanks," Pratt said.

"No prob," the Raider rumbled.

One by one, three more Nordic Raiders appeared, each toting a two-handed sword. The Mastodons backed away. They evaporated like the morning dew. They had suddenly turned extinct. The biggest Raider stood about six five. The hirsute cannonball who'd come to Pratt's aid had to weigh 300.

Pratt dropped the chain and stuck out his hand. "Josh Pratt."

"Lars Larsen," the cannonball rumbled, gripping Pratt with the soul clasp.

When Pratt looked around, the War Bonnet was long gone.

CHAPTER 15

Pratt followed the Nordic Raiders to their camp where a javelina roasted on a spit over a barbecue made from a fifty-gallon drum split in half. A bulbous Raider in a purple Bret Favre jersey turned the spit. Two Raider old ladies dished up potato salad, coleslaw and beer from the tailgate of a double-cab F-250. Biker etiquette demanded that Pratt drink and chow down with the gang that saved his life.

Pratt realized he was starving. The War Bonnets weren't going anywhere. It was only the first day. He joined Larsen and two other Nordic Raiders, Sven and Steve, hanging around the barbecue.

"You always travel with swords?" Pratt asked.

"Yeah. We're historical reenactors." Lars winked. "At least that's what we tell the cops."

Pratt gestured to the long sword poking up over Lars' shoulder. "Can I take a look?"

Lars drew the sword with a metallic ring and handed it over. It weighed about five pounds and appeared to be hand-forged. "Where did you get this?"

"Albion Armorers in New Glarus. We're putting on a show with some Indians on Sunday. Premise being the Nordic Raiders got here first and may even have ventured as far west as the Black Hills."

"Is there any evidence to support such a theory?"

"Quite a bit," Lars said, warming to the conversation. "I did my doctoral thesis on it. Traces of bronze found in the Black Hills, evidence that early Nordic Raiders may have mined for gold."

"What do you do for a living?"

"I teach history at Elgin University. You?"

"I'm a private investigator," Pratt said. He always felt silly when he said that. "Last week I recovered a couple of dogs the Mastodons stole to feed their pit bulls. Hence the rumble. I should have guessed they'd show up here."

The Raider in the Bret Favre jersey handed Pratt and Larsen paper plates with barbecued hog and a roll of paper towels. Larsen was about to dive in when Pratt bowed his head.

"Lord," he said softly, "for this food we are about to receive we thank you."

"Amen," Favre said.

"So what are you doing out here?" Larsen said.

"Somebody hijacked a truck last week, stole four Ducati V-4s." It wasn't a lie. Pratt couldn't say why he was reluctant to discuss Ginger's case but some still-small voice urged caution.

"Man," Lars said, "I haven't done toes down since I was in college. I used to have a GPz550. It's a miracle I didn't kill myself on that thing. I couldn't bend myself around one of those crotch rockets today if I tried."

They decried the squids whose antics made it difficult for all bikers. Pratt tossed down more ibuprofen. Pratt and Larsen drank Irish whiskey and swore eternal allegiance to one another. Lars removed a card from his fat Harley wallet. Pratt took out one of Bloom's and wrote his number and e-mail address on the back.

Pratt left his bike in front of the stage and made his way to the Bedouins' camp on foot. You could leave your bike anywhere in Sturgis with the key in and nobody would touch it. Bullshit

Pratt lay in his sleeping bag listening to a non-stop chorus of revving engines, shrieks of joy and pain, cursing and the distant throbbing of the band. He screwed in his ear plugs and fell into deep sleep.

Pratt rose at seven, crawled out of his tent, walked to the fence to piss and climbed a rock to survey the Chip, which looked like the aftermath of battle, bodies lying everywhere and smoke rising from countless campfires. There would be no action until the Chip heated up around eight or nine that evening. Pratt decided to go into town.

His bike was where he'd left it. He started her up and joined the long dusty line snaking back from the exit. A deputy directed traffic in and out of the Chip. Traffic into Sturgis was thick and slow. Nobody tried to pass, wheelie or do anything crazy. An SDHP cop stood next to his blue strobing bike.

The line moved so slow, Pratt may as well have pushed his bike into town.

By the time Pratt found a parking spot it was ten. You could literally walk across Sturgis stepping only on motorcycles. Main Street looked like the world's biggest motorcycle showroom. A line stretched out the front door and down the block from Sturgis Breakfast and Brunch. Pratt bought a corn dog and a raspberry Slurpee from a vendor and ate it standing up along with a couple of ibuprofens.

Pratt saw several "John Deere" Harleys, a Confederate Wraith, Big Dogs, Indians, Beemers, restored Vincents, Excelsior-Hendersons, Ducati Monsters and speed bikes, Aprilias, Bimotas, Bourgets and one-off customs of no discernible heritage. He saw every kind of bike but the Desmosedici. Since that vehicle had not been officially released in the United States, the one that passed him had to be hot.

Not that he was prepared to do anything about it. A block off Main were the vendors, tat studios, massage therapists, every kind of leather, hop-ups and add-ons. Pratt walked the route, stunned by the sheer press of humanity. The air smelled of sizzling meat, suntan oil and pine.

Traffic cruised Main Street at five miles per hour under the watchful eyes of local deputies. By eleven it was ninety degrees out and the women were showing off their breasts. A couple cruised by on a Harley that looked like a buffalo, draped with skins, horns sprouting from the furred fairing. The woman must have weighed two hundred pounds, her gut bulging over her leather skirt, showing off her gigantic boobs like rare fruit. A cop turned away in disgust.

It took Pratt an hour and a half to get back into the Chip. He rode his bike all the way back to the camp where half the Bedouins were still zonked out. Pratt crawled into his tent, opened both ends to catch the nonexistent breeze, and fell into a shallow slumber in which he dreamed he was still in the joint, in the lunch line, and a man who was pure scar tissue was about to grab the last piece of lasagna. Pratt tried to break free but the other cons kept pulling him back.

He woke covered with sweat.

He knew what he had to do.

It was going to be a bitch.

CHAPTER 16

Saturday night Jonny Lang was the headliner. A Guns 'N' Roses tribute band was onstage when Pratt tossed down his coffee can lid at the end of a long semi-circle of bikes facing the stage. He'd talked to Cass earlier. She'd just come back from making the rounds of her fireworks stands in Wisconsin and Minnesota. Her employees had proven slothful and mendacious. She had no assets. She was thinking of going back to dealing blackjack. Pratt told her they'd talk when he got back.

If she was looking at Pratt for money she was shit out of luck. "Son," his dad had told him. "Never play cards with a man called Doc. Never eat at a place called Mom's. And never go to bed with a woman who has more problems than you." Probably the only worthwhile advice Duane had ever given him, even if it wasn't original.

The sheer craziness of the scene banished all thoughts of Cass. Children in Harley diapers ran through the crowd. Hundreds had put down blankets to watch the show. It looked like Family Picnic Day in Heavy Metal Hell. The Hells Angels sold balloons filled with nitrous. The Sons of Baal worked the crowd with lids.

At nine-thirty Pratt spotted the War Bonnet from the previous night, face like a fist, doing business in the shadows between a pizza joint and a tattoo parlor. His patch showed a skull wearing a war bonnet. Pratt shadowed the guy for over an hour as the Bonnet unloaded his stash, baggie by baggie.

Finally the Bonnet exhausted his supply. Pratt watched him explain to a bearded giant, hold a hand up indicating he'd be back. The War Bonnet headed up the dirt road away from the stage with a herky-jerky power walk indicating he'd been sampling his wares. Pratt was almost jogging, ribs pulsing dull red. Over a slight hill a mob had converged, a sea of black leather. The Rum Wranglers New Orleans met up with the Minneapolis branch. Guys kissing each other on the lips.

The War Bonnet had disappeared.

All those non-conformists looked alike.

"Fuck!" Pratt said, hustling around the mob. His detour expanded as most land next to the road had been staked out. By the time Pratt got back to the road, no sign of the War Bonnet remained. Pratt hustled up the road hoping to catch up with the distinctive patch.

Pratt was reluctant to ask after the War Bonnets because word would spread. He cursed himself for not taking time that morning to walk the camp when most of the bikers were sleeping off binges, inactive wasps in the cool of dawn. He stood on a rock and did a three-sixty, clenching his fists in frustration.

Double fuck.

He'd lost him.

But the night was young. Pratt decided to follow the road as it zig-zagged back through the trees. A drunken biker pursued a laughing nude woman through the trees, tripped and fell on his face. A thousand boom boxes blasted from all sides, heavy on the blues 'n' boogie. Unmuffled engines shrieked until it seemed they would explode. Some exploded.

It was louder than Cheap Trick Live. A boiler factory didn't come close. An engine revved and revved, grinding on Pratt's nerves until he saw red and started looking for the source to punch him out.

And then, the most beautiful sound in the world—click-WHUMP as the engine tossed a valve and died. Like someone had removed a nail from between Pratt's eyes. He shook his head in relief and looked around. No War Bonnets. Ahead lay a mini-encampment of two of the biker motor homes with the garages in back, a cluster of bikers gathered around something, a bike or a gang bang. Their patches were so dirt-besmeared he couldn't read them.

He was level with the group when an incredible sound broke from the cluster and rose into the trees, raising the hair on the back of Pratt's neck. Only one engine in the world made that sound.

Desmosedici.

Pratt couldn't stop himself. He turned toward the cluster of men and elbowed his way to the front, where a greasy figure in leather and denim straddled the carmine red space age bullet working the throttle. The man looked up.

President Robles of the Aztec Skulls.

CHAPTER 17

Robles' mouth formed a perfect circle inside his parenthetical mustache. Pratt braced for flight or fight. Robles unexpectedly grinned. "*Praaaaatt.* Choo get chur dogs back?"

"Yeah, thanks. Sorry about ruining your evening."

Robles turned the engine off, kicked out the stand and got off. Pratt steeled for a boot or brass knuckles. Instead Robles threw wide his arms and embraced Pratt. They slapped each other on the back.

"That's okay, ese. Least we didn't lose no dogs."

"Where'dja get the Desmo?"

Robles grinned snarkily. "Aztec magic, what can I say? Want to buy it?"

They were hiding in plain sight. No one would think to look for a hot bike on the streets of Sturgis because you couldn't get anywhere faster than five miles per. Nor could the cops search every van and pick-up. The South Dakota Chamber of Commerce made sure of that.

"Maybe," Pratt said.

Robles tilted his head back, a gold tooth reflecting light from a passing bike. "Choo serious? Choo know, fool me once, chame on you. Fool me twice. . . . Let me put it this way." Robles threw an arm over

Pratt's shoulder. "I can't say choo lied to us but you did attend that dogfight under false pretenses, choo know what I'm sayin'? On the other hand I like chour style. The way you took on three Mastodons, that ain't something choo see every day. When they started kicking choo on the ground, man, it looked like an army of fire ants on a dead coon." Robles tilted his head back and brayed. His nostrils were wet and red-rimmed. Twin slicks ran through his mustache.

A crazy idea popped into Pratt's head. It was ten-thirty at night. If he returned to the main stage he might pick up the War Bonnet, he might not. In any case the War Bonnets would be back the next night and the next until they ran out of crank or the event ended. Eric had been missing for sixteen years. Another day wouldn't make much of a difference. There was no urgency.

No one had done more for him than Danny Bloom. Delivering one of the stolen Ducatis would be a nice feather in Bloom's cap.

"I want to take it for a ride," Pratt said.

Robles stared and guffawed. "Choo know what that bike is worth, man?"

"Well how much do you want for it?"

"I can get fifty grand from some dudes I know. Choo got that kind of dough?"

"Not right now but I can get it."

"Choo gots to be shittin' me, bro. Where's a butt-ugly private ass investigator get that kinda dough?"

"You'd be surprised."

"Surprise me."

Pratt pulled out his wallet attached to his belt with a chain, opened it, and took out ten hundred dollar bills. He held it up like a dog treat. "How 'bout you sit on this thou for me while I take it for a test ride? What am I gonna do? Steal it? I'm already in deep shit with you guys. This is my way of making it right. I put a ding in it, the thou's yours."

Robles tucked the thou into his vest. "How 'bout the thou's mine already? Okay. I let choo take it for a ride but to make chure you don't suddenly go off the reservation, ahmina have my man Taco ride along with choo, okay? And don't try to lose Taco, he's been racing dirt bikes since he was seven."

Taco appeared at Robles' side glaring at Pratt with raw hatred, pinpoint pupils screaming mean little thoughts.

"Taco, dude, I feel we got off on the wrong foot," Pratt said, stepping forward and offering his hand.

Taco stared. Robles nudged him. "Do it, bro."

As Taco reluctantly put his hand out, Pratt grinned and brushed back his hair. "Just joshin', dude! Get it? I'm Josh! It's what I do! It's okay to hate me, bro! We all need someone we can cream on."

Sensing ridicule, Taco worked his jaw and deposited a wad of phlegm that narrowly missed Josh's boot.

Minutes later the Aztec Skulls had unloaded a modified Hayabusa. Taco put on a black leather jacket, gloves and aviator goggles. Pratt straddled the Desmo, hunched over like a Doberman humping a poodle, and hit the starter. He had a bandanna tied around his head and wore ski goggles courtesy of Robles.

The Aztec prez made an "after you, Alphonse" gesture. Pratt clicked the Italian V-4 into gear and let out the clutch. The machine lurched forward. Fussy clutch. Taco followed. It took them twenty minutes to traverse the half mile to the front gate, stopping for every dog, Dick and Harry that crossed their path.

They got fresh stamps at the gate. Pratt turned west toward the Hills. Revelers wandered Sturgis in packs clutching plastic beer cups and souvenir tees. Traffic had thinned to a reasonable rate and soon they were riding through Sturgis, circling Main Street via a series of detours until they came out the other side facing Deadwood Canyon. As soon as the road opened up Pratt scouted for heat and goosed it, hoiking the compact bike into a fifty-yard wheelie before setting down the front tire with a squeak. The more Pratt twisted the throttle the faster the Desmo went until the rush of wind obliterated all sound, leaving only a sensation of speed, of rushing endlessly forward with eyeball-flattening thrust, canyon walls streaming by like man-sized carbon paper.

He glanced at the digital speedo: 150. So was his pulse. He had one of those head-smacking moments. *Was he insane?*

The road curved and Pratt squeezed the brakes, feeling the pulse of the ceramic brake disc through the levers. Taco was on his ass in an instant, sticking with him through the twisties like a draft racer, daring Pratt to make a mistake so they could both go down in a heap of twisted metal. Pratt came up on the rear bumper of a Wayfarer land yacht, bicycles bungeed to the rear, trailer hitch pulling a Jeep. Even at eleven, traffic was dense throughout the hills as tourists sought to circumvent or flee Bike Week, joined by burnt-out bikers who'd had enough.

Pratt juked left, sticking his nose into oncoming traffic. SUV coming a hundred yards down the road. No prob. He yanked the throttle and rocketed into the opposite lane of traffic, passing the land yacht in a blur and pulling in tight. The SUV was almost on him. The angry driver flashed his high-beams and honked. Taco was forced to jerk back into lane behind the land yacht.

The road twisted through the canyon like a sidewinder, just enough traffic to make passing impossible. Rounding another hairpin Pratt pulled way to the right to avoid a semi pulling two segments, its bigfoot encroaching into his lane. The Desmo's horns resonated in the narrow canyon as Pratt flipped the startled driver the bird.

Pratt came up fast on the bumper of a Porsche Cayman. The driver grinned and downshifted. A quarter mile opened up before them. Pratt downshifted and twisted the throttle, momentarily lifting the front tire and accelerating past the Cayman as if it were parked, seeing a white Suburban coming way too fast, standing on the brakes and cutting in front of the Porsche with mere feet to spare.

Taco, bug-eyed with fury, waited until the Suburban passed before shooting into the opposite lane in a desperate attempt to keep Pratt in sight. They approached a decreasing radius turn around a piece of rock that looked like Gibraltar. Pratt saw the pick-up first—the automotive equivalent of a linebacker. The massive pick-up was ten miles over the limit. Taco was about twenty miles over the limit. The distance between them closed faster than a Chrysler dealership.

Pratt glanced once in his rearview.

SPLANG! A nanosecond of flesh and metal in a Cuisinart.

The enormous impact smacked Pratt like a slap to the back of the head. He swooped around the bend grinding his teeth, leaving chaos spread across two lanes of traffic. The highway would be closed for hours. Angry cell phone calls would reverberate through the night. *Sic transit gloria, Taco.*

My God, what have I done?

Regret blossomed in his gut like one of Cass' Roman candles. Had he deliberately led Taco to his death? Was that who he was? He hadn't let that thought coalesce while he was leading the Skull in near suicidal fashion but it had always been in the back of his mind. What kind of game had they been playing? Before prison he wouldn't have given Taco's death a second though.

He's fucking dead, Josh.

Pratt knew nothing about Taco. What if he had a wife and kids? What if he had a mutt he'd adopted that waited for him every day?

Was it the wind through his goggles that caused his eyes to tear? He could barely see. Pratt slowed down and noted that the Cayman was at least a quarter mile back, chastened by what had happened.

Pratt found a runaway truck ramp and pulled off. He shook so bad he nearly dumped the bike. He got a kickstand down, semaphored his right leg and collapsed by the side of the road on a discarded piece of plywood. His heart went *thub-a-duh, thub-a-duh. He'd just killed a man.*

God forgive me.

It wasn't until an SDHP cruiser and an ambulance shrieked by with all lights blazing that he got on his bike and headed west, scrupulously obeying the speed limit.

CHAPTER 18

The sun was rising as a weary Pratt turned into a strip mall on the outskirts of Rapid City. The mall contained a Walgreens, a veterinarian, a karate school and a Trans-Continental office. Pratt parked the bike in front of the insurance office, locked the fork, and went across the highway to McDonald's for coffee and an Egg McMuffin.

The familiar smell hit him like a wall of warm fat. This McDonald's was done Western style, with faux-aged wood booths and prints of Boot Hill. Pratt took his coffee and McMuffin to a booth in the back and settled in with a groan. It was five-thirty. Too early to call Bloom. He was the only patron. He swallowed two ibuprofens and read the *Sioux Falls Argus Leader*, the *Rapid City Shopper* and the *Rapid Daily News*. The rally dominated the headlines, as it did every year at this time.

Newspaper editors liked perennials. They trotted out the old observations and homilies and breathed easy until a real story occurred and they had to work.

STURGIS OFF TO ROARING START
ESTIMATE 550,000 AT RALLY
STATE POLICE CLOSE I-90

FATAL ACCIDENT CLOSES NEEDLES HIGHWAY

The Entertainment section: Edgar Winter at the Chip, Gretchen Wilson at the Full Throttle.

Sports: Duane Newsom of Mt. Vernon, WI, Dominates Hill Climb.

Lifestyle: "Dear Abby: I am a biker widow. Every year my husband and his friends take off for ten days and leave me and the kids by ourselves . . ."

Police blotter: "A man became enraged when a tattoo artist mistakenly gave him a Honda tattoo instead of the Harley he had requested, and assaulted the tattoo artist with a chair and the tattoo needle. Ralph T. Bromley of Belleville, CO, has been charged with Atrocious Assault, Public Indecency and resisting arrest . . ."

Total Sturgis-related deaths since rally began: four.

By the time he'd had a refill and polished off the papers it was seven-thirty. He called Bloom.

Bloom answered on the second ring. "Why so early, Josh?"

"I recovered one of your Desmos."

"What?"

"I recovered one of your Desmos. I'm leaving it with the local Trans-Continental office in Rapid City. He'll open in a half hour and I'll call you from there."

"Just one?"

"You're welcome. I'm not working the case. It fell into my lap."

"Well thanks. One is better than nothing. How'd you do it?"

"Aztec Skulls pulled the heist. They were selling hot bikes. I took one for a test ride. You owe me a thou for expenses and whatever you think it's worth. Unfortunately, there was a fatality involved. The Skull following me ran into traffic."

"Are you in any trouble?"

"The Skulls could be a mite ticked off. I'm not going to let them stop me."

"How's your case coming?"

"I have a lead. With any luck I can wrap this up quickly and devote myself full-time to your Desmos."

"There's no rush on that. I've got Hank Meyer on it."

"Hank Meyer couldn't find his feet in his socks."

"Well all the more reason for you to wrap up whatever you're doing and get back on it. Let me know if you need anything."

A new Ford Taurus had pulled in next to the Desmo. A man in a light gray suit got out, giving the motorcycle an appreciative stare before unlocking the door to the Trans-Continental office.

"The insurance guy's here. I'll call you back in fifteen."

"Okay."

Pratt gathered the newspapers and put them in a wall rack on his way out. Traffic on the interstate had picked up. Pratt waited until a kamikaze Honda screamed by and dashed across the street full sprint. Lots of bikers heading north.

The name on the door was Ed Kazynski. Pratt pushed through into a reception/office area, the man in the gray suit looking up from his gray desk near the front. He was a big man with a large oval head, a ruddy complexion and the easy bonhomie of the born salesman.

"Is that your Ducati?" Ed Kazynski boomed.

Josh stepped forward and stuck out his hand. "Yes sir. Josh Pratt. I'm a private investigator."

Kazynski stood and pumped Josh's hand. "Well then I guess that's our Ducati!"

"That's right, sir. I'm actually on another case right now, and coming across this Desmo was a fluke."

Kazynski frowned. "Our man in Madison said he had someone working on this full-time."

"That's true, sir. An investigator named Hank Meyer."

"Well this is a lucky break for us. Do you need anything from me?"

"A receipt. And I could use a ride to Sturgis."

Kazynski looked at his calendar. "Why don't you bring that motorcycle around to the back door. I'll run you up myself."

Pratt rode around the strip mall to the back, where Kazynski had opened a steel door into the back of his shop. The Desmo slotted neatly through the door. Pratt left it in a crowded storeroom next to the ink erasers with the key in it.

Kazynski typed up a receipt and signed it. They headed north in Kazynski's Taurus.

Once on the interstate he floored it. A giant hand pushed Pratt back into his seat.

"Wow," he said. "What's under the hood?"

"Twin turbo 3.5-liter V-6. It's the new SHO."

The thrills did not last long as they came up on the end of a gelatinous line of traffic headed for the rally. It was Monday morning. They cruised at thirty-five between cycle cavalcades. State troopers with flashing lights stood by the side of the road.

"Normally this is a forty-five minute drive," Kazynski said.

"These are the rains that let a thousand businesses flourish," Pratt said.

"Buddy, you said it. Sturgis accounts for fifty percent of all South Dakota tourism. You got your Rushmore, you got your Crazy Horse, Corn Palace, Wall Drug, whatever. None of them hold a candle to the granddaddy of all cycle rallies."

Krazynski's cell phone rang. He took it. Kazynski talked policy with a client as they inched forward. Pratt pulled out his own cell and called Bloom.

"The baby has been delivered." Pratt gave Bloom the details off Kazynski's card.

The abrupt wail of a police siren three feet from their rear caused them both to jump.

A state bike cop was keeping pace. Kazynski lowered the window. Heat poured in.

"Put the cell phone away, sir. It's against the law." The cop bent down to give Pratt the hairy eyeball.

"Gotta go, Danny." Pratt hung up.

Kazynski hung up. "I know that, Officer. I'm sorry. I shouldn't have taken that call."

The cop gave a slight nod. A whoop sounded from behind them. The cop glanced back down the long line of stalled cars and bikes and fingered the speakerphone pinned to his shirt.

"What's going on?"

"We got shots fired at the Chip," announced a staticky voice. "The Aztec Skulls and the Vandals are going at it."

CHAPTER 19

Without another word the cop clicked into gear and tore off down the shoulder. The whoop from behind was joined by a half dozen sirens from every direction.

Pratt glanced at Kazynski. The insurance agent looked pale and had begun to sweat.

"I'll get out here, thanks," Pratt said, opening the door. "No need to fight your way through town."

Kazynski smiled in gratitude. "'Preciate it, Josh. I'll see that the bike goes to the right people."

With a salute Pratt shut the door and stepped out on the shoulder. He heard more whoops converging on the Chip to the north. The highway was a solid mass of chrome and metal, hirsute and overweight bikers sitting by the side of the road stripping off leather.

With gang activity tying up law enforcement and likely shutting down all traffic, Pratt would be better off walking. Pulling the bill of his gimme cap low over his nose, he strode north up the shoulder, passing numerous bikers and ordinary families on vacation who had elected to get out of their vehicles.

The temp was in the low eighties. Pratt was thirsty. He passed a family having a picnic with a cooler stuffed with soft drinks. Pratt stopped and pulled out his wallet.

"Like to buy one of those sodas from you," he said to the father, a portly man in a white Lacoste shirt and Bermuda shorts sitting on a blanket with his wife and two children, a boy and a girl.

The man waved Pratt's money away. "Just take one. We got plenty."

"Daddy, is that a biker?" the little boy said, peering out from behind his father's shoulder.

"I'm a biker all right," Josh said. "I just don't have a bike."

He waved and moved on, popping the top. The cold Coke went down like a frozen avalanche. He drank it all, crushing the can into a flat disc, which he put in his rear pocket. Pratt saw Sturgis from a slight incline. It had been transformed into a glittering brooch with the addition of hundreds of thousands of chromed bikes.

"You got the right idea, brother," a stalled biker called from traffic.

Twenty minutes later he was walking down Junction Street. Pratt made it to the Broken Spoke. He stopped, stretched and entered the bar. He used the facilities and ordered another Coke. Everybody was talking about the fight.

"I heard the Vandals started it," said a dude at the bar wearing a wife beater that showcased his tribal tats. "Now they're scattered all over the plains and the Highway Patrol is rounding them up one by one."

"Anybody killed?" the bartender asked.

"I heard three Skulls got shot but nobody knows if they died."

The talk filled Pratt with a great weariness as he contemplated the futility and stupidity of inter-tribal warfare, as ritualized and pointless as any obscure government bureaucracy. The Bedouins had been locked in a debilitating feud with the Quad City Rockers for many years, which eventually led to the dissolution of both gangs.

Pratt hitched a ride with a vendor in a pick-up. The drive out to the Chip was glacial. The laconic vendor said, "Sturgis comes but once a year. And when it comes it brings good cheer," before lapsing into calm resignation. Pratt fell asleep in the truck. He woke when two ambulances screamed by on the shoulder heading into town.

"Bad for business," the vendor groused, chain-smoking Camels. It took forty-five minutes to reach the Chip from the Broken Spoke. Pratt thanked the man and jumped out at the gate, flashing his bracelet to the guard.

Six SDHP squad cars crowded the shoulder just outside the gate. Pratt made his way through the milling mob toward the main stage where he'd left his bike.

Three cop cars occupied the area in front of the main stage. Most of the bikes had been moved. Pratt waited at the yellow tape for a cop to permit him to retrieve his bike, which he'd left in front of the stage. He got the story while waiting.

The Vandals and the Skulls had a long-standing beef that began when three Skulls jumped a Vandal in Reno in 1999. They'd taken their feud to Daytona Beach and Laughlin, Nevada. They'd taken their feud to Canada and Mexico.

In the wee hours of the morning, while the Skulls partied in front of the stage, two Vandals with bandannas over their faces unloaded with Mac-10s, shooting four Skulls, two fatally. The Vandals split the scene before the cops got there. The cops hadn't released any names.

Nobody knew if the show would go on. Prior to this, there hadn't been a comparable incident at Sturgis in twenty years. The gangs had all learned to get along. The big worry was that the shooting would result in the Chip's being forced to close, losing a major chunk of change, and that the bad publicity would affect Bike Week for years to come. Most bikers were outraged and would have cooked the Vandals on a spit and served them up as barbecue.

Pratt rode/walked his way through the choking dust back toward his camp. Monster wasps vibrated the air as hands twisted throttles. Many bikers saw this as heaven but Pratt saw it for what it was, a pathetic gathering of perpetual adolescents clinging to a mock image of toughness, outlaws excluded. For them the toughness was real and often resulted in injury or premature death. They were pretty far down the list of enlightened species.

Pratt's camp was as he left it. There was virtually no theft inside the Chip. It was like Hong Kong in that respect. The Vandals had broken a sacred trust and henceforth would be cast out even among the lowest of the low. Maybe that was the point. The Vandals had lowered themselves to legendary status. Pratt was glad none of the Bedouins were around. It was one-thirty in the afternoon and the heat was fierce. He had barely crawled inside his pup tent when he lay down on the mat and crashed.

Every time he woke up he heard sirens wailing.

CHAPTER 20

Pratt woke to a howling cacophony of voices, bikes and country music. The sun barely hovered above the hills, lasering in at an angle, turning bikes to gold and leaves to emeralds. Pratt rolled over and checked his watch.

It was seven-thirty. He'd slept for six hours.

He checked his phone. Cass had left a "I love you, baby." He called her back, got her phone and left her one.

Pratt crawled out, relieved himself against the barbed wire and prepared for the long haul to the showers. He felt stitched together with duct tape and baling wire. The morning incident had left powder charge in the air. More booze- and drug-crazed bikers howled at the full moon, already rushing the sun offstage.

Some loon kept shrieking, "Yeeeeeee-HA!" with a Southern accent. More bikers flying the stars and bars. Pratt stood in line for fifteen minutes for his turn at the shower. The water was lukewarm but at least he'd sluiced. He took two ibuprofens.

Dusk had fallen by the time he got back to his camp. It was going to happen tonight. He could feel the electric tide rising in his bones. He changed into a fresh shirt, underwear and Packers cap and packed his tank bag with water, gloves, a light backpack, maps, goggles and rain suit and headed back to the stage. He wore a pair of Gargoyles.

The sonic throom of the blues vibrated through the ground. Jonny Lang was opening for Lynyrd Skynyrd. Bikers were still pissed about Harley's 100th anniversary party where they'd booked Elton John. Why not just book RuPaul and be done with it? The Chip knew its audience better than Harley.

The cops had left and taken their crime tape. The Chip was back to normal, with several thousand people milling in front of the stage as Jonny Lang went down on one knee, face twisted in exquisite agony as he plucked a chord that would make a banker weep.

Pratt hung back near the concessions, purchased a smoked turkey leg, of which he could only consume half, and handed the rest to a starving biker. Pratt watched people for an hour. A lot of people were letting it all hang out when they shouldn't have let any of it hang out. There was something about biker cons and Sturgis in particular that erased the inhibitions of men and women of a certain age.

Pratt spotted the War Bonnet between Jake's Tattoo and Domino's Pizza, furtively trading with a wan blond who looked like she'd been left in the rinse cycle too long. Pratt hung back and observed.

Over the next hour, while Jonny Lang finished and Lynyrd Skynyrd came on, the War Bonnet did a dozen deals. Then he was out. Like before, he headed toward home base. This time Pratt would not be distracted.

The War Bonnet walked right by him. The War Bonnet had a pronounced occipital brow and a full face beard. The full moon lit the campgrounds like Stalag 17. The War Bonnet had a bald patch on the crown of his head that looked like an eagle's nest. He moved with a herky-jerky motion. People stepped aside for him. He broadcast bad juju.

The dusty road was chock-a-block with drunks, stoners, tweakers, shooters and trippers. Pratt was invisible. He followed the War Bonnet for a half mile through the campgrounds to an ivory LaFarge Motor Home parked in a copse of cottonwood, two rat bikes in front.

Pratt stood behind some cottonwood and alder as the War Bonnet knocked on the door. A second later the door opened. Lights went on in the motor home but Pratt couldn't see anything. The angle was wrong and the rear windows had their blinds shut. He knew what was going on. The vendor was replenishing his supply. The War Bonnets kept their stash in the motor home.

Fifteen minutes later the vendor left the motor home walking more spasmodically than before and headed back to the stage. Pratt stayed where he was. The blinds on the motor home went up and Pratt could see inside. There appeared to be only one dude. Of course there may have been more in the bedroom but with Lynyrd Skynyrd just tuning up that was doubtful.

If the trailer's a rockin', don't bother knockin'.

The trailer was not rocking. Pratt watched and waited. The dude in the motor home seemed to be straightening up the joint. That open blind was going to be a problem. The War Bonnet peered into the darkness and closed the blind.

Don't think about it, just do it.

Pratt let his gut go slack before heading to the motor home. What he was about to do made his asshole ride up between his shoulder blades and gave him the heebie-jeebies. He strode up to the door as if it were his own, glanced around once. Nada. The door hinged outward. Pratt knocked on the door.

The motor home shifted as the dude inside jumped. A second later the door opened two inches, dude inside peering down with an evil brown eye.

"What the fuck," he said.

Pratt ripped the door open with his left hand and punched the guy in the balls with his right hand. The man immediately collapsed in agony. With a quick glance around Pratt leaped into the motor home, dragged the War Bonnet away from the door by his collar and shut the door. The Bonnet had a shaved skull and a 'stache and for an instant Pratt thought he'd got lucky and found Moon.

Pratt looked down. This dude wasn't old enough to be Moon although his face bore all the signs of hard living, crackle-finish skin from a lifetime of smoking, pinpoint pupils from sampling his product. The War Bonnet curled up like a carpet worm, looking up with tiny rage-filled eyes.

"You're a dead motherfucker, you know that?" the Bonnet said through gritted teeth.

Pratt kicked him in the ribs with his pointy-toed boot. "Where's the shit?" he seethed. Blood rose in him like a gusher. He was Gut Wrench again. The violence fed off itself as his instincts urged him to finish the job. He plunged a knee into the man's bruised rib and pulled his boot knife.

Pratt stuck the point under the War Bonnet's chin. "Where's the shit?" he growled in a voice he didn't recognize. Green with pain, the man pointed at an overhead compartment. Pratt kicked the War Bonnet's legs apart, dug a buck knife out of the Bonnet's side pocket and stomped on the man's hand. Pratt grabbed a greasy cast-iron pan from the stove and brought it down sideways against the Bonnet's temple with a temple bell gong. The War Bonnet banged down sideways and lay inert.

Pratt ripped open the compartment. Inside was a patched-leather duffel bag. He yanked it out, set it on the sofa and ripped it open. Inside a jumbo zip lock contained about a pound of gleaming meth. There was a triple beam balance in the cupboard as well as a pack of little baggies and several sterile hypos.

Pratt looked around for CCTV. Nada.

Quickly Pratt stepped to the bedroom and threw wide the card paper door. The tiny room was empty, sheets in disarray, smelling of stale sweat and cigarette smoke. Pratt turned off all the lights, stepped over the inert War Bonnet and fled into the night.

CHAPTER 21

Pratt made a beeline for the nearest concrete privy, a hundred yards away. The beeline veered around campsites and trees. From ten feet the privy smelled like the devil's asshole, an acidic stench that peeled the bark off trees. Eyes watering, Pratt went up to the sprung wooden door and pushed it aside with his foot. Inside he could see the floor covered with feces, used condoms, toilet paper, rags and two feet poking out from under a pile of rags. Dude was folded on his side snoring like raw static.

How fucked-up was that dude, to fall asleep in the Chip's privy? Pratt didn't want to think about it.

Pratt couldn't even imagine using one of the privies, let alone sleeping in it. He tossed the zip lock of crank into the toilet. An instant later there was a moist splat. Pratt got away from there. There were people right there at the Chip who would gladly dive into that privy if they knew what was down there.

On the way back, his cell buzzed in his pocket. It was Cass. He was immediately resentful. Couldn't the bitch leave him alone? As certain as night follows day came the shame. She loved him, or at least she thought she did.

"Are you all right?" she asked breathlessly.

"I'm fine."

"I heard about the riots. It's all over the news."

"I wasn't around when it happened, babe. But thanks for your concern."

"And then I read that a guy I knew died in a traffic accident last night."

That would be Taco.

"I don't know anything about it, babe. I can't really talk right now. I'm in the middle of something. I'll call you back."

"Love you."

"Love you."

Pratt returned to his perch across the way from the trailer. Folded against the base of a tree he was nearly invisible. The lights went back on in the motor home. The first thing the War Bonnet would do was phone his supplier. Next he would phone the cave man and any other War Bonnets in the Hills.

The War Bonnets would seek vengeance. Pratt was pretty sure he would be hard to identify. He'd worn a cap and Gargoyles the whole time. Long sleeves covered his ink. They'd be perplexed. And furious.

Ten minutes later the caveman jogged up to the motor home, sweat popping on his bony face, panting like a winded dog. Caveman's eyes bulged from the exertion. Pratt half expected him to have a thrombo right there. One hand on his knee for support, the caveman knocked.

The door popped open and caveman went inside.

For long seconds there was relative silence as the War Bonnet explained the situation. Pratt could practically see crimson bolts of fury radiating from the motor home.

"Why do I have to go?" caveman wailed, followed by the smack of flesh on flesh.

"Because I say so, asshole."

A window cranked shut.

Seconds later two War Bonnets rumbled up to the motor home on rat bikes, tossed down plates for their kickstands, got off and knocked on the door. They went inside. The bikes were rat bastard Harleys, one with twin leather saddlebags.

More shouting from inside. Glass breaking. Cries of anger and astonishment. "Motherfucker!" escaped the cone of silence.

It was only the third day. The War Bonnets couldn't afford to turn their franchise over to somebody else. They'd never get it back. So they had to come up with more crank for the rest of the weeklong celebration. Pratt believed the War Bonnets would send a rider. Pratt would follow the rider to the source.

About twenty minutes later one of the War Bonnets, not caveman, came out and got on the rat Harley with the saddlebags. The rat Harley had a brake light hanging off the right chassis near the axle, just above the vertically displayed license plate. No turn signals. The Bonnets weren't the type who signaled turns.

Eric, here I come.

Pratt stared a hole in the Bonnet's colors knowing that each rugged individualist looked more or less like the next rugged individualist. The Bonnet started his Harley. Pratt ran for his bike.

Pratt pissed off a few people in his mad scramble to catch up with the Bonnet. Someone threw a full can of beer at him, followed by, "Hey asshole!" Pratt didn't turn. He kept on moving. He sympathized with the can thrower. He reached the front gate in twenty minutes and joined the queue waiting to get out. The Bonnet was two bikes ahead of him. It was nine-thirty.

A few minutes later he showed his ticket stub and got a yellow bracelet to wear back in.

The Bonnet turned west toward town and Pratt followed. The Bonnet trolled sedately through town before turning west on Highway 14 toward Deadwood.

Here we go again, Pratt thought.

Traffic was intense even at the late hour, thousands of bikes roaming the Hills, motorized Conestogas hauling families hither and yon, trucks bearing bawling cattle and bales of hay. The Bonnet was in no particular hurry and went with the flow. Pratt was happy to lie back and keep an eye out for the low red brake light.

The Bonnet stopped in Deadwood to gas up at a Kum & Go. Pratt motored past and filled his own tank at a Conoco, lining up behind a full-dress Kawasaki with a teddy bear bungeed to the sissy bar. The dresser's owner tried to talk to Pratt, but Pratt smiled and said, "Gotta go. Have a good ride."

He paid via credit card at the pump and waited in the shadow of a closed supermarket until the Bonnet passed him heading west. They were in Wyoming an hour before the sun cast low beams on the western horizon. There were enough bikers heading every which way to conceal Pratt for a while, but sooner or later that would thin out and he'd be on his own.

West on 90 through Gillette headed toward Buffalo. A wash of wind rolled over Pratt with every eastbound semi. The capricious wind threatened to blow him off the road. At other times it was meek as a clam. Sun and wind sucked water out of him like a giant ShamWow. Pratt thought of T.E. Lawrence crossing *Al Rub al Qali*—the "Empty Quarter," on the way to liberating Aqaba. He rode to Maurice Jarre's stirring theme to *Lawrence of Arabia* echoing in his head.

When the camels die, we die. And in twenty days they will begin to die.

They rode for hours beneath the blinding sun. Pratt drank water on the go, one hand on the bar. Three and a half bottles left. When the Bonnet stopped in Buffalo to fill up, Pratt held back, watching from a promontory on the edge of town until the biker moved off. His own tank was on reserve. Pratt had no choice but to gas up and hope to catch up with the lone Bonnet.

He watched from afar as the Bonnet turned south on 196.

Lonely 196.

Pratt filled up at the Last Chance Gas! at the edge of town and took off like a bat at dusk. Crosses with plastic flowers sprouted from the shoulder of the rough-hewn road. This was high desert, sunbaked rocks rising thousands of feet to the right—the Bighorn Foothills. The land was sand and gravel, worthless save for the hardiest of predators—rock-eating lichen, road-kill-eating turkey buzzards.

Buzzards and hawks gyred overhead. Maybe they were waiting for someone to crash. The occasional pick-up or truck passed him heading north. The road peaked gently and Pratt saw his quarry a mile ahead, an intense black presence against the rust and beige background, like the after-spot from staring at the sun or a morning floater.

The rat Harley's rear-views were worthless. The bike made so much noise the rider wouldn't hear a semi. Dude never looked back.

Pratt hung a mile back, pausing atop each promontory, sticking to the shadows. Forty-five miles south of Buffalo the Bonnet slowed and carefully turned west onto a gravel road that looked like it hadn't been traversed since the Civil War. Basketball-sized rocks littered the rutted path. The only signs of life were some scrub, ground-hugging juniper and Spanish bayonet, all coated with a patina of brown dust, and the omnipresent turkey buzzard. It was always up there, like the Air Force's 24/7 Early Warning Mobile Command Platform.

Pratt waited until the Bonnet had disappeared into the folds of the earth before easing his Road King onto the treacherous gravel. Pratt hadn't messed with his bike's baffles. He never dug straight pipes. He didn't need to hear the fucking engine to appreciate the sensation of speed. He shimmied up the gravel road using his boots, winding through a tight "S," and shut off his motor. The cackle of the Bonnet's engine spoke clearly, reverberating off the rock walls.

Pratt cinched into the shade of a half dome, tossed out the coffee can lid and left his bike. He shimmied to the top of the rock outcropping, covering his jeans and shirt with dust. One hundred yards ahead the Bonnet had stopped at a barbed wire gate. The land beyond was desolate and unforgiving, part of the Great American Siberia that stretched from Minnesota to the Rockies.

The Bonnet got off his rat bike, opened the gate, rolled his bike through and closed the gate behind him, looping a length of wire over the wooden post. The dirt road wound into the foothills. Pratt hunkered on the hot rock, motionless in his desert camo hat. For a long time the Bonnet's engine echoed, fainter and fainter until finally it fell silent, the choking dust falling to earth.

Pratt shimmied back down the rock and sat in the shade, his back to the half dome. He pulled out a bottled water and drank it in one chug. He waited fifteen minutes. He looked around. The turkey buzzard circled high overhead, its widening gyres covering half its arc with rock. Pratt got on his bike, scooped up the lid and thumbed the starter. He followed the Bonnet through the wire fence, carefully locking it behind him. He rode into the hills dead slow using his feet to fend off rocks. Canyon walls turned abruptly vertical ahead. The Bonnet's tracks showed sharply in the sand.

Pratt stopped.

Pratt pulled his bike off the rutted trail, up a desiccated wadi filled with baseball-sized stones, around a mushroom cloud of ancient juniper and kicked the stand out on a flat rock. The bike was not visible from the rutted dirt road. Not even its chrome.

Taking the remaining three bottles of water connected by a plastic collar, Pratt shrugged into his daypack and stepped back into the canyon. He cupped his ears with his hands and listened for five minutes, hearing the sigh of the wind, the caw of an invisible crow and his own blood pulsing in his temples.

Pratt headed up the canyon, hat pulled low against the westering sun.

CHAPTER 22

Now Pratt really regretted not bringing a gun. He figured the road could not go on forever. It would eventually run into the Bighorns. Pratt pulled a map of Wyoming from his backpack. The dirt road was not marked. Wherever the Bonnet was headed could not be much further.

Sand made for difficult riding but easy tracking. Pratt was about to set his foot on some gray-beige rocks when the ground came alive and slithered away. Pratt watched the five-foot timber rattler work its way into the shade of a natural cairn. Even here there was life. Life that could kill you. Pratt looked up. He had almost developed warm feelings for the turkey buzzard, like they were in this together.

"See anything?" Pratt whispered. The buzzard circled.

A mile up the trail Pratt saw an old wagon wheel sticking out of the earth, the same dun brown as the trail. It had been there for decades, half-buried by a flash flood. What blind fool had tried to coax a wagon up this wadi? Someone driven by lust, greed or fear. Pratt imagined he'd unearth a skull if he dug. He automatically touched his cell phone. He pulled it out and opened it. Of course there was no service.

Pratt needed a horse.

The canyon zigzagged west. Pratt stopped at each turn to listen, smell and feel, laying his ear against the canyon's smooth brown walls. He had not heard the Bonnet's unmuffled exhaust since the man had disappeared into the hills. Certainly the road was not something to which most bikers would subject their rides, but a determined rider could work his way back here.

The walls closed in to no more than four feet, smooth sandstone worn away by eons of wind and rain. The canyon floor was solid granite where it wasn't buried in rocks and gravel. The tracks disappeared but there was no place the biker could have gone save onward. There was no place to turn around. It was late afternoon and shadows crept forward from the west-facing walls, casting bizarre patterns on the opposite rock. A wind-ravaged juniper became grasping claws. A stack of boulders became a grizzly. Pratt looked up at the stack. It was a man-made cairn, a pile of rocks on rocks to indicate that this was the right path.

Pratt clung to the shadows gratefully. He was down to two bottles.

A hundred feet ahead the slot bowed to the left. Pratt inched along the convex surface until the sun had turned the opposite wall blazing yellow. He heard loud flapping, some predator, the clucking of crows. Crouching, Pratt stuck his head around the corner. The rat Harley was down, rider splayed against the rock wall like a discarded action figure. A six-point stag lay on its side panting, bloodied eye staring at the sun. A couple of crows danced around the biker's brains, eyeing Pratt with suspicion and cawing at him. The turkey buzzard removed its beak from the deer's side long enough to give Pratt the once-over before returning to its feast.

Pratt saw the instant replay. Bonnet came around the corner too fast and T-boned the buck, which somehow managed to gore the Bonnet before slamming him into the wall. Pratt rose silently and padded forward until he came to the stag. The turkey buzzard flapped its wide wings, slowly at first, then faster and faster as it jerked itself into the air. The buck's eye clouded over, muzzle open, tongue protruding. Pratt checked the Bonnet. The crows hopped in the air cawing madly, then withdrew to the wind-blasted limbs of a scrub oak shrieking bird obscenities.

The biker's head lay at an awkward angle in one of the dry rivulets that debouched into the gulley, sightless eyes staring at the sun. His skull was staved in. Pratt saw slick gray brains. Flies settled on the dead biker's eyes and brains. Pratt waved them away. They whirled, hovered and settled right back. They gathered in the dead biker's nostrils and mouth. The land was as dead as the moon until something died and then *bam*! Out of the stones themselves the insects appeared, to be followed by the birds, then the coyote and larger predators.

Pratt thought about returning to the highway, to try and get a signal or failing that, riding back to Buffalo and telling the cops. He thought about it for two seconds. He knew cops. He might as well voluntarily check himself into jail. Pratt searched the fallen biker. A Nevada license plate said Saul Grundy. A caveman's name. Grundy had a .357 Magnum in one of his ratty tank bags.

Thank you, Jesus.

He had a quart bottle of Gatorade in the other. Pratt stuck the Magnum in the back of his belt, put the Gatorade in his backpack. Grundy's cell phone appeared to be intact but of course there was no signal. Pratt took it. He checked the last number Grundy had called. He didn't recognize the area code. It could be anywhere. He checked the address book. There it was. The name Moon next to the last number dialed.

For a long second Pratt squeezed the Gatorade. He had put together a premise as Chaplain Dorgan had taught him; that Moon was a War Bonnet, that the War Bonnets would be at Sturgis, that he could track a War Bonnet back to his source and find Moon.

All good.

Being proved right was like his first snort of good coke. It filled him with exhilaration and a sense of triumph.

Yes!

He'd done it. He was good for something other than raising hell and serving process.

So far so good.

Pratt considered covering Grundy's body with rocks, but it would take time and energy and would prove fruitless against high-desert predators. The best he could do was shut Grundy's eyelids and offer a few words.

He hath scattered the proud in the imagination of their hearts. He hath put down the mighty from their seats, and exalted them of low degree. Lord take this sinner. Amen."

Spying the tiny broken-off mirror by the shattered bike, Pratt picked it up and stuck it in his cargo pants.

A half mile on a deadfall of kindle-dry timber blocked his path. Pratt used a tree limb and leverage to clear the path. A cycle could have made it thus far. The trail might have been an abandoned fire path dating from a time when the arid hills held more ponderosa. Grundy wouldn't have come this way if it didn't lead somewhere.

Somewhere he'd find Moon, and Moon would help him find Eric.

It was dusk by the time he hauled himself atop a rock promontory and looked west across a range of low dun-colored hills, the blue-black shadow of the Bighorns beyond. He was atop a mini-bluff in a natural bowl. As he settled in with his legs stretched behind him he saw a cigarette butt a foot from his chin. A Marlboro filter bleached white by the sun. It may have been there for years. Ahead lay shadow and a hint of coolness, some trick of the light suggesting a possible oasis in the searing desert.

Further up the trail he came to big cat spoor. Pratt tried to remember what he knew about pumas from his prison reading. *The Worst Case Scenario Survival Handbook* had been much in demand. Get big. Stand on tiptoes and hold your arms up. Wave your jacket.

The mountains held rattlers. And bear for all he knew. He chuckled. He was scaring himself. He was more likely to die from a heart attack or thirst than wild critter.

For the nth time he wondered if he'd brought enough water. The Bonnet carried only the one quart of Gatorade, but the Bonnet had expected to ride right through. It couldn't be much further. The going was too slow and the day was mostly gone.

Pratt caught a glimpse of green through the rocks.

At eight-fifteen, as the sun was sinking below the Bighorns, Pratt crawled out on a jutting granite shard and gazed down into a hidden oasis. A Quonset hut crouched amid a copse of cottonwood centered around an old well with a two-foot stone lip. A tepee tucked under the trees, walls of white canvas painted with pictographs, buffalo, Indians on horseback, an entrance flap facing east. Some buffalo grass retained its tint in the trees' shadow. The well must have tapped an underground spring that was the source of this green bounty. Several feet away was an old-fashioned hand pump jutting from a concrete base, painted green.

A pyramid of gallon tins and chemical jars twenty yards from the hut. The wind shifted from the west and a sliver of chemical glass stabbed at Pratt's membranes, something that made the Buffalo Chip privies seem fragrant in comparison. His eyes watered and he fought the urge to sneeze, pressing his index finger tight against his septum. A dirt road wound northwest out of the oasis and curved out of sight behind a series of massive outcroppings that jutted out of the earth. Pratt could see no vehicle. He lay atop the rock and carefully scanned the valley for fifteen minutes. The only movement came from the occasional breeze ruffling the trees on the cottonwood. It was now dusk, the valley a deep blue-black. No light came on in the hut.

At dusk the temperature was still in the high eighties. Pratt's shirt was soaked. Having finished his bottled water, he had drunk two-thirds of the Gatorade. Thirst and hunger tugged at him like willful children. That well looked good. An old wooden crank held a corrugated iron bucket on the end of its rope. Turning that crank would shatter the stillness like an air-raid siren at vespers. He saw himself drawing a bucket of cool water. He saw himself finding something to eat in the hut—cold cuts and a cold beer. Maybe a frozen pizza.

He reached for the Gatorade.

Night rose. Emerging from behind a curtain of cumulus the full moon shone a spotlight on the hidden valley. Stars spattered the sky. There was no animal life. No deer, mountain goats, squirrels or pikas. No birds sang in the trees. As the only source of water for miles around it should have been a gathering place. Unless the well was empty, but if that was the case, what sustained the trees and the patch of green?

Who could live in such a terrible place?

The hut remained dark. Pratt eased himself down off the rock, set the empty bottle of Gatorade on the ground and crept toward the hut.

CHAPTER 23

Perhaps it was the taint of chemicals—of man himself—that kept the creatures at bay. Perhaps the well was tainted. Pratt hoped not. He'd drunk four twelve-ounce bottles of water plus the Gatorade and he was still thirsty. He was punchy from being up for 36 hours but the lure of the cabin drew him to it with the force of a power winch.

It could have been me.

Pratt didn't think Duane was evil, not in a malicious sense. He was evil in the sense that he refused his responsibilities as a father and a man. The pettiness of withdrawing Pratt from his mother, whom he'd never met. Pratt had been around casual cruelty his whole life and he was sick of it.

If I find this boy, he thought, maybe I can find my mother.

Then what?

He crouched at the edge of the clearing between alder and ageless juniper that split a granite slab. He watched. He listened. He smelled. The acrid chemical odor was stronger here, overpowering the scent of the juniper berries.

Where was the cook?

It seemed inconceivable that the War Bonnets would leave their lab unattended, especially with the boys needing to re-up. Grundy had intended to meet someone. Where was he?

Pratt used shadow as he sidled up to the edge of the hut, the curved, corrugated aluminum siding overgrown with a brittle vine that cracked and rustled to the touch. Pratt saw a square window at the end of the hut, and one set into the curving side with a little box gable jutting forth to keep the glass vertical. A window box held dust and long-dead vegetable matter.

Trying to look in the windows would announce his presence like a flare gun, so bright was the moon. Pratt had been watching the hut for hours in the baking heat and he was convinced that it was empty. Not even meth-addled bikers would choose to stay inside a baking oven on a day like this.

It was possible the hut was booby-trapped. Pratt had had an excellent education in booby traps while he was in the penitentiary. But there were risks here as well. You never knew when innocent bystanders might come along, even in this wilderness. There were liability issues. Did meth-addled bikers care? You didn't run a successful franchise like the Buffalo Chip for fifteen years without some semblance of professionalism.

Pratt drew the Magnum and pussy-footed toward the front door. He used the broken side mirror from Grundy's bike to peer around the corner, using the stiff gorse that grew like armpit hair for cover. The door stood open a foot, hinged inward, revealing a black vertical slot. An airstream of chemical reek rolled out, causing Pratt's eyes to water. Beyond the chemicals was the taint of fleshly corruption as in a cancer ward.

There were two large dog crates stacked next to the door. The bottom one held a long-dead dog, withered muzzle pressed against the gate. It made Pratt want to vomit and kill someone at the same time. He set the mirror on the top crate.

Pratt leaned back with his back against the wall, gun in hand, panting, trying to see, feel and hear around the corner. The interior remained as still and mysterious as an unopened tomb. With a silent fuck it he rolled in front of the door at a 45-degree angle, supporting the gun on his elbows. He stared into the cool reeking interior and waited for his eyes to adjust. They streamed like a broken water main. He wiped tears away on his arm and looked.

Cool moonlight penetrated through four windows and a skylight revealing a long, dark, messy lodge. A deep corrugated steel tub sat beneath one of the side windows next to a wood workbench, on which rested a two-coil hot plate, jars, tubing and several gallon metal tins. Acetate and paint thinner. A garden hose snaked in through the partially opened side window. A jumble of cardboard boxes obscured Pratt's view to the rear of the hut, about thirty feet.

Pratt got a knee under him and slowly stood holding the pistol in a two-handed grip and sweeping the interior. A twine dangle brushed his cheek. It was attached to a bare bulb fitting in the ceiling. They had to have electricity to cook the meth. Pratt spotted another fixture halfway down the ceiling. He refrained from turning on the light.

There was always a possibility somebody else was watching. The hair stood on the back of his neck. He could feel someone's gaze as a paper-thin weight.

Stop it, Pratt, you're freaking yourself out.

He shuffled past the sink.

An animal grunt issued from the jumble of trash at the rear of the hut.

Goosebumps rose on his arms and ice glided down his spine. It was the sound of some primordial beast, an atavistic warning that cut straight to the lizard brain. Fetid breath carried with it a hint of the grave. A light breeze caused the trees outside the window to dance and cast their limbs on the filthy interior. The foul reek of animal waste emanated from the back of the hut.

"Shit." Pratt swallowed, aiming the gun toward the rear, praying that whatever it was would just permit him to walk backward out of the hut. A fucking wolf or God forbid a puma. Something nocturnal lying up out of the sun all day.

Pratt stepped backward. His heel landed on something rubbery that squeaked and Pratt overreacted, nearly falling on his ass.

"Squeaky toy," the creature croaked in an unearthly animal growl.

"What?" Pratt gasped. He thought he saw something beneath the rear window—a flash of red like a wolf watching from the forest.

"M . . . squeaky toy." The voice was hoarse, unused to speech.

A cloak of ice-cold dread settled over Pratt. The speaker did not sound human—the words were barely understandable, accompanied by harsh breathing and a liquid gurgle.

"Who are you?" Pratt whispered.

Something rose from the jumble of old blankets and carpet segments. It rose past the window, blotting out the moonlight. Its silhouette was fuzzy and indistinct.

"I . . . am . . . Eric," it snarled. "Who . . . are . . . you?"

And then, God help him, it turned on the light.

CHAPTER 24

The creature stood five six but may have been taller. An unnaturally curved spine forced it into the posture of an elongated question mark. Coarse fur sprouted from its shoulders, arms and tapered torso. Its head was a matted tangle: Cousin It from the Addams Family. It looked like a fucking wolf man. A rank animal odor flowed like fog from dry ice. The thing took a step with a crooked leg. Metal clanked on metal. Pratt looked down. The creature had an iron band around one hairy ankle connected to a short length of chain.

The chain was not anchored. It hung from the creature like a leash from a dog.

A wad of aluminum foil lodged in Pratt's throat. His eyes streamed uncontrollably from the chemical miasma. "Eric?"

The thing shook itself like a wet Labrador. Its claw-like hands went to its head, sweeping aside the cascade of matted hair, revealing a sand-blasted young/old face mottled with tufts of multi-colored fur. Sunken eyes peered from beneath a bony ridge like woodland creatures from a burrow. It looked like a toy troll from the sixties. Its lip curled up over elongated yellow teeth and it growled from deep within, a disturbing subterranean rumble.

"*You . . . go . . .*" it snarled with overtones of grief and desperation. This couldn't be Ginger's little boy, stolen at the age of two. This wasn't even human. The name was all wrong. "Eric" belonged to a clean-cut boy with a crew cut, a ready grin, a grasp on life. Not this, this *thing*. This was some kind of sick nature joke, like pinheads and Siamese twins.

Pratt's eyes swept the room seeking refuge from the sight before him. Dozens of empty cereal boxes: Frosty-Os, Count Chocula, Cap'n Crunch. Industrial bags of popcorn and oats. Dozens and dozens of candy bar wrappers—Snickers, Hershey's, SweeTarts. Frozen-food packages, a microwave sitting on a table made from a telephone company spool. And the creature's nest—blankets and cushions jumbled into a fur-lined sleeping hole. A dream catcher twisted overhead as an errant breeze wafted through the chemical lodge house.

Was it house-trained? What was that shit smell?

The creature scratched its neck, revealing a studded leather collar.

I'm not equipped to handle this, Pratt thought. It called for child psychologists and animal behaviorists. It called for a pastor, a rabbi and a priest. The creature made no hostile move apart from the omnipresent growling that issued from the back of its throat like surf. Pratt tucked the pistol in his pants and showed his empty palms like you would to a strange dog.

"I'm Josh Pratt," he said in a soft, gentle voice. "I'm a private detective. Your mother hired me to find you."

"*My mother?*" the creature snarled. It reached up and switched off the light. Josh was momentarily blinded.

"I have . . . no mother." Consonants stripped of all sharp edges yet Pratt understood him clearly almost as if a tiny voice inside his head was speaking at the same time.

"Of course you do and she loves you very much." Pratt groped, caught in a whirlpool, desperately trying to recall the social workers who'd worked so hard to make a difference and never had. Pratt had to go to prison to straighten out his life and find Jesus.

Where could this thing go?

Pratt regretted his thinking instantly. *It isn't a thing. It's a human being.*

Who could do this to their own child?

"You have a father, don't you?"

Emotional confusion overwhelmed Pratt. Duane was in his head. The thin line between love and hate, it was all over him. He started to weep. It wasn't just the chemicals. He cursed himself for his weakness like some silly bitch on the rag. Why did he suddenly feel this way? In that instant he would have welcomed a joint, a line, a drink, anything to move him off the emotional spot.

"*Daddy,*" Eric said with a heartbreaking mixture of love and fear.

"Where is he?"

Eric gestured toward his hairy chest. "*My job . . . to guard the lab . . . until Daddy returns.*"

"Where is Daddy?" Pratt said. A wave of anticipation and dread rocked his ticker, followed by a sense of suicidal dread.

"*Daddy . . . is here.*"

A massive arm snaked around Pratt's neck, fingers gripping the back of his shoulder. "Right behind you," a voice whispered in his ear. The arm clamped tight, shutting off the carotid artery. Pratt reached for the pistol in the small of his back but a hand grasped his wrist and jerked it up between his shoulder blades.

Pratt's last thought before he passed out was, "Careless . . ."

CHAPTER 25

The rancid smell of public toilets. Something foul splattered onto Pratt's face. He opened his eyes. Dark, all dark except for straight up where the sky had been reduced to a deep blue plate. The silhouette of a man standing on the well wall, impossibly foreshortened from Pratt's angle. Golden droplets falling down.

The man was pissing on him. Pratt jerked his head aside and found himself sitting on cool, hard-packed earth. He looked around. He was in a hemispherical chamber lined with red bricks, flow holes open at ground level. An empty gallon container made of steel that smelled of chemicals lay on the ground next to a rug segment.

He was in the well.

Moon was pissing on him.

Pratt scrabbled backwards on his ass out of the line of fire.

"Good morning!" Moon sang in a surprisingly mellifluous and friendly voice. It echoed around Pratt's head like reverb. "Josh, is it? Wow. I really can't believe Ginger's got a bee up her butt after all these years."

Pratt choked on his fury, struggling to bring himself under control. "What did you do to him?" he said, voice cracking.

"What, my boy Eric? He's a good'n, ain't he? He's my faithful pal, isn't that right, Eric?" Moon's voice drifted in another direction. "Who's Daddy's good little boy?" he cooed.

Pratt retched. His stomach heaved a whiffle ball. There was nothing to throw up. He was thirsty and needed to piss. He needed something to wash the sour taste from his mouth. Something hit the ground with a dull thump. A bottle of water. Pratt twisted off the cap and drank gratefully.

"Don't want you to think I'm inhospitable," Moon said. "I'm damned proud to know you. Was that you broke into the LaFarge, beat the crap out of Ringo and took our stash?"

"Yeah," Pratt gasped between gulps.

"That took balls. All kinds of balls. Balls to the wall! And then you followed Grundy. Hell of a thing, hitting a deer like that. You know his brother died the same way. Must run in the family."

Moon had to have gone back down the canyon to know about Grundy. Pratt felt outsmarted.

"Tell me where my shit is, I'll make it easy for you."

"I flushed it down a toilet."

Moon sighed dramatically. "Pratt, you're not helping yourself."

"What did you do to him?"

"Who?"

"Your son."

"I raised him as a dog boy. It's an ancient Chinese custom. 'Every day, starting with the back, the captors would remove a bit of the unfortunate child's skin and transplant pieces of the hide of a bear or dog in its place. The process was tedious, for the hide adhered only in spots and the children had a habit of dying in the midst of treatment.' Of course having my genes, my boy survived." Moon's voice turned indulgent. "He not only survived, but thrived! And now he helps his Daddy, doesn't he?"

Pratt felt rather than heard a faint whimper. His gut did dry belly flops. He retched again and reached for the water. He drained the bottle.

"He's a tracker, Pratt! This boy could track a fart in a hurricane!"

"Can I have another water?"

"Well I don't know. You drank that already? It's not like you're going to be around much longer."

"People know where I am, Moon."

Moon hunkered down on the well's rim like a big frog. "I checked your cell phone. You're talking about an old friend of mine. I guess Cass is your friend now, huh? Well I'm just going to have to pay her and Ginger a courtesy call after all these years. Yes sir, I just may have to do that."

Pratt's breath came shallow and fast and he felt lightheaded like the first time he'd found himself in jail. Recognizing the signs of a panic attack, Pratt scooted to one side of the oubliette from where he was invisible to Moon and leaned back against the inward curving wall. He watched the disc of sunlight in the middle of the floor. How long had he been out? He put his head between his knees and practiced square breathing. Inhale—one, two, three, four—hold it—one, two, three, four—exhale—one, two, three, four—hold it.

Not working. Pratt's heart sounded like a bass drum. The tach needle was way past red.

All Moon had to do was walk away. Pratt would die of thirst. Like the dog in the crate.

"You know Cass is short for Cassandra, 'She who entangles men.' I'm doing you a favor, Pratt. You'd just get sick of her and not be able to get rid of her. 'Course either way I'm doing you the favor."

"Don't do me any favors."

"Well I was wondering what to do with this mangy old mountain lion I trapped and you come along. You ever see that film, orca versus great white shark? It's a classic. You can find it on YouTube. Guy got lucky in the North Pacific. I mean the guy with the camera. It's not much of a battle. That orca kicked major shark butt. We don't get to see that kind of thing too often. I wish there were more of that kind of thing. A reality show, y'know? Thing versus thing."

Feeling queasy and thirsty, Pratt said, "Did you say mountain lion?"

"Yes that's right. I hope you're as excited as I am."

Pratt patted down his pockets. His gun, wallet and cell phone were gone. For some reason he still had his buck knife and the bottle of ibuprofen. He looked around for other potential weapons. Some rocks. A brick. When he stuck his fingers into the groove next to the wall they came away wet. White spots appeared before his eyes.

"Bullshit," Pratt said.

Moon giggled girlishly. "You may very well think so but I'm not fuckin' around." His voice segued from flirtatious to ominous rasp in the same sentence. A headache launched a stabbing attack behind Pratt's left eye. Death by dehydration was awful. Maybe being killed by a mountain lion wasn't as bad.

Get off it, Pratt. He's full of shit. He's playing you.

"Eric, you make sure you water the lion after it eats this motherfucker," Moon said, his voice echoing eerily down the sides of the well. "I don't want to be accused of mistreating an animal."

The outline of Moon's head and shoulders appeared in the sun disc on the ground. "Well I hate to bug out on you and all but I got some deliveries to make. Let me just leave you with this thought: Joker in the well. Mountain lion chowing down. Soon joker is gone."

The silhouette withdrew. Pratt heard Moon speaking to someone but couldn't make out the words. He couldn't stop shaking. The disc of light on the floor squeezed into a crescent.

"It's in God's hands," Pratt whispered.

A terrible silence descended.

CHAPTER 26

It was cool in the well. It would be cold at night. Anxiety added to Pratt's thirst. He looked at the empty plastic bottle. He jammed his fingers into the slot at the base and they came away damp. There was no water. Pratt could last three, maybe four days before delirium set in.

He dismissed the mountain lion. That Moon was a master of psychological warfare was a given. But the threat against Cass and Ginger was real. Pratt had to get out of there. For the nth time he surveyed his prison. It was lined with bricks. There was the gallon tin. It had been an artesian well. Pratt felt the bricks. Some were loose, the mortar worn away by decades of water. The aquifer had long since drained, leaving nothing but a wet spot.

Where did the facility draw water? Was there a tank on the property? The ground pump had to be connected to a deeper well. Electricity? You could cook meth over a Sterno flame. Why the one empty can? Why didn't Moon dump all his empties in the well? Maybe he'd discovered Gaia. Maybe the boy threw it in.

The boy.

If indeed he was the boy. It was impossible to tell the creature's age. Pratt had deliberately steered clear of that mental black hole but if he had understood Moon correctly, Eric had stayed behind. To deliver the puma.

Yeah, right.

Pratt was in solitary again. Been there, done that. He pissed carefully against the wall opposite where he'd been sitting.

"Eric?" Pratt called.

Silence. Utter silence save the faint susurrus of the wind blowing across the well's lip like breath on a bottle.

Pratt got to his feet, cupped his hands to his mouth, aimed straight up and wound it up from the gut. "ERIC!"

His words shot out of the bottle like a spitwad and whisked away in the wind. Pratt eyed the top. Had to be thirty feet. Pratt worked a brick loose. It fell to the ground with a moist thump. Eyeing the aperture, he heaved it underhand with his best fast-pitch softball arm. It scraped the inside of the well two feet below the lip.

"ERIC!"

Pratt caught himself hyperventilating again. Square breathing. Think about the boy.

No, it was better not to think about the boy. Pratt was torn between existential anxiety and horror. He stared at the ground and balled his fists.

The back of his neck tingled as if he were being watched. Anxiety and anticipation nibbled at his gut and somehow it was not his own, but an alien presence in his mind.

"*Shut . . . up,*" fell into the well like a feather. Pratt looked up. A shaggy silhouette disturbed the gibbous outline.

"Eric." Pratt heard himself sob in relief. "Thank Christ. Eric, you've got to help me out of here."

"*Just shut . . . the fuck up. I'm not helping . . . you. Gene told me . . . what to do. I have . . . my orders.*" There was an undertone of desperation to the barely human speech. Although the creature's—*the boy's*—speech lacked sibilants and all hard-edged consonants, Pratt had no trouble understanding him. Again, that sense that someone was talking to him in his head.

Pratt consciously relaxed his gut as he arched his back. "Eric, your mother sent me to bring you back. She loves you very much."

"*I have . . . no mother. My mother . . . was a wolf.*"

"Eric. Think about this. You have a mother who loves you. You hurt all the time. She can help you get better. Think about this, Eric. What if Gene is lying?"

A hissing gasp. "*Gene . . . does . . . not . . . lie!*" Eric rasped. "*You are . . . a bad man! You came . . . to hurt me!*"

"Eric! How could I possibly hurt you any more than you've already been hurt?"

Pratt heard Eric's labored breathing as he leaned over the well.

Wendigo. An American werewolf in the Old West. Pratt had read about them in a book about old legends he'd taken out of the Mayville, Iowa library once when they were stopped for a few days, Duane working at a grain elevator. Young Pratt had gravitated toward monsters like iron filings to a magnet. He sought reassurance in a world more sinister than his own.

That world never existed.

Until now.

The boy was a mental black hole. Pratt would have preferred not to think about him but that was impossible. No longer an "it." Only the boy could help him now. Thinking about how the boy got that way accomplished nothing. Pratt was forced to compartmentalize, furiously hurrying down a mental corridor slamming doors. He had no use for the strangely intense emotions assaulting him.

The entity leaning over the well was unknown but human. Certainly the boy would respond to any sincere and meaningful overture. That was only natural. He remembered a *Fantastic Four* comic book he'd read in prison wherein Sue Richards extends the hands of kindness to some Kirbyesque monster, saying all living things responded to kindness. He'd dated a hippie once who believed all men were basically good.

What was her name? Dar something. Darryl.

Darlene. She talked a good game but when push came to shove, she folded like a cheap tent. She was proud of her "progressivism." She made Pratt her project. When he failed to respond to her unselfish love and devotion, she waited until he was at work one day, cleaned out the apartment, sold his stereo, microwave oven and TV to a pawn shop and disappeared.

Pratt learned years later she'd died of AIDS in Mexico.

Get him talking. The more the boy talked, the more human he became.

"What do you eat?" Pratt forced a conversational tone.

"*What?*"

"What do you eat out here? What does Gene feed you?"

"*I eat . . . apples . . . protein bars . . . venison . . . peanut butter . . . Red Vines.*"

"You ever had a thick, juicy steak? How'd you like a thick, juicy steak?" His own stomach rumbled like a Panzer Division. He could see the steak. He could practically taste it. Medium rare with grilled mushroom topping. The boy's teeth had to be a disaster. He'd never seen a dentist. Pratt wondered if Moon had fed him lots of sweets.

"Do you like candy?" Pratt called.

"*Yeah . .*"

So the boy's teeth were shot.

"How 'bout tossing down another bottle of water?"

Silence. Pratt gazed up. The shaggy outline withdrew. A sense of calm settled on Pratt like a shroud. He zoned out, momentarily unaware of his surroundings and condition. The sound of a twelve-ounce bottle of water thwacking the floor snapped his head off his chest. Pratt scooped it up gratefully and chugged it down. He looked up. No outline.

"Eric!" he called.

No answer. Was the boy even within earshot? Where had he gone? Pratt sat down Indian style. All things being relative Duane didn't seem quite so bad by comparison. Sure there'd been physical abuse— the drunken beatings, that time Duane kicked Pratt, age nine, out of the car five miles from home in the middle of a blizzard and told him to walk.

At least Duane hadn't engaged in systematic crippling torture. Yeah, Duane was a real prize. He failed the Dr. Mengele test. Pratt still had Duane's cheap digital watch. Fucking thing had been keeping time for twenty years. Go figure. An hour passed as Pratt considered his options. It was possible that all his clothes, torn into strips, might make a twenty foot rope. He had an idea regarding the discarded gallon tin.

Pratt wondered how long he should wait. It was possible Eric had deserted him, left him to die on Moon's orders. The anxiety made him thirsty. He stood, looked up, cupped his mouth.

"Eric!"

Nada.

"ERIC!"

No response. Well there you have it. He was on his own. He reached for his belt buckle.

He heard a grunt.

"Eric, is that you?"

Another grunt, imperceptibly louder as something approached the well, someone struggling with a bulky or heavy object.

"Eric, I need a rope!"

The shaggy outline appeared briefly.

"Eric?"

More grunting. A large, rectangular box hove into view as Eric rested one end atop the low well rim. The box had rounded corners. It was an animal container similar to those Pratt had seen outside the hut.

A wild feline snarl shot the tube.

Pratt watched petrified as a shaggy arm reached around to the door, which hung over the well. The arm released the latch and opened the door. An instant later Eric tilted the other end of the box up, emptying the mountain lion into the well.

Fuck.

CHAPTER 27

Pratt's head slammed into the wall as he jerked back. He pulled his Buck knife from his pocket and opened the four-inch blade.

The sinewy tan creature dropped like a load of laundry, landing un-erringly on four wide-spread paws, using the impact to spring at Pratt as it was born to do. Shrieking slightly through his teeth Pratt lashed out with a right front kick that caught the cat square in the chest with a jar-ring thump. The cat dropped to the ground, turned around and sprang. It was a perpetual-motion machine, a foaming buzz saw.

Pratt threw up an arm. The cat's hind claws scrabbled at the duct tape, cleaved through skin and muscle leaving furrows, its yellow eyes inches from Pratt's, its breath a hot charnel wind. Pratt grabbed it by the scruff of the neck with his left hand, pulled it tight and hacked down with the knife. Each of its clawed extremities tentacled from his grip and found purchase in his skin. Pratt yanked its neck back, stop-ping the inch-and-a-half incisors from reaching his face. He fought a tornado of razor blades at his belly, slash after slash on his forearms and chest, the intimate shocking parting of the flesh, furiously lashing out with the knife. Over and over and over, his arm flinging blood every time he drew it back. The lion's spittle struck his face.

Would his tiny blade even penetrate to the cat's vital organs through the matrix of bone and sinew? The mountain lion dropped back snarling and spitting, limping from a slash across its forepaw and sucking holes in its side. Pratt reversed his grip so that the blade protruded from the thumb side. He grabbed the carpet segment and wrapped it around his bleeding left arm. The cat circled and pounced, jaws clamping on the carpeted forearm as he thrust it forward, nearly crushing his ulna. Pratt brought the blade up with all his force, driving it through the soft underbelly beneath the breastplate, working it back and forth like a recalcitrant cork.

The cat mewled piteously and collapsed, panting. Its torn side bellowed quickly in and out. It looked at him with an odd mix of defiance and regret, as if it knew it had burned through its nine lives in one fell swoop. A pool of blood spread across the hard-packed earth. The light in its eyes dimmed. It lay on its side, fat pink tongue protruding at an odd angle.

Pratt slumped on his ass, panting. He waited for the giant fist that had seized his heart to unclench. He practiced his square breathing. He thanked God. He examined his wounds. The gouges on his left arm had penetrated to the bone and ached in pulses with his heartbeat. His clothes were drenched with sweat and blood. The cat had ripped off his shirt and bandages.

Pratt wiped the buck knife off on the cat's fur and used it to cut his shirt into strips, which he used to bandage the wounds on his arms, the claw scrape across his hairline that sent tendrils of blood into his eyes.

Thirst scorched him to the bone. He thought about drinking his urine. He'd read a book about Marines on a prisoner-of-war ship during WWII drinking their own urine. They just puked it back up. He couldn't stop sweating despite the cool air. He looked at his buck knife, tufts of fur projecting from the serrated part of the blade.

He looked at the mountain lion. Had to weigh one hundred and fifty pounds. Cat muscle wasn't like human muscle. It was stronger and faster. The cougar was a threshing machine and somehow he'd killed it. Could you eat the meat? It didn't matter. He'd be dead of thirst long before he'd be hungry enough to eat a mountain lion.

Pratt got to his knees and straightened the big cat's body. Seven feet from tip to tail. It was beginning to stink already. Pratt must have pierced the abdomen. All that fur. What a trophy.

Pratt looked up at the disc of deep blue sky. If only he could reverse gravity.

All that fur.

Using the buck knife Pratt field-dressed the carcass as he would a deer, splitting open the thorax from neck to anus. The reeking innards plopped out, a plate of purple sausage. The skin was extremely slippery and difficult to separate from bone and sinew. Pratt had to stand on the carcass to hold it in place while he drew the blade longitudinally, carefully slicing the skin into two-inch strips. It was difficult to get a grip against the slippery skin, and he slipped several times, landing hard and sending furious bolts of pain ricocheting throughout his body.

It was grueling, backbreaking work. When he was done he'd turned the cat's skin into sixteen strips varying in length from two feet to six. He looked up. The quality of blue had deepened. The sun had begun its long slide into the mountains. Weak from loss of blood and hunger, Pratt worked feverishly, fearing if he waited until morning he wouldn't make it.

The skin was already stiff as he forced it end to end, tying knots with his whole body. Blades assailed him from without, his own bones from within. The skin was as flexible as a wire coat hanger. He worked it. He bent it back in on itself like an accordion, over and over. He wrapped it tightly around a brick and smacked all sides against the hard-packed ground. When he finished he estimated he had about thirty feet.

He went to work on the gallon tin, flattening it with the brick, hacking through it with the buck knife. The well stank like an abattoir. Flies descended en masse. Flies swarmed his face and arms and settled on the bloodied carcass. It was a fly buffet. It was a fly Sturgis.

Light was fading as Pratt cut, bent and hammered the tin into a crude hook with a puncture at one end for the rope. He tied a brick fragment to the hook for weight. His fingers were torn from the lion's claws and gouged by the ragged tin edge. Slick with blood, they refused to obey him. He couldn't grip the metal. He caught himself whining, stopped, breathed, slumped. He flexed his fingers, wiped them off on his jeans and went back to work. At last he had a rope and a grappling hook. Did he have the energy to throw it and after that make the climb?

Pratt pissed again at the wall, his urine chrome yellow. He picked up his stiff, reeking lariat and stood in the center of the floor. He looked up. Using his best fast-pitch softball underhand, he heaved the hook at the sky. It clacked against the bricks several feet from the top and tumbled back to earth. Pratt stepped back to avoid getting smacked. The buzzing of the flies filled his prison with an eerie drone.

Hungrily he eyed the fly-specked carcass.

What are you, crazy?

He looked up. Second throw. Get that Zen thing going. You don't need to look—you know which way is up. Bending at the knees, he used the same technique as a kettlebell hoist, swinging straight up with his thighs, hips, whole body. The weighted hook sailed toward the blue sky, brushing the bricks just below the rim. It fell to the ground and lay in a pool of congealing blood. Pratt was at the limit of his range like a good place kicker on the fifty-yard line. He had to dig down deep and find that extra six inches.

Pratt was exhausted, weak from loss of blood and anxiety. He didn't have that many throws in him before he reached diminishing returns. Breathing deeply he centered himself and threw again. The hook cleared the rim—barely—but failed to catch. Pratt prayed for strength.

Nine tosses later his prayer was answered.

CHAPTER 28

Pratt tested the cat-skin rope with his weight. The skin stretched with a slight squeaking noise but held. Dried puma blood provided an adhesive grip. Wrapping the reeking rope around his forearm, Pratt began pulling himself up, cat rope clamped between his shoes, glad that he'd been practicing chin-ups religiously. Eight feet off the floor the chamber narrowed to a four-foot tube. The diameter was too great for him to brace himself but bricks protruded from the wall, allowing him to place some of his weight. Fifteen feet up he paused to catch his breath, each foot resting on a slight protrusion while he gripped the rope and tried to ease the screaming pain in his upper back and ribs.

Pratt craned his neck. The blue sky had darkened and deepened. A star twinkled. It was almost eight. Rationing his breath, he heaved himself up, foot by foot, brick by brick. A cramp seized his right calf, threatening to twist it into a pretzel. Pratt struggled to stretch his leg but the cramp pushed back like a steel vise. He overpowered his own alien flesh, willing the leg to relax while the rest of his body tensed and coiled like a steel spring. Cramping came from dehydration. His fingers cramped. His jaw cramped.

The cramps went away slowly, leaving him scared of extending those muscles. He needed water. He looked up. Disc was closer now. With eyes on the deep blue disc he inched upward. Four heaves. Then three. He got his hands over the rim and hung there panting for five minutes, feet braced against a couple of protrusions, gathering strength to heave himself up and out.

He raised himself on protesting arms. For the first time in hours he saw the horizon. The little valley was deserted. The silence was immense. Even the omnipresent crickets and katydids had ceased their constant sawing. Pratt grasped for the outer edge and got it. With both hands gripping the outer edge, he got his right leg up and over until finally, gratefully, he tumbled from the low rim to the matted brown grass and lay there panting.

The impatient North Star had already emerged in the sapphire sky. Pratt felt the cramps gathering in his limbs, massing for attack. He relaxed his gut, willing his overheated body to calm down. He had to relax it in stages. It wouldn't all go at once. He started with the toes, an old yoga trick. The cramps retreated.

Water. He needed water.

Pratt sat up and looked around. There was no sign of other living creatures save a lone turkey buzzard.

Is that you, my friend?

"Thank you for saving my life once again," Pratt said. He arched his back looking up at the heavens. Pratt staggered to his feet. He felt lightheaded, fresh off the boat and hadn't got his ground legs yet. Darkness flowed through the hills into the little valley. The Quonset hut was a black silhouette.

"Eric!" Pratt yelled once. His voice cracked. The place felt empty.

Pratt stumbled for the hut, automatically glancing to his right and left. The tepee glowed pale ivory in the starlight. Pratt gripped the Quonset door frame and stared into the darkness of the interior. A slow river of reek invaded his sinuses.

"Eric," he said. Nothing. Pratt stood in the door frame, listening. The crickets and katydids were back at it.

Pratt needed water badly. He had never felt such a thirst. He found a light switch next to the door but it clicked uselessly. Some light filtered in through ivy-covered windows and the lone skylight, revealing a Coleman lantern resting on some cardboard boxes inside the door. Pratt took the lantern and looked for matches.

He found them on the workbench, crowded with Bunsen burners, chemicals and latex gloves. The matchbook said, Vern's Place, 421 Main St., Hog Tail, WY. Pratt lit the lantern. It cast a yellow glow into the jumbled hermit hoarder's lair, boxes everywhere, an old sofa shoved up against the side beneath one occluded window. American Pickers would have a field day. There was a sink in the worktable surface and beneath that several picnic coolers. Next to the sink was a small glass vial labeled "ketamine" with a warning and what looked like a pharmaceutical bottle labeled "Ciclosporin." Several spent hypodermic needles lay in the bottom of a ten-gallon tub used for trash. Another ten-gallon tub served as an umbrella stand. It held a pump-action air rifle and a nine iron.

Pratt pried the lid off one of the coolers. A flesh-eroding stench latched onto his skin and he slammed it shut without looking. Breathing now through his mouth he pried up the lid of the second cooler and found three quart bottles of lime-flavored sports drink, still cool from the water in the bottom of the chest.

"Thank you Jesus," he muttered, twisting the cap off one and up-ending it. He chugged it down and opened another. Half of that and he was finally sated. Holding the lantern before him Pratt began a careful search of the interior. A stained coffee table in front of the sofa was virtually invisible beneath piles of old magazines, empty take-out food wrappers and bottles. An old compound bow poked up from behind the sprung sofa.

The fumes made Pratt's eyes water. He made his way toward the rear of the hut. A scurrying sound froze him in place. Mice. In the back beneath an open window he found the nest. Piles of old rags and blankets formed into a crude hollow, like a dog might make, covered with fur. There was so much fur, the pattern of the fabric was invisible. Pratt reached down, pinched a wad and stuck it in an open envelope he found in the trash. The envelope was addressed to Arnold Daggett, Spearfish, SD. The postage marking was three years old.

Next to the pile of rags was an aluminum water bowl. An iron ring had been sunk into the floor of the hut. The nest smelled like feces. Taped to the wall about four feet off the floor was a picture cut from a Sunday magazine: the Simpson family all together smiling for the camera. Pratt stared at it a long time thinking the same thoughts Eric had.

The combination of assaultive smells pushed him inexorably back to the door.

On the way out he paused to take inventory of the work surface. Unbelievably, his wallet and cell phone lay on the bench half-covered with a BUDK catalog. Pratt flipped the cell phone open. No signal. He checked his wallet. His money and credit cards were intact. Pratt stuffed them back in his pockets. He grabbed a roll of gray duct tape. He saw cotton peeking from a cardboard box, peeled back the lid. Dozens of pale green shirts with a wild flame-colored logo depicting a fierce Sioux warrior in war bonnet and the legend, "STURGIS—THE ONE, THE ONLY, THE ORIGINAL."

Pratt used his buck knife to slice the shirts into strips, which he used to stanch his blood.

Pratt pulled one out. It was a large. He struggled painfully into it, a spastic ballet. The fumes gave him a headache. Grabbing the two remaining bottles of sports drink, he went outside and inhaled deeply of the sweet night air.

He looked around.

Where had the boy gone?

Maybe he was watching from the surrounding hills. Maybe Pratt was the first human being other than Moon the boy had ever seen, other than his mother. What was he doing? What must he think, his home invaded, forced to participate in savagery? Eric's anxiety level had to be over the moon.

Don't think about the boy.

Don't think about the elephant in the room.

Pratt needed to alert Cass and Ginger that Moon was coming for them. He had to tell the police. He had to get his ass back to Wisconsin pronto. He dismissed going back the way he'd come. There had to be an easier way in and out. A dirt road ran from the yard up a rocky ridge and southwest, doubtless connected to some road somewhere. Pratt hadn't heard a vehicle last night when Moon had grabbed him but that meant nothing. Moon might have stashed the vehicle over the ridge to creep in. Why would he creep in unless he suspected there might be an intruder? How had he known?

When Grundy didn't show, Moon must have smelled a rat.

Pratt walked outside the copse, up the sandpapered rock to a slight promontory and did a 360. Shadows flickered across a ridge in moonlight. Coyotes barked weird yipping ululations. There—in the creosote. A pair of red eyes.

Pratt stared until his vision blurred. Wolves had red eyes in the moonlight. Men did not.

An icicle entered his heart. A sense of hopelessness seized Pratt in iron jaws like the first time he'd been thrown in jail, age sixteen, car theft. They got him when he ran the new Chevy Tahoe he'd hotwired in a mall parking lot into the ditch. A cop with a face like a bulldog took one sneering look at him, pumped and inked in his wife beater, and tuned him up by the side of the road with swift, brutal little punches to his kidneys that left him pissing blood for days.

The bull had cranked the cuffs behind his back and tossed him in the back of his cruiser. The back seat smelled like vomit. The jail stank of urine. There was no mattress on the hard iron cot.

Pratt remembered sitting in the stinking cell by himself Saturday night thinking of ways to commit suicide, thinking, *Of course people kill themselves in jail. All the fucking time.*

They did it when the future looked worse than the past. They made that calculation in their minds—is it worth going on? Are things ever going to get better or is it all downhill from here?

Duane weighed in. "You ain't worth a glass of warm piss, boy. I don't know how you're gonna make it."

Fuck you Duane, I'm gonna make it.

Pratt shivered uncontrollably, sat right there and did the breathing thing. The desolation, the smell, the awful things he'd seen—he had to get out of there.

The pale white tepee decorated with Sioux pictographs beckoned like a beacon.

Pratt stiff-walked over and looked inside.

An ivory and rust colored tank gleamed dully in the moonlight, the word "Indian" painted on its side in elegant script with a gold out-line. Ape hangers stuck straight up like a praying mantis' antennae. Indians had been around since 1901. The original manufacturer was in Springfield, Massachusetts. It went bankrupt in 1953 but ever since, venture groups had been buying up the name and introducing new "Indians," capitalizing on the full-skirted fender look. This Indian was from 1999, with an 1800-cc chunk of iron in the cradle frame.

The key was in the ignition.

CHAPTER 29

The Indian was one of those legacy jobs based on the original tooling but with a modern engine. Art deco fenders covered most of the wheels. It had fishtail pipes and floorboards. It was long and low and weighed seven hundred and fifty pounds.

Pratt laughed when he saw it. Who would have thought the day would come when he would prefer four wheels to two? His cracked rib was incendiary and the rest of him looked like it had gone through a wood chipper. He'd bandaged himself as well as he could with rags and duct tape. There were bungee cords on the pillion. He used these to strap in his sports drink, gingerly sat on the saddle and unscrewed the gas cap. Good to go. He was seeping.

It occurred to him that with Moon gone there was no reason for Pratt to flee. He could stay the night, start fresh in the morning.

Maybe the boy would come back.

He thought about entering the hut and his flesh prickled. The place gave off a bad vibe. A long, slow, dangerous ride into town was preferable to staying there.

Pratt turned the key. The telltale lights in the huge instrument nacelle blinked on: red and green. Pratt thumbed the starter button.

The machine whirred mechanically for an instant then exploded in an eruption of power. Pratt let out the clutch and eased the beast out of the tepee toward the dirt road that disappeared in a fold in the rock.

The headlight turned the world a sickly yellow as Pratt used first gear to negotiate the rock-strewn path.

If he can ride in, I can ride out.

Pratt's feet left the floorboards to control his balance when they hit the gravel. The road surface hardened to clay a quarter mile up the road and Pratt was able to get into third gear. At one point as he traversed a narrow wadi, the hairs stood up on the back of his neck. He glanced up and thought he saw two red eyes peering at him from atop a promontory. He laid on the throttle, paying the price in pain as the big machine lurched and rolled over obstacles.

The road meandered through the hills before picking up the remains of a barbed wire fence on one side. Pratt subsumed himself in the task of guiding the machine, achieving for a time a blissful amnesia, a blessed release from the scare he'd just had. The hills retreated and the horizon expanded. Pratt and the bike functioned as one. Total concentration yielded to no concentration and the bike rolled flawlessly on. Pratt lost all sense of time. Eventually he was joined by a trickle of creek. Emerging from a stand of cottonwood next to the creek, a white-tailed deer dashed across the road.

Pratt checked the odometer. He'd gone twenty-five miles. He shut off the engine, reached behind him and snagged the last bottle. He drained it and stuck it back under the bungees. After a few minutes he heard the whoosh of traffic from beyond the next ridge. He started the engine and snicked the big bike into gear. Moments later he topped the crest and looked down at a busy two-lane blacktop. The dirt road ended in a locked gate set ten feet back from the highway. Ten feet back from the gate was a tiny pre-fab shed with a green metal roof. Down the road was a green highway sign, "HOG TAIL 6 MILES."

Pratt rode to the gate, found a flat rock and kicked out the stand. The aluminum gate was part of an electrified wire corral enclosing a stable and an empty water trough. The gate was held shut by a Master padlock. Pratt hefted the lock and tested the connection. It was on tight. He looked up and down the barbed wire fence. A lot easier to breach the barbed wire then fight with the lock.

A truck whooshed by. The driver waved through the window as he passed. Pratt waved back. The moon glared balefully down. A Toyota whooshed by and abruptly stutter-stepped as the driver registered what he'd seen. There was a flash of brake lights, then the guy took off. Maybe phoning in what he thought he saw.

Pratt walked over to the shed. The door was shut, the hasp turned, but there was no lock. He opened it up and found a pair of bolt cutters in a rusted red tool box. He also found the fuse box and shut off the power going to the fence. Cutting another man's wire used to be a hanging offense.

Pratt cut through the three strands of wire. They fell inert to the ground. Pratt got on the Indian, started it up and rode through the fence, across the shallow ditch at an angle, onto the hard shoulder and up the road toward Hog Tail. His body achieved an uneasy equilibrium, pain evenly distributed like side saddles, vibrations soothing his angry nerves. Maybe he should just stay on the bike until he ran out of gas. He followed an old Ford pick-up and a PT Cruiser filled with whooping teenagers down a long slope toward the clustered lights of Hog Tail.

Hog Tail was six blocks of bars, a Piggly Wiggly, a post office, a grain elevator, a hardware and appliance store and real estate. A blinking sign on the bank said 10:15. A gleaming new Chevron station occupied one corner at the crossroads. Four choppers sat outside Vern's Place, a faux redwood dive with a horizontal window sporting a neon Hamm's sign.

Feeling light headed and shaky, Pratt backed the big Indian to the curb next to a well-worn FXLH. His multiple stab sounds and contusions had coalesced into a steady red alert pulsing through his whole body. He sat there for a minute while he waited for his vision to settle down. He was seeing double. High school harries cruised past in tricked-out Hondas. The Fast and the Furious had come to Wyoming. The ripping shrieks of their exhausts provided a suitable soundtrack for how he felt.

After awhile he carefully got off the bike, nerves like arcing sunspots. The ground lurched beneath him and he swayed, caught himself. Even his hair hurt. Using the seat for support, he stepped up onto the curb and walked slowly to the front door.

Using both hands to spread the pain evenly, he opened the door, pulling it back with his whole body to avoid bending his arms, and sidled inside. The interior was cool and dark, long bar running three quarters the length of the room on the left, booths on the right, pool table in back. Four bikers occupied a round table in the back. They were all Indians. They all had long black hair fastened in a braid. Their colors said Lakota Nation. They glanced at Pratt. Two of them did double-takes.

Pratt eased himself up on one of the sofas and planted his elbows gingerly on the bar. The bartender, an ancient ginseng root, floated his way. The bartender had a sloping forehead over a sharply pointed nose and a receding chin, giving him the profile of an arrowhead. He wore a faded blue bandanna around his forehead, keeping his long salt and pepper hair out of his face. "Vern" was stitched across his green bowling shirt in red. He stopped in front of Pratt. He had gray-blue eyes.

"What the hell happened to you?" Vern croaked in a nicotine-stained voice.

"I got in a fight with a mountain lion. May I have a glass of water?"

The old man drew water in a Coke glass and set it on the bar in front of Pratt. "Hang on. I got a first aid kit in the back."

Pratt put up a hand. "And a shot of Jack before you go."

Vern wordlessly poured the shot and ambled toward the rear of the building. Pratt held the amber liquid up to the light—the Budweiser Clydesdales in their endless plod around the lamp, and downed it. Like a miniature depth bomb, it fell into his gut and detonated spreading heat. He could hardly wait for the bartender to return so he could have another.

Vern returned at a measured pace holding a big cardboard box. He set it on the counter and opened it. "You ought to get them gouges looked at. Could be septic."

Pratt flexed his left shoulder, causing a thermonuclear detonation that left him gasping. "You got a doctor in town?"

Vern removed two rolls of bandages and a container filled with iodine. He grabbed Pratt's arm in one hand and drew the moistened applicator through the grooves in his flesh, imparting white-hot sting that made Pratt want to shout, *I'm alive!*

"Mountain lion," Vern said.

Pratt barked. "It sounds crazy!"

Vern shot him a suspicious look. "Where the fuck you find a mountain lion?'

"Do you know Eugene Moon?" Pratt said.

Vern shrank back as if he'd almost stepped on a rattler. He looked around. He leaned in close. His breath smelled like citrus with telltale alcohol. "Mister, I don't have a thing to do with Moon. Ahmina patch you up but then you got to hit the road. Them drinks are on me."

"I'm a private investigator," Pratt said. "Moon did this to me. He left me for dead with a fucking mountain lion."

Vern peered at Pratt hard with his arrowhead face. "Mister, when you put it that way I don't doubt you. Any enemy of Moon's a friend of mine. Vern Lovejoy." He stuck out his hand.

"Josh Pratt." Pratt winced from the grooves on his hands. "Can I have another shot then?"

Vern poured the shot. Pratt peeled off his shirt and went to work with the iodine.

"Give me a minute I'll get Dr. Keith down here. He's a mighty fine veterinarian, that's the best I can do."

Pratt nodded and tossed back the shot.

CHAPTER 30

Dr. Keith was eighty if he was a day. He had a face like a russet potato beneath a rumpled campaign hat and wore a safari jacket with breast pockets and shoulder straps. He ushered Pratt into the back room, a combination storage shed and office, and bade Pratt sit in an ancient captain's chair while he cleaned up Pratt's wounds, stitched shut the rips and administered a shot of antibiotics.

"When's the last time you had a tetanus booster?" the doctor asked.

"Two years ago."

"Then you should be good then, although I would advise you to take it easy for a few days, give these cuts a chance to patch over."

"That ain't gonna happen, Doc. I got things to do."

"Up to you. Vern says you tangled with a mountain lion. Your injuries are consistent with such a diagnosis so I must ask myself, how did this come about? Normally I would be obligated to report your injuries to Sheriff Archie DeWitt. So what's your explanation, son?"

"I had a disagreement with a mountain lion."

The doctor sat back and stared at Pratt through round lenses that appeared opaque as they reflected the desk lamp. "A-huh. And how did this come about?"

"Doc, you wouldn't believe me if I told you."

"Try me. Now I'm not charging you a fee, so the least you can do is level with me. How in hell did this happen?"

Pratt told the doctor about his search for the missing son, leaving out the part where he actually found Eric. He didn't want that to get out before he had a chance to talk to Ginger. He glanced at the phone. Just what was he going to tell her?

Your son has been irreparably damaged by his deranged father.

After he finished, Dr. Keith pursed his lips, reached into his black bag and removed a small sterling silver flask. He unscrewed the cap and upended the bottle, handing it to Pratt. "Brandy?"

Pratt took a swig, feeling the fiery liquid land on the whiskey base. *Whoa.* Enough of that shit.

"Eugene Moon. I have heard that name before. It seems he's a local legend, some kind of bad guy. I have treated dogs alleged to have belonged to him. Sadly they had to be euthanized. Well, young sir, this is most certainly a matter for Sheriff Archie DeWitt."

Doc Keith reached for the ancient black Bakelite phone with a rotary dial. Pratt placed his bandaged hand on the doctor's wrist. "Doc, I really wish you'd hold off on that. I can't hang around. I've got to get to Madison ASAP. I don't know how I'm even going to do that. I'm gonna have to ride that Indian. You got anything I can take for the pain that's subscription-based?"

"You mean prescription. You've been up a long time too. You need to rest before you go running off, young sir. The way you're wincing, 'pears you've got a cracked rib, am I right?"

"Right as rain, Doc. Can't do it. Gotta go. What do you have for pain killers?"

"How about PCP? You look like you might have tried it."

"Not in a long time, Doc. No I don't think so. Don't you have any morphine?"

"You want me to pump you full of morphine so you can ride all night. That doesn't strike me as a good idea."

"Doc, I'm afraid Eugene Moon is going to kill two nice ladies."

"Then you had better notify the police."

Pratt stared at the doctor for a second then picked up the phone. He called Cass' number from memory. Cass answered on the fifth ring, laughing. Pratt heard music in the background.

"Cass," he said.

"Oh my God! It's you!" Cass turned away from the phone. "Turn the music down," she said urgently. "How are you? What's going on?"

"I'm all right. Listen. I believe Moon is headed your way."

"What?"

"I think both you and Ginger are in danger and you both need to get the hell out of your respective homes and hole up somewhere else for a few days and not tell anybody."

"You're scaring me, Pratt. What's going on?"

"I found Moon. I can't go into it right now. I'm heading back there tonight. I should get there sometime tomorrow around midday if I can rent a car. As soon as I'm done talking to you I'm going to notify the Madison PD and the FBI."

Pratt heard Ginger asking Cass what was going on and to speak with him. Cass shushed her.

"The police can't stop him," Cass said with despairing finality.

"If he can't find you, he can't hurt you. Don't even tell Ginger's husband."

"Like that's gonna fly. She wants to talk to you."

Pratt did not know how to avoid that conversation. Ginger came on the phone weak and breathless.

"Did you find him?"

And there it was.

"I have every reason to believe he's alive."

"*Did you find him?*"

"No. I'll give you a full report as soon as I get there."

"Godspeed," she said before hanging up.

CHAPTER 31

Pratt eased out his wallet and checked the bills. Amazingly, Moon hadn't touched his money. He had eight hundred sixty bucks.

Dr. Keith shook his head. "You don't have to pay me."

"I need a vehicle, Doc. Where can I buy a vehicle on short notice?"

Doc peered at him from beneath a hedgerow of white eyebrow. "First of all, I would not suggest you go running off anywhere, young man, until you've had some rest and given those meds a little time to work themselves out of your system. I would advise you not to operate a vehicle."

Pratt spread his bandaged hands. "Can't do it, Doc. Gotta roll. Some lives may depend on it. Moon's a killer."

Doc nodded. "I've heard that. Seen him once up at Fisher's Lake."

"How long ago was that?"

"Three, four years. I was out hiking with my Molly. I saw he had some old pick-up truck backed up to the cliff and it looked to me he was looking to unload something. Trail's kinda narrow so I came right up on him. He had that truck back there on a fire trail. The look he gave me, well, I'm sure glad I had Molly with me. It was like staring into two pits of dry ice. Molly's a rotty-bulldog mix. She is one ugly critter and highly protective."

"You heard anything about Moon recently? Like he might be running a meth lab?"

Dr. Keith shook his head. "No sir. The sheriff and I meet for coffee regularly. I'm certain he'd tell me about something like that, nor would Sheriff Archie tolerate such a thing in his county. Why? Was he?"

"Yeah. Place is gonna need a hazmat team."

Pratt didn't want the little valley crawling with cops. They might scare Eric off, or worse. Nor could he tell them about the boy. That information had been purchased by Ginger. Pratt had no idea how to handle it. He needed expert advice. The last thing Eric needed were sheriff's deputies tramping the hills with dogs. But now it looked like that's what he was going to get. He knew how these things worked.

"Doc, I need a vehicle. Where can I rent or purchase a car around here?"

Dr. Keith scratched his white head. "The nearest car dealers would be over at Buffalo. Used to be Mason's Autos down on Main Street, but they got closed down when the government took over Chrysler."

"What about Vern?"

"Vern won't let go of his F-150, but you might ask him about that old Rambler he's got out back, if it's running. Also, you don't mind, you smell like the coyote cage at the zoo. You might think about a shower, you get the chance."

Pratt was so taped, doped and drunk he nearly slid off the chair. Dr. Keith took him by the arm and led him to a cot in a corner next to a stack of Cutty Sarks and eased him on down.

"I gave you a little something to help you relax. Best not fight it, son. You're in no condition to go anywhere. Don't worry I'm going to tell the Sheriff. I won't do it until you're bright-eyed and bushy-tailed. Don't see where it would do any good anyway."

Pratt tried to tell the doctor about the dead War Bonnet in the gulch but he was slipping down a black ice luge. He dove into unconsciousness like a rock dropping into a pond. Sploosh. He dreamt of being stuck in a cavern with the Minotaur, and of ill-treated dogs. He was running along the interstate, semis roaring past five feet away, screaming and crying, "Daddy!" He was in the pen. Big ruckus in the cafeteria. The bulls tased him and tossed him into solitary.

Long time in solitary.

CHAPTER 32

Pratt came back to consciousness by degrees. First he was aware of the scraping of furniture in another room, muted voices. The smell of dust and sawdust. Orange light through his lids. He lay there feeling good until he shifted and all the cuts and bruises woke up, 911 calls from the furthest reaches of his extremities. He opened his eyes and stared at the dim light on the desk. The clock said nine a.m. He'd been out for twelve hours.

The slightest movement reminded him where he was. He was wrapped like King Tut. Moon had had a fourteen-hour head start. Pratt cranked himself to a sitting position, got his feet on the floor, leaned on a wooden liquor case and slowly stood. He stiff-walked to the bathroom, to its rust-stained porcelain sink, and gave himself a sponge bath with paper towels and a sliver of soap. He dropped three ibuprofens. He looked at himself in the cracked mirror. He was ready for his zombie close-up. Pratt found a box of Vern's Place T-shirts, rust with yellow lettering, and eased his way into an XL, which hung on his lean frame like a flag. Pratt went over to the ancient desk and sat in the creaking captain's chair, on a well-worn sponge cushion. Even his ass hurt. He fished out his cell phone. Still dead. The charger was with his bike.

Pratt reached for the ancient black dial phone and saw the note: "Pratt—back at ten. Milk in fridge, cereal beneath bar. Vern."

Pratt dialed Detective Heinz Calloway's number from memory. It rang once.

"Calloway."

"Heinz, it's Josh Pratt."

"What's goin' on? You involved in that shoot-out at the Buffalo Chip?"

"No. Listen. That guy I asked you about, Eugene Moon? I found him. He tried to kill me. He told me he's heading back there to kill Cass Rubio and Ginger Munz." He told Calloway everything except the boy.

"What about that kid you're looking for?" Calloway ineluctably asked.

"Still searching." Not a lie, exactly.

"Phone numbers?" Calloway said.

Pratt recited Cass' from memory. "Can't tell you Ginger's. It's in my cell phone and I don't have a charger. I'll pick one up on the way and charge up in the car, but I can tell you how to find them. Ginger's husband Nathan is a big-shot builder. He can't be hard to find. Munz Construction."

Big sigh. "All right. I'll try and get in touch with them."

"You have to get them into police custody, Heinz."

"That ain't gonna happen. All I have is your word and there's no heat on this guy Moon. He's been off the books since 1992. I'll do what I can."

Pratt dry-swallowed. He heard the front door to the bar open. "You know me, Heinz. I'm not an alarmist."

"Believe me, I'm taking this very seriously."

"Okay. Thank you. I'll phone you as soon as I get back."

"Don't get arrested for speeding," Calloway advised and hung up.

Vern appeared in the doorway. "How's it goin'?"

Pratt smiled and spread his hands, expanding his chest against the confines of the bandages, hearing the chair squeak. "I feel a thousand percent better 'cause I slept. Vern, I need to buy, steal or borrow a set of wheels. I've got to get back and I should have left yesterday. Doc said you had a Rambler you might let me use."

Vern put his hands behind him and shuffled his feet. "Well now I hate to tell ya this, son, but last night the sheriff dropped by after you fell asleep and before Dr. Keith left. Sheriff started asking about that Indian out front and Dr. Keith told him everything."

Pratt sat down on the bunk. "Oh shit."

"Yeah and in fact here he is."

A tall man in khakis and a Sam Browne belt pushed through the door. His big head came to a bald point. A whisk broom hung from his substantial nose. He confronted Pratt with his hands on his hips.

"Mr. Josh Pratt, how you doin'?"

Pratt stayed where he was. "Sheriff."

"Now tell me you were plannin' on letting me know about that meth lab Vern says you found."

Pratt glanced at the old Indian. Vern stared at the floor. Well fuck it. Vern had to live here. Pratt didn't.

"Sir, I was going to phone you as soon as I alerted my client to a threat on her life."

"Mmm-hmmm. Well I just got back from Moon's little meth lab in the hills and we got cadaver dogs out there, 'bout shit when they got a whiff of that well. Whooo-eee. That must have been some battle. You look like shit."

Pratt grinned. "You should have seen me last night."

"I'm looking at you right now and I'm seein' jailhouse tats. Now when I went to check on you, you didn't have a record so I called a few friends of mine in the Wisconsin Highway Patrol. My friends have long memories. You did time at Waupun for all sorts of nasty stuff. You used to ride with the Bedouins. You look to me like forty miles of bad road."

"Sir, I'm not that person no more. I came to Jesus in prison."

DeWitt shook his big head with a smirk. "Lots of prison conversions these days. The blacks flock to Islam. You crackers always find Jesus."

Pratt didn't know what to say so he said nothing.

"Can I see some identification?"

Pratt dug out his wallet, removed his driver's license and handed it over. The sheriff stared at it for a long time. No one spoke. Vern shuffled his feet. A beam of light coming through the dusty window froze motes in the air.

Finally DeWitt handed the license back. "Mr. Pratt, you're under arrest. Stand up and put your hands behind you."

Pratt goggled. "What for?"

"Killing an endangered species."

CHAPTER 33

"Oooo-WEE!" Sheriff DeWitt exclaimed, opening all the windows in his Crown Vic. "You stink!" The roasted outside air did little to alleviate the pong.

"I could use a shower," Pratt said.

"You don't have to talk, Pratt," DeWitt said from the front seat of his Crown Vic, his left wrist draped over the wheel, arm along the seatback. "But you being a private investigator and all can appreciate that you're going to need police cooperation from time to time. You see where I'm headin?"

"Yes sir."

"So if you don't mind, what were you really doing out there?"

"Sir, I was searching for a missing person on behalf of my client."

"What missing person?"

"Sir, that's privileged information."

"Don't give me that crap. You're not a lawyer. You're just a bottom-feeding peeper far from home with no friends."

"Sir, I'm going to have to talk to my lawyer first."

"Your choice." DeWitt took his arm off the seat back and focused his attention on the road. The Robbins County Jail was located in the basement of the Robbins County Courthouse, a Greek revival temple built of Rocky Mountain granite sitting like a wedding cake in the center of a manicured green lawn overgrown with oak and ash two blocks from Vern's. An emerald in a sandbox. The Sheriff drove around to the back, where a ramp led down to the lower level and the sheriff's offices. DeWitt parked in a marked spot, got out, opened the rear door and helped Pratt out of the vehicle. Pratt had his hands cuffed behind him.

The sheriff held the door as he ushered Pratt into an air-conditioned front office with a yellowish linoleum floor, a linoleum counter top and yellowish acoustic tiles on the ceiling. Yellowish light flickered from three fluorescent installations mounted flush in the ceiling.

A bulletin board on one wall was jammed with overlapping notices and mug shots of the FBI's Ten Most Wanted, including several jihadi types. A "Lost Dog" Xerox. Postcards from friends, clipped cartoons and the odd picture.

With an arm on the shoulder, the sheriff directed Pratt to a middle-aged Indian woman in a deputy's uniform. "Marie, please book Mr. Pratt in. The charge is killing an endangered species."

The woman set aside her Peter Brandvold Western and waited while the Sheriff released the cuffs. She put a deep metal pan on the counter, wrinkled her nose and stepped back with a disgusted expression.

"Empty your pockets please."

Wallet, change, watch, buck knife, phone, pen, pad, ibuprofen, parking receipt.

"Shoelaces."

Pratt bent down and undid his laces. He placed them in the tray.

"Step over to the wall please and put your hands on the marks." Two black palm prints five feet off the ground. Black shoe prints for his feet. While Pratt leaned against the wall Marie patted him down efficiently and professionally. A lanky deputy stood nearby with thumbs in belt.

Marie painstakingly wrote a list of Pratt's property and had him sign a receipt. She sat at a keyboard and seconds later the printer disgorged a booking warrant. She produced an ink pad and fingerprint form. "Please do all five fingers in the indicated boxes." She took his hand and used each finger like a rubber stamp.

"You know what one of those fingerprint scanners cost?" the sheriff said. "Fifty bucks. That's right. Fifty bucks. I am sore tempted to reach into my own pocket. Norm, would you take Mr. Pratt to his accommodations?"

The lanky deputy held the door for Pratt. A short corridor ended in a metal door that led to the lock-up, three side-by-side cells. No windows. One was occupied by a heap of rags that rattled like Venetian blinds in a wind. Pratt went in the middle, an eight-by-ten iron box with a stainless steel bed, sink and toilet. A sign on the cinderblock wall said, "ALL TELEPHONE CALLS ARE MONITORED."

"There you go," Norm said, sliding the cell door shut. It locked automatically and could only be opened electronically.

"What about my phone call?" Pratt said.

"Let me check with the sheriff."

The deputy departed the cinder block chamber, the door hissing shut behind him. Pratt sat on the bunk. The bundle of rags in the next cell shifted position and gears, reaching down for a low grinding sound. A moment later the deputy reentered the jail holding a wireless land line no doubt hooked into the department system. Norm handed the black phone through the bars, went down to the end of the room twenty feet away, sat in a wooden kitchen chair with its back to the wall, pushed off and hit the wall with a thwack. The deputy pulled a rolled-up magazine from his hip pocket and began to read. *Field & Stream.*

Pratt went to the far side of the cell, turned away and dialed Bloom's number.

"Bloom Law Agency!" Perry brayed. Every word capitalized. Bloom was in a meeting. Pratt told Perry it was an emergency.

A minute later Bloom came on the line. "What?!"

"I'm in the Robbins County Jail, Hog Tail, Wyoming. I killed a mountain lion. It was self-defense. They got me locked up on an endangered species rap. Is that for real?"

Pratt could practically see Bloom staring at the phone as if it were a strange insect. "Why the fuck you kill a mountain lion?"

"I had no choice. It was self-defense. Moon trapped me in a dry well and dropped it on my head."

"Oh Jesus. What are you into?"

Pratt gave him the brief version. He could hear Bloom sucking air through his teeth. Even the abbreviated version was hard to take.

"Jesus," Bloom said.

"Yeah. Can you get me out of here? And I want you to call Cass and tell her to come get me."

"I can't. I'm in court every day this week. I know a good lawyer in Cheyenne, Mason Mazin. I'll give him a call. Give me Cass' number and the sheriff's department."

Pratt gave Bloom Cass' number, then put his hand over the mouth-piece and called to the deputy. "Hey deputy, what's the number of this office?"

He relayed the number to Bloom.

"Okay. Hang tight. I promise you, you'll have representation by the end of the day."

"ASAP, buddy. Every second I'm in here that kid gets farther away."

"Don't worry. You have my word."

"Thanks, Danny."

"Okay, talk to ya."

The deputy heaved himself forward, bringing the kitchen chair's front legs down with a bang. Pratt was dialing Cass when the deputy stuck his hand through the bars.

"One call's all you get."

Pratt handed it over. "All right. Thanks."

The deputy took the phone and left the jail area.

Pratt was alone save for the sawing pile of rags in the next cell. Pratt did fifty push-ups. He tried to do sit-ups but he was afraid his stitches would pop. He lay down on the thin mattress and went to sleep.

Werewolves and fire. He woke with a start. He had the feeling he'd been out for several hours despite the lack of windows or clocks. The dude in the next cell sat on his bunk Indian style regarding Pratt with keen interest. Rags draped the wizened homunculus like laundry on a pole.

"You remind me of someone," the creature said in a phlegmy voice.

Pratt could find no speech. A mystic sine wave rippled through the

building, momentarily distorting Pratt's thoughts and flesh and pluck-
ing at his bones like a mandolin player. The old dude reminded Pratt
of someone too. He couldn't quite put his finger on it.

The dude's light bulb-shaped head poked up out of a black turtleneck pullover three sizes too big. It was covered with dog hair.

"You look like a turtle," Pratt said.

The ancient face creased in a beatific smile. "My name is Herman
Hightower."

"Josh Pratt. How ya doin.'"

"Doin' okay. You know what you remind me of?"

Pratt waited, forearms on his knees. "I'll bet you're going to tell
me."

"A cougar."

Pratt touched the stitches on his forearms. "Funny you should say
that."

"When you killed that cougar you absorbed its spirit. And you
killed it in a good way."

"I guess the whole town knows, huh?"

Hightower shrugged, barely visible through multiple layers of
clothing. "It's all they been talking about. You drove Moon away. No
one else even had the guts to try."

"You think the sheriff knew Moon . . ." Pratt quickly lowered his
voice and moved to the grille. Hightower moved close too, bringing a
miasma of graphite body odor.

Pratt whispered, "You think DeWitt knew Moon was running a
meth lab?"

Hightower shook his hairless head. "No way. The sheriff is a good
man. But he knew Moon was around in the same way a prairie dog
knows there's a coyote waiting for him. A force, an atmosphere that affects everyone. You feel anxious but you don't know why. Well he don't
feel anxious anymore."

The door squeaked open. Deputy Norm came through, followed
by a bantam rooster who could not have been taller than five five in
his stocking feet, wearing hand-tooled leather boots with a three-inch
lift, a light gray seersucker suit, a string tie with an opal the size of a
robin's egg surmounted by an elegant squarish head, extravagant white

handlebar mustache, hedgerow brows and matching Stetson. His engraved silver belt buckle depicted a bull rider whoopin' on a Texas longhorn. He wore a gold signet ring with a ruby the size of a dime.

The cowboy stepped up to Pratt's cell. "Josh Pratt? I'm your attorney, Mason M. Mazin."

"Glad to see you, Mr. Mazin. Danny must have called you, huh?"

"Norm, can we let Mr. Pratt out of here now?"

CHAPTER 34

Sheriff DeWitt was seated at the booking desk when the deputy brought Pratt and Mazin out of the cells. Mazin nodded to him.

"Sheriff."

The sheriff nodded back. "Mason. Marie, give Mr. Pratt back his personal belongings. And Mr. Pratt, I'd appreciate it if you'd stick around for a few days in case we have any more questions. You with me, counselor?"

"That is entirely at Mr. Pratt's discretion but as his lawyer, naturally I advise him to cooperate fully with law enforcement."

Marie produced the metal bin, checking the items off against a list one by one as she named them and handed them over. Pratt signed the receipt and redistributed his goods back in their pockets. He swallowed two ibuprofens, washing them down at the bubbler. Mazin indicated an exit up a flight of stairs through the front of the building. They emerged next to the main entrance of the courthouse into the afternoon heat, oppressive even in the shade. Mazin headed down the concrete path to the street toward a black Ford Excursion with a set of Texas Longhorns mounted on the hood. The license plate read, "CWBOY."

Mazin fingered his fob. The Excursion beeped and flashed. "Step into my office," he said, climbing up into the driver's seat using both a step-up and a hand hold.

Pratt stiffly got in the passenger's side, also using the hand hold. Mazin started the engine and turned the air conditioner on full blast. A police scanner hung beneath the dash on the passenger's side.

"I knew that chickenshit charge wasn't going to last. Sheriff's been combing the books looking for some other charge with which he could hold you. His pride is hurt 'cause you uncovered something he should have known about. By the way, he impounded your bike. Found a dead War Bonnet in a gulch."

"What do I owe you, counselor?" Pratt said.

Mazin waved a hand, pointed toward the glove compartment. "Gratis. I owe Danny some favors. Open that up why don'tcha and hand me one."

Pratt popped open the glove compartment. Inside was a miniature refrigerator holding a six-pack of Fat Tires. Pratt handed one to Mazin and took one himself.

"There's an opener on the lid there."

Pratt removed the bottle opener from its clamp inside the glove compartment and opened his bottle. He handed the opener to Mazin.

Mazin held his bottle up. "To liberty." They clicked bottles. "Danny gave me the short version but I'm not sure I know what this is all about. You mind bringing me up to speed?"

Pratt told the story of his search for Ginger's missing son, omitting nothing. Unlike law enforcement officers, Pratt had an instinctive and well-earned trust in criminal defense attorneys. They had always helped him. His best friend was a lawyer. And they knew how to keep their mouths shut. Like all good lawyers, Mazin was a good listener. He was silent for a minute when Pratt finished.

"That's unbelievable. This Moon sounds like a raging psychopath. What are you going to do now?"

"Well sir, I was hoping to go back out there and take another look around for the boy."

"If what you say is true he's unlikely to trust anyone ever again."

"Maybe. I have to try. I can't just leave him out there to forage like a wild animal."

Neither put into words what both were thinking.

"How you feeling? You're moving pretty good for a man who fought a mountain lion."

"If I slow down I'll stop moving."

Mazin glanced at his Tag Heuer. "I've got to go. Drop you someplace?"

"Vern's, I guess."

The same four choppers were at the curb outside. The same four Indians were at the same table playing with the same deck of cards. Vern saw Pratt enter and automatically reached for the bourbon. He had the shot poured by the time Pratt eased himself carefully onto a bar stool.

"I knew that chickenshit charge wasn't gonna stick," Vern said. "DeWitt's all right 'less you cross him. How'd you get out so quick?"

"I got a good lawyer. Vern, I wonder if I could impose on you a little more."

"Whatcha need?"

The four Indians at the table shot surreptitious glances Pratt's way. One of them detached himself and walked toward the bar. He was about six feet tall with thick bones, pepper-salt hair tied in a ponytail, sad eyes beneath patchy brows. He paused next to Pratt.

"Pratt, this here's Richard Longtree. What's up Rich?"

"Want to buy this man a drink."

Pratt turned toward the man and stuck out his hand. "Josh Pratt."

Longtree shook his hand ceremoniously. "That was slick, what you did, man, taking down a mountain lion. We didn't even know Moon was around."

"I'm sure he's gone now," Pratt said. "Half the country's going to be looking for him by the morning."

Vern leaned on the bar, lowered his voice. "I got a friend whose brother's a deputy, says they pulled two bodies out of the ground out there this morning. One of 'em may be that missing fed guy."

"What fed guy?" Pratt said.

"Couple years ago, federal marshal went on the Pingree Res looking for an AIM guy named Little Danny. He disappeared. No one's heard from Little Danny either."

"I always figured Little Danny for the fed job," Longtree said. "Maybe Moon killed 'em both."

"Rich," Pratt said, "I've got to take care of some business. Then I'll come over and join you guys for a drink."

Longtree clapped a big hand on Pratt's shoulder, causing him to wince. "We'll be waiting."

Longtree returned to his table. Pratt pulled out his cell phone. "Vern, I need to charge this."

Vern held out his hand. "Give it here. I got a universal charger back in my office. You can pick one up at the Walgreens in Buffalo."

"And I need to use your phone to call my old lady."

Vern handed him the phone. Pratt dialed Cass.

"Where are you?" she demanded. "I was worried sick about you! Then that lawyer called and said you'd been arrested!"

Pratt heard Ginger's querulous voice in the background. "I'm out now. I wonder if you'd come get me. I'm in Hog Tail, Wyoming."

"Jesus, Pratt. That's the ass end of the universe! Are you all right?"

"I'm a little torn up. I'm really in no condition to ride." Pratt wanted Cass for another reason. He suspected Eric might react more favorably to a woman. He could be wrong. He wasn't about to leave without taking another crack at finding the kid. The boy had been on his mind since their encounter. How could he survive out there on his own, without the most rudimentary skills?

"If I leave now I can be there in the morning."

"You'd have to drive straight through. I don't want you to do that."

"No prob. I got shit to stay up."

"Cass, no. I have some shit to take care of anyway. Leave now but don't try to make it in one sitting. It'd be a real bummer if you crashed. I'll still be here tomorrow night."

"Did you find him?"

"I'm not sure."

"What's that supposed to mean? Ginger wants to talk to you."

"I can't talk to her right now. Cass, just come get me. I'll explain everything."

"What am I supposed to tell Ginger?"

"Moon is looking for her. He's looking for both of you."

"They've hired a private security firm."

"Who?"

"Flintstone.

"They're very good," Pratt said. "Ginger should be all right."

"Okay, baby. I'll leave in an hour. I love you."

"I love you too," Pratt automatically answered, feeling like a fraud.

CHAPTER 35

The Indians seated at the round table regarded Pratt with awe. They solemnly shook his hand, drawing strength through the skin. He was something out of the old times when adolescents were sent into the wilderness on their dream quest armed with a knife and a bow. Only by proving themselves in elemental struggle with nature could they become men and warriors. Now the young men drank and did drugs and hung around the reservations waiting for their welfare checks.

Pratt read awe in their eyes and felt unworthy.

"That Moon," Longtree said. "He was always trouble, even when he was a little boy."

"You knew him?" Pratt said.

"Oh yeah. He was the class bully out at Crazy Horse Middle School. You know how hard it is to get expelled from a reservation school?"

A thin man named Pat said, "He was rapin' girls in junior high."

The other two Indians were Burt and Paul.

"He was always a freak," Paul said. "He was into Satanism and death metal before he decided to become an authentic Injun."

"Claimed he had second sight," Longtree said.

Burt asked Pratt about the Sturgis shooting.

"I wasn't there," Pratt said.

"Last thing the rally needs," Pat said.

"This won't hurt the rally," Longtree said. "Just means they're gonna eighty-six the Skulls and the Vandals."

"Ain't no loss," Burt said. The others nodded solemnly. None of them had gone to the rally anyway.

As Pratt finished a second shot Dr. Keith entered beneath the wheezing air conditioning unit carrying his little black bag. Pratt excused himself and met the doctor at the bar.

"Sorry you got arrested," Dr. Keith said, setting his black bag on the bar. "Sorry about that, but the sheriff had me dead to rights as I was leaving the other night. It's one thing not to volunteer information, quite another when the sheriff's got you dead to rights."

Pratt eased himself down on a stool. "I understand, Doc. So they went out there?"

"Oh yeah," Dr. Keith said, sitting on a stool and opening his bag. "Found two bodies. One of 'em might be that missing fed. I think back to that day when I ran into Moon about to unload his truck up in the high country I can't help but wonder maybe it was that federal agent. Take your shirt off, son."

Pratt peeled off his shirt. A couple field hands burnt red by the sun glanced at him as they took up two bar stools toward the back. A silent TV monitor over the bar showed a baseball game. Vern drew two drafts without being asked and carried them down the bar.

Dr. Keith poked and prodded, checked the seams, took out his stethoscope and held the welcome cool against Pratt's back. Had Pratt cough several times, looked in his eyes. "Son, you have got the constitution of a dray horse. You could just as easily gone into shock and died out there. If I was younger I might try and write you up for some medical magazine. Those antibiotics seem to be doing the trick. How you feeling?"

"Just glad to be alive, Doc."

"Try not to rip these stitches."

Vern came back. "Offer you gentlemen a beer?"

Pratt shrugged. "Why not."

Dr. Keith nodded. "Might as well. I just got done helping McGillicuddy's cow give breech birth. How we got that tangle of limbs outta there I still don't know, but we had three people pushing and pulling at one point."

Pratt hoisted his glass. Vern and Dr. Keith hoisted theirs. They clanked. They drank.

"Vern, do you know any trackers?"

"Lester," the doc said.

"My cousin Lester can track a sheet of white paper in a blizzard."

"Can you get Lester to meet me here in a day or so? I'll pay you two hundred and I'll pay Lester eight hundred." Pratt figured it wouldn't hurt to give the sheriff's department another day to sift through the ranch.

"Boy that money sure do sound good to me and it'll sound good to Lester, but Moon, he ain't one to hang around, not without a reason."

"Can you do it?"

Vern shrugged. "Let me give him a call."

"Where can I book a room?"

Vern nodded toward the door, his Adam's apple doing a slow wobble. "Chic's Best Western straight up the street. Ain't nothin' else, 'less you want to crash on my sprung and beer-drenched sofa."

Pratt grinned, feeling the stitches at his hairline draw tight. "I appreciate it, Vern, but I have an expense account."

"Chic's ain't bad," Vern said. "They got cable and an indoor pool."

"Used to be the Buffalo Bill but that closed down years ago," Dr. Keith said.

Again Pratt tried to pay Dr. Keith. Again the doc refused. Hungry and in need of a shower, Pratt excused himself, leaving his cell phone behind. He walked slowly down the baking Main Street toward the two-story Best Western at the edge of town, across the street from Frody's Bar and Grill, which appeared to be doing a bang-up business.

The pimply teenage girl behind the check-in desk blanched when Pratt entered the air-conditioned office. "What happened to you?" she said, chewing gum.

"Crashed my bike."

"Wow."

"Do you have a single?"

"You can have any room in the place, just about."

Pratt gave her his credit card and checked into a second floor room in the rear. The girl supplied him with a toothbrush and a mini-tube of Colgate. Pratt went into the darkened room and turned the air conditioner up full blast. He switched the TV on to

Fox News and took a shower as hot as he could stand. Water stung his cuts and gouges from head to toe but it was worth it. He gently toweled himself off, sat on the springy bed and gingerly put on his shoes and socks. Had to find a thrift store or something. His underwear was getting rank.

It was eight-thirty, dusk by the time he stiff-legged across the highway to Frody's. The parking lot was nearly full. Inside ol' Waylon was wailing on the jukebox and the bar was busy. Three mesomorphs stood out with their baggy, low-hanging trou and Tapout hoodies. They watched Pratt make his way to a booth and sniggered.

A cute blond waitress brought Pratt a short menu. She tried not to stare. "Can I get you something to drink, sir?"

Pratt smiled. "I hit a deer," he said. "How about a shot of Jack and a Hamm's back?"

As the waitress brought Pratt his drinks and a glass of water, one of the Tapouts said, "Hey Brianna! When you gonna go for a ride with me?"

Brianna didn't drop a beat. "In your dreams, Gus."

"Hey Brianna," said another one. "When you gonna take me and Cal for a ride?" They grinned and elbowed one another. The waitress ignored them as she set the drinks down.

"There you are. Are you ready to order?"

The one called Gus stepped away from the bar. "What happened to your friend, Bri? Did you cross your legs too fast?"

The trio guffawed. The bartender gave them a dirty look. Pratt ordered a steak and a salad. The food came quickly. Pratt ate like a starving dog. The steak was good but it hurt to chew. When he looked up the mesomorphs were gone.

Pratt left a generous tip, went outside, waited for a semi to pass, and herky-jerked across the highway inhaling diesel. He let himself into his chilled room, stripped, and was out in ten minutes.

He dreamed about Bosselman's, that sheer panic in his chest when he realized what had happened. He ran from gift shop to restaurant to showers searching for his wayward father.

And then he tripped and fell down the well.

CHAPTER 36

Pratt slept like shit. Every time sleep tossed him back up, he fixated on the kid out there in the hills peering fearfully as strange men ripped apart the only home he'd ever known. He finally rose at seven, carefully put on his clothes, tossed down a couple of ibuprofens and headed out. There was no point picking up his impounded Road King if he couldn't ride it. May as well wait for Cass.

Pratt went back across the highway and into Frody's. Brianna was on duty.

"Don't you ever sleep?" he asked as she handed him a menu.

"I went home at eleven, caught six hours. Coffee?"

"Yes please."

Pratt perused the menu while Brianna got a pot. He decided to pass on the Rocky Mountain Oysters.

"Those fools ever give you any trouble?" he asked when the waitress returned.

"I can handle those boys," Brianna said, pouring coffee into a mug. "They've been nothing but trouble ever since I've known them. They know they pull any shit in here, sheriff's gonna land on them like a load of bricks."

Pratt ordered the Denver omelet. It was perfectly cooked and easily chewed. Pratt felt better after eating and several cups of coffee. He felt he could talk to Ginger and explain what had happened, but he'd left his cell phone at Vern's and Vern didn't open until eleven. He glanced at Duane's cheap digital watch, which had survived flood and famine. Three hours to kill.

He would have loved to go back out to the ranch and search for the boy himself, but he didn't know what he was doing and there was a good chance the sheriff still had deputies out there, understaffed as they were. Finding a dead fed would bring the feds in on it. Pratt had a nightmare vision of scores of law enforcement officers tramping up and down the little valley rendering it forever uninhabitable for Eric.

The image of the boy's furred figure broken at the bottom of a ravine would not desert him. Broken like the boy's heart.

And yet there was something deep in Pratt's soul, a candle flame of hope, that refused to accept that.

Eric was alive! Look at what he'd already survived. Boy like that, he doesn't quit easy.

Stop it, man. You're freaking yourself out.

After breakfast Pratt borrowed a Cabela's cap from Frody's lost and found and walked into Hog Tail. The sun beat down. Pratt's shadow jigged before him razor sharp. He sat on a bench outside Small's Drug until the proprietor, an older woman in a severe bun with pince-nez dangling from her neck on a pink beaded chain, unlocked the doors at nine.

Pratt went inside and took a basket. He bought a razor and a traveler's tube of Barbasol, floss, a toothbrush, Axe body spray, earplugs, more ibuprofen, a cell phone charger and the latest issue of *The Horse*. The saleslady rang them up without looking at him.

As she handed him his receipt she finally looked up with a twinkle in her eye. "So what's it like to fight a mountain lion?"

"Does everybody know?"

"You bet. This is a small town and my sister-in-law works for the sheriff."

"Well I guess it's like riding in a clothes dryer with a thousand razor blades. Where can I buy clothes?"

"Sid's Men's Wear, a half block down toward the courthouse."

Sid's had a dusty window display that looked as if it hadn't been changed since the eighties. Inside the store was redolent with hardwood floors. There was a rack of leisure suits in one corner on sale seventy five per cent off. Sid himself was a natty septuagenarian in a seersucker suit, tufts of white hair crouching above the ears.

Sid didn't bat an eye at Pratt's appearance. "Good morning! How can I help you today?"

Pratt bought Levi's, his first new pair in years, underwear, and a gaudy Hawaiian shirt with crimson blossoms on a sky blue background. Throughout the transaction Sid never commented on Pratt's injuries or rough appearance. By the time he was finished it was ten.

Pratt killed an hour in Babe's Diner across the street from Vern's. He read the local paper. It was twelve pages and consisted mostly of livestock prices and high school sports. Bikers blatted through town. Even here, three hundred and fifty miles from the rally, there was spillover. At five of eleven, Vern unlocked the front door of his bar and opened it from inside.

Main Street had two traffic lights. Pratt waited patiently at one of them even though there was no traffic and walked across the street. He pushed into the dim coolness. Vern looked up from behind the bar, shielding his eyes with his hand.

"Good morning, Vern," Pratt said, taking a stool.

Vern brought up two glasses and filled them with orange juice from a carton. Pratt washed down a couple more ibuprofens.

"You don't look too bad, considerin'."

"Thank you."

"Well I talked to Lester and he says pick him up here tomorrow at nine."

"You gonna be open?"

"Special for you."

Pratt thanked Vern, got up and went into the back, where his phone was fully charged. Sitting in the creaky old captain's chair, Pratt phoned Cass. She answered on the third ring. Pratt could tell from the highway sound she was on the road.

"I just went through Brookings. I should be in Hog Tail by five."

"How's Ginger holding up?"

"The same. She's always been kinda fatalistic."

"Security?"

"Those Flintstone boys mean business. She's well protected. I miss you, baby."

"I miss you too," he said automatically, feeling his penis stiffen. Pavlovian. Every time he made love to her he was more banged up than before.

"Love you," Cass said with a plaintive tone Pratt instinctively resented.

"Love you too," he said, feeling a heavy weight on his shoulder. Sighing, he closed the phone and put it in his pocket. He went back out front and shot the shit with Vern. The drought was bad for everyone. If they didn't get some rain soon the ranchers and farmers were going to have a shit year and so was Vern.

A few customers staggered in from the heat. While Vern served them Pratt got up and left. Cap pulled low, he walked back out to the Best Western as bikers and trucks rumbled by raising dust.

Alone in his room Pratt stretched. He could do push-ups but sit-ups still threatened to tear out the stitches across his gut. He slept. He watched *Judge Judy*.

Pratt pumped a fist as Judge Judy read the riot act to a feckless young man. "You *go*, girl!"

At five-thirty his cell phone rang.

"I'm in the lobby, baby. What room you in?"

He told her, excited as a little boy on Christmas morning. Oh boy, he was going to get laid. He went into the bathroom and doused himself with Axe. He hurriedly straightened up the room. He cursed himself for not getting a bottle of tequila or something—not that he craved a drink but he knew she would.

A minute later she knocked on the door. Pratt opened it, Cass dropped her overnighter and folded herself in his arms. They didn't speak. She kicked her bag inside and shut the door behind her. They raced each other to the bed. This time Pratt got on top.

"I'm famished," she said fifteen minutes later. "Let me take a shower and then you're taking me out to dinner."

"Cass, are you on some kind of birth control?"

She shot him a funny look. Little late for you to be asking, don'tcha think?"

Pratt flushed. "I know."

"I have an IUD."

Thank God, Pratt thought, and flushed again.

Cass went to shower.

CHAPTER 37

Cass' truck was in the parking lot. They held hands and dashed across the highway to Frody's, Cass pulling Pratt like a trailer. It was just after six and the joint was half full. A waitress named Sandy took them to a booth opposite the bar. Willie Nelson sang softly over the sound system.

"I could eat a horse," Cass said, looking at the menu.

"Well you're in luck," Pratt said.

"Would you folks like something to drink?" Sandy said. She looked like she was in her teens and would have been pretty were it not for a chin the size of a cowcatcher.

Cass ordered a vodka and tonic. Pratt ordered a Hamm's. As Sandy returned to the bar the front door swung inward and the three mesomorphs in Tapout hoodies entered.

They noisily sidled up to the bar, turned and leaned against it backwards, insolently surveying the field and fixating on Cass. One of them said something and grabbed his crotch and they cackled like jackals.

Sandy returned with their drinks and they both ordered buffalo burgers. Cass said, "I'll take another," and finished her drink before Sandy could get back to the bar. The three hoodies turned their attention to the TV over the bar, which was showing some kind of mixed martial arts competition.

Pratt washed down a couple of ibuprofens with a beer. Sandy returned with their order.

Cass polished off her burger and had a third vodka and tonic, folded her hands and looked intently at Pratt. "I figured it out, Pratt. I'll tell him I'm his mother. He's not so crazy he doesn't want to meet his mother."

"You can't do that, Cass. It's a lie. Kid's had enough lies."

"It's guaranteed to bring him in. That's what we want, isn't it? I mean you can't help him if he doesn't come in. He'll be happy enough when he meets his real ma."

Could something positive come from a lie? Of course. It happened all the time. The kid had to know the difference. He was human, wasn't he? If the full depth of Eric's betrayal at his father's hands became clear to him, he might never trust another human being again. It came down to trust. Pratt worried that Eric was incapable of the concept.

The hoodies stood with their backs to the bar examining Cass' every move, commenting to each other and chuckling salaciously. They couldn't see Pratt, whose back was to them, although they'd seen him when they entered. Psychologists said sex was a great tension reliever. So was beating the shit out of someone. Pratt was frustrated with the Eric situation, apprehensive about his upcoming meeting with Calloway and the feds, and didn't know whether to shit or go blind in regard to Cass. Sewn together as he was he had to restrain himself from getting in the hoodies' faces. With every comment they lowered his flash point.

Red dead redemption rose from his toes.

Cass glanced at the bar.

"Are those men bothering you?" Pratt said.

"No more than usual."

"'Cause we could switch places."

"I've been dealing with that kind of trash my whole life, Pratt. They remind me of my brothers."

"Yeah well do me a favor. If they start something step back, pull out your phone and film it."

"Excuse me?"

"You heard me. Your phone takes video, doesn't it?"

"Yeah."

"Well all right then."

Her bare foot snaked up inside his pants and Pratt was instantly hard. Like Pavlov's dogs. He'd learned about Pavlov from Chaplain Dorgan. He signaled their waitress.

"How 'bout some of our world-famous pecan pie, honey," Sandy said to Pratt with an ease belying her youth.

"Just the check, thanks."

Sandy pulled her pad from her apron and totaled it up. "You can pay me when you're ready, honey. You take care now."

Pratt left cash on the table. Cass started to get up, fell back and tried again. As they walked toward the door the biggest hoodie detached himself from the bar and drifted between them and the exit. He had a weightlifter's build, a mullet, luxurious pointed sideburns and no neck. He smelled of road sweat and cheap aftershave.

"Hey hey hey little lady," he said, "why don't you dump the ragman here and get with a real man."

Pratt glanced at the bar where his buddies stood grinning, empty shot glasses lined up like soldiers.

"I'd sure like a piece of that pie, Unca Donnie," one of the hoodies said, to the delight of his pal.

Pratt put his hand on Cass' shoulder. "Start filming."

"The fuck you say?" the neckless hoodie said.

Pratt stepped up. He and the hoodie were eye to eye. "Do I look like some kind of faggot to you?" Pratt said softly, standing perfectly still but relaxed, crouching atop a thermonuclear trigger twitching to explode, seeing in his imagination as he head-butted this fool on the bridge of the nose, grabbed him by his mullet and kneed him in the balls. Radiating menace from every pore, his hand hovered disconcertingly near Unca Donnie's crotch.

The hoodie met him with angry brown eyes, little balls of hate at the bottom of sand washes. His hands twitched. For five long seconds electricity hummed. The neckless hoodie blinked and stepped back.

"Just havin' a little fun, folks."

The waitress sighed with relief and put the phone down.

The mojo is with me.

As Pratt led Cass out by the hand she wagged her finger at the hoodies. "You don't know how lucky you are."

She took his hand and practically danced across the interstate.

When they got into the motel room Cass removed four or five silk scarves from her overnighter. "Now I want you to tie me up and gag me, and I want you to gag me real tight 'cause I plan to scream like a cat in heat."

CHAPTER 38

Cass was rarin' to go in the morning too but Pratt had too much on his mind. He was eager to get back out to the ranch and try to find the boy. They drove into town in Cass' truck and ate breakfast at Babe's Diner. At a quarter of ten an ancient Ford pick-up parked at an angle to the curb in front of Vern's. Pratt could see a figure behind the wheel smoking a cigarette.

Cass read a travel mag she'd picked up at a rest stop. "I want to stop at this Lakota Casino on the way back."

"That ain't in the cards, baby. As soon as I check out the ranch we're out of here."

"What for?" she whined. "Ginger and Nathan aren't in any danger. Just for a couple hours."

"Forget it." Was she crazy? Didn't she realize he had a job to do, that there was a maniac on the loose?

Vern's front door opened. Vern peered out like a March groundhog, saw his cousin and motioned him inside. Lester got out of the truck. He looked like a stiff breeze would knock him over. He wore wraparound sunglasses over a shirt so big it looked like a spinnaker. His long unkempt hair fell to his shoulders. Only his shoes were brand new, some kind of high zoot sneaker.

Cass and Pratt crossed the street and entered the bar. The air conditioner over the front door sounded like it was self-destructing. They paused inside the door for their eyes to adjust.

"Hey there, Pratt," Vern said. "This here's my cousin Lester."

Lester took off his sunglasses and turned toward them. His black hair, beak, and squinty eyes suggested Moe Howard. He smelled of tobacco, graphite and something atavistic.

Pratt moved around Cass and put out his hand. "Josh Pratt. Pleased to meet you."

The thin Indian took Pratt's hand in a surprisingly strong grip. "Lester Lovejoy, how ya doin'?"

Vern washed glasses behind the bar. "I told Cuz about the deal." Vern went in the back.

Lester fixed timeless patient eyes on Pratt. Pratt removed his wallet and counted out four hundred dollars. "Half now, half later."

Lester folded the cash and stuck it in the breast pocket of his worn flannel shirt. "What is it you want me to track?"

"Wendigo."

Lester grunted. "Ain't no Wendigo."

"A man, Lester. I want you to track a man."

"That's what I thought."

"Y'all better skedaddle before the sheriff notices your truck," Vern said.

"Doesn't he have better shit to do right now?" Pratt said.

"I'm just sayin'."

Pratt turned to Lester. "You ready?"

Lester gazed longingly at the massed booze bottles behind the bar. "I reckon."

They went outside, putting on their sunglasses and tugging their caps down low.

"I'll follow," Lester said, getting in his truck.

"Be easier you ride with us," Pratt said. He wanted the benefit of Lester's wisdom on the way in.

"All right." Lester followed them across the street and got in the back, leaning in the corner with his legs stretched across the rear seat at an angle.

They drove east on the state highway until they came to the turnoff to Moon's valley, a wire gate between fence posts like thousands of others they'd passed. No one had repaired the cut wire. There were a lot more tire tracks than before. The truck jounced over sink-sized potholes and rocks.

What a bleak, terrible place, Pratt thought.

"We're looking for a sixteen-year-old boy who has been turned into a sort of animal man." Pratt explained the procedure as best he could. Lester kept his eyes on the sere landscape and did not comment.

"Kid reeks to high heaven," Pratt said.

"I ain't no dog. I don't track by smell. I track by what I can see and what makes sense to me."

"Sure. I mean he's got problems, curvature of the spine. I wonder how far he could get on his own. He can't be too eager to change his surroundings if this is all he's ever known. I have a feeling he's hanging around, keeping an eye on the place, waiting for everyone to leave and for Moon to come back."

Cass put a hand on his thigh. Pratt removed it. She put it back. It crept closer to his package. He removed it again.

"Casss . . ."

She giggled. She thought it was funny. Pratt needed all his concentration to keep the truck on the road and avoid scraping the transmission off on the rocks. Cass put her hand on his thigh. He bent back her little finger and placed the hand back in her own lap.

"OW!"

Pratt kept his eyes on the road. Cass crossed her arms and pouted. Lester stared out the side window, oblivious.

"Coyote," he said softly. Pratt looked in time to see a shadow disappear behind a rock. Twenty-five minutes later they wallowed up and over a ridge and beheld the little valley, the Quonset hut, the well, tepee, and stand of cottonwood. Yellow crime tape had been strewn around and a Caterpillar backhoe blazed yellow in the noon sun. There were six shallow depressions where it had gouged the earth.

There was no sign of life. Robbins County didn't have the bucks to leave a deputy watching a defunct meth lab. Pratt piloted the big

Dodge down the boulder-strewn trail and parked it in the shade of a cottonwood.

They got out. Pratt headed for the hut. Cass walked toward a nearby hill to show her displeasure. Lester followed Pratt. The door was open.

Lester stuck his nose in and jerked his head out. "Bad medicine," he spat.

"Meth lab," Pratt said, forcing himself in. Breathing through his mouth he walked to the far end of the hut where Eric had made his nest and gathered a handful of fur. Some of the bedding had been taken. The empty water bowl and another containing a crust of dog food remained. The chemicals were gone.

When he came out Lester crouched atop a nearby sandstone hummock surveying the landscape. Pratt stepped into the blazing heat and walked up the grippy stone. Sweat trickled down his forehead and back. By the time he got to Lester his collar was wet. Pratt pulled his cap lower on his forehead and hunkered down next to the tracker. He held out a tuft of fur.

"Kid sheds like a Bernese. He's got all kinds of fur: brown, white, black . . ."

Lester put a finger to his lips. Pratt shut up and tried to see what the tracker saw. He let his eyes slowly swivel one hundred and eighty degrees. Hills and scrub. Creosote and Spanish bayonet. To the west lay mountains covered in a green furze—Ponderosa pine. Pratt looked up. Black raptor shapes flitted against the sky. Lester rose like smoke and took off down the hill. Pratt had to run to catch up.

Lester circled the top of the next hill and proceeded to the one after that, southeast of the hut. He stood atop this hill with feet a shoulder width apart, stuck his finger in his mouth and held it up. Feeling the wind. The Indian went down on his haunches and focused his attention on the ground. The hill was covered with a stubble of straw, a wino's five-day growth. Carefully Lester reached out and plucked something from the weeds. He held it up.

A tuft of fur.

Pratt crouched nearby. Lester swept his gaze from horizon to horizon. His eyes didn't move in their sockets. His head moved. He stood and did a three sixty. He reached into his voluminous trousers and removed an Altoids tin, which he opened. Inside was a crushed leaf. Lester dumped the contents into his hand and flung them into the air. A breeze caught and fanned them out like brown confetti. Lester watched them flutter until they disappeared.

Lester crouched and stayed that way without twitching a muscle. Pratt timed it. The sun beat down. Pratt thought of Lawrence and the *Rub al Qali*. Civilizations rose and collapsed. Seas swallowed the earth and receded. Pratt was about to say something when Lester rose and turned to him. Eleven minutes.

"Give me the other four hundred dollars," he said.

Pratt stepped up. "Half now, half when you deliver."

"The boy went that way." Lester pointed southeast. "He's terrified of men, of cars, especially of trucks, but he knows how to track and he knows how to hide."

"How do you know this?"

"I just know. Something else I know."

"What's that?"

"There's the sheriff." Lester turned and loped off into the hills.

Pratt had that "oh shit" feeling as he turned around. The sheriff had arrived unheard in his new blue and white Dodge Charger, which exuded jackboot authority. Cass was talking to DeWitt near the car's front fender. He loomed over her like a butte. The sheriff looked Pratt's way and smiled. Cass saw him and motioned him in.

Pratt made his way to the bottom of the hill, a dried-up coulee. He was no longer visible to the sheriff. He could just ease on outta there, hook up with Cass later. He could read the sheriff's malice from a hundred yards, never mind the smile. Pratt knew the kind too well. Never had much luck with cops.

Pratt reminded himself that he had sworn on the Holy Bible to tread a righteous path, unpleasant though that might be. He'd promised Chaplain Dorgan and he'd promised God. He'd promised himself. Pratt pulled a water bottle from his fanny pack and drank it in one swallow. Over the hill, don't step on the rattlesnake and there he was, all six four of him.

"Mr. Joshua C. Pratt!" the Sheriff boomed in rotund tones. "We meet again."

"How can I help you, Sheriff?"

"This is a crime scene, Mr. Pratt."

"I have a job to do."

"The only reason I don't re-arrest you for interfering with police business is sheer pity and sympathy for your ideal."

And fear of Mason Mazin.

"I wish you'd told me about this boy sooner, Mr. Pratt."

"Sir, honestly, I thought Moon was going to run straight back to Wisconsin and kill Cass and my client."

"That's a matter for the police."

"I know."

"Now we got the FBI involved and I don't know what all. I do have some good news for you."

"What's that, Sheriff?"

"Moon's outta the country. FBI tracked him to LAX, where he boarded a Korean Airlines flight to Hong Kong."

CHAPTER 39

Pratt watched the sheriff in his rear view as Cass drove up and out of the little valley. The big man stood with his legs spread, hands on hips. He didn't twitch a whisker until he disappeared from Pratt's view. Pratt tried his cell phone. Nada. It wasn't until they reached the outskirts of Hog Tail that he had service. He phoned Calloway.

Calloway answered on the second ring. "Calloway."

"Heinz, it's Josh Pratt. Is it true about Moon?"

"That he left the country? If you believe the FBI. Why wouldn't you? They got him on camera boarding the plane. Where are you? What's going on?"

"I'm in Wyoming searching for the boy."

"Lotta people think there is no boy. They think you're shining them on."

"Why would I do that? Did they talk to Ginger Munz?"

"I believe you, but there are people here who look at your background, and they look at Mrs. Munz' background, and they see a pattern. Your friend's a druggie. I hope for your sake you're not back into that shit. They don't know what's going on but they're damn sure it ain't about no boy."

"I've been straight since I got out of the joint!" Pratt declared, instantly remembering the line he'd done with the Skulls and the joint he'd smoked with Cass. Well one was part of the job and the other, well it was just a fucking joint. It was practically legal now anyway.

"Like I said, I believe you," Calloway said. "When will you be back? The feds want to talk."

"Sometime tomorrow if we leave soon. We have to get my bike."

"There's another problem."

Pratt stared out the window as they rolled down Main. "What?"

"Word is the War Bonnets are looking for your scalp. So Moon spread the word. I really don't have anybody I can put on you. Best steer clear of your usual haunts for a while."

"All right."

"Call me."

Cass stopped at one of the two streetlights. "Where's your bike?"

"County impound lot. It's on the way out of town, back the way we came. We have to check out first."

They returned to Chic's Best Western, retrieved their personal belongings and settled with the teenage clerk.

The impound lot was a quarter mile off the highway on the way out of town, two acres surrounded by a hurricane fence topped with concertina wire. Pratt's bike sat on a concrete slab next to a rat Honda 750 by the refrigerator-white trailer that served as an office.

Pratt inspected his Road King like the DEA going over a box from Panama. They'd done a nice job impounding. Although covered in dust, the Road King was blemish-free. Pratt went into the office and used his credit card to pay the $125 impounding fee. The clerk was a buzz-cut Pillsbury dough boy in Oshkosh B'Gosh coveralls.

"You know where there's a loading ramp around here I can use to get the bike in the truck?"

"You might try the Piggly Wiggly down at Ahrens Plaza. You passed it on the way out of town."

"Thanks."

The bike started with the first nudge. Pratt led the way back into town to the modest shopping mall anchored at one end by Piggly Wiggly. They drove around back. There was a loading dock at exactly the height of the pickup's tailgate. Pratt carefully rode his bike up the concrete ramp to the dock, then guided Cass in so that the truck bed was level with the dock. With Cass pushing down, Pratt bungeed the bike, front and rear.

On the way out Pratt sat in the truck while Cass ran into the PW for a quart of orange juice, bananas and granola. She came out and bumped Pratt from the driver's seat.

"Let's roll."

Cass drove while Pratt tried to sleep. His eyelids kept popping open like a sprung window blind. His gaze roamed. McDonald's, Arby's, Auto Zone, Shell. Anywhere USA. Shiny franchises gave the world a happy, homogenous face. They passed through the exurbs and entered a bleak terrain of wind-smoothed rock and sere prairie.

How long had it taken Moon to achieve his desired affect? A year? Two? Was he still at it, interrupted only by Pratt's arrival? Is that why he had a mountain lion? Sioux/Chinese juju swam in Pratt's head. His desire to destroy something was almost overwhelming.

Cass jerked the wheel and the truck juked like a fullback with the ball. "Pratt, what are you doing? Stop banging the dash! You scared the shit out of me!"

"Sorry, sorry," he said, staring out the window at the flat, featureless landscape.

"You're thinking about that kid, aren't you?"

"I can't get him out of my head."

"You've got to."

"I won't get him out of my head until we find him, one way or another."

Pratt's cell phone rang. He checked the lead—Calloway. "Pratt here."

"Pratt, Calloway. Got word the War Bonnets have put out a contract on you."

"Seriously?"

"Pretty reliable shit."

"Shit fuck piss, cunt cock crap. Sorry, Heinz. It's been a rough couple of days."

"We got an OPB on your boy Moon with the FBI, Homeland Security, DEA and local jurisdictions."

"I thought he was in Hong Kong."

"I hope so."

"What about the War Bonnets? You tell the Munzes?"

"I spoke with the Flintstone guy. Very impressive bunch. Ex-military. The Munzes are very well protected."

How do you protect against a ghost?

"Pratt? You there?"

"Sorry, Heinz. I'm not so sure."

"'Bout what? Trust me, this dude ain't coming within a thousand miles of Wisconsin right now. Half the state is looking for him."

"Yeah. Right."

"Gotta go. Don't do anything stupid, and if this kid turns up let me know."

"Yeah."

The rally was winding down. There were fewer bikes on the road, although they were still everywhere. Everybody in America who ever dreamed about a motorcycle already owned one. Gold Wings bearing bulbous couples pulling trailers, bumper stickers on the trailer. Hard-core bikers on hard-tails, numbed up on painkillers. Squids on sports bikes, asses in the air, heads down. They all passed the truck. America was on the move.

Halfway across South Dakota, Pratt fell into some real sleep. He jolted out of it three hours later as they crossed into Minnesota. It was dark but he could smell the change. The air was redolent of living things and moisture, the faint sweet smell of horse manure.

"Where are we?"

"Pipestone," Cass said. "How you feeling? You need to stop?"

"Yeah. Pull in at the next rest stop."

The next rest stop said CLOSED UNTIL FURTHER NOTICE and had orange plastic mesh across the entrance.

"Budget cutbacks," Cass said.

They drove on until the lights of a truck stop beckoned.

CHAPTER 40

The sign hovering over the freeway said LITTLE AMERICA. A black Tahoe pulled away from the pumps as they pulled in. Cass took its place.

"I'm going to go freshen up a little. Can you take care of the gas?"

"Sure."

She blew him a kiss. "Love you."

Pratt grabbed the pump. "PLEASE PAY BEFORE PUMPING," said the little sign. There were seven Harleys parked in and around the pumps. Dudes in face scarves, black leather vests and beards nodded as Pratt walked to the front door. Pratt nodded back. It was still in the mid-eighties at two o'clock in the morning.

Pratt laid forty dollars on the counter. "Pump eight."

The zit-scarred youth behind the counter took the money, set it on the box and pushed a button.

Pratt returned to the pump, popped the cap and pumped regular. A yellow sign said, "10% ETHANOL FOR A CLEANER AMERICA." There wasn't a biker alive who didn't hate ethanol. It screwed up old engines, melted plastic fuel tanks and slowed the bike.

Bullshit, Pratt thought. Riders pulled in and pulled out. Semis roared by two hundred feet away. It was louder than a Tool concert. A dog yelped in terror. The sound sawed its way through the aural storm like a heat-seeking missile and hit Pratt's ear. He looked around.

Was he hallucinating?

There it was again. A dog crying. Not fake crying, real crying as if it were in pain. Pratt looked around. Men were busy pumping their rides. No one else appeared to have noticed. There it was again. Had to be coming from the sides or back. Leaving the pump on auto, Pratt stiff-walked briskly toward the corner, feeling stitches and bandages flinch and stretch. The Patchwork Man. He turned toward a green dumpster. The yelping was louder here, coming from beyond the dumpster. Pratt rounded the corner.

A man held a shaggy mutt on a short chain, whacking it with a flashlight. The man wore coveralls and had a gut like a watermelon. He wore an Xtreme Energy Drink hat turned sideways. He had a gold chain around his neck.

"You stupid son of a bitch!"

Whack!

"That's the last time you piss in my truck!"

Whack!

Pratt wasn't aware he was running, wasn't aware stitches snapped and bandages tore. Pratt grabbed the man by his greasy black hair and yanked backward, jamming his right foot into the back of the man's right knee. The beater hit the worn asphalt with a thump. Pratt stomped the dog beater in the sternum with his foot. The dog beater let out a loud whoosh, eyes screwed shut and grimacing. Pratt kicked him in the ribs, exulting in the snap of bone. He kicked the man repeatedly, using his heel for maximum penetration.

"*How . . . do . . . you . . . like it?*" Pratt grunted, maneuvering to attack the dog beater's gut and sides.

"Help!" the man screamed. "Somebody help me!"

Pratt was in a red haze. He was unaware of the popped stitches, blood oozing from his arms and face. Just him and evil incarnate and this time he had the upper hand. This time he would not stop until he killed it.

Strong arms seized Pratt and dragged him away from the writhing and screaming man. Pratt looked from side to side. Two jumbo-sized bikers had him in a vise-like grip.

"Okay, calm down," one of them said.

"What the fuck's goin' on here?" said the other.

"He . . ." Pratt was suddenly exhausted, his entire body shrieking in protest. If pain were noise he would have sounded like a tornado siren. He went limp. "He was beating that dog . . ."

"I told you I heard something," one of the bikers said. His patch said "Tiny." He must have weighed 330 pounds. He had a ZZ Top beard and snakeskin boots.

"Yeah," the other biker said. He was trim and muscular and had a shaved skull. "Well good on you brother for delivering that righteous beating. Now I suggest you get the hell away from here before somebody calls the cops."

"You really did a number on that dude," Tiny said.

Pratt looked at the dog beater. He lay on his side in a fetal position. A man stooped to ask him how he was feeling. Pratt shrugged loose.

"What about the dog?"

"We'll take care of the dog. Don't worry. That motherfucker isn't getting it back."

"I'm gone."

What the fuck was I thinking?

Pratt went back to the truck. Cass was behind the wheel giving him the stink-eye.

"What happened to you? Oh my God you're bleeding again." She waited until he climbed in the truck and examined him in the harsh lights of the truck stop. "Let me get out the kit and we'll get you patched up. What happened?"

"Please, Cass, let's just go."

They drove in silence for ten minutes.

"Stop the car!" Pratt wailed.

Cass swerved hard to the right, pulling off into the entrance to a cornfield. Pratt was out of the truck even before she stopped rolling. He went into the corn a little ways, knelt and vomited energy bars, banana, chocolate and jerky. Cass stayed behind the wheel until he was finished, came back to the truck and used some napkins to wipe his mouth. He got back in, rummaged through the glove compartment for a tin of Altoids and tossed one back.

"You okay?"

"I feel better," Pratt said.

Cass cautiously put the truck in gear and pulled back onto the highway.

CHAPTER 41

Three hours later they came to LaCrescent, winding down the steep embankment, crossing the Mississippi on a series of span bridges anchored in islands, nose out to LaCrosse, Wisconsin. They took a break in the Welcome to Wisconsin Center on the Wisconsin side. The lot was filled with bikes either going to or coming from. While Cass hit the john, Pratt stretched, splashed water on his face and looked in the mirror. His face resembled a catcher's mitt mauled by a bear. A dark blue circle surrounded his left eye.

All in all not too bad. He wasn't sleepy. Quite the opposite despite the fact he'd been up for over twenty hours more or less. His nervous exhaustion translated into alertness.

They pulled into Pratt's driveway at seven in the morning. Callaway had told him to steer clear of known haunts but fuck it. Moon wasn't a superman and wouldn't waste time watching an empty house. Even so, Pratt insisted on going in first through the rear door and swiftly checking all the rooms. The place felt empty as he'd left it. He'd thought about getting a dog but he was on the road so much it wouldn't be fair to the dog.

Now that he had an old lady, she could watch the dog.

But who was going to watch the old lady?

Pratt went out through the front door, grabbed Cass' bag and led the way back in. "I'll unload the bike later. We need sleep."

Leaving Cass' bag in the bedroom Pratt went downstairs. His man-cave was furnished with red shag carpeting, a 42-inch plasma TV and a fake zebra hide rug. Bike and babe posters decorated the walls. Pratt went through the door to the utility room and his vertical gun safe. He dialed the combination and opened the safe.

He reached for his Ruger .40 S&W. He reached for boxes of ammunition. And he reached for a Sanyo voice recorder. He stuffed the gun, recorder and clips into a leather fanny pack. He headed upstairs. He went into the bedroom. Cass was splayed across the bed in her birthday suit smirking.

Fifteen minutes passed.

Pratt stared at the ceiling, naked body cooling in the AC. Cass lay next to him, resting her head on her arm, an unlit cig dangling from her mouth, a half bottle of vodka on the nightstand.

"Don't worry about it. It happens."

"Not to me."

"It happens to everybody," Cass snickered. She brushed his hard chest, fingers trailing over the stitches. "You look like a Persian rug that's been torn apart and stitched back together by sail makers."

Cass turned around and reached for the lighter. Pratt looked at the tat on her rump. Harley Davidson. Like they were making women now. Cass lit her cig and lay back, blowing a perfect smoke ring. The AC whisked it away.

"Is there anything I can do?" she said.

"It's that kid. I can't stop thinking about him."

"Well stop."

"Yeah right."

The susurrus of the air conditioner wrapped them in a protective cocoon. Pratt might never sleep again if he couldn't turn off that eidetic image of Eric in the Quonset hut. That nest of filthy blankets. His phlegmy voice.

Pratt would pursue Moon to the ends of the earth if necessary. His hatred was an obsidian crystal lodged in his chest. You think *you're* a hunter?

That time that big kid, what was his name, Vazquez, gave Pratt a black eye. He remembered it vividly because Duane had brought home pizza for dinner, which he had done maybe five times in his life. Pratt tried to hide the shiner beneath his cowlick but Duane reached across the linoleum kitchen table and tilted Pratt's head back.

Not *what happened*? but, "Where is he?"

Pratt didn't want to give it up.

"Where is he?" delivered in the exact same flat voice. SMACK.

Pratt led Duane back to the playground and there was Vazquez' old man, two hundred and fifty pounds of Mayan beef, and Duane went straight up to him and cold-cocked him with one punch. Spent the night in the pokey while the police farmed Pratt out to CPS.

Duane conned some buddy into posting bail and picked his son up the next morning.

Cass lay on her side snoring lightly. Pratt lay back knowing he wasn't going to be able to sleep. The enormity of Moon's crime had created a singularity in his soul. He fought with all his strength to prevent being sucked in. Those images, the idea would live with him as long as he lived. He recognized the temptation to pull the switch.

Pratt thought about his guns downstairs in the locker and the ones he'd brought upstairs. So close. That's how he'd do it. That's why he—and a lot of his friends—had guns. When the time came they'd decide for themselves.

Pratt could almost convince himself he'd hallucinated the whole thing and would wake up any minute safe and secure in his cell at Waupun. The wish segued into a shallow dream where he knew he was sleeping and every detail stayed with him when he woke up.

Chaplain Dorgan was making his rounds. Pratt went to the bars.

"Chaplain," he called, but Dorgan ignored him. Passed right by without looking at Pratt.

"Hey Dorgan!"

Without looking the chaplain held one hand behind him, throwing Pratt the bird.

"Well fuck you, Dorgan! And fuck God too!"

A great fear came upon him, a tidal wave of wrath, an oceanic wall of destruction. It rolled over him and crushed him down into the black depths of despair. Was there some point to all this? He was less than a mote, less than a flicker, almost gone. Hanging on by a thread. He shivered uncontrollably.

"In my wrath, I will unleash a violent wind," he said in his dream. "And in my anger, hailstones and torrents of rain will fall with destructive fury."

Someone shook him. He woke up gelid and bone tired. Cass looked at him with saucer eyes. "Are you all right? You were shouting."

"What did I say?"

"Biblical shit."

"Just a bad dream."

She planted her fists on his chest and looked straight in. "Don't do that to me, Pratt. I love you. You scared the shit out of me."

"Sorry, babe. It was only a dream."

Pratt thanked God that it had only been a dream.

Then he remembered the boy.

CHAPTER 42

Pratt woke with a jolt. It was ten-thirty. He'd been out for three hours. The stomping of prison feet in his dream became steady knocking at the front door. Cass sawed away beside him. Pratt swung his legs out of bed, pulled on his jeans and headed for the front door. Louise Lowry stood on the stoop with a bundle of mail.

Pratt opened the door and stepped out into the morning sun. Louise's expression of happy anticipation morphed into alarm. She put a hand to her mouth. "My God, Josh! What happened?"

Josh grinned. "I got caught in a cement mixer. Thanks for taking in my mail, Mrs. Lowry."

"Josh, please. It's Louise. What really happened?"

"I had a motorcycle accident. I'll be fine." Twinge of guilt for lying. When Jesus came to Pratt, he came hard. Sometimes it was okay to tell little white lies. Chaplain Dorgan had told him that. The truth was too complicated and would only have burdened Louise.

"Thank God for that. You know Dave and I are having a little party tonight for some friends of ours and we'd love it if you could attend."

"We'd love to come," Cass said, appearing behind Josh wearing his old blue plaid robe. She stepped outside and elbowed Josh over. "Hi, Louise."

"Good. We have a pretty interesting crowd."

"We'll be there. What time?"

"Fivish."

Pratt wanted to kick Cass. He hated parties and wanted to get out of town, but he kept that grin plastered on his face and nodded agreeably.

Inside, Cass turned on him. "What?"

"I was hoping to get out of town."

"And go where?"

"Danny's got a place nobody would think to look. He got it off some drug dealer."

"Do you mind? Only for an hour. I'd love to see it!"

Pratt sighed with resignation and headed for the shower. When he came out Cass had whipped up an omelet with cheese and onions. After she'd rinsed the dishes and stacked them in the dishwasher she tried to lure Pratt back to bed.

"Come on, babe, later. I've got to take care of business."

Pratt phoned Calloway and agreed to meet him at police HQ downtown. He phoned Bloom and told him he would be over as soon as he finished with the police. Pratt grabbed an old gym bag from the basement, threw in some underwear and toiletries. He put on the fanny pack while Cass gathered her things. They rode downtown in her truck and parked in the Doty Street ramp.

Pratt removed the voice recorder from his fanny pack, put it in his pocket and got up in the truck bed. He pointed to the Northern Industrial toolbox snugged up against the cab, held shut by a laminated Master padlock.

"Got the key?"

Cass reached into her jeans pocket and tossed her key ring to Pratt. It had a rabbit's foot fob and a tiny silver coke spoon. Pratt unlocked the padlock, pulled it off and opened the toolbox. Inside were a case of Dragon's Tears Roman Candles and a case of Hasta la Vista Baby Cherry Bombs which were illegal in 49 states.

"Nice," he said, putting his guns inside and locking it. He and Cass walked down Doty toward South Carroll toward the City/County

Building. She took his hand and he felt awkward, like an adolescent. The City/County Building loomed five stories high overlooking Wilson and Hamilton. They paused outside the double glass doors.

"You coming up?" Pratt said.

Cass sucked lemon. "I don't think so. I think I'll go to that café on the square and get a coffee. You can meet me there."

"Okay."

Cass reached out and grabbed his head for an intense kiss. It worried him. In addition to his long-lasting fear of commitment, he felt that circumstances were lending unearned emotional gravitas to his and Cass' relationship.

The thought of her tight body made Pratt want to throw her down and fuck like a coked-up bunny. But bells kept going off in the darkness. That crack about Jews. The dogfights. Was he setting obstacles for himself? Were his standards unreasonable? Was he ignoring instinct? Where was the book?

Enjoy it while it lasts, son, Duane had told him.

CHAPTER 43

Pratt entered the police department and signed in with a desk sergeant, who called up to confirm Calloway was waiting for him. The sergeant gave him a laminated visitor's badge to wear around his neck and motioned him through a metal detector, where a stout black policewoman in navy blue slacks and crisp white shirt hand-wanded him. The wand beeped at his pocket.

"Please empty your pockets, sir."

Pratt pulled out his wallet, keys, a handful of change, a bottle of ibuprofen, his buck knife and the Sanyo recorder. The policewoman picked up the knife in a latex-gloved hand. "You can ask for this on your return."

The hall and elevators smelled of pine disinfectant. There were cameras everywhere. Pratt got off on the fourth floor and turned to a young woman at a reception desk beneath the blue and gold Madison Police logo mounted on a wall made of striated oak.

"Mr. Pratt?" she said.

"That's right."

"Down that corridor, second door on the left."

Pratt thanked her and moved on. The walls were decorated with framed photographs of notable Madison police. Pratt paused to look at a black and white picture of the Capitol Square from 1920. The men in bowlers, the women in full skirts. A Model T sat outside Baron Brothers Department Store. The door to Calloway's office was open. Pratt knocked and went in. Calloway looked up from his desk, one eye on Pratt, the other at a corner of the ceiling. His gunmetal-gray desktop was neat and clean, with a stack of reports in the center precisely lined up at the corners. A flat-screen computer doglegged around the side of the desk.

"Have a seat."

Pratt sat in the institutional steel chair facing the desk. On one wall were Calloway's trophies, awards and photographs. Calloway with the governor. Calloway with Obama. Calloway with Morgan Freeman. A framed photograph of wife Doris and their two boys, Ike and Parker.

The opposite wall contained a chalkboard and a large bulletin board, case after case, face after face affixed with thumbtacks. The tops and bottoms were perfectly horizontal. The sides were perfectly vertical. Behind Calloway a large window looked out on Wilson.

Calloway slid a photograph across the desk. "Is this your boy?"

Pratt picked it up. It was a mug shot of a pumped-up dude in a black wife beater, tats covering both arms, staring sullenly at the lens. Dark eyes peered from beneath a unibrow of black electrician's tape. High, almost Oriental cheekbones. Black hair pulled tight and fixed in a ponytail. The date on the photograph was July 12, 1983. Moon in his twenties.

"I never got a clear look at him."

"Well you look like shit, I'll give him that. There's good news and there's bad news. How do you want it?"

Pratt flipped a hand. Already he wanted this interview to be over.

Calloway peeled a sheet of white paper from near the top of his stack. "Fine. We'll start with the bad news. The feds are charging you with interfering with a federal investigation."

"That's bullshit, man."

Calloway stared at a fax transmission. "You know it and I know it, but they don't know it. There's more. Sheriff Archie DeWitt is charging you with breaking and entering and failure to render roadside aid."

"Breaking and entering!? What the fuck! Has Moon complained?"

"Don't have to. The sheriff can charge you with whatever. If the DA doesn't agree he'll throw it out."

"I'm through with DeWitt."

"You might want to let him know. Here's his phone number." Calloway turned the sheet around and slid it across the desktop. He'd highlighted the number with a yellow marker.

"I already got it. What's the good news?"

Calloway put his hands behind his head and leaned back, accompanied by the squeak of stressed leather and springs. "LAPD has your boy Moon boarding a flight to Hong Kong last night at eleven-thirty Pacific time.

Pratt stared at Calloway's good eye. He felt a sucking sensation in his gut.

"What's the matter, Pratt? You look like you swallowed a bad oyster."

"I don't believe it."

Calloway riffled through his stack and withdrew another sheet. "Eugene Strong Eagle Moon, United Flight number 346. That's your boy, right?"

"Come on. Would he use his own name? Do you have confirmation that he got off in Hong Kong?"

"He'd just be landing now but I'll check. If half the charges against him are true he'd be a fool to hang around."

There was a knock on the door. Without waiting for permission, a wiry dude carrying a briefcase, in a military cut and gray Brooks Brothers suit, red tie and black pancake holster on his hip entered. He came around the chair and stuck out his hand.

"Ward Barlin, DEA."

Pratt shook his hand, shot a glance at Calloway who shrugged.

Barlin sat in the other institutional chair half facing Pratt. "You mind answering a few questions about this meth lab?"

"What about dropping those charges?"

"Those were just to get your attention. Cooperate and there's no problem."

Pratt stuck his hands in his pockets and shrugged, turning on the little recorder.

Barlin pulled a credit card-sized metal box from an inside jacket pocket. "I'm going to record this if that's all right."

"That's fine."

"What happened at the Buffalo Chip?"

"Sir, I'm not sure I should talk to you about this without a lawyer."

Barlin put his forearms on his knees and leaned forward. "Why is that?"

"Sir, if you'll permit me, my lawyer is five minutes away. I could call him and he could come over."

Barlin fired his lasers. Pratt didn't flinch. "I could arrest you on behalf of Robbins County, Wyoming."

"Sir, yes you could but you'd just be tying up badly needed resources in the investigation."

Barlin stared hard. Pratt slowly closed his eyes.

"Look. Maybe we got off on the wrong foot here."

Pratt opened his eyes.

"You're reluctant to talk because you may have committed some crimes in finding this meth lab."

Pratt blinked noncommittally.

"I don't care about that. I care about busting up meth rings. From what I've heard you accomplished something we haven't been able to do, infiltrating the War Bonnets and locating their lab."

Pratt glanced at Calloway. Both eyes swept the sky.

"I can't really talk about it unless you give me a written statement to the effect that I will not be prosecuted for any crimes I may have inadvertently committed in discovering this so-called meth lab."

Barlin leaned back. "Jailhouse lawyer. Look, Pratt, I give you my word, so long as no innocent persons were harmed by you, I won't file charges on anything you tell me."

"And you won't hand it off to somebody else to file charges."

"That too. Detective Calloway is my witness."

Calloway looked at Pratt and winked. Calloway was the only cop Pratt had ever trusted.

"All right. First off, I didn't exactly 'infiltrate' the Bonnets." Pratt told them his plan to steal the War Bonnets' stash and trace the runner who would have to get more. As he described bush-whacking the dude in the trailer Calloway smiled.

"My man, my man."

Barlin shot Calloway a look.

"What did you do with the meth?" Barlin said, pulling a spiral notepad and a pen from inside his jacket. He made notations.

"I threw it down a toilet at the Chip. It's gone."

Barlin nodded. Pratt continued. He talked about the boy with clinical dispassion in as few words as possible. The well and what Moon said. The mountain lion.

Barlin slapped his notebook on the desk. "Get the fuck outta here."

Pratt pointed at the three parallel slashes on his left cheek. "What do you think did this? A garden rake?" He lifted up the front of his shirt to show his stitched and bandaged belly.

"What about this feral boy?" Barlin said.

"He's still out there. I'm hoping I can bring him in. I'm not certain he's my client's son. I'm afraid he is."

"Sheriff brought in a backhoe and cadaver dogs. They found the remains of two adults near the hut, one male, one female. As of yet no identification."

"Do you think Moon left the country?" Pratt asked.

"Yup. We got a positive ID and video."

"May I see it?"

Calloway swung around to face his computer. The flat screen was mounted on a swivel. He turned it toward his visitors and stroked the keys. A black video screen appeared within the computer screen, grainy color footage of a boarding area at Los Angeles International.

"Here he comes," Barlin said.

A man in a dark blue hoodie joined the line waiting to board. The bulky sweatshirt did not conceal his nervous energy. He carried a small flight bag. He looked up once, a featureless oval with a Fu Manchu.

"And this," Barlin said, removing a piece of paper from his briefcase and placing it on the desktop, "is a computer projection of what he looks like today."

CHAPTER 44

The eyes were sunken. The electrician's tape was thinner now, the cheekbones more pronounced. Moon was clean-shaven. A gold hoop dangling from one ear. Pratt had seen the face a thousand times in his nightmares. It was the face of a killer.

"We done?" Pratt said.

Barlin looked at Calloway. Calloway shrugged. Barlin handed Pratt his card.

"Need a place to stay?"

Pratt stood and tucked the card in his pocket. "Got one."

He reclaimed his buck knife at the front desk and turned in his visitor's badge. He walked a block and a half to the Square. The State Capitol gleamed like a frosted wedding cake. Cass sat at a café table on the sidewalk outside Josie's reading the *Wisconsin State Journal* and smoking a cigarette.

She folded the paper as Pratt approached and looked up. "How'd it go?"

"That fuckin' sheriff wants to charge me with breaking and entering. Jesus. Now DEA's involved."

Cass stood. Two high school kids in baggy tees on skateboards nearly collided staring at her.

"God I hope they get him," she said.

"Guess what. Moon left the country. They got video of him boarding a United flight to Hong Kong."

Cass' gray-green eyes slitted. "Left the country?"

"They're waiting to confirm he landed in Hong Kong. Relax. He's not coming after us." He held out his hand. "Come on. Let's go see Bloom."

"Why not," she said taking his hand.

They walked past the Park Motor Inn down South Hamilton to the Kipgard Building.

They walked up the steps and entered through the pebbled glass door. Perry Winkleman whispered intensely with a distraught older woman wearing a potato sack dress, ankles bulging over her flat black shoes. Perry glanced at Pratt and held a finger up to indicate one minute. Perry talked a few more seconds, levered himself up out of the wheelchair and leaned forward to give the woman a one-armed hug. She turned with a slight smile and headed for the door.

Perry sat back down and did a huge double take at Josh. "What in heavens happened to you, object of my heart?"

"Dude dropped a mountain lion on my head."

Perry stared. "What really happened?"

"Dude dropped a mountain lion on my head."

"Fine. Be that way. Go ahead. Who's this ravishing cowgirl?"

Cass stuck her hand out. "I'm Cass."

Perry took her hand and kissed it. Pratt cringed.

"Go on down. The master is in."

Pratt and Cass went down the hushed corridor to Bloom's office.

"He seems kind of gay to me," Cass whispered.

"No shit."

The door was open. Bloom sat at his desk rolling a joint on a copy of *Wisconsin Bar Review*. He looked up and shrank back in his chair as if trying to submerge himself beneath the leather.

"Jesus, Josh! You said you had a couple of scratches!"

"It's no big deal. This is Cass Rubio."

Bloom licked the paper and slickly rolled the joint. "This is medical marijuana. I have a prescription." He opened a drawer and dropped in the works.

"Cass doesn't care."

"Cass might want some," Cass said.

Bloom retrieved the joint and lit it with a lighter shaped like a Transformer.

Pratt and Cass sat on a leather sofa facing the desk. "This sheriff where I found the meth lab is charging me with breaking and entering. What kind of trouble am I in?"

Bloom inhaled deeply, leaned forward and passed the joint to Cass. He placed his elbows on the desk and lasered in. "Tell me again what happened." Smoke surrounded his head like Mount St. Helens.

Pratt recounted everything that had happened from the Buffalo Chip on, leaving nothing out. He recounted his meeting with Calloway and Barlin. From time to time Bloom wrote on a yellow legal pad. When Pratt finished, Bloom opened a drawer in his desk and pulled out a bottle of bourbon.

"I don't know about you but I need a drink after that. You want?"

Pratt shook his head. "Too Duaney for me."

"What?" Bloom goggled.

"I meant too early."

Bloom gestured toward Cass.

"Sure," Cass gurgled, holding her smoke.

Bloom poured a shot in a Wizards of the Coast shot glass and handed it over. He opened a drawer, found another shot glass, filled it and tossed it back. "What kind of father could do that to his child? He could go to prison for life on this. And probably should. I wouldn't worry that he's stalking either you or your client. Guys like that, they know when to fold 'em. You've made it too hot for him around here. He probably threatened the women to throw you off."

"Danny, he thought I was going to die. He had no reason to lie."

"These guys lie to themselves as much as anyone. That's why they're called compulsive liars!"

"I never got a good look at him."

"And this sheriff, he's blowing smoke. He already had you in his cell. He'd look like a fool if he rearrested you, particularly on such a trumped-up charge. All you have to do is claim that you acted to save the life of a child."

"I'm not going to quit until I find him. You still have that old farm out near Baraboo?"

"Yeah. Why?"

"Mind if we stay there a coupla days? Cass and me?"

"Sure. Got the keys rightchere." The counselor reached into his middle desk drawer and pulled out a set of keys on a ring. He tossed them to Pratt. "But really, I wouldn't worry about this character. I'm pretty sure you've seen the last of that guy."

"I hope you're right. I just left the MPD and the DEA." Pratt reached into his pocket and removed Barlin's card and the voice recorder. He set them in front of Bloom and turned on the voice recorder. They listened to Barlin's offer.

"Hold on to this."

Bloom put the recorder in a drawer. He glanced at his watch. "Just got time for one. An old blind cowboy wanders into a lesbo bar by mistake. Orders a beer. Pretty soon he says to the bartender, 'Hey! Want to hear a blond joke?' The bar immediately becomes absolutely silent. Then, in a deep husky voice, the woman next to him says, 'Before you tell that joke, cowboy, I think it's only fair, given that you're blind, you should know five things. One. The bartender is a blond girl with a baseball bat. Two. The bouncer is a blond girl. Three. I'm a six foot five blond woman with a black belt in Brazilian Jiu-Jitsu. Four. The woman sitting on your other side is a professional weightlifter. And five. The lady to my right is a blond professional wrestler. You still wanna tell that joke?'

"The blind cowboy thinks for a minute and mutters, 'No. Not if I'm gonna have to explain it five times.'"

Cass burst into laughter. Even Pratt had to smile.

"I've got an eleven-thirty. I'll walk you out."

Bloom accompanied them to the reception area and said goodbye. As they were leaving he turned to his next client.

CHAPTER 45

They drove to Pratt's place. Cass honked at a bicyclist who was a foot outside the bike lane. "Fuckin' retard!" she yelled, accelerating past him. "These goddamn bicyclists think they own the road." She switched gear to cloying nasal. "Oh, I'm a vegetarian earth person! I'm better than you because I ride a bike!'"

Pratt laughed. "You got that right. In Portland, dozens of them will surround your car and beat it to death with their bikes."

Cass parked in the driveway. Pratt borrowed her key and got his weapons out of the toolbox. He stuck the Ruger in his fanny pack with the zipper open, went into the house through the kitchen and back out through the garage lugging a fold-up black steel ramp which he unfolded and fastened to the truck's lowered tailgate. Carefully, he un-bungeed his bike and backed it down the ramp. The stitches stretched to breaking as he wheeled the Road King into the garage next to the stealth Honda.

Cass carried her overnight bag into the house through the garage while Pratt got his mail. As Pratt was walking back from the mailbox, he heard a voice.

"Josh! Josh!"

Pratt turned around. It was Lowry, coming down the smooth blacktop of his house wearing navy blue Bermuda shorts and a white Hawaiian shirt with purple and pink gardenias. Pratt waited as Lowry crossed the road, a bead of sweat on his brow.

"What's up, Dave?"

"You didn't RSVP. Are you coming to the party tonight?"

Pratt recalled the unopened invitation in the pile of mail. "We'll be there, Dave."

Lowry left. Pratt found Cass in the bedroom putting her clothes in Pratt's dresser. She'd unceremoniously shoved the drawer's previous contents into the drawer below it, which now bulged with socks peeking over the rim.

"Don't bother. We're not staying here."

Cass pushed herself into him. "Come on. We've got plenty of time before the party."

Pratt was instantly hornier than a teenager playing footsie with the head cheerleader. Like a switch had been thrown. *Lord, am I that weak?* "Okay. Wait a minute."

He locked the front and rear doors and followed Cass into the bedroom. She went into the bathroom. Pratt heard the sounds of toothbrushing, a flushing toilet, running water. He sat on the bed and pulled off his shoes and shirt.

Cass came out of the bathroom wearing a pair of Pratt's gym shorts. Fifteen minutes flew by. Pratt pulled up short.

"You're thinking about that kid again."

He was. He was thinking about the black hole.

By six-thirty Lowry's long driveway and turn-around had filled with Volvos, Lexuses, Infinitis, Mercedes and BMWs.

"I want all these cars," Cass said as she and Pratt walked hand in hand up the drive. Cass carried a rum and Coke in a plastic cup.

Louise Lowry met them at the front door sausaged into tight black jeans and a frilly white shirt, a ruby the size of a dime nestled in her cleavage. "Josh! I'm so glad you could make it."

"Wouldn't miss it, Louise."

The older woman took Cass' hand. "Did Josh tell you how he saved our doggies?"

George and Gracie capered up on cue, dancing and barking.

"He talks of nothing else."

Pratt felt an enormous surge of affection. "Actually, Cass was there."

"Oh really. You must tell me about that later. Please—the party's out back by the pool. I'm on greeter's duty."

Another couple was hot on their heels. Josh and Cass walked through the Spanish-style vestibule with blue and yellow tiled floor and rustic chandelier, past the winding staircase through the sunken living room, white shag rug, white furniture, fieldstone fireplace, out the sliding glass doors onto the broad patio, where about two dozen people had broken up into conversation clusters standing around a sky blue rectangular pool.

A college kid in white shirt and red and white Bucky tie mixed drinks at a portable bar. Cass made a beeline, pulling Pratt like a dinghy.

The bartender handed two sixteen-ounce plastic cups filled with draft beer to a sunburned guy in a Lacoste shirt and khaki shorts, feet planted in two-hundred-dollar Skechers.

The bartender swiveled to Cass. "What'll you have?"

"Rum and Coke please."

"A Cuba Libre. And for the gentleman?"

"Just a Coke."

Cass made a face. "You're no fun."

Pratt grinned. "Yes I am."

They walked around the pool, heads swiveling in their direction. What rough beast and a real fine slut. Some dude in crimson trousers arrived and the crowd gathered round like children at an ice cream truck. Turned out he was the UW athletic director, a former college and pro football great.

Cass stood on her tiptoes. "Wow! Blake Torkelson. I remember watching him on TV. Didn't he used to play for the Broncos?"

"And the Pack."

They spotted David Lowry doing meet-and-greet by the open patio doors. "Come on," Cass said leading Pratt by the hand. "Let's explore." She pulled him toward the house.

"Josh!" Lowry said. "Glad you could make it. And Cass!" Lowry moved in for a gratuitous squeeze.

Cass bubbled. "Oh, Mr. Lowry."

"Oh please! Call me Dave." He turned to Pratt. "Jeez, you look like you were in a real crash. I was going to say something this morning but I didn't think it was appropriate."

"It's embarrassing. You'd think I'd know how to ride a bike by now."

Another party caught Lowry's eye and he swiveled with the finesse of a long-term politician. Cass pulled Pratt into the house.

"I don't know if he wants us wandering around in here," Pratt said.

"Oh come on! I thought you were fun. Let's see what's in the basement. I'll bet there's a pool table."

Pratt let her lead him to the staircase descending into the basement. A fully finished family room with a large flat-screen TV, a computer desk, sofas and framed prints, several depicting the UW campus and Camp Randall, where the Badgers played. A photo of Lowry with the athletic director. The walls were knotty pine, the ceiling was ecru acoustic tile. One wall contained a large shelving system filled with golf trophies, books and testimonial plaques.

A pool table dominated one end of the room. Cass turned in triumph. "See?"

"You're good," Pratt said.

"No I'm not," she said, pulling Pratt by his belt toward a door. She opened it. Inside was a guest bedroom, one wall completely covered with books, a shallow window closed with drapes but letting in enough light to show the king-sized bed, the Queen Anne dresser, a door opening onto a full bath. She pulled Pratt in and shut the door.

Cass turned and attached herself like a suckerfish to Pratt's chest and hips. "I'm bad, Pratt. I'm very very naughty. But in a good way."

She began to unbuckle his belt. Pratt pushed her hands away.

"Stop that! This isn't our house!"

Cass played him like a theramin. "Come on, Pratt," she purred, sitting on the bed, hanging on to Pratt by his belt as she tried to undo the buckle. "We won't be long. What's this in here? Something with a mind of its own."

With a snarl of lust, Pratt unzipped his pants and pushed Cass back on the bed. She squealed, turning to the side to remove her jeans and panties. Pratt pinned her down and entered her, white ass bouncing.

The door opened and the light went on.

"Oh, excuse me!" said a startled female voice.

CHAPTER 46

The woman immediately shut off the light and closed the door. Pratt stood and pulled up his pants, mortified.

"Hey!" Cass said. "Hey, where you going? She's not going to come back!"

"You want to fuck, we'll go back to my place. I'm sorry but I just can't do it here."

Cass put on her pants. "You're so romantic."

"Come on. I'll buy you a frosty shake."

"Gee thanks!"

Pratt cracked the door. The family room was blessedly empty. He quick-stepped across the floor to the stairs, Cass right behind him. As they eased their way out to the patio Pratt noticed a stout, older woman with a cap of white hair looking at him. She waited until Cass went back to the bar before approaching.

"Don't worry. I won't tell anyone," she said softly. "I'm dreadfully sorry I stepped in on you two."

"That's all right. Josh Pratt."

"Yes," the woman said. Up close she had wide-set brown eyes that were almost mesmerizing. She could have been anywhere from fifty to seventy. "You're the man who saved George and Gracie. I know all about you. Good work, young man. I'm Morgan Teitlebaum. Now if you'll excuse me, I'll go back downstairs and get the book I was looking for." She turned and went. She'd come upstairs to spare them any possible embarrassment when they emerged from the bedroom.

Pratt backed up against a stone wall and observed. Most of the guests were older, well-dressed and had that academic look—the BoBo clothes, the studied casualness. Cass was chatting up a Mitt Romney look-alike with a pale yellow cashmere sweater tied around his neck. A college kid had fired up the grill and was setting out plates of hamburgers and hot dogs. Another table had been set up with condiments, paper plates and napkins. A couple sat on the end of the diving board eating from paper plates balanced on their knees.

Morgan Teitlebaum reappeared next to Pratt holding a copy of Bruno Bettelheim's *The Uses of Enchantment*.

"I read that book," Pratt said.

Morgan stood next to him watching the party. "Really. Was it assigned to you?"

"Yeah, by the chaplain at Waupun. He helped turn me toward Christ."

"Glad to hear it. How does an ex-con get a private investigator's license?"

"It helps to know someone who knows a judge."

"Ah."

They watched Lowry work the crowd like a maestro, cupping elbows, laughing, a hand to the back, a gesture toward the bar. George and Gracie lurked beneath the buffet table, eyes fixed on hands holding food.

"Is Dave raising money?" Pratt said.

"Dave is always raising money."

"Do you give him money?"

Morgan had a hearty laugh. "No, we're just old friends. I'm faculty. I teach child psychology, mostly for special needs kids."

Pratt looked at her. "You know, Morgan, I don't put a whole lot of stock in fate, but this is just too weird. Can I tell you about this case I'm working on?"

"Well, sure, if you're not divulging any confidences."

"No names. Let me just tell you the situation. Let's sit down." Pratt led the way to a pair of Adirondack chairs on the lawn near the tree line. Through the trees they saw the bones of another incipient Mc-Mansion.

Pratt went through the story from his meeting with Ginger. When he got to his discovery of Eric Morgan gripped his wrist like a vise. Her face turned to ash.

"You saw this?"

"It was dark but yeah, I saw enough of him to know he was real. Well enough to see that his spine was out of whack, his teeth were a mess, he could barely speak."

"This is the worst case of child abuse I've ever heard in my life," Morgan said. "I'm not even sure therapy would do him any good, but we've got to try. Where is he now?" "He ran off. He's mistrustful of everyone, probably has a love/hate relationship with his father. Probably dreams about killing Moon, but fears to do so because he doesn't know how to survive on his own."

"That's very insightful. Have you studied psychology?"

"Just books in the prison library. My old man was a worthless piece of shit. I used to think about killing him a lot."

"Is he still alive?"

"I don't know and I don't care."

"You might benefit from therapy too."

"Are you a shrink?"

"I'm a psychologist. The first thing is to find this boy and get him into a clinical setting. Unbelievable as this may seem, there are precedents. Kaspar Hauser is probably the most famous. Werner Herzog made a film about him. More recently there have been several from India. I don't know why, but India has more feral children than any other country in the world. Alex the Dog Boy from Chile. In each case, these children were without socialization, no social skills. They don't even know how to use a toilet. Fortunately we know a great deal more today than we used to. Unfortunately, the prognosis for any feral child is grim."

Pratt watched a hawk circling over the tree line. "I'm heading back out there as soon as I can clear my schedule with the intention of bringing him in. Any tips?"

"By yourself?" Morgan said.

"My girlfriend Cass will help. That's her chatting up the movie star." Did he just say girlfriend?

"It's not going to work if either of you drinks or does drugs."

Pratt sucked air through his teeth. Did they look like that? "We won't be drinking or doing drugs."

"He might respond better to a woman."

"That's what I was thinking although he did speak to me. Probably the first human other than Moon he's ever spoken to."

"I'd like to help. Let me give you my card."

"That's what I was hoping you'd say, Doc."

"Call me Morgan." She rummaged through her feedbag and drew a business card. Pratt tucked it in his wallet, wrote his phone and e-mail on the back of one of Bloom's and handed it to her.

When Cass looked up the hill, Pratt waved his arm. She came toward them weaving slightly and holding a drink. Pratt cringed.

"I was wondering where you went," she said, oblivious to the fact that the woman with whom Pratt was seated had walked in on them making love.

"Cass, Morgan. Morgan's a child psychologist. She might be able to help us."

Cass stuck out a hand. "Very pleased to meet you." At least she wasn't slurring.

Pratt stood. "I'll call you. Come on, Cass. We've got to get going."

CHAPTER 47

Pratt went through the house one last time. Everything was up tight and out of sight.

They left at seven-thirty, Cass' pick-up laden with drinking water, food and blankets. They ate trail mix, granola bars and apples. Cass played Queen loud on her six-speaker system.

Pratt turned it down. "Loud music makes me want to drink and do drugs."

Cass laughed. "Life makes me want to drink and do drugs." She cracked the window, pulled a cig from the armrest and lit it with a Zippo. They drove north toward Sauk City, inspiration for Sinclair Lewis' *Main Street*, sun blazing in from the west. Four riders appeared around a bend heading toward Middleton. Pratt slouched in his seat as they passed.

As soon as the last one passed Pratt popped up and stared out the rear window trying to see their colors. Couldn't make them out.

There was an APB out for the War Bonnets but you never knew. The Bonnets were bat-shit crazy. They'd do whatever their supreme commander demanded. Moon would know how to get Cass' license number, the make and year of her vehicle. Pratt put nothing past him. He drew comfort from the lump of metal at his waist.

They crossed the river at Sauk City. The town was chock-a-block with bikers, choppers lined up outside every tavern, dozens of them slowly cruising the two main drags. Pratt slumped in shadow as they drove with the windows open. At the red light a skinhead on a Warrior pulled up next to Cass.

"Hey pretty mama! Whatchoo doin' out here?"

Pratt leaned forward in his Gargoyles and gave the man a hard look.

"Whoops. My bad."

Cass headed north alongside the Wisconsin River as Pratt straightened up and pulled out a dog-eared copy of the *Wisconsin Atlas*. "Turn left in two miles at Factory Road." They passed the deserted Baraboo munitions plant, hundreds of acres fenced off and filled with bunkers.

The road cut west through rolling farmhand toward the blue Baraboo Hills. All other traffic disappeared. Pratt directed Cass through two more turns. The road wound through cottonwood and alder. Through the trees Pratt saw an old red barn lit by the setting sun.

"There it is. Pull in at that mailbox."

The mailbox sprouted from a milk canister filled with concrete. Next to it screwed into a solid wood fence post was a sign. PRIVATE-NO TRESPASSING!

The eastern sky turned velvet. The farmhouse was set a hundred yards back from the road, a typical two-story wood frame job with a front porch and a slanted exterior cellar entrance. The barn was trash, leaving only a few vertical piles and a floor that had rotted through.

Cass pulled up in front of the house and shut off the engine. The silence was shocking.

"What a dump," Cass said.

"Bloom got it from some druggie he represented." The druggie begged Bloom to get his ass out to the farm and clean out the refrigerator before the cops came. Bloom found several eight balls and a half pound of killer weed which he dutifully relocated to his own house. He called up Pratt and they had a victory celebration.

Pratt went up the creaking wooden steps to the front door, opened the shredded screen door and inserted the key Bloom had given him. He had to joggle it around for several minutes before it clicked. He opened the door and stepped inside. The interior was musty and smelled as if it had been closed off for a long time.

He flipped a switch. The electricity had been shut off. There was a pump in the backyard from which they could draw shivery ground-water. Pratt expected Cass to squawk. The air weighed heavily. Pratt wished he had a laptop, then realized there would be no service. He felt cut-off without his computer.

Pratt went back out. Cass came up the porch stairs with her bag and stepped inside.

"Phew! Let's open some windows."

Pratt went around the ground floor opening windows with intact screens—at least nobody had broken out the glass—while Cass went upstairs to investigate the tiny bedrooms. There was a Coleman lantern in the kitchen with fuel in it. Pratt lit it and carried it with him.

Pratt was bone-tired. He actually dreaded Cass' teasing. Men would kill to have her. He remembered a time when he seldom went to bed before two a.m. He'd turned his life around in more ways than one.

"There's no water!" Cass said from upstairs.

"There's a pump in the back. I'll bring some in for drinking and washing."

"Great. I'm going to crash."

Thank you Jesus.

A moment later something flew out of the bedroom and smashed against the wall with the sound of breaking glass.

Pratt went up the steep stair. "What the fuck?"

Lying on the landing was a shattered picture frame holding a picture of Jesus and the Holy Heart. The bedroom door was shut. Pratt decided to let it be. He stooped, picked up the shattered print, carefully placing each piece of broken glass on top, took it downstairs and threw it in a paper bag he found beneath the kitchen sink.

Was that bad, trashing Christ's picture? Was it bad of him to have thrown it out?

Lord, I sure could use that rulebook.

He went out to the truck and brought in the victuals and his overnighter. As he was walking back to the truck his cell phone rang. He pulled it out. The little screen showed Bloom. A minute fracture opened in the evening's perfect stillness. Pratt flipped the cell open.

"What's up, Danny?"

"Danny can't come to the phone right now," said a voice as dry and cool as a root cellar.

CHAPTER 48

A lead fist sunk into Pratt's gut. Bloom was dead. A crushing mantle of guilt settled on his shoulders. Diesel rage seethed. Pratt looked around half expecting to see a shadow lurking in the trees. It was a beautiful sundown, sky violet against the deep dark of the hills. A red cardinal perched on a limb at the edge of the yard. A hawk circled over the Baraboo Hills.

"Where are you?" Pratt said softly, as if he might wake Cass.

"Now you see me, now you don't," Moon said.

"Call it off, Moon. The feds, DEA and half the state are looking for you. Your only hope is to get out of the country as fast as possible." Pratt's hand went to the Ruger in his fanny pack.

"They can't stop me, Pratt. They've been trying for years. But you! You! What a warrior. What a worthy opponent. I am astonished at your perseverance and ingenuity! I salute you, Pratt. How the hell did you get out of that well?"

"I've got powers too, Moon. I was born with a caul on my face. I'm the seventh son of a seventh son. I've got a black cat bone and I know how to use it."

Silence.

"It's me you want," Pratt continued. "I'm the one who burned your crew, stole your crystal, chased your pet freak away. Meet me and we'll settle it just between us. Those women have nothing to do with it." It hurt to refer to the boy that way but Pratt couldn't afford to give Moon any emotional leverage.

"Don't they?" Moon hissed and for the first time emotion crept into his voice. "I told that bitch what I'd do if she ever betrayed me."

"She didn't betray you. She's dying. She just wants to see her son."

"She's not dying fast enough to suit me, and as for her son, I doubt Eric could survive more than a night or two by himself in the wild."

"How could you do it, Moon?"

"I got kids all over. I won't miss him."

"You'll burn in hell for this."

Moon chuckled. "So they say, but I won't die. Haven't you heard? I'm immortal. I've got the second sight. You tell those two bitches to enjoy it while it lasts. You too, Pratt."

The cell went dead.

Pratt dialed Calloway.

Calloway answered on the fourth ring. "What the fuck, Pratt. It's eight-thirty."

"Moon just phoned me on Danny Bloom's phone. I'm afraid Bloom's dead."

Calloway's annoyance evaporated. "What did he say?"

"He said he intends to carry out his threat against Cass and Ginger Munz. You've got to send people over to Bloom's house. It's adjacent to the zoo. Two thirteen Lafayette Street."

"I'm on it. Where you at?"

"We're in a safe place, Heinz. I've got Cass with me."

"I'm gonna need to talk to you. You want to come in here or am I coming out there?"

Pratt calculated. The safe house was shot. Bloom would have talked. "Cass and I are leaving now. We'll meet you at Bloom's."

"Don't—"

Pratt hung up. He dialed the Munz residence.

"Nate Munz." Munz was up early and expected the same of others.

"Mr. Munz, Josh Pratt. May I speak to your head of security?"

"What's this about?"

Pratt told him about the call. Munz was blasé.

"I appreciate the head's-up, but these boys have got it covered. One of them's ex-Special Forces. Another was an Army Ranger. We're safe as Fort Knox."

"May I speak to one of them?"

"I'll convey the message. Anything else? Any news on the matter for which you were hired?"

"No sir."

"Don't call unless you have some news."

Munz hung up. Pratt went back into the house and up the stairs. Cass was flaked out belly-down on the queen-sized bed in the master bedroom overlooking the front yard. There was a half-smoked joint in a glass ashtray on the nightstand.

"Cass."

She snorked in exhalation.

Pratt gently shook her shoulder and she turned over with an arm across her forehead. "What is it? Let me sleep."

"We've got to move. He knows we're here."

"Who knows?"

"Moon."

Cass sat up. "What? What did you say? How is that possible?" Her voice carried an edge of hysteria.

"He got to Danny, Danny Bloom. The guy who owns this place."

"How do you know that?"

"He phoned me."

"Who, Bloom?"

"No. Moon. I just got off the phone with him."

Her eyes went wide-angle. She said in a tiny, disbelieving voice, "You talked to Moon?"

"Yeah. If he got to Danny he knows about this place. We've got to leave."

Cass got up and went into the tiny bathroom. The toilet flushed and Pratt heard running water. She came out a minute later with water dripping from her chin.

"Let's go."

CHAPTER 49

"Isn't there someplace you can go until this is over?" Pratt asked as they waited at a traffic light in Sauk City on the west side of the Wisconsin River.

"What are you talking about, Pratt? I'm with you. You're stuck with me. I don't have any place to go. Where? Back to the farm? I'm with you."

Behind the wheel Pratt stifled a sigh. He knew places, but if she wouldn't go she wouldn't go and he couldn't make her. "I have a .38 in my backpack, you want to carry that."

Cass twisted around in the passenger seat and snagged the kelly green backpack, pulled it onto her lap. She opened the flap and rummaged around, pulling out the steel Python and a box of ammo. Cass filled the five-shot cylinder.

"Don't blow your foot off."

"I know how to handle guns, Pratt, in case you forgot."

They hit the Beltline around nine-thirty, joining a thick line of cars circling the city. Pratt took the Nakoma exit. Traffic was stop and go on Laurel. Trader Joe's, Capital City Comics, Gullesarian Carpets, and a Wi-Fi hot spot on every block. Pratt flipped around AM looking for news. Nada. Sirens wailed in the east. They crawled toward the center of town past Camp Randall Stadium.

The Vilas neighborhood, where Bloom had owned a house since student days, consisted of narrow two-way streets and mostly older one-family dwellings, ivy-covered with putting green lawns. The police had set up a barrier on Franklin Street and were turning back all traffic. Pratt found a parking spot in front of a four-unit apartment block and snugged the big Ram to the curb.

"Better leave the hardware," Pratt said, taking the Ruger from his waist and tucking it under the seat. Cass did the same with the revolver. They got out, locked the truck and walked south toward Lake Wingra. The cop hailed them from across the street.

"Hey, people, nobody in here but residents. I'm going to have to see some ID."

Pratt veered toward the cop, pulling out his wallet and producing his driver's license and private investigator's license. The cop was young with the face of a choirboy.

"I'm Josh Pratt, officer. I alerted the police this morning to the situation at Daniel Bloom's house. I'm meeting Detective Calloway there."

The cop examined Josh's ID and pulled the rectangular transceiver from his shoulder. He spoke into the transceiver. Pratt looked around. He'd always liked the neighborhood with its canopy of oak, elm and alder. A quarter mile across the hill an elephant trumpeted at the zoo. Children squealed in delight. A seal barked.

The cop replaced his transceiver. "You know where it is?"

Pratt nodded. The cop waved them through.

Lafayette Street backed up to zoo property. The backyard ended in a ten-foot bluff surmounted by a six-foot hurricane fence. There were police cars double-parked in the street and an ambulance in the driveway. Calloway came out on the front porch to greet them.

Pratt introduced Cass to Calloway.

"Ma'am, I'll ask you to remain on the porch." He handed Pratt two plastic baggies and rubber bands to slip over his shoes. Pratt sat on Bloom's glider and put them on.

They stepped inside the foyer. It was a comfortable old family home from the thirties, two-story brick. Just inside the entrance stairs went up to the second floor. The living room was to the left and the kitchen in the back. Calloway led the way up the stairs. They emerged on a landing overlooking the living room, a short hall leading to two bedrooms and a bath.

"Don't go inside, just look from the door."

Pratt moved to the entrance to the master bedroom. A medical examiner stood between Pratt and the bed, momentarily obscuring the view. Red. Everywhere red. You wouldn't think a human body contained that much blood. The sheets were soaked.

Crimson pools of blood lay at the foot of the bed. The ME stepped aside.

Bloom lay spread-eagled, arms and legs tied to his four-poster. The skin was missing from his neck to his thighs. Strips of waxen skin lay on the floor curling like fax paper. The room smelled like an abattoir. Pratt's stomach flip-flopped.

"Moon flayed him. He couldn't cry out because he was gagged. You and your friend are going into protective custody."

If not for Bloom, Pratt would still be in Waupun. Bloom got Pratt's record cleared, gave him a job serving process, encouraged him to go to school and get his private investigator's license. Paid the fucking tuition.

Pratt rubbed his eyes hard.

He stared at the chunk of raw meat on the bed. Calloway gently positioned himself in the doorway, edging Pratt out.

"I'm sorry, Pratt. I know he was a friend of yours. Did he have any family?"

Pratt was in shock. Bloom's corpse looked like the skinned cougar. Moon did this deliberately. Moon was in his head.

"Hey!"

A brat-sized finger poked Pratt's chest.

"I'm sorry, what?"

"Did Bloom have any family?"

"His mother in Evanston, and a brother in Los Angeles. I think he's an entertainment lawyer. You'll find their contact information in his red date book in the downstairs office."

"Come on." Calloway pushed Pratt ahead of him like a bulldozer herding a puppy. Pratt led the way down the steps, around the corner to Bloom's home office with a view of the zoo, one wall entirely covered in bookcases and books. The red datebook lay on the polished maple wood desk. They stood on a Persian carpet that covered most of the hardwood floor.

"Anything look different to you?" Calloway said.

Pratt looked around. Nothing seemed out of place. Pratt walked over to a framed Badger poster and tilted it away from the wall. Bloom's wall safe was closed. "Hunh-uh. But I wouldn't bet on it. This guy's a fucking ninja."

Calloway pulled out a mini-recorder and a little black pad. He sat in the leather sofa, set the recorder on the coffee table and gestured for Pratt to sit. He turned on the recorder. "Tell me about your phone conversation. Tell me exactly what was said, as best you remember."

Pratt recounted the conversation. "Cass and Ginger both say that payback is a religion with this guy. He's like Captain Ahab. He'd rather go down with the whale then let a slight pass unanswered."

"At risk of losing his life?"

Pratt shrugged. "He's insane. Mean crazy evil insane."

The boy had a collar around his neck.

"All right," Calloway said. "I'm assigning Officers Higgins and Kellogg to you and Rubio. They should be here shortly."

"What about Ginger Munz?"

"That's Lake County's problem but I understand they have private security."

The front door opened. Ward Barlin stepped into the foyer. "Gentlemen." He wore plastic baggies over his shoes.

"The body's upstairs," Calloway said. "We'll wait down here if you don't mind."

Barlin tramped up the creaky stairs.

"I have to visit the Munzes," Pratt said.

"If you leave the city my men can't go with you. I'd rather you stayed here."

"I understand that, but my first duty is to my client. We'll be fine. Flintstone Security's top of the line."

"I can't stop you."

"I'll wait for Barlin. Then we're out of here."

CHAPTER 50

Barlin came down the stairs ashen-faced. He sucked it up and went into the office. "We've put Moon on the Homeland Security Watch List and the FBI Most Wanted. I learned this morning that remains found on his ranch match those of DEA Agent Robert Fisker who disappeared in South Dakota on April 19, 2006. We identified him through dental records. Warrants have been issued for murder one, murder of a federal agent, as well as all the drug stuff."

"What about the other?" Pratt said.

"Not a clue."

Barlin took out a small pad and a tape recorder, which he set down next to Calloway's and turned on. "You spoke to Moon?"

Pratt told Barlin what he'd told Calloway. Pratt excused himself. He used the downstairs half bath. Cass was sitting in the swing chair on the porch smoking a cigarette. Two kids with skateboards gawked from across the street.

Cass stopped rocking when Pratt appeared.

"Call Ginger. Tell her we're on our way and that we'd like to stay the night if that's all right with them."

"What? Why?" Cass stubbed out her butt, field-stripped it and tossed the parts into the hedge. She got to her feet.

"'Cause Flintstone Security is the best and we need to sleep. We can figure out where to go from there in the morning. Will that be a problem?"

Cass shook her head. "They've got plenty of room. Nate'll bitch but he'll put up with it."

They walked hand in hand back down the block toward Cass' truck. The cop car was gone and normal traffic had resumed. Cass used her remote to unlock the truck with a flash and a beep.

"Is Nate a pompous ass?" Pratt said, getting in the passenger side.

Cass got in and fastened her seat belt. "You noticed. He comes from a very proper Whitefish Bay Protestant family. His father was a lawyer and then a state Supreme Court justice and his mother is one of those high falutin' society types who's always throwing charity balls. The first time he brought Ginger home, his mother about had a cow. I mean, a biker chick? Nate's old man called him in for a talk and that's when Nate's old man found out Nate was a chip off the old block.

"Nate stuck to his guns. He knew a diamond in the rough when he saw one and he stuck up for Ginger, tats and all. The more his family saw of her the more they realized that she was a woman of real quality. Everybody except Agnes. The old bitch still has a hair up her ass."

"How'd they meet?"

Cass smirked. "I'll say this for Ginger—once she made up her mind to improve her situation, she went about it in a real workmanlike fashion. Cleaned up real nice and got herself a job at Leonard's, fanciest restaurant in Lake Geneva." Gripping the wheel, Cass extended the pinkie on her right hand. "Carriage trade, don'tcha know. That's where she met Nate. It's a target rich environment for young ladies of a certain bent."

Cass worked her way through the Vilas neighborhood to Fish Hatchery Road. "Why don't you dial Ginger and give me the phone."

"Don't crash."

When the phone began to ring he handed it to Cass. They pulled up to a red light at the Beltline.

"Nate? It's Cass Rubio. I've got Josh Pratt here and we're coming out. May I speak to Ginger?"

Cass listened. She rolled her eyes. "Nate, it's important."

She placed the phone face down on her thigh. "He's getting Ginger. On the plus side he's very protective." She picked the phone up. The light changed and they drove around the clover leaf onto the Beltline heading east.

"Hi babe," Cass said. She explained what they were doing. There was some back and forth.

"Okay, see ya."

Cass closed the phone and handed it to Pratt. "All systems are go. Nate has a lot of respect for you. I think he envies you."

"I envy him. Who knows how I might have turned out if I hadn't wasted most of my life."

"Don't badmouth yourself, Pratt. You're a good man. You saved your neighbor's dogs."

Pratt grunted. His whole life had been unsettled except for that stretch in Waupun. He hated unsettled.

He'd bungled the job. If he hadn't bungled the job, Moon would not now be creeping after them.

Where did he fuck up? He began at the beginning, at Cass' farm, and walked it through.

The image of the dog boy lurked in the shadows at the edge of consciousness, a rabid predator threatening to seize him in its iron jaws and drag him into the singularity. The emotional black hole from which there was no retreat and only one way out.

Do. Not. Think. About. The boy.

His skin peeled back to expose raw flesh, pain in every joint, unable to relax in any position. Spine fucked up. So bad. Pratt didn't know how to turn it off.

"Pratt!"

"What?" He found himself staring out the window at an endless series of warehouses abutting the Beltline.

"Don't zone out on me."

"Sorry."

They headed south on 14.

CHAPTER 51

Lake County cruiser was parked on Makepeace across the entrance to the Munz' driveway, lit by two sconces set in both of the stone pillars. Cass stopped the truck and waited for the officer to approach.

He shined his flashlight on both their faces. "May I see some identification please?"

Cass and Pratt handed over their driver's licenses. The deputy examined them minutely. "Wait here," he said, returning to his car.

"What's he doing?" Cass said with irritation.

"He's phoning the house, giving Flintstone the head's up."

"What kind of operation is Flintstone, anyway?"

"Ex-military. They do a lot of contract work in the Middle East. Very competent from what I understand. They do security for a lot of big companies, celebrities."

Pratt reached beneath the seat, snagged his fanny pack and fastened it with the pouch forward, the weight of the pistol reassuring against his thighs.

The cop returned and handed over the licenses. The electronic gate slid silently to one side. The long green tunnel leading to the house was as Pratt remembered, the truck's headlights picking out moths. What had seemed natural and secluded was now an invitation for trouble. At the house all exterior lights were ablaze. A black Chrysler 300 was parked in the roundabout. A Flintstone agent in a blue blazer and khakis sat in the front seat, feet on the ground through the open door. He got up as Cass pulled up behind him.

Cass and Pratt got out of the truck.

"Hey, how are ya? Jimmy Bonner," the Flintstone agent said, sticking out a hand. He had a military haircut and the bearing that went with it. He wore a blue tie and shiny black shoes. His grip was cool and dry. He shook Cass' hand. "I know that cop vetted you, but I'd like to see some ID too, because we're obsessive-compulsive sumbitches."

Pratt laughed and handed over his driver's license. "How many of you are there?"

"Foucalt and Stuart are around here somewhere. You'll meet them later. Whatcha got in the fanny pack?"

"A 40."

Bonner nodded. "Well I can't tell you not to wear it, but try not to shoot any of us, okay?"

"No prob."

Munz met them at the front door. The builder wore a purple, green, and orange Hawaiian shirt with the tails pulled out over Bermuda shorts and Skecher sandals, a poorly concealed automatic jutting up from his waist. He grudgingly shook their hands.

"So the detective," he said. "We finally meet."

"Mr. Munz."

"Call me Nate. Everybody else does. Ginger's in the breezeway." He gestured down the corridor toward the rear of the house, falling into step behind Pratt. Most of the drapes and blinds were drawn, casting the interior in cool gloom. Ginger lounged on a sofa in the screened-in breezeway sipping from a tall glass of iced tea. She smiled wanly as they entered but made no attempt to get up.

"Forgive me for not standing up," she said. "I'm feeling a little rocky this evening."

"Would you like something to drink?" Nate said with an air of resignation.

Cass and Pratt asked for coffee. Nate headed for the kitchen.

"Usually I have someone here," Ginger said, "but Nate thought it better if we had no extraneous personnel on site. You know this may all be a set up. Moon loves to play mind games. He's probably in Mexico right now having a tequila and laughing at us."

Cass sat next to Ginger and touched her hand. "Ginger, don't you remember what he was like? He's coming after us."

"You know, I have learned a few things over the years. We were so young and naïve to ever think he was some kind of god in the first place. Moon's a smart guy. It just doesn't make sense for him to risk everything on a pointless vendetta. We've got Flintstone Security out skulking through the woods. We've got the FBI, DEA and Homeland Security looking for him. I choose to think that he's not coming, and even if he does, we've taken all the proper precautions. It's not worth worrying about."

Hardly, Pratt thought. Proper precautions would involve a completely anonymous safe house far from home until Moon was apprehended or confirmed dead.

Munz returned with a carafe of coffee, cream in a white ceramic tureen, sugar in a sterling silver bowl with spoon. The tray contained a plate of English tea biscuits. *Tally ho*, Pratt thought as he helped himself to the coffee.

Munz set the platter on the coffee table in front of Cass and Ginger. "Any news?"

Pratt shook his head. "You know as much as us. He's out there somewhere."

Munz sat in a leather recliner, took a biscuit and crunched. "We're ready," he said, patting the pistol at his side. "You packin'?"

Too many cop shows, Pratt thought tapping his fanny pack. "Yes sir."

Munz nodded. "Tried to arm Ginger, she wouldn't have it," he said with a tone of disapproval.

"I'm sorry, dear, I'm just not a gun person."

"Well I am," Munz asserted pulling a Glock, dropping the mag and slamming it back in, careful to keep the muzzle pointed away at all times. "I was a gunnery sergeant in the Army, did two tours in Iraq, back in the day."

"Thank you for your service to our country," Pratt said.

Munz looked at him funny, realized Pratt was sincere and nodded. "Got you two in the basement guest suite. You've got your own bath down there and a kitchen if you want to cook. Opens up onto the pool deck."

"Thanks, Nate," Cass said.

"I figure there's strength in numbers, not that these Flintstone boys can't do the job. These boys know what they're doing. All ex-military."

Cass stretched. "I'm fried." She shot Pratt a smoldering look. "You coming?"

"Josh," Munz said, "we need to talk. Shouldn't take more than a few minutes."

"I'll be waiting," Cass said.

CHAPTER 52

Munz led Pratt up the stairs to the first floor, down the hall to a study that overlooked the woods. The man cave had walnut paneling, a wall of books, many with fat leather bindings, a free-standing globe, a mounted deer's head over a field stone fireplace, a flat-screen TV mounted flush with the wall, a rich cocoa carpet and leather furniture. Munz went directly to a wet bar in one wall and took out two tumblers. He poured a couple fingers of Macallan in each, added ice from a mini-fridge, came back and handed one to Pratt.

"Cheers," Munz said. They clinked. They sipped.

Munz sat in a leather wing-backed chair, gestured for Pratt to take the sofa. "I appreciate the risks you've taken on behalf of Ginger."

"That's why I get the big bucks."

"Yes. I'd be interested in knowing how much this has cost me so far."

Pratt did a quick audit in his head. Thought about billing Munz for the thou he'd laid on Robles. Took a nanosecond for the shame to set in. "About sixteen hundred dollars."

"How 'bout I pay you off and you and Cass can be on your way in the morning?"

Pratt stared at his drink. "Is that how Ginger feels?"

"Don't be a smart-ass. I know about Ginger's past. She's left all that behind. You and Cass have brought it all back in again. She cries at night and gets night sweats. Do you know how long it took for her to feel halfway normal?"

"Nate, she asked me to find her son."

Munz reached over to the cherrywood desk, snagged a wood cigar box and pulled it over. He held a fat cigar toward Pratt.

"No thanks."

Munz shrugged, took out a cigar cutter and nipped the end. He lit it with a gold flame thrower, turning the end slowly until it glowed red. The room smelled of tobacco and aftershave. Manly smells.

"You've done all you can and I thank you. I'm willing to round your fee up to an even five grand."

Pratt shrugged. "It's your house."

"Good man." Munz got up, went behind the desk and found his check ledger in a black leather folder. He sat back down again and pulled a Montblanc pen from his breast pocket.

"Nate, that's not necessary. You can wait until I submit a voucher."

"Not a problem."

Pratt heard a car door slam. He looked out through the window at Cass getting something out of the truck. Bonner spoke with her briefly. Pratt was dog tired. He hoped Cass didn't expect him to fuck her but of course she would.

Munz peeled the sea green check out and handed it to Pratt. Pratt folded it and stuck it in his vest pocket. "Ginger tells me you were in a gang."

"The Bedouins," Pratt said. "I was young, dumb and full of come."

"Let me see your gun."

Pratt removed the Ruger, released the magazine into his hand, checked the chamber, handed it over.

Munz held the pistol in a two-handed grip and aimed at a stuffed deer head over the fireplace. "I won't lie to you, Pratt. I fear what the discovery of this child will do to our marriage."

"I can understand that."

"Ginger should have thought of that before she hired you to whack this particular hornet's nest."

Pratt didn't know what to say so he sipped his drink. The old West-clox on the mantel ticked loudly. Munz blew a perfect smoke ring.

"I will give you ten thousand dollars to make this boy go away."

Pratt thought of all the ways he could do that, all the ways it might already have been done. When you don't know what to say, Chaplain Dorgan had told him, count slowly to ten. Pratt counted.

"That would not be in my client's interest."

"Bullshit! Who knows her interests better? You or me?'

Pratt counted. Cass was waiting.

"I can't do that, Nate. It's been a long day. I'm going to turn in."

Someone pulled the front door clapper. Pratt's cell phone rang. Munz heaved himself to his feet. Pratt opened his phone. It was Calloway.

"Turn on Channel 13."

"Why? What's going on?"

"Looks like the War Bonnets staged a little war party on Bloom's receptionist."

CHAPTER 53

Pratt found the remote on the desk and turned on the television. He heard Munz opening the front door, muted conversation. Pratt scrolled through the channels until he came to WMAD Channel 13, a news channel. There was a live-action feed from a row of one-story apartments in the old Triangle region near the Capitol.

Pratt remained standing as Munz returned accompanied by Agent Bonner. All three stood and looked at the television. Four cop cars and an ambulance pulled up on the lawn of the federally funded housing unit designed for the handicapped. Perry had lived in an apartment with smooth floors and no sill with most of the drawers and appliances lowered to wheelchair level. There was a body covered by a tarp in the harsh glare of a half dozen police spotlights.

"We're at the Greenbush Housing Project on West Washington. Apparently there was a shoot-out in one of the apartments involving members of the War Bonnets motorcycle gang. There are two confirmed dead, including the apartment's occupant who fought back with his own gun. . . Police are withholding the occupant's identity pending notification of the next-of-kin. We'll know more in a minute. Chief Johansen is going to say something."

"It was Perry Winkham," Pratt said. "Danny Bloom's receptionist."

"Why kill him?" Bonner said.

"He's sending me a message," Pratt croaked.

"That doesn't make sense unless you and Winkham had a special relationship. Did you?"

"He liked to tease me because he knew I was uncomfortable around gays. Moon's saying it's scorched-earth time. He's coming after me and anyone who is close to me."

"Do you think we need more ops, Mr. Bonner?"

Bonner laughed. "Those clowns aren't getting within a hundred miles of this place. Are you kidding me?"

"How many War Bonnets can there be?" Munz said.

"One hundred to two hundred members," Pratt said.

Munz picked up his glass and headed for the bar. "Jesus! What if they all come here?"

"Not even a factor, Mr. Munz. Every law-enforcement agency in the country is all hopped up over outlaw cycle gangs. They can't gather anywhere without drawing heat."

Munz held the bottle out to Pratt. Pratt shook his head. "What's your feeling, Josh?"

"I can't rule anything out. Moon wants to kill us personally but he might use his boys to soften us up."

"Reason I knocked," Bonner said, "the Lake County Deputy out front alerted me. We're on top of this. They won't get within a hundred miles of this place. If they did, any one of us is more than a match for all of them. You were in combat, Mr. Munz. You know what it's like."

"Yes, and I don't ever want to see it again," Munz said unconvincingly. Pratt knew the look of a man itching to use his gun. Just what they fuckin' needed.

"Guys, I really have to turn in," Pratt said.

He went downstairs to the basement—there was an elevator next to the stairs—and found Cass sitting up in the guest bedroom watching Letterman wearing a teddy. Pratt was beyond exhaustion. He just wanted to sleep.

"Baby, I gotta crash. Give me a rain check."

Cass smiled. "We'll see." She reached for his cock as he neared the bed. Pratt swatted it away.

"I mean it. We just learned that the War Bonnets killed Perry, Danny's receptionist."

"That fag?"

"He was a friend of mine, Cass."

"Sorry. I can make you forget about that."

"Cass, if you don't let me go to sleep I'll go sleep in the rec room."

"Fine," Cass flounced, turning her back. She lay at the edge of the bed staring at the wall. Pratt sat on the bed, turned off the table lamp, took off his shoes, shirt and pants and lay next to her, drawing the cover up against the air conditioning. Exhausted as he was, he didn't feel sleepy. He wished he could take a pill.

Cass spooned up to him and reached for his joint. Silently he fended her off.

"I love you," she cooed in his ear.

Pratt tensed. The words jammed in his throat. A second later Cass' foot shoved him hard in the small of his back and he landed on the floor.

Silently Pratt took his pillow and went into the rec room, where there was a blanket on the old sofa.

CHAPTER 54

Pratt woke to the sound of chairs moving in the kitchen overhead. Light crept around the perimeter of the blinds covering the view to the patio. Pratt sat up. He had a slight hangover from the booze and was stiff all over. The door to the guest bedroom was closed. Pratt stiff-walked to the half bath beneath the stair, relieved himself, splashed water on his face and washed his hands. It was just past ten.

Pratt went up the stair smelling bacon, down the hall to the kitchen, which had a twelve-foot beamed ceiling with a fan and a hanging rack of iron pots. Ginger stood at the stove in a pink terry cloth robe flipping eggs. Munz sat at the breakfast table opposite Bonner, who was digging into a plate of eggs.

"Where's Cass?" Ginger said. She sounded strong and refreshed.

"Still sleeping," Pratt said.

"How do you like your eggs, Josh?"

"Over, medium well."

Munz clicked on the flat-screen television stuck to the wall and cued in the local news station. They watched the weather report and a loud ad for American TV. There was nothing about the killings. The forecast called for rain, possibly heavy at times.

"'Bout time," Munz said. "Our cropland is hurting."

Bonner pushed himself back from the table. "Thanks, Mrs. M. I'm sending Bob in now."

"They named your friend this morning," Munz said. "Apparently he put up quite a struggle and managed to take out one of his assailants."

Perry with a gun. Pratt was still trying to get his head around it. Perry had embraced every liberal cause from global warming to white guilt and had repeatedly declared that private possession of a handgun should be illegal.

You never really knew people.

Ginger slapped a plate of bacon and eggs in front of Pratt.

A man appeared at the door. He was squat and powerful and spoke with an Australian accent.

"Greetings, mates. I'm Bob Foucalt. Thanks for the tucker."

Pratt introduced himself and Cass. Foucalt carried a sidearm in a pancake holster and a two-way clipped to his collar. "Normally I'd tell you to stay away from the windows but I hear this cobber likes to work up close and personal."

"He doesn't use guns," Cass said. "He doesn't like guns."

Expect him to use a gun.

"You know him then?" Foucalt said.

"A long time ago but some people don't change. They just get more so."

"Ain't that the truth." Foucalt saluted.

"Sit, Bob, sit," Ginger said. "How do you like your eggs?"

"Scrambled."

"Bob's a sniper," Munz said. "Most of the time he's out there in the woods with his rifle. Served two tours in Afghanistan with the SASR."

Pratt turned to Foucalt. "What's that, sir?"

"Special Air Service Regiment. And call me Bob. You calling me sir makes me think I'm back in the bloody Army and I wouldn't care to relive those days." Foucalt winked.

"Honey, the TV," Ginger said.

Munz used the remote to turn on the sound.

Dane County sheriff Mason stood in front of a podium. He looked like Ward Bond. "Warrants have been issued for members of the War Bonnets motorcycle gang. Deputies are in the process of serving those warrants now. . ."

"Sheriff!" The camera cut to a slim blond in a power suit. "Do you have a motive as to why the bikers would attack this man?"

"We think it was a drug deal gone sour."

"Bullshit!" Pratt exploded.

The press conference continued but there was no new information. Munz cued the mute. Foucalt finished his breakfast, thanked Ginger, and went out front with a coffee-filled thermos.

"Well look who's here," Ginger beamed.

Cass in the morning still gave Pratt a hard-on and he regretted his moment of truth the night before. Cass didn't look at him. Ginger immediately picked up on it.

"How do you like your eggs?"

"Just one, please, sunny-side up."

"How'dja sleep?" Munz said.

"Fine," Cass said listlessly. "Anything new?"

"Since the War Bonnets hit that guy, no," Ginger said.

"Do you have any coffee?"

Before Ginger could move, Cass got up and helped herself to a mug from the cupboard and coffee from the Mr. Coffee machine on the counter. She poured in a couple ounces of milk and three spoons of sugar. She sat, stirred, and drank.

"Hey folks," a deep voice boomed from the hallway. A tall black man with a shaved skull and a diamond earring wearing a sleeveless black tee that highlighted his enormous biceps, baggy cargo pants and steel-toed boots entered the kitchen. He had his own gravitational pull that made you want to get next to him.

Charisma, Pratt thought.

"I'm Rob Stuart."

Pratt got up to shake hands. "Josh Pratt. And this is Cass Rubio."

Cass looked away.

"Cass," Pratt said.

Cass waved wanly. "Hi."

"Just the three of you?" Pratt said.

Stuart showed perfect teeth. "That's all it takes. And two of us are redundant."

"Moon's dead meat if he comes anywhere near this property," Munz said. "What kind of eggs do you like, Rob?"

"I've already had breakfast but I will take a cup of that coffee."

Ginger handed him a mug. "Help yourself."

Stuart took it black. "Well I just wanted to introduce myself. We would prefer if nobody leaves the house, and it wouldn't hurt to keep the drapes, blinds, and shades drawn. There's no use advertising what's inside."

"Which one of you is in charge?" Pratt said.

The ivory grin. "That would be me." Stuart dipped into a pocket and handed Pratt a card between his index and middle finger. "Call if you must—but please make sure it's important."

Stuart withdrew.

"Let me give you the grand tour," Munz said.

Pratt stood. Cass remained where she was.

"You go ahead. I've seen it."

As Munz and Pratt left the breezeway the two women huddled in intense conversation.

CHAPTER 55

The first floor had an open floor plan with the kitchen segueing into the dining room into the living room. Nate's office was to the right as you entered. There were two half baths. The décor was Old West with Navajo rugs, kachina dolls, and paintings of stolid Indians gazing into storms with titles like "Early Winter." There was a Dali print on one wall. A proud buck gazed down from the living room.

Munz pushed a button on the wall and the dining room blinds retracted with a clacking noise. Broad vertical windows seemed to let the forest in, casting the whole room in a green glow. Pratt noted how easy it would be for a sniper to conceal himself with a clear shot of the house.

But that wasn't Moon's way.

The stair to the second floor began in the foyer and split into two curves halfway up. "We can take the stairs or we can take the elevator," Munz said.

"Let's take the stairs."

Pratt followed Munz up the broad winding stair to the second floor. A balcony overlooked the foyer. The floor was oak parquet. Munz turned east.

"This is the master bedroom suite," he said, gesturing Pratt in. The big room had a balcony looming over the patio that was in the trees, creating the impression of a luxurious tree house. Limbs provided easy access to the deck.

The bed was fashioned from twisted limbs, the headboard a solid slab of hand-carved oak depicting a herd of buffalo. Pratt went to the sliding doors leading to the deck. Locked. He unlatched the door and slid it to one side. He stepped out onto the deck. The scent of blossoms walloped him in the snout. It was like stepping from an antiseptic chamber into a floral stew.

Munz followed. "You're worried about these trees, aren't you?"

"Guy could pop right into your bedroom with those limbs."

"That's a hundred-year oak. I'm not going to mutilate it for some maniac."

"In that case it wouldn't hurt to string some cans and bottles up here. Crude, but effective."

"Good idea. I have a shitload of both."

Munz showed Pratt the bathroom. It had a skylight, whirlpool tub, two-person shower stall and two sinks all outfitted in Kohler modern. His and hers walk-in closets. Each was bigger than Pratt's bedroom at home. An Imelda Marcos display of shoes.

"What do you know about Cass?" Munz said, leading the way out of the suite toward the other side of the house.

"Not much. Met her last week on a job."

"Listen, it's my business because I think she's a deleterious influence on Ginger."

They entered a guest suite, king-sized bed handsomely made up with Navaho blankets, paintings of canyon lands on the wall.

"How so?" Pratt said, walking around the room, pulling aside the blinds and peering outside.

"I don't know how she is now but she used to do a lot of drugs and drank like a fish."

"If she's doing drugs I don't see it," Pratt said. "And we've been pretty close these last couple of days."

"She's also committed to magical thinking. So's Ginger. It just so happened that I came along and fulfilled her fantasy so she thinks it's true. That if you do A, B will happen. This whole thing with the missing baby . . . I don't know what she expects but I'm afraid it won't be good for her or any of us."

"That kid is in a bad way. We've got to help him."

"Listen, I'm not entirely convinced it is her son. I'll believe it when the DNA test comes back. If they ever find him. I have to say you're not at all what I expected. I mean that in a good way. I thought you were going to be some kind of cowboy. You're thoughtful, meticulous, and you keep your word. I just can't see what a guy like you is doing with a girl like that."

"Can't you?"

"Well I mean apart from the obvious."

"I'm not a complicated guy, Nate. I'm not looking for Kim Kardashian."

"Well listen. You're a detective. Go through her purse when you get a chance, why don'tcha?"

"I'll think about that."

A third room between the suites served as an office and overlooked the patio and pool. It was warm from several monitors and a printer quietly disgorging pages. Across from it was the elevator. Munz pushed the button. Seconds later the elevator beeped and opened.

They stepped inside. Munz pushed the button for the basement. The doors sighed shut and the elevator descended to the bottom floor. The elevator opened into a game room with South Seas décor: tiki dolls behind the bar, bamboo curtains, a pool table, a thatched roof over the bar, tile floor. Faux palm trees drooped in the dim light coming off the patio. A huge flat-screen TV sat opposite the sofa. It reminded Pratt of the monolith from *2001: A Space Odyssey*.

Pratt had been too exhausted last night to notice.

"Was the room okay?"

"Fine."

Munz looked at the rumpled blanket and pillow on the sofa.

The deck was concealed behind the electrically controlled blinds. Munz stepped to the wall and pushed a button. With a soft clacking sound the vertical blinds withdrew to one side, revealing a lush green landscape, soft light coming through the woods.

"There's beer and soft drinks in the fridge. Help yourself to whatever you need."

"Appreciate your putting us up."

"Sometimes my boy Russell and his wife visit but that's about the only time we have guests. I'm out of the house most days on site and I just like to relax when I get home, maybe watch a little golf. Ginger doesn't entertain as much as she used to."

Pratt gazed out at the forest. They were sitting ducks for anybody prepared to break glass. That was without the Flintstone factor. Pratt scanned the trees and the uppers. He saw no sign of them.

"Nate, if you don't mind my saying, we'd all be a lot safer if we checked into a hotel under a different name."

"That may be, but I'm not going to let some psycho chase me out of my own house. That's what Flintstone is for. They're going to nail this son of a bitch if he's stupid enough to show up here. Bet on it."

Munz headed for the door. "You want to help me string those cans and bottles?"

CHAPTER 56

Ginger insisted on cooking dinner with a lot of help from Cass. Together they made salad out of spinach, mustard greens, roasted corn nuts, red onions and cherry tomatoes. Ginger removed four huge steaks from a gargantuan freezer in the garage while Munz fired up the grill on the deck off the kitchen.

Ginger used a walker to maneuver. It had a bicycle cage affixed to the handlebars and a squeeze-bulb horn. Cass and Ginger killed a bottle of Chardonnay. Munz and Pratt drank a croaker of triple hops from the Great Dane Brewery. Conversation flowed like sludge until Munz mentioned he had a BMW 1200S in the garage.

They went into the garage and looked at Munz' bike.

Munz lit a cigar and offered one to Pratt, who declined. "So you were in prison, huh?"

"Six years at Waupun for a crime I did commit."

"Well that's refreshing. And that's where you found God?"

"That's where I welcomed Jesus Christ into my heart and soul."

"That works for you?"

"Has so far. What about you? You religious?"

Munz sighed. "Hardly. I was raised Episcopalian but Sunday school didn't take. My folks dutifully dragged us to church every Sunday but I sensed that they didn't believe, and when you're a kid, you figure out the ropes. If my parents didn't believe, why should I? I understood they were doing it for appearances. My father was a Rotarian, an Elk and a Mason. I wish I believed, know what I mean?"

Pratt nodded. "We all need to believe in something bigger than ourselves or we're just passing time."

Munz blew a smoke ring and nodded. "That's right. That's exactly right. I guess I've always believed in the endless opportunities of being an American. I like to think my homes are loved by generations."

Pratt nodded. "A-hunh."

"I wish I had your faith," Munz said.

"Well faith's a gift. Prayer doesn't hurt."

"What do my prayers matter? I'm not sincere. I don't believe in a God up in the heavens who made the universe in seven days. Christ. Try to get a permit in seven days!"

"You may not believe in God, but God believes in you. You want to pray with me right now?"

"No thanks. But we will have some bourbon."

"Come on," Pratt said. "It doesn't hurt. Give me your hand."

Reluctantly Munz extended his hand. Pratt gripped it and looked down. "Dear Lord, please watch over our loved ones and keep them from harm, and please help Eric find peace and his family."

"Amen," Munz said choking.

CHAPTER 57

Munz excused himself. Business. He went into his den and shut the door.

Pratt went out front where he found Foucalt.

"What's up?" Foucalt said.

"I'm going for a walk. You might tell the others so they don't shoot me by mistake."

"Well I can't tell you not to walk, but be careful, huh? If you're not back here in fifteen, someone will come looking."

Pratt patted his fanny pack. "Make it thirty." As he went back through the house to exit on the pool side, he ran into Cass carrying glasses into the kitchen. She didn't look at him.

"Look, baby, about last night," Pratt said.

She stepped around him. "Forget it, Pratt."

"I'm just scared, okay? I've never been in a serious relationship before."

"And you're not in one now. You've made that perfectly clear."

"I just wanted to say I'm sorry and I'll make it up to you."

"Yeah. Right." She turned her back and went into the kitchen.

Pratt watched her go with lustful regret. He toted up the pluses and minuses. The pluses: totally hot bod. She loved him. Knew how to fire a gun and drive, which in Pratt's limited experience was rare. Wasn't afraid to get her hands dirty.

The minuses: she seemed to have an animus toward Jews and blacks, and who knew who else. She seemed to have a teeny drinking problem. She apparently had no use for organized religion and Jesus in particular. Then there were the dogs.

"Jesus," he said quietly, "I can't ask your guidance on this since you are involved. I'll just have to figure it out by myself."

Pratt exited the first floor onto the rear deck. Bonner stood at the rail in camo fatigues surveying the woods through a pair of binocs. He put down the binocs and turned. "Ron says you're going for a walk."

"You guys get any sleep?" Pratt said.

"Oh yeah. We spell each other, grab a couple hours here and there. We'll probably sleep some today."

Pratt wore sunglasses to hide his tired eyes and a ball cap. "Omma walk around a little. I'll be back in thirty."

"Well naturally we'd prefer you remain at the house and confine your outdoor activities to the deck, but I can't stop you. You going up near the road? I'll alert the deputy."

"Nahh. I just want to stretch my limbs a little. I hear there's a lake over there."

"There is. Well how's this? If I don't hear from you in thirty minutes we're going to start looking. What's your cell number?"

Pratt took out one of Bloom's cards and scribbled his number on the back. "You boys are reading from the same hymnal."

"Bear in mind that we've set up an infrared perimeter, so you might get a call if you trip the line."

"I wondered about that. What do you do at night?"

"We have night vision goggles."

Pratt stepped down off the wide redwood steps and headed into the woods. Cass had told him that the estate contained six acres including waterfront property for a small lake. He could smell the lake but not see it. The day was overcast with a hint of rain. Dark cumulus clouds stacked up over the western horizon. Pratt had always loved walking in the woods with summer in his nose.

The wind whistled through the trees. Birds chirped. Squirrels scuttled through the ground cover. He saw a gleam of green through the trees. The lake. Pratt moved silently from rock to root, taking care not to step in crackly leaves. As a child he'd spent endless hours in the woods playing Indian. He could creep with the best of them.

Pratt thought he saw movement off to his right but when he looked there was nothing. Maybe it was Stuart. Pratt froze and listened. The woods felt empty of humans, the birds unperturbed in their search for bugs and berries. Pratt pressed on Injun style. The lake grew until he stood on its rocky shore watching the whitecaps whipped up by a sudden wind. The lake comprised about twenty acres with two baronial mansions visible, each extending a pier from the opposite side, each pier festooned with a boat lift holding a buttoned-down speedboat.

Pratt stood at six. The houses were at eleven and twelve. At three was a county park indicated by open space and a concrete ramp leading into the water. A fisherman was pulling out an aluminum skiff ahead of the rain. Woods came right up to the water except for these three features.

Suppose Moon wanted to sneak up on them. He'd put in a boat at the park and get out here, Pratt thought. Nothing to stop him but three Flintstone guys.

And Munz and Pratt. The builder suffered from Big Man syndrome, the need to assert himself, to lead, to solve the problem. He got a kick parading around the property with a pistol on his hip. Made him feel dangerous. Pratt worried that Munz might yank that gun out and blow his foot off. Or Pratt's head.

He imagined the Flintstone boys felt the same way about him.

Pratt was at a turning point. With the exception of Lowry's dogs and Ginger's son, every job he'd taken had come through Danny Bloom. The lawyer had been his friend and champion. Pratt wasn't a natural entrepreneur. He could do the job but he was lousy at selling himself. He was too blunt. He didn't know how to schmooze. A lot of people didn't like the Jesus thing.

He might advertise. Take out an ad in the Yellow Pages. Go on Craig's List. Go on Angie's List. Maybe he should take one of those business classes on how to be a better executive. He did not want to serve summonses and repo cars forever.

If he ever found the boy. Try as he might to steer clear of that dark star, the image of Eric had burned itself into his retina and was always there, just over the horizon, waiting to overwhelm him with its tidal force. He nourished a hatred so profound it could burn a hole in steel plate. Maybe Moon was just a surrogate for Duane.

Dear Lord let him come. And let me kill him.

Was it right to pray for another man's death? Pratt wished he knew someone he could ask.

His cell phone tickled his thigh. He pulled it out. "Pratt."

"Stuart here. Looks like they got your boy. Come on back to the house."

CHAPTER 58

Pratt found them all in the living room: Cass, Ginger, Munz and the three Flintstone ops. A television the size of a card table showed police vehicles and fire trucks gathered around the remains of a smoking farmhouse. Stuart stood, hands on hips.

"DEA agents found Moon this morning by following a stolen vehicle to this rural Lake County property. Sheriff's deputies said shots were fired from the house. They returned fire and the house burst into flames. They found his body in the kitchen."

Cass leaned forward from the sofa. "Holy shit. That's my place."

Stuart looked at Cass. "They've tentatively identified Moon from some body ink but they're sending in the fingerprints just to be sure."

Munz sat with an arm around his wife. "Looks like your job here is through."

"Up to you, Mr. Munz. You may want us to stick around until we get a positive confirmation."

"How many crazed fucking Indians are there? They know what he looks like. That's it. It's over. Good job."

It didn't feel right to Pratt. "It's a fake-out."

Stuart looked at him. "What makes you think so?"

"This guy's a ninja. He's not going to get caught in a shoot-out with cops. I don't think he even uses guns. Check his rap sheet. No guns." Pratt turned to Munz.

"Nate. You need to keep these guys around for a few days."

"Do you know what Flintstone charges? Come on. He's toast."

Ginger put her hand on her husband's arm. "Nate. One more day."

Munz looked at her and caved. "What the hell. It's only money! We'll give it another twenty-four, see what the situation is tomorrow."

Stuart nodded minutely as if Munz had just confirmed something he'd suspected. Bonner and Foucalt were indifferent. They were getting top dollar. It was a sweet gig compared to keeping American civilians alive in Baghdad.

"How do you people feel about staying in the house or on the deck for the rest of the day?" Stuart said. "Better safe than sorry."

A far-off rumble rolled through the still air. Munz shrugged. "Going to rain anyway."

Stuart nodded to his boys. Bonner and Foucalt left via the front door exuding confidence. Munz headed toward the stair. "Might as well try to work."

Cass and Ginger went back to the breezeway, leaving Pratt alone in the living room. Cass wasn't going to make it easy for him.

His woody had taken on a life of its own. He could hide in a bathroom and jerk off or make up with Cass. Pratt didn't know whether to shit or go blind. The last thing he needed was a distraction. But it wasn't up to him—not any more. The Flintstone boys had relieved him of responsibility. Too bad they couldn't relieve of him of his hatred or fear.

He went out onto the deck via the kitchen so he wouldn't have to pass through the breezeway and phoned Calloway.

He got the detective's machine and left a message. From the upper deck, the lake was just visible through the trees. The forest thrummed with the wind and there was a cool nip in the air. Fall was coming. A lone drop flew through the canopy of trees and smacked him coldly on the cheek.

Pratt folded his hands and looked down. "Dear Lord . . ." He stopped. He'd been tugging on God's ear a lot lately, and called in some big favors. He was in no position to implore the Lord. Rather he thanked him.

Pratt could hear the ladies in the breezeway. At least they were laughing although God knew, neither one had much to laugh about. Like a compass needle in the grip of a powerful magnetic force, Pratt's imagination returned to Eric and the concentrated evil of what had been done to him.

The scope of it never ceased to take his breath away. Since Pratt had gotten religion he'd accepted the idea of pure evil in the world. But he had never imagined he would encounter someone who was pure evil.

Pratt leaned against the rail. He was exhausted. He'd had hardly any sleep for two nights running. It was all he could do to drag his tired ass downstairs, flop on the sofa and pull the Afghans over his head. He was instantly asleep, a sweet, dreamless, velvet-lined plunge into oblivion.

Thunder woke him and the sudden dash of rain on the patio glass like a bucket of gravel. Pratt sat up momentarily bewildered. Lightning illuminated the tiki-themed rec room and he remembered. It was dark outside. He looked at his watch. He'd been out for ten hours. It was seven pm. Normally it would still be light outside but the summer storm that had been brewing all day had arrived, cutting off the sun with an iron curtain.

It took him a second to realize the pool was dark. The lights were out. Pratt made his way upstairs and found Ginger, Cass, and Munz in the dining room eating cold cuts by the light of candles. Pratt sat at the table. Cass didn't look at him. No doubt she'd spilled her guts to Ginger and they were seated in judgment against him, a worthless rat.

"How long has it been raining?" Pratt said, blinking.

"About fifteen minutes," Munz said, holding a seeded bun in one hand. "One minute the air was still, the next like we were in a tunnel with a freight train and wham, a wall of water."

Ginger used her arm rests to get to her feet. "I'm going to take a nap."

Munz rose next to her. "Let me help you, dear." Ginger took Munz' hand and they headed toward the stairs. Cass remained, staring into a cup of coffee.

"You're right," she said. "I should have kept my big mouth shut."

"I just need a little more time, is all," Pratt said, hating himself. He'd been through this shit before although never with a woman of Cass' class. Sexually speaking. He wasn't talking to Jesus now.

"Come on," he said extending his hand. The hand would lead to the hug, the hug would lead to bed.

Cass looked at his hand for a minute and took it, as he knew she would. Her scent drove him wild. Something named after an *American Idol* winner.

They went out on that part of the deck that had a roof over it. Water cascaded over the rim like a curtain. The air had taken on a slight chill. They leaned against the rail and Pratt put his arm around Cass as she snuggled into him.

In like Flynn.

CHAPTER 59

Pratt and Cass lay in the dark in the same position they had last night when the trouble began. This time Cass kept her mouth shut. Let it ride for now. Pratt liked the feel of her next to him, the snug curve of her hip. Let her think that with time he would warm to the idea of commitment. It could happen, he kept telling himself.

Lightning lanced through the night followed by cannon fire. The blinking light on the TV box had stopped. Rain lashed the windows. They were in for an old-fashioned goose drowner. Pratt tried out the thought of marital bliss: coming home from a long day tracking stolen cars or delivering summonses, the little lady greeting him on the stoop with an apron and a cocktail. More likely leather hot pants and a joint.

Pratt had no clue what domestic bliss looked like. His father was a one-man wrecking machine. Duane claimed to have been married, three, four, or five times. All questions about Pratt's mother were turned away with, "That bitch. You don't want to hear about her."

When pressed Duane would smack him with the flat of his hand.

Light shifted in the stairwell, a sudden flickering and shadow dance cast upon the wood-paneled wall.

"Hey Pratt," Munz stage-whispered down the stairs.

"Yeah?"

"Come up here a minute, would you?"

Cass was instantly awake. "What is it?"

"Nothing. Stay here. Keep that gun handy."

Pratt pulled on his jeans and slipped his feet into his Velcroed Nevados. He put the Ruger in the fanny pack and buckled it around his waist. He ascended into a dark house lit by a handful of flickering candles and the occasional lightning flash. Munz stood at the top of the stairs in cargo pants, gun worn over his tucked-in shirt, pushing back against his belly. He looked strained. Pratt glanced at his watch. It was only eight-thirty but the skies were dark as a tunnel.

Munz shut the basement door and led the way into the kitchen, where a skylight admitted flashes of harsh white light.

"What?" Pratt said.

Munz set the candle holder on the granite-surfaced island. "It's about the boy."

"What about him?"

"Is there a chance he's not Ginger's?"

This again.

Pratt shrugged. "There's only one way to find out, if we find him. With every passing day that seems more and more unlikely. I'm afraid this is a soul who is simply unequipped to exist in our world. Moon stole his life. Murder might have been kinder. I doubt very much we'll ever see him again, much less find him alive."

Munz sagged against the counter and for a moment seemed far older than his forty-plus. "I pray that it is so. You've got to understand something, Josh. I love my wife. The moment I laid eyes on her I knew she was the girl for me. God, that sounds so clichéd, but it's true. Most women prattle on about soul mates without the slightest clue what they're looking for. Ginger's past never bothered me. The tats, they didn't bother me. She cut way down on the drinking.

"But this business with the kid terrifies me. I already raised two kids and got 'em out of the house. If they find this kid and God forbid, there's something wrong with him, I'd be for putting him in an institution. I'm afraid it's going to break up my marriage."

Pratt shook his head. "Don't worry about something you can't control. Chances are we'll never see him again. But if he does somehow manage to survive, and we find him, I've already looked into counseling. People at the university would be eager to help."

Munz reached into a cupboard over the sink and removed a flask of bourbon. He poured himself a couple of fingers in a juice glass, looked at Pratt. Pratt nodded.

They silently toasted. Pratt sipped his bourbon. Like lava pouring down his throat. The bourbon triggered an atavistic longing for a line of coke or meth to bring him fully up to speed. Pratt smiled. He would no sooner dive back into that barrel than he would take his own life.

"What?" Munz said.

"Oh, I was just thinking about the way I used to live. I can identify with Ginger. We both sort of came out of that biker scene and lived to tell about it."

"I asked a doctor once if all that shit she did before she met me, the meth, the blow, the smack, whatever, might have brought on the Crohn's. Not likely."

"Like it or not, she's the woman you fell in love with."

"I'll drink to that." Munz did so. He refilled his glass and held the bottle up for Pratt. Pratt shook his head.

"When'd the lights go out?"

"About two hours ago. Happens all the time. They should be up soon."

"Have you heard from Flintstone in the past hour?"

Munz frowned, pulled out his cell phone and pushed buttons. He put it to his ear and frowned. "The cell phones are out. Nothing. No signal."

Pratt reached into his pocket, pulled out his own cell phone and confirmed. The lights were out. Cell phone service was out. As if some *brujo* had sacrificed a lawyer and brought the storm.

"Shouldn't there be somebody out front?" Pratt said, walking toward the front door.

Munz strode fast to keep up. "I looked about a half hour ago but I didn't see anyone. I just figured they were on patrol."

Pratt paused at the front door and peered out the mullioned window. Rain reduced everything to a washed-out dark gray and concealed all movement. Pratt opened the door. A blast of cool moisture assaulted him. The agents' car rested at the curb, dark and inscrutable.

Pratt reached for an umbrella in the stand next to the door. "Wait here." He stepped out beneath the porte cochere and popped the black brolly. Clutching the umbrella just beneath the brace, he stepped out into the driveway. The wind tried to yank the umbrella from his grip. Pratt stepped down to the drive.

Rapid percussions echoed down the long drive, the sound of automatic gunfire.

CHAPTER 60

Pratt looked around. Where was Flintstone? A flash of lightning illuminated the black Chrysler. It appeared to be empty. Munz came out on the stoop.

"That's gunfire!"

"It came from up toward the road. Shit!" Pratt was dying to know what happened but he dared not leave the ladies. Someone ran around the corner of the house into the drive. In the rain and dark Pratt nearly shot him. Bonner did a massive double-take.

"Don't shoot! It's Bonner!"

Pratt lowered his pistol. He hadn't even remembered pulling it. "Did you hear that?"

"Yeah. The radios are down. Foucalt and Stuart are on perimeter. Our transceivers are still working. I'd sure like to know what happened."

"I'm going up there," Pratt said. Somebody had to do it. If something had happened to the deputy they had to know.

"Don't be stupid," Bonner said. "I'll go."

"No. Your job is here protecting the women. If I'm not back in fifteen minutes. . ." He let it die.

"Wait a minute!" Bonner said. He opened the Chrysler's trunk and removed a heavy device that looked like binoculars with a head strap. "You know how to use this?"

"Show me," Pratt said.

Bonner fitted the device over Pratt's head and switched it on. An electronic hum reverberated between Pratt's ears as the landscape suddenly stood forth in an unnatural green. He could see each raindrop as it zipped by. He could see the outlines of the towering blue spruce.

Pratt made the "okay" sign with thumb and forefinger and trotted down the drive holding his pistol before him in both hands. The driveway curved to the right, concealing the end. An old oak lay across the drive, felled by the wind. Pratt stepped gingerly over it and pounded on, sticking to the side of the pavement, where every footfall created a little wave. He rounded the bend and saw the deputy's car at the end of the drive through the closed gate. He paused and took in the scene. The only motion came from the rain and the trees sighing in the wind.

Pratt slowed down and approached cautiously, rounding one of the massive stone pillars on the outside. Concealed by the pillar, he looked at the scene. The patrol car's windshield was punctured with dozens of bullet holes. An old Chevy pick-up rested with its butt in the air, nose in the ditch nearby, the driver's door open. A dude sprawled out the driver's side with his head on the tarmac staring sightlessly into the black sky, his legs still in the truck.

Pratt crept up on the deputy's door, hunkering low. The door was ajar and one booted foot rested on the ground. Pratt got up to the door and looked inside. The deputy lay across his bench seat, face pulped, hand curled around his service automatic. The deputy had worn horn-rimmed glasses, which had split, one lens jutting up at an angle. Brass lay on the seat and on the dash. His vest hadn't saved him. Whoever had opened up on him unloaded several clips through the cruiser's windshield. It was some kind of miracle the deputy was able to shoot one of his assailants, if that's what had happened.

Pratt opened the door wider. The rain and wind drowned out all sound. He tried the deputy's transceiver. Dead. Pratt found it awkward to maneuver his head inside the cab with the night vision goggles but he could see the radio had caught a ricochet.

Pratt reached for the deputy's shoulder radio and pulled it close. He keyed it. Nothing but static. Pratt eased himself out of the cruiser, went around the back and approached the pick-up on the passenger's side. The door was open. There was nobody inside. Pratt went around the back of the truck and up to where the driver lay in the road. His long black braid snaked beneath the truck. Prison tats crawled up his neck. The driver wore a denim vest with a tiny War Bonnets patch.

There'd been a passenger. Filled with a sense of urgency Pratt cut off his inspection and headed back toward the house. Pratt ran on the mossy shoulder close to the trees so as not to present a clear profile. If he had night vision so could they. He approached the curve in the driveway and jerked to a stop as if he'd reached the end of his chain.

Wait a minute.

The hairs on Pratt's neck stood straight up. He backed into the woods, wet fir scratching him head to toe. He stopped with his back against a sycamore as ice water rolled down his back and peered through the glowing green landscape. Each tiny motion drew his attention. The wind howled, rain flew. It was like trying to find a pattern in a foaming sea. The tree erupted next to his head, sending a sharp splinter into his cheek. Simultaneously he heard the report of a big bore weapon so close it slammed his eardrums shut.

Instinctively Pratt sunk, whirled and fired. The Bonnet was standing six feet away. How had he missed? Pratt's bullet struck the Bonnet's Mac-10 below the barrel and it arced up and out of the man's hands. The Bonnet was not wearing goggles. In the split second before he jerked into the trees, Pratt registered it was the caveman from the Chip—the retailer.

The fucking goggles now restricted Pratt's vision. The caveman had juked beyond. Pratt whipped off the goggles and whirled wildly. A piece of the forest detached itself too close to identify. The caveman lunged at Pratt with a knife. Pratt instinctively swung the gun barrel down on the caveman's wrist with a satisfying crack. Pratt put the gun to the man's chest. The caveman lurched, staggering backward with each squeeze of the trigger. The caveman died with his mouth open, showing meth teeth like tombstones in a vandalized cemetery.

Pratt stared at the body. He'd never killed a man before. He didn't count Taco.

And Jesus said unto him, *Pratt, I don't know shit about combat, but doesn't this seem like a diversion?*

Scooping up the night vision goggles, Pratt spent one second looking for the Mac-10. Fuck it. He had to get back to the house. Holding the pistol before him, Pratt booked.

He splashed back to the turnaround breathing hard. Fitting the goggles around his eyes, he turned them on. There was no sign of life. All lights in the house were off. The rain poured down. Angling into the wind, Pratt dashed to the black Chrysler and opened the passenger door.

The overwhelming smell of sheared copper smacked Pratt in the face. Bonner lay sideways across the seat, eyes open, gaping black maw where his throat had been cut.

CHAPTER 61

Blood pooled on the leather upholstery and ran onto the floor. Bonner's holster was empty. There was no sign of his gun. Pratt felt a presence at his elbow and looked. Munz had joined him.

Pratt stepped aside, allowing Munz to look. Munz bent down, gripped the door frame and looked. He jerked back. His face went white. "My God," he said, taking an involuntary step back.

Pratt slammed the door. "Let's get back in the house." Mind reeling. Moon could be anywhere. He might already be in the house. Pratt didn't wait. He ran. Munz ran right behind him, slammed the door and threw the dead bolt.

Munz drew his pistol, a Glock 17, and ratcheted a shell into the chamber.

Pratt put a hand up. He stood in a puddle of water. "Don't shoot your foot off. Or me. Is the safety on?"

"It's a Glock," Munz said.

They spoke quietly, words drowned out by the storm.

"I'm turning on the alarm," Munz said.

"The electricity's off."

"Right! Right, damn it!"

Pratt looked down. The wet footprints on the hardwood floor belonged only to him and Munz. All the doors and windows were locked. If Moon were in the house he had to have broken something to get in. The wind picked up, louder than the tin cans they'd strung among the branches with pennies inside.

"Flashlights," Pratt said. "We've got to make sure he's not in the house."

"Oh shit," Munz moaned softly, turning to the broad stair leading to the second floor.

Pratt followed. Munz reached the deck overlooking the living room and raced down the corridor to the master suite. Pratt followed him. Ginger lay asleep on her half of the king-sized bed, hair fanned across the pillow.

"Thank God," Munz whispered while Pratt went to the window and pulled aside the curtains. The deck outside looked down on an empty patio. Pratt checked the locks. Munz had inserted a pipe to prevent the sliding door from being opened. Pratt let the drapery fall back into place.

I fucking knew it, he thought. He tapped Munz on the shoulder. "Flashlights," he whispered.

Munz nodded. "Office," he whispered.

"I'll be right back," Pratt said.

Pratt turned and ran down the corridor, down the stairs three at a time, through the door to the basement, across the rec room into the guest bedroom where Cass lay where he'd left her softly snoring. Wake her and drag her upstairs? Pratt checked the sliding door. The brace was in place. He let the heavy curtains fall back, plunging the room into darkness. His night vision was excellent. He preferred it to the goggles.

He checked the rec room, looked behind the bar, in the closet and the utility room. Satisfying himself that the house had not been breached, he ran back up the stairs, around to the front stairs, up those two at a time back to Munz' office.

Munz produced two black plastic C cell flashlights, long and heavy clubs.

"Let's keep these off until we really need them," Pratt said. "We've got to check all the closets on this floor. And look under the bed."

Munz goggled. "Really?"

"Really. And if you see the son of a bitch shoot him."

"How will I know if it's him?"

"Who else is going to be hiding under the bed? We'll stick together, do a systematic search of the house."

Munz led the way back to the master suite. Pistol extended, he lay on the floor five feet from the bed and pressed the flashlight button. The beam illuminated dust bunnies and a shoe box.

They checked the bathroom, the shower stall, the two walk-in closets. They moved to the office. The closet, the half bath, beneath the desk. They moved to the guest bedroom and checked under the bed, the closet and the bath. There was no moisture on the hardwood floors other than their own. Pratt stared up at the access panel to the attic.

"There's no outside access," Munz said.

They quietly descended the stairs and searched the first floor, Pratt guarding Munz' back. Outside the storm raged. The living room, the dining room, the breezeway, the den, the kitchen and numerous closets, all cleared.

In the kitchen Munz opened the door into the cavernous garage. Pratt followed, shutting the door behind him. A pair of windows in the far wall admitted just enough light to illuminate the outline of vehicles. Munz switched on his flashlight and kept it low to the ground. Pratt did likewise.

They searched between the vehicles and in the half bath off the garage. They got down on the ground and searched beneath the vehicles. They checked the floor for footprints. Pratt shined his light up and searched among the girders and ducts, thinking now would be a perfect time for Moon to move around the house.

They went to the basement, Pratt leading with his pistol clutched in both hands. Lightning strobed around the edges of the blinds. Pratt cut across the rec room to the guest suite and stepped inside. Cass lay where he had left her, one arm flung across the sheets. He stood over her for a minute watching the telltale pulse in her neck.

Pratt got down on his knees and checked under the bed. As a child it had been a nightly ritual until Duane caught him at it and the ridicule began.

"You know that goddamn boogie man is real, boy, and one of these days he's gonna grab you by the hair and drag you straight to hell."

Moon was not under the bed. Pratt checked the closet and the bathroom. He went to the door. Munz came out of the utility room.

"All clear," he said.

They met in the center of the room between the bar and the patio. "What else is there?" he said.

Munz pointed to a door behind the bar. "Just that closet."

Pratt braced his elbows against the bar and pointed at the closet as Munz reached for the knob and swiftly yanked it open, stepping out of the way. Darkness. Munz held his flashlight around the edge and shined it in. The closet contained only stacks of boxes.

"I think," Pratt said, "We should all get in your car and get the fuck out of here."

"Okay. Wake Cass and bring her. Let's all stick together from now on."

Pratt nodded and headed for the guest bedroom.

Three flat smacks interrupted the rain's white noise. Munz and Pratt looked at the patio door from where it had issued. Lightning flashed. Through the slits in the blinds the outline of a man.

Three more raps as he slapped his open palm against the glass.

Pratt went into a shooter's stance. Munz moved to the wall next to the sliding glass door. Quickly he reeled in the blinds.

The tall figure of Rob Stuart, barely visible as a black outline, watch cap pulled low over his ears, cupped his hands against the glass. "Let me in," he mouthed.

CHAPTER 62

Stuart dripped water on the parquet floor. He was dressed in a black turtleneck, black holster, black trousers tucked into black boots, all of it soaking wet. He moved quickly to shut the blinds and draw the others away from the door. He appeared agitated.

"Did you find Bonner?" Pratt said.

Stuart nodded his head grimly.

"What about Foucalt?"

Stuart shook his head. "Can't find him. He's not where he's supposed to be."

"Fucking great," Munz said, going behind the bar and picking up a bottle of Famous Grouse. He poured several ounces into a tumbler and drank it neat. He gestured with the bottle toward Pratt. Pratt shook his head.

"I'll have some of that," Stuart said, taking the bottle and chugging.

Creases radiated from the bridge of the Flintstone op's nose. He put the bottle down on the bar and shook himself like a dog, spraying water everywhere

"Let's get both women down here if you don't mind."

Munz headed for the stair, gun in hand.

Pratt gestured toward the bedroom. "Cass is in there."

Cass appeared in the bedroom doorway wearing a white T-shirt and jeans. "What's going on?" She walked toward Pratt.

Stuart ushered them back. "Let's all back away from the window."

They gathered at one side of the great room by the brick fireplace. A stuffed muskie hung above the mantel. Stuart appeared excited, totally alive. He thrummed with nervous energy. "Okay. There's no reason to panic. He's out there but we have him outnumbered and outgunned. Both you gentlemen are trained shooters. Are there any neighbors around who might respond to the sound of gunshots?"

"Nearest neighbor's a quarter mile," Munz said. "Doubt if he'd hear anything in this storm."

"In that case we can assume that anyone found lurking around whom you can't immediately identify is our quarry."

Cute word, Pratt thought, turning Moon from nightmare to prey.

"War Bonnets hit the deputy at the end of the drive," Pratt said. "He's dead, so was one Bonnet. I killed another one on the way back to the house."

"I heard the gunfire," Stuart said. "I thought Moon didn't use guns."

"He doesn't. But his boys do," Pratt said.

"What's going on?" Cass said. "What happened?"

Pratt put an arm around her shoulder. "Bonner is dead. Foucalt is probably dead too."

She shivered uncontrollably. "Moon is here?" she whispered.

"So it would seem," Stuart declared. "Is there any exit directly from the basement to the outside, other than the patio?"

"There's an entrance off the spare bedroom," Pratt said. "He'd have to break the glass."

Stuart looked around. Munz had gone upstairs to get Ginger. Stuart headed for the stairs.

"Stay away from the windows," he said. "We'll be right back."

Cass went limp with fear. "He's going to kill us," she moaned.

Pratt gripped her firmly by the shoulders. He had to physically hold her up. "Bullshit! He tried to kill me and it didn't take. This time it's his ass on the line."

Bravado was better than meth. Strength surged through his legs. He gathered himself for a fight.

Bring it on, motherfucker.

If Moon were to pop through the door, Cass would be in the line of fire. The basement bedroom had that sliding door open to the patio. But the utility room's only door opened into the rec room. Pratt steered Cass back to the utility room. A large, unfinished room, it contained a washer, dryer, freezer, and a spare sofa. A window high up on the wall opened into a window well on the side of the house. You could get out of the house through the window in an emergency, just put a chair under it. Pratt put Cass on the sofa. She moved like a zombie. Pratt took an old wool blanket folded over the back and laid it across Cass, who curled up in a near-fetal position.

Pratt took the Ruger from the fanny pack, its weight like the Old Testament in his hand. He released the magazine and filled it with bullets from his pocket.

"Yea, though I walk through the valley of the shadow of death," he whispered to himself away from Cass, **"I will fear no evil; for you are with me; your rod and your staff, they comfort me." He stepped into the rec room and shut the door behind him.**

Pratt leaned on the bar facing the patio, projecting his radar through the blinds and the glass and the rain. No go. He wasn't Superman. Footsteps. Munz came first, leading Ginger, who hung on his arm and the banister. He held her up as she tentatively crossed the room, face creased with pain.

"Where's Cass?" she whispered.

"In the utility room. I figure it's the safest place."

Munz nodded and led Ginger into the utility room.

Stuart silently appeared.

"I say we put a man on the first floor and two down here. Anybody sees him, we start shooting."

The storm tossed a load of gravel against the patio window. Through a crack in the blinds Pratt saw white pellets. The house rang like Billy Cobham's snare drum.

"Hail," he said.

Munz came out of the utility room. "Fuck. Hail means tornadoes. Well this is the safest place in the house."

The three men huddled at the bar, Pratt and Munz in back, Stuart in front. Stuart told them his plan.

"What good does that do?" Munz said. "Wouldn't it make more sense for all of us to pile into the Infiniti and make a run for it?"

Stuart gripped Munz' shoulder. "We don't know what's out there. He may have more War Bonnets and I don't think we should be in a car in this weather. I say we put an end to this motherfucker once and for all." Stuart's eyes glowed. He was happy as a pig in shit.

Munz looked like he'd eaten a bad shrimp. "You're the expert."

Lightning flickered through the vinyl blinds, which chattered in the wind that forced its way in through the porous door.

Stuart stepped away from the bar and faced his audience. "I just go by what. . ."

An electric crack insinuated itself into the mix. Stuart looked mildly surprised. He looked down. A black point emerged from his chest just below the diaphragm.

Stuart collapsed, an arrow jutting from his back.

CHAPTER 63

Munz and Pratt ducked behind the bar. It was made of wood with a bamboo façade, unlikely to stop either an arrow or a bullet, but three stainless steel dish pans rested on a sub-shelf. They might. Munz was sick with fear, his eyes yellow.

"How can he see?" Munz said with a hitch in his voice.

"Maybe infra-red—it can pick up heat signatures through glass."

But Moon supposedly eschewed technology. How had he done it?

"He's picking us off one by one!"

"He's still outside," Pratt said, mind careening wildly over strategy and tactics. The window in the utility room. If he could get outside, he could circle the house and maybe find Moon. The arrow had come from up in the trees off the deck.

It would be like a blind man searching for a mouse in a cave. Better to wait for Moon to enter the house. While Munz and Pratt hunkered behind the bar, Moon was undoubtedly moving.

Pratt realized that if he were Moon he would now run around to the front of the house to gain entry. "He's coming around the front," Pratt hissed. "You stay with the women."

Pratt sprinted for the stair. He hated to leave the women without his protection—he had doubts about Munz. Up the stairs three at a time, into the entry hall pointing the Ruger's muzzle at the big front door. Again Pratt projected his "radar," his every sense seeking anomalies that would signal an intruder. The storm increased its fury, lashing the roof and windows with wave after wave of gravel-sized pellets. The air seemed to carry a charge.

The wind built toward a crescendo. Pratt hoped it was a tornado—pick Moon up and dump him in Kansas. The sound grew in intensity until it was like standing inside the cockpit of a hurtling locomotive. There was a resounding crash from the second floor as a tree smashed through a window.

Pratt jumped, swiveling like a turret toward the second-floor balcony. His con sense said it was a diversion, intended or not. For an instant Pratt was torn. He headed back toward the basement stairs, stopping at the top to listen. He thought he heard a muffled grunt.

Pratt inched down the hardwood stairs, pistol at his side. He stopped at the bottom, hidden from the rec room by the wall. The sky turned white with multiple lightning flashes. Pratt waited for the roll of thunder.

He stepped into the rec room with pistol raised, gripping with both hands.

A figure straightened up behind the bar. Lightning flickered.

Moon smiled, his bald head eerily skull-like, heavy black Fu Manchu framing his rictus grin.

Pratt pulled the trigger, three quick shots where Moon had stood. They struck the door to the utility room and the back wall. Pratt lowered his sights and perforated the bamboo bar, right to left, a foot between shots. Each shot produced a metallic clang. That was seven. He had eight left. Pratt had deafened himself. His ears rang with tinnitus.

Dear God don't let the women open that door.

The door looked closed. In the dark it was hard to see.

"Moon?" Pratt called.

"Pratt, you insane motherfucker!" Moon called from behind the bar, voice filled with admiration. "You owe me thirty grand!"

"Why aren't you dead, Moon?"

The women had to have heard. If they had any sense they'd crawl out the basement window. Go. Go now. Run into the forest where he'll never catch you.

"Why aren't *you* dead, Pratt? You mean the bar? Bunch of steel saucepans down here on shelves."

"Whose body did you leave at Cass' place?"

"That was Rollie, the guy you sucker-punched to get my stash."

Pratt eyed the bar. Obviously Moon didn't have a gun or he would have used it, but a bow and arrow were just as lethal. Pratt hyped up. Run to the bar, stick his gun hand over and *shoot shoot shoot.*

Do it.

Do it now.

Pratt exploded from the base of the steps. Three leaps to the bar. He jammed his gun hand over and shot down behind the bar from one end to the other, handheld novas casting black and white tabloid light.

Pratt stepped behind the bar.

Munz lay where Moon had dropped him, with four post-mortem holes Pratt put in him. Munz' gun was nowhere to be seen.

Pratt looked at the door to the utility room. His heart exploded and jammed in his throat. The door was open.

"Stand away from the door, Pratt," Moon called.

Numbly Pratt stepped back. Cass came first, face like concrete, Moon's arm around her neck. At the end of the arm was a bowie knife with a twelve-inch blade that caught the lightning like fireflies in a jar.

"One false move, I slit this bitch's throat like a harvest pig," Moon grinned.

The point of his knife indented her throat. Both her hands were on his knife arm.

"Set your gun down on the bar and step back."

Pratt hesitated.

The knife bit until a drop of blood trickled from Cass' neck. Pratt stepped forward and put the Ruger on the bar. Moon edged forward with Cass and grabbed it. He turned and propelled Cass into the utility room with a mighty shove. Moon meant for Cass to hit the floor and she did. Moon pulled the door shut. He wore a black muscle shirt, black jeans, and black biker boots. Tribal tats encircled his biceps. A beaded knife sheath hung from a beaded belt.

Moon leaned on the bar holding the pistol casually. He reached down and brought up a bottle of bourbon that had survived the shootout. He reached down and brought up two glass tumblers. Laying the pistol down behind the bar, he unscrewed the bourbon and poured two fingers in each glass.

Pratt watched, mesmerized. Moon picked up his glass and his pistol and walked out from behind the bar toward the sofa. He gestured toward the other glass with the Ruger.

"Here's to you, my resourceful friend. Under other circumstances we would have been boon companions."

"Never," Pratt said.

Moon made a face. "What's the matter? Don't you like me?"

"What you did to that boy . . ." Pratt searched for words.

"Big fucking deal. Eric's father owed me seven thousand dollars. I gave him an ultimatum." Moon drained his glass and set the tumbler down on the bar.

For a second Pratt wasn't sure he'd heard right. "What did you say?"

"We could have been friends!"

"You took him from his *father*? You mean he's not Ginger's kid?"

"Fuck no! Do you think I'd do that to my own flesh and blood? I placed the real Eric with a wealthy Cuban couple in Miami. He's living in the lap of luxury. I don't know if that's going to make Ginger happy or sad. I guess we'll find out, won't we?"

"Why call him Eric?"

Moon grinned. His teeth were perfect. "Well maybe he is my kid. I guess you'll never know. Come on, Pratt! I'm fuckin' with ya! When I look at that boy my heart soars like an eagle. He can track a jackrabbit through a blizzard. I taught him how to *smell*, how to *see*, how to *listen*." Moon touched his nose, eyes and ears. "Many's the time that boy went out in the morning and brought back dinner in the evening. He can crouch like a rock for hours. Patience? You don't know the meaning of the word. Speed? He can outrun a coyote."

Pratt envisioned the stoop-shouldered, spine-twisted Eric running. Was everything Moon said a lie? Or like all great liars, did he pepper his lies with the truth? A black and twisted thing clawed its way out of Pratt's gut, a hatred so intense it threatened to consume him.

It must have showed on his face. Moon looked surprised and took a step back, training the pistol on Pratt. "Wow. I'll bet you suck at poker. You'd really like to kill me, wouldn't you?"

"It would give me great pleasure."

"Now I'm really sorry, Pratt. I like you more every time we meet. But I can't let you live. We are known by our enemies. They will sing about me around the council fires so long as there are Lakota. I will sing for you in a minute."

Moon pointed the Ruger at Pratt with both hands. He began to chant slowly in a loud, ritual voice, moving from foot to foot like a sumo wrestler. "*Hey na na na na hey—nokia na na . . .*"

Pratt waited for death.

Lord, it's in your hands.

The door to the utility room slammed open and Cass leaped out holding the .38 Pratt had given her. "YAHHHHH!" she screamed.

CHAPTER 64

Moon swiveled and fired at the same instant as Cass. Twin geysers of flame lit the basement. Cass crashed on her face. Pratt slammed into Moon, planting his head under Moon's jaw and grabbing Moon's gun hand in both his hands.

Control the weapon hand. They slammed into the sofa and fell over it onto the floor, Moon on top. Pratt got his foot beneath Moon's hip and thrust, twisting the pistol up and out of Moon's grasp. Pratt seized the Ruger by the barrel and tried to turn it. Moon kicked Pratt's hand, sending the Ruger skittering across the floor into darkness. Moon straddled Pratt and rained down elbows. It was the mountain lion all over again. Stitches ripped. Pratt jammed his pointed fingers hard against the indentation in Moon's throat. He thrust his finger beak deep and twisted.

Moon choked.

Pratt tore loose, lashing out with a back kick that caught Moon in the gut. Moon grunted. Pratt and Moon got to their feet. Moon's hand went to his waist and pulled out the bowie. His teeth reflected lightning. They circled one another in the center of the rec room. Pratt sprinted for the pool table, swept up the cue, swiveled and lashed out with the thick end, barely missing Moon, who danced back.

Pratt held the cue in both hands, rotating it over his head and out with a swishing sound. He dared not glance at Cass, not for an instant. She was lost in shadow. They circled one another, each looking for an opening. Pratt fixed his gaze on Moon's chest.

"You think this storm just happened?" Moon hissed. "I *made* it happen. I control the elements, the seasons, the creatures of the prairie. You can't beat me, you could never beat me. I wear the belt of quills and the medicine lodge shirt. My father was a medicine man, as was his father, and his father's father. My great-great-great-grandfather fought with Crazy Horse at the Little Big Horn. I am the son of the sun and the moon's lover."

"You're nothing," Pratt spat.

With a roar Moon attacked, the tip of his blade describing wild helixes as Pratt yielded ground, sweeping the cue to keep Moon at bay. Pratt gripped the cue and swung for the fences. Moon corkscrewed into a reverse spin kick, catching Pratt in the ribs.

Pratt grunted but held on to the cue, jamming it into Moon's chest. Moon stepped back, gasping. The two men faced each other, panting. Moon's face morphed into a leering mask like a Mohican lodge pole.

He began to chant. "*Hey na na na—hey na na na.*" He lifted each leg in turn and stomped. Eyes fixed on Pratt, Moon danced backwards toward the sofa. He danced behind the sofa, his gaze sweeping the floor.

Looking for the gun.

Pratt exploded, banishing his pain to the outer boroughs of his thoughts. He leaped over the sofa, swinging the pool cue in a downward arc at Moon's head, which gleamed dully in the flickering light.

The pool cue struck a bolster. Moon lay on his belly reaching beneath the sofa. Pratt came down on both knees but Moon rolled out of the way, away from the sofa, and uncurled to his feet like smoke rising. He held the black Ruger like the Olympic torch.

He pointed the automatic at Pratt. In the dark only Moon's head was visible, disembodied, floating in space like a ghost moon.

Pratt got up and leaned on the sofa.

Both men grinned.

"Damn," Moon said panting, "you are one resilient motherfucker! Where do you want it?"

Pratt stepped behind the sofa. He could dive, but Moon would be on him in an instant. It will be interesting, he thought, to see if Chaplain Dorgan's interpretations of heaven were accurate.

"Your ass."

"Well turn around."

Pratt wasn't about to take a bullet in the back. He held his hands behind him and faced the bullet.

Moon squeezed the trigger.

The utility room door opened in a blaze of light.

Ginger stumbled forth spitting flame from her hands.

CHAPTER 65

Eyes glassy in the moonlight, Ginger advanced, holding a Roman candle before her like a dousing rod. Like a tiny volcano it spat flaming fragments across the room. Grimacing and whining deep in her throat, Ginger aimed the tiny meteorites at Moon's face. Moon was too quick for her. With a ducking motion he weaved out of the way, went down on one knee and swept Ginger off her feet with his leg.

The Roman candle rolled to one side, where it continued to disgorge its flame for several seconds. The room stank of burnt gunpowder.

"Hello, darling," Moon snarled. "Been a long time. . ."

As Pratt lurched forward Moon brought the gun up and aimed.

Ginger lay beneath Moon's grasp. She put a hand on his wrist and choked, "Tell me the truth, Gene. Is Eric our son?"

"Of course he is, darling. You don't think I'd let a stranger raise my own flesh and blood?" Moon stood, letting the pistol fall to his side half-aimed at Ginger. Moon stared at her with loathing, lips curled in an animal grimace. Pratt saw that Moon was a razor's edge from pulling the trigger.

"You're afraid of her!" Pratt said.

Moon's eyes seemed to retreat beneath his brow until they were two dull gleams. The muzzle fixed on Pratt. "I'm not afraid of anything."

"You're afraid of everything! Look at the way you live. I'll bet you don't even have a driver's license."

Moon shivered with delight. "Most people are sheeple. You know that to be true, Josh! Look at the life you've chosen to lead. You've been through the criminal justice system. Do you know that in Greek, Joshua, is the same as Jesus? The Lord said unto Moses, 'Send thou men, that they may spy out the land of Canaan, which I give unto the children of Israel; of every tribe of their fathers shall ye send a man, every one a prince among them.' And he sent Joshua to lead them."

"And Moses sent them from the wilderness of Paran according to the commandment of the LORD; all of them men who were heads of the children of Israel."

"Christ I wish I didn't have to kill you Pratt!"

Ginger struggled to her knees and put her hand on Moon's arm. "Gene . . ."

He whipped away as if scalded, swinging the automatic in a tight arc that clipped Ginger on the temple. She said, "Ooh," and went down. The gun snapped back to Pratt.

"I told this bitch what I'd do if she ever betrayed me."

"You, you, you. It's always all about you, isn't it? You don't believe in anything bigger than yourself."

"Why should I? Show me proof that God exists."

"It's a matter of faith. You can't see it, hear it, or touch it."

"I understand mass delusion when I see it. Look at Nazi Germany—all those good Germans. They went with the herd. It's happening right here. They're just going with the herd."

Ginger moaned and grabbed Moon's leg. He tried to shake her off but she held on tight. "Where is he, Gene? Where is our son?"

"Get . . . off!" Moon dinged her on top of the head with the butt of the pistol.

Pratt fought the detonation of fury in his belly, the image burned indelibly into the back of his skull. He heard the rhythmic whacking of a wind-driven limb against the roof. He tasted copper at the back of his tongue. He caught a scent of something atavistic. Something strange yet familiar touched his mind, and his rage was doubled as if joined by another.

Pratt sensed movement and turned. A blurred shape detached itself from the base of the stairs and rolled at Moon, shoving Pratt out of the way with enough strength to send him stumbling into the bar. The bolus of fur fell on Moon like a mother bear protecting her young, claws slashing. The jaws clamped down on Moon's gun hand and nearly tore it off. The gun skittered across the floor and disappeared in shadow.

The dog boy gripped Moon behind his head, pulled him to the ground, and used his legs and feet and teeth to tear into Moon's gut and neck, the way he'd been taught. Blood flew. Warm viscera struck Pratt in the face.

Moon never uttered a word.

Slowly, ever so slowly, Eric got to his feet. He stood over the body panting, blood dripping from his hands and mouth. Ginger looked up from the floor.

"Eric?"

Eric crumbled and crawled into her arms, mewling.

CHAPTER 66

Pratt ran to Cass. Two holes in her torso oozed blood. One was in her abdomen near the right side. The other was up under the armpit. Pratt felt for a pulse in her neck. It was barely there. She opened her eyes and tried to smile.

"Hold me, Pratt," she croaked.

Pratt took her head on his lap, bent over her so that his lips brushed her hair.

"Hang on baby," he whispered. "Help is on the way."

"Don't shit a shitter, Pratt. Is he dead?"

Pratt glanced over at Ginger and Eric holding one another on the floor.

"Ginger's son showed up and took care of Moon."

"Eric is here?" A bubble of blood appeared at the corner of her mouth. She smelled of mimosa.

Pratt nodded. "Don't speak. Save your breath."

"I'm cold, Pratt."

He looked around. The blanket from the sofa. "Wait here."

Pratt got up and quickly fetched the blanket. When he returned Cass was dead. Pratt covered her with the blanket and knelt next to her.

"Fuck me," he said to himself.

Pratt was grateful for the dark. It hid his tears.

The hail stopped. The rain stopped. Pratt found a flashlight behind the bar. He flicked it on the slumped figure of Munz, whose head lay at an odd angle to his body. Moon had broken his neck.

Stuart lay where he had fallen. That left only Foucalt unaccounted for. Pratt had no doubt they'd find his body in the woods.

Pratt knelt next to Ginger. He looked at the pathetic creature she held in her arms. Eric's mouth was streaked with gore. "You remember me? Josh Pratt?"

Eric spoke in a lugubrious honk, "*I remember . . .*"

"You tracked Moon?"

"*I followed his scent.*"

A brief image appeared in Pratt's head of an old pick-up truck rolling across the prairie, an explosion of fury in the driver's seat.

In cars on highways? Through the air?

Pratt helped Ginger to her feet and up two sets of stairs to her bedroom. Although she felt too light it wasn't easy. He had to support most of her body weight. The boy couldn't help—there wasn't room. He followed, snuffling. They put her to bed and she collapsed immediately into a deep sleep.

"Come on," Pratt said. "You must be hungry."

He could hear the boy's stomach growling as he went back down the stairs and into the kitchen. The sudden harsh glare of fluorescents pinned them as power was restored. Eric covered his eyes and moaned. Pratt skipped to the wall and turned off the lights. The clock on the microwave blinked 12:00 over and over. The refrigerator hummed.

Pratt found some baked ham in a Tupperware container, put it on a plate, got out a fork and knife and set it on the island counter. "Go ahead. Dig in."

Eric seized the piece of meat in both hands and ate it like an apple with a growling, slurping sound, crouching over his food and staring defiantly at Pratt beneath his shaggy mane. The sky began to clear. A slice of the moon poked through. Pratt leaned on one side of the counter studying the dog boy. The fur sprouting from his face and arms obscured the human being, making him a fuzzy, shambling horror.

The kind of thing you'd pay a buck to see at a carnival.

Pratt pulled out his cell phone. Still no service. He tried the Munzes' land line. Dead. If he wasn't able to get through in the next fifteen minutes he'd pack everybody into the truck and drive into Janesville.

Eric looked around hungrily. Pratt gave him an apple and a banana. After starting on the apple the boy set it down. His teeth couldn't handle it. He finished the banana.

Three sharp raps on the front door. Pratt looked through the peephole. It was a fresh deputy. Pratt opened the door.

The deputy's nameplate said Hopkins. "You folks okay in here? Storm toppled an oak right across the driveway. I had to walk."

"Then you know about the shoot-out at the end of the driveway."

"Damn shame. Ed Foster was a good man. Leaves a wife and child."

"I'm sorry. I'll pray for him." He heard sirens in the distance. Pratt glanced at the Flintstone car. "You didn't look in the car?"

The deputy followed Pratt's glance. "No. Why?"

"Moon killed the three Flintstone ops, Nate Munz and Cass Rubio. Mrs. Munz is alive. The boy, Eric, is here. He killed Moon. Two other Bonnets got through. Your deputy killed one and I got the other."

Pratt did the math. Seven bodies. Deputy Foster made eight.

Hopkins' mouth hung open. His shoulders stiffened and he touched the radio at his shoulder. He went down the steps to the black Chrysler and stared in the window. He opened the passenger side door and looked. He quietly but firmly shut the door and, eyes on Pratt, began to fiddle with the transceiver at his shoulder. He spoke quietly and urgently for several minutes before approaching Pratt.

He looked hard at Pratt. "You look like hell. Show me the bodies."

"Officer, the boy Eric is a wild child and may have been taught to hate policemen. You won't get anything out of him. He barely speaks English."

"I'll keep that in mind."

Pratt led the way inside and down the basement stair. Ginger had taken Eric into the bedroom. Hopkins shone his flashlight first on Stuart, arrow protruding from his chest, then on Moon, who lay twisted and bleeding, torso black in the flood of blood Eric had unleashed.

Falling back on routine, the deputy checked Stuart and Moon for a pulse, busied himself with notations on a tablet.

Pratt withdrew the blinds, admitting morning light. He rapped softly on the bedroom door.

"Yes?" Ginger said in a surprisingly firm voice.

"Ginger, it's Pratt. There's a deputy out here wants to see you and the boy."

"I don't think that's a very good idea right now. Eric is very upset."

Pratt looked to the deputy.

"Ma'am," Hopkins said, "I'm just going to stick my head in for a minute to satisfy myself you're not in any danger. As long as everyone remains where they are there won't be a problem."

"Okay," Ginger said after a minute.

The deputy stuck his head in the door.

CHAPTER 67

A beautiful summer day bloomed with the arrival of four police cars, an ambulance and a fire truck. Firefighters used chainsaws to remove the fallen oak blocking the road.

The Lake County Sheriff's Department questioned Pratt for two hours while crime scene techs photographed the bodies. They recovered the Ruger to match it against holes in the wall and in Munz. They had a hard time accepting that Munz was already dead when Pratt shot him but they were just being cops. Deputies found tufts of fur clinging to the broken glass in the second-floor bedroom invaded by a falling tree. Eric had come into the house through the second-story window.

Police were dubious when Pratt explained that Eric had tracked his father across the Midwest.

"Tell me how, Pratt," Lake County Sheriff Edmund Little said, seated across from him in the dining room, recorder and notepad on the table. He wore beige khakis and a brown tie with a pig tack. His balding head and mild features, burnt by the sun, gave him the appearance of a toasted acorn. "Tell me how a feral boy even survives while crossing twelve hundred miles on foot without being seen."

"Sir, I have no idea. It's no more incredible than Moon taking out three Flintstone ops in a storm. You need a child psychologist. Maybe an expert in paranormal activity."

Pratt fished in his wallet and found Morgan Teitlebaum's card. The sheriff took it, pausing to read her credentials.

"May I have this?"

"Sure."

Calloway appeared in the door, nodded at Little and winked at Pratt.

DEA agent Barlin arrived at eight-fifteen and went immediately to view Moon's corpse. The coroner had already sealed Moon's hands in plastic but there was no mistaking the shaved skull or the tats. Pratt couldn't resist looking. In daylight and death Moon seemed diminished. It was hard to imagine he had wreaked such damage.

A plump female deputy with a master's in psychology gently questioned Ginger, who held and stroked her boy on the bed in the guest bedroom.

By the time Morgan Teitlebaum arrived, two television crews were camped out on Makepeace Road offering the first tentative reports against a backdrop of massed police vehicles and law enforcement officers. Someone switched on the flat-screen TV in the den. News reporters characterized the crime as a "mass slaying" by a "disgruntled former boyfriend of Mrs. Munz who may have been active in a methamphetamine ring."

Teitlebaum spoke with police for a half hour before introducing herself to Ginger and Eric. Taking the deputy's place, she closed the door behind her. Teitlebaum remained in the room with mother and child for two hours.

The police finished questioning Pratt at eleven forty-five. He was free to go but chose to remain until Teitlebaum came out of the room. Agent Barlin found Pratt on the back deck helping to clear storm debris.

"The DEA is offering a reward for information leading to the breakup of a major drug ring."

"That would be the boy's," Pratt said, using pruning shears he'd found in the garage. "How's Mrs. Munz?"

"She left in the ambulance a half hour ago. She wanted to stay but she's having some kind of flare-up that requires hospitalization."

"And the kid?"

"Still in the bedroom with the shrink. Jesus Christ, Pratt. Every time I see you, you look worse than the last. Maybe you ought to go to the emergency room."

"I just want to sleep."

"You're free to go as far as I'm concerned. You have my card? You need me for anything just give me a holler."

"Thanks, Barlin."

"Stay out of trouble."

Pratt threaded his way out front, where he found Calloway talking to the Lake County sheriff. Little shook Pratt's hand.

"Son, you done a good thing, busting up this meth ring. Very sorry for your loss."

For a moment Pratt went blank.

Cass.

They were talking about Cass. Numbly, he looked around. Cass' truck remained at the curb. He couldn't just take it. He looked at Calloway.

"I need a ride."

Calloway nodded. "Let's go."

Pratt slid in the passenger side of the city's Crown Vic. By the time they reached the end of the driveway he was asleep.

CHAPTER 68

Calloway poked Pratt on the leg. "Wake up."

Pratt blinked himself awake and saw that they were in his driveway. He opened the car door and swung his legs out.

"Mind if I come in with you, see what Moon might have left?"

Pratt pulled himself to his feet with the door frame. "No. Come on."

Pratt fumbled with his keys. The nap had only served to focus his exhaustion. He got the door open and stumbled into the living room. He collapsed on the sofa. Calloway followed him into the house and went room to room. When he had finished the first floor he went down the stairs to the basement.

Before Pratt went to prison and found Christ, he never would have permitted a cop anywhere near his home, warrant or not. But Calloway was different. Calloway had showed respect. And Pratt had nothing to hide. The only evidence of sin was a half-empty bottle of Wild Turkey in the kitchen cabinet and a roach Cass had left in his bedroom.

Pratt's cell phone sang. He reached into his pocket, didn't recognize the number, and turned it off.

Calloway was a long time in the basement.

Pratt was sound asleep on the leather sofa when Calloway came back upstairs. Calloway quietly let himself out and shut the door.

Steady knocking woke Pratt. He checked his watch. It was four o'clock. He sat up, parted the blinds and looked out the window. There was a WMAD news van at the curb. A familiar-looking news babe and her cameraman were at the door.

Pratt opened the door.

"Mr. Pratt, I'm Sonia Tyrell from WMAD News. What part did you play in the death of alleged drug kingpin Eugene Moon?"

The camera guy replaced his head with the camera. Pratt flipped them the bird and shut the door. The pounding resumed.

With an inarticulate noise of animal desperation, Pratt headed for the basement. The spare bedroom in the basement was in the rear of the house. When he shut the door he couldn't hear the knocking. Pratt flopped down on the bed and pulled the pillow over his head.

Now the rush of blood through his head kept him awake. He'd arrived at that stage of exhaustion where he was jazzed by everything that had happened. Too much nervous energy to sleep. He considered talking to the news crew, but they'd get it all wrong anyway and he didn't trust himself not to play the fool.

He didn't know what to do. It was the type of situation that cried out for Bloom. Pratt was drained, running on fumes. The reserve tank was empty.

He flipped the TV on with the remote. The five o'clock news was on in five minutes. Pratt went into the bathroom, relieved himself and splashed cold water on his face. Back in the bedroom he flopped on the bed.

The storm led the news. Tornado touched down in northern Illinois, two people missing and feared dead. The Munz massacre was next. A helicopter view showed myriad police and emergency vehicles jamming the broad turn-around in front of the house.

The voiceover sounded like the info babe at the front door. "The Lake County sheriff says alleged drug kingpin Eugene Moon used the cover of the storm to attack this residence. Five people are dead, including the couple who lived here and three Flintstone Security agents who had been hired to protect them. Sheriff Edmund Little will hold a news conference tomorrow at nine a.m. to discuss the killings. In the meantime they are withholding the names of the dead pending notification of next of kin."

The view changed to the front of Pratt's house. "According to Sheriff Little, private investigator Joshua Pratt triggered the series of events culminating in the horrific tragedy. The couple who lived at the murder house allegedly hired Pratt to locate a missing child.

"Earlier today we tried to speak to Mr. Pratt . . ."

Pratt watched himself flipping the bird on TV. A black dot covered his finger. Pratt turned it off.

Danny, Danny, what do I do about these jackals?

Pratt's stomach yowled. He went upstairs, through the kitchen to the living room, and peeked through the blinds. No news vans. He went into the kitchen and opened the freezer, surveying the field of Marie Callender and Stouffer's. Lasagna was always a good bet. He zapped it in the microwave and popped a Point.

Pratt turned the microwave container upside down over a chipped plate, took his meal and beer out on the back deck. It was dusk and the woods twinkled with thousands of fireflies. Mosquitoes dive-bombed Pratt until he got up and switched on the yellow lights. A raccoon scurried through the brush.

Through the trees to his left Pratt could make out the ribs of another McMansion rising from the soil. The whole neighborhood was on the chopping block. It was only a matter of time before somebody offered him a half mil for his home and lot. Well he'd cross that bridge when it came to him.

Pratt took his dish into the kitchen, laid it in the sink and went into the bathroom to apply Chiggerex to his mosquito bites. He was still exhausted but a toothed edge of raw anxiety sawed at his soul. There was always the Wild Turkey.

No. He didn't want to wake up tomorrow with a dirty sock in his mouth. TV was crap. Chaplain Dorgan said, when all else fails, read. There was always the Bible. He went into his bedroom to get it and his eyes fell to a pile of sky blue cotton beneath the bed.

Cass' panties.

The sky fell. He was overwhelmed by a sense of loss so keen it threatened to obliterate him. He couldn't breathe. Something had sucked all the air out of the room. Too late he realized what he should have known.

She had really loved him.

She had given her life for him.

Pratt sank to the floor and moaned in misery. He stayed that way for a long time, thinking about the guns in his safe.

CHAPTER 69

The knocking woke him. Pratt lay in bed twisted up in the sheets like a croissant. At some point he must have gotten off the floor and fallen asleep. Making a pit stop Pratt padded barefoot through the house, wearing only pants. The cable box told him it was 7:45 in the morning.

Sun glared in through the blinds. Pratt didn't have to look. He knew who it was. He opened the door on three separate clusters of news people, two from local affiliates and one from CBS.

Without Danny he was lost.

"Mr. Pratt! What can you tell us about the so-called 'dog boy?'"

"Mr. Pratt! How were you able to locate Eugene Moon when the FBI and DEA couldn't?"

Across the street Lowry came out on his front porch, folded his arms and watched. George and Gracie charged the curb, barking hysterically.

Sonia Tyrell was back, inching forward with her mike and cameraman. Pratt had played his biker card and was smart enough to realize he had to make a living. If he didn't manage his image, they would. He had to say something. He held his hands up palms out and there was a sudden bristling among the media as their antennae quivered.

George and Gracie barked and barked.

"Folks, Mrs. Munz hired me to find her son, Eric. I was able to find the father through my connections and he turned out to be a full-blown psychopath. Had I known it would end like this I might have reconsidered. What happened yesterday was a tragedy that didn't have to happen. Moon should have been brought to justice years ago."

All yammered at once. Sonia elbowed her way to the front and stuck her mike in Pratt's face. "What connections?"

"My connections with motorcycle clubs."

"Don't you mean gangs, Mr. Pratt? Weren't you a member of the Bedouins and didn't you serve six years at Waupun for various offenses including aggravated assault and trafficking in guns?"

"That's all true, Sonia, but with the help of my Lord and Savior Jesus Christ, I have put my past behind me. I now walk in the light of the Lord."

Sonia rolled her eyes. Pratt smiled.

The crowd squawked. Pratt tamped them down. "Folks, that's all I'm going to say. I say any more I might embarrass myself. Good morning and God bless."

Some of them got it but they yelled anyway. Pratt went inside and shut the door.

He found his cell phone on the coffee table in the living room next to the V-twin engine. He turned the phone back on. He had fifteen phone calls, some with voice messages, mostly from news organizations. He listened to his messages. Two were from Trans-Continental asking him to call at any time. One from Ginger. "Call me, Pratt. You brought my boy back to me and I want to thank you."

She sounded weak but happy. She was better prepared than most to deal with tragedy. He wanted to call back but she was probably sleeping. He wanted to speak to Teitlebaum but it was too early. He wanted to call a lot of people. As far as Pratt was concerned the only advantage to living in California was you could call anybody on the East Coast as soon as you woke up.

Pratt went into the kitchen and made breakfast with English muffins, cream cheese, a banana, an apple, and yogurt. He mixed a killer pot of coffee. He got up, went to the living room, bent at the knees and lifted the V-twin off the asbestos pad, carrying it like a kung fu acolyte into the garage, where he gently maneuvered it into the custom frame he'd commissioned from Thunder Mountain Harley Davidson in Fort Collins.

At nine he phoned Teitlebaum, got her box. He phoned Calloway.

"Calloway."

"What's going on?"

"Dude from the university took samples for a DNA test. The boy and Ginger just left for University Hospital. You can probably catch 'em there in a couple of hours. You're in line for a DEA cash reward."

"How much?"

"Ten Gs."

"You're shitting me."

"It's real. I gotta go. Talk atcha later."

Pratt called Trans-Continental. They wanted him to recover the three missing Desmos and offered five thousand per machine, including the one he'd already found.

The Ducatis could be anywhere. Pratt told them he'd think about it.

Somebody opened his unlocked front door. "Josh?" It was Lowry, sent by his wife to make sure everything was all right.

"Come in, Dave."

Lowry went up to Pratt and embraced him like a long-lost brother. Pratt was shocked. It's what a biker would have done. "Josh, I'm so sorry for your loss. If there's anything Helen and I can do, please don't hesitate to let us know."

"Thanks, Dave."

"You need a place to hide out, come on over."

"I appreciate that, Dave. Would you like a cup of coffee?"

They took their coffee out on the back deck. The sound of hammers and saws drifted through the trees.

"That was a fine thing you did, putting Morgan together with that boy."

"You have any kids, Dave?"

"Carson, she's just starting with a big law firm in Chicago. And Blake, he's twenty-two, he's at the Air Force Academy in Colorado Springs. Do you?"

"None that I know of," Pratt automatically answered.

"You see things differently when you're a parent," Lowry said.

"I guess."

"Welp, I got a tee time. I'll be seeing you."

"Thanks, Dave."

Lowry let himself out. Pratt went for a ride around New Glarus, grabbed a brat at the New Glarus Apple Orchard, got home around two, spent the rest of the day in the garage without his cell phone working on the basket-case Harley. He watched some *Ultimate Fighter* reruns and turned in around ten.

Pratt got up at seven, finished off the muffins and went for a jog slower than his usual pace due to injuries. All the stitches held. Back at the ranch he showered and continued to work on the basket case.

Pratt's phone hummed. It was Ginger. It was ten a.m. She sounded weak.

"What up?" Pratt answered.

"I need to see you, Josh. Can you come down here?"

CHAPTER 70

Pratt saddled up the Road King and hit the highway, stopping for breakfast at a Burger King on the Beltline. Ginger was back on Makepeace Road. Her sister-in-law Gwen, Nate's sister, was with her. Behind Gwen's Porsche Cayenne sat a black Chrysler 300 identical to the one in which Bonner had died. Behind the Chrysler was a van with "BEST GLASS" stenciled on the side. Behind the van was a pickup truck that said, "HARRISON TREE SERVICE." Pratt heard sawing and pounding.

Pratt went through the open front door. A vinyl runner had been set on the hardwood floor and stairway to protect them from the workmen's boots. A man in coveralls came down the stairs carrying a paper bag filled with broken glass. He nodded at Pratt.

Pratt found Ginger and Gwen on the deck seated at a round table with an overarching umbrella tilted toward the late-morning sun. Ginger relaxed on a chaise lounge wearing loose-fitting cotton trousers and a beige blouse, one hand resting lightly on her stomach. Gwen, a matronly redhead, sat with her elbows on the table going through a stack of papers. Two tree guys sawed up a fallen limb in the yard.

Ginger waved but did not get up. "Josh. Thank you for coming." She introduced him to Gwen, who stood and hugged him. She was one of those women who unself-consciously hugged people whom she liked.

Pratt sat. "Where's Eric?"

"Morgan took him to University Hospital," Ginger said. "They're going to see what they can do about his spine, his hair, his skin and his teeth."

Pratt thought about the basket-case Harley. He'd been working on it for years.

"The funeral's tomorrow at Redeemer Episcopal Church in Janesville."

Pratt took out his pad and made a note. "What did you want to see me about?"

"Morgan rushed the DNA test through the school. Eric is not my son."

"What?"

Ginger looked adrift. "He's not my son. He's not Eric."

Pratt looked at the trees. "Jesus."

"Pratt, I want you to continue looking for Eric."

"Ginger, I wouldn't know where to start. I had one idea. I'm not that good a detective."

Ginger sat up and gripped Pratt's knee with a steely claw. "Now you listen to me, Pratt. You darn near accomplished the impossible. You found that boy and you removed an evil man. You're a better detective than you know. I have faith in you. Please. Give it one week. Money is not an object."

"What about the boy?"

Ginger breathed deeply. "I'm adopting him."

"You know you're never going to have a normal relationship with him."

"Maybe so but I feel at least partly responsible. I should have stopped Moon years ago before all this happened. Besides, what else am I going to do? Nate turned me into a creature of leisure, a lady who lunches. I have the money, the time and the love that boy needs. He responds to me, and he feels love. He may never lead a normal life but he might have a chance at happiness."

"What are you going to call him? He's used to Eric."

"That's what I'll call him." Ginger reached down to something at her side and handed it to Pratt. It was an envelope.

Pratt opened it up. Another ten thousand. "Ginger, the first check was more than enough."

"Shut up and take it. I'll be very pissed if you don't take that check."

Pratt put his hands up and put the check in his billfold. "Yes ma'am. I do have one idea."

CHAPTER 71

One week later on a Monday morning Pratt arrived at Dane County Airport in the company of a tall, handsome high school student named Mario Echeverria. Pratt paid for the taxi to his place, sixty bucks.

"Make yourself at home, Mario. I got to make a phone call. We'll leave in a half hour."

"Okay, Josh."

The kid was polite to a fault, had a grade-point average of 3.7 and was starting quarterback for the South Latin High School Marauders.

Pratt phoned Ginger.

"Well Josh. What's going on?"

"It's Monday morning, time for my report. I'd like to deliver it in person if you don't mind."

"You want to drive down here?" Ginger said in a hushed voice. She was afraid to ask the next question.

"Just wait until we get there. We should be there around twelve-thirty."

Pratt found Mario in the garage ogling his bikes.

"Go on—have a seat. You ever ride?"

"No sir," the boy responded, swinging a leg over the Road King's two-tone tank. "My parents would shit a brick if I bought a motorcycle."

"You ax 'em?"

Mario gripped the midrise bars. "Yeah. 'Not if you want me to pay for college!'" he said in a dead-on impersonation of his father.

"He who pays the piper calls the tune. Let's roll. Pretty sure she's gonna feed us."

They got into Pratt's ten-year-old Honda Accord and headed south, arriving at the Makepeace Road residence at twelve-fifteen. Gwen's Cayenne sat in the drive. Pratt parked behind her in the shade of the portico. Pratt lifted the heavy brass knocker and let it fall. Seconds later he heard footsteps approaching on the hardwood floor. The door opened and there stood Gwen with fresh lipstick and an expectant look.

She peered around Pratt at the boy. "Is that him?" she said quietly.

Pratt shrugged. "We won't know until they test. Where's Ginger?"

"She's out on the deck. She'd have greeted you herself but she's feeling a little weak today. Hello, young man. I'm Gwen."

"Mario Echeverria. Pleased to meet you." They shook hands. Gwen led the way down the hall to the deck.

Ginger sat up in her chaise as they appeared, tried to get to her feet, staggered. Pratt ran over and steadied her. Mario came up and smiled.

"Hi."

Ginger stared at the boy a minute. The resemblance was undeniable. Her eyes filled with tears. She hesitantly offered a hand and then fell on Mario, hugging him tightly. Most boys would have been acutely embarrassed but this kid kept his cool. He hugged her back.

"I don't know if you're my birth mother or not but I think maybe you are."

Sniffling, Ginger pushed herself back and smiled. "I think so too."

Gwen tapped Pratt on the shoulder. "Help me with lunch."

Pratt followed her into the kitchen, where she began to unload sliced deli meat and cheese from the refrigerator onto a big platter. "How on earth did you find him?"

"Moon said he'd placed the boy with a wealthy Cuban couple in Miami. I went to Miami and contacted every Cuban American agency

I could, especially those dealing with families. I looked for male babies adopted sixteen years ago. At first the agencies were reluctant to help but when I explained where I was coming from they enthusiastically agreed. I went armed with news stories.

"Felipe and Isabel adopted Mario at two months—exactly the time he was stolen. They admitted to me privately that they paid a baby broker five thousand dollars. There's nothing anybody can do about it now. Of course they still have to run a test."

They looked out the window. Ginger and Mario were deep in conversation, knee to knee.

CHAPTER 72

Morgan Teitlebaum's office was in the Psych Department in the Humanities Building, a Borg-like hive built in the seventies. Pratt parked the Road King in the State Street parking lot and walked. It was the first time he'd ridden since the storm.

Teitlebaum's office was on the sixth floor. The narrow concrete corridors were lined with bulletin boards filled with Psych Department notices, yard sales, kittens, cartoons and humorous posters. The heavy oak door to Teitlebaum's office was open.

"Come in Josh," Teitlebaum said from her seat at the gun sight window, rotating an old oak office chair away from an antique roll-up desk. Behind her was a computer stand with computer. The bulletin board on the wall looked like a tossed paper salad with pictures and notices peeking out from six layers. There was a Karastan carpet on the floor, a bronze and ceramic hookah mounted on a cherrywood planter and a framed picture of Einstein sticking out his tongue.

Pratt sat on the old cloth sofa, which looked as if it had come from student moving day.

"Would you like an iced tea?" Teitlebaum said.

"Sure. How's it going?"

Teitlebaum bent to open a cube fridge, from which she removed two trendy green teas, handing one to Pratt. "Well the good news is that I've created a rapport with Eric and he is learning to trust me. That will take time. Trust is always the first casualty in bad parenting."

Pratt snorted. "Bad parenting."

"Yes, well this is an extreme case. Mostly he sits in his room and listens to songs on his iPod. He's especially fond of the Electric Light Orchestra. We did have to sedate him once, to shave the fur. As you can imagine, his skin is covered with lesions. He's responding well to antibiotics. The next step will be to get him into a dentist chair. He has some verbal skills and that puts us miles ahead."

"Any idea who he is?"

"No. We've sent a DNA sample to the NCIC but that's a long shot. He could be anybody. Thousands of children disappear every year in this country. Some never get reported."

"That's hard to believe."

"So it is. I'm not saying he's about to get a job. He'll be in therapy for the rest of his life, I suspect, and may never overcome his mistrust of strangers and men in particular."

"What I want to know, Doc, is how he tracked Moon. I don't believe it was by scent. You don't just stick your snout in the air and smell somebody two hundred miles away in a car."

"I wondered about that too and have only a tentative explanation, which we will be investigating for years to come. Did you know our Defense Department has been conducting paranormal activity tests since the fifties?"

"Whooo-EEE-ooo," Pratt intoned.

"The Soviets began a crash program in '53 to develop 'mind reader' spies. We got wind of it and soon we had our own program trying to develop precognition, telepathy, telekinetics and clairvoyance. The Army has a program called 'Silent Talk' in which soldiers will communicate telepathically on the battlefield. They hope.

"Now I don't have any better understanding of these phenomena than you. I'm not sure they even exist. But I'm not sure they don't exist, either. Is it possible that Eric and Moon formed a telepathic bond? I don't know. But consider that Moon was the only person with whom

Eric came in contact . . . I'm not certain of that but getting that boy to talk is like pulling teeth. Bad analogy. We can be sure that they had an unusually intense relationship, particularly while Moon was grafting pieces of animal fur to the boy's skin.

Maybe Eric was able to track Moon because he had a mind image in his brain of what Moon saw, of Moon's surroundings.

"There is ample anecdotal and empirical evidence that telepathy is real. I've got reams of material. Right now that's the best I can do."

Pratt thought about the presence he felt whenever he talked to Eric, and why Teitlebaum didn't feel it.

"You don't feel sometimes he's communicating with you via telepathy?"

Teitlebaum's bright blue eyes widened. "Why no. Do you?"

"No."

Teitlebaum shrugged and took a slug of tea.

"God works in mysterious ways," Pratt said.

"Amen."

They sat in companionable silence for a minute.

"Whelp," Pratt said rising, "thanks for your time, Doc."

"Any time. If you want to see Eric, we can arrange that but for now I don't think he's comfortable in the company of men."

"I understand."

"What are you working on?"

"I have to find some stolen bikes."

"The tabs are going to be on your ass like a hawk on a June bug. Are you ready for that? You might want to get a lawyer to deal with the shit storm headed your way. I could recommend someone if you like."

"Thanks, Doc. I'd appreciate that."

CHAPTER 73

On September 4 Pratt went for a run. He ran all the way to County PB and back.

It was five-thirty by the time he returned to Ptarmigan Road. Mc-Mansions sprouted on both side of his modest ranch, a pair of lions guarding a mutt. Pratt's yard was overgrown with weeds. Vines crawled up the sides and into the window slots of his Camaro. The only reason the Lowrys hadn't complained was because they were now friends. Louise was picking up his mail.

Pratt didn't doubt that whoever moved in on either side of him would waste no time forming a neighborhood association and declaring his domicile unfit.

Pratt let himself in, opened windows and took a shower. He had a frozen pizza for dinner. After dinner he cracked a Capital lager, went out on his deck. The fireflies were still at it. Looked like Indian summer, at least for a while. Pratt phoned Teitlebaum.

"Teitlebaum," she answered.

"Doc, it's Pratt. How's Eric?"

"We are making steady progress," she said guardedly. "He carries on conversations and makes himself understood. Better yet, he understands others. Physically he's still in a lot of pain. His physical therapist is helping with the spine but several discs are gone and they're talking about an operation. We did get him to sit still for the dentist and they're making him a new set of choppers. He asked about you."

"He did?"

"He said, 'Where's Pratt?'"

"You're shittin' me."

"I shit thee not."

"Can I see him?"

Short pause. "How about you come by tomorrow afternoon around two. You know where Nakoma State is? Ask for the K Building. I'll tell the main desk. There's a fenced enclosure in back where we'll be. Walk around so that you're outside the fence. We'll let him have a look at you and decide for himself if he wants to see you."

Pratt fell asleep to *Antiques Roadshow*.

CHAPTER 74

September 7 was a Thursday. There was a hint of frost in the air, oak leaves turning crimson. Pratt rode his Road King clockwise around the north shore of Lake Mendota toward Nakoma State, the psychiatric and rehabilitation hospital on the northeast side.

Pratt parked in the visitor's lot and headed for the administration building. Nakoma State looked more like a college campus than a holding facility for the criminally insane, in which capacity it had functioned since its founding in 1954. Ed Gein was its most famous alumnus. Broad, sloping lawns led down to blue Lake Mendota, Governor's Island extending off a small peninsula like a dew claw.

The buildings were made of blond brick, fifties modern, one-story with flat roofs. Pratt went up three concrete steps to the entrance, let himself in through the glass double doors. Inside was a desk with a smiling, middle-aged secretary, and several benches, each with a coffee table covered with the usual institutional magazines: *JAMA, National Geo, Style*. Ceiling fans lazily stirred the air.

Pratt went to the counter.

"Yes sir?" the woman said.

"I'm Josh Pratt. Dr. Teitlebaum said she'd leave a note about me observing Eric, uh, Munz. The wild boy."

The woman nodded, her rimless glasses momentarily reflecting the morning sun. "I'll have one of our custodians take you to them. Please have a seat."

Pratt sat beneath a painting showing a cornfield and a red barn. He picked up a copy of *People* and read about the Kardashian sisters, who were famous for some reason that escaped him. There was an article about a woman who survived an acid attack and suddenly he realized it was only a matter of time *People* came after Eric.

And him.

He had a new phone to escape the tab hounds and badgers. The front door opened and a man wearing an institutional gray jumpsuit, his hair a rat's nest of flying blond tresses, came up to him. The nameplate on his breast said Sykes. He smelled of the outdoors.

"Mr. Pratt?"

Pratt looked up. The man had piercing blue eyes and the lean bones of an athlete. "I'm Norbert Sykes. Dr. Teitlebaum asked me to escort you back."

Pratt flipped the mag on the table, stood, and shook hands. "Great."

Sykes led the way to a locked door, which he opened with a key card. They walked down a spotless, disinfectant-smelling corridor past several offices, some with caseworkers. At the back of the building Sykes opened another door and they exited into the crisp fall air. Following a concrete path that wound through the park-like setting, they headed toward a building set a little ways off from the others at the north end of the compound.

Pratt saw faculty eating lunch at a picnic table, people he took to be patients. Some smoked cigarettes. Sykes led the way to a one-story red brick building with green shutters. A rectangle-shaped area enclosed by a five-foot chain-link fence extended toward the lake. Sykes stopped a hundred feet from the building and held up his hand.

"There they are," he said in a hushed voice.

Pratt looked at the enclosure. Teitlebaum sat on a concrete bench—Pratt guessed there would be a dedication plaque behind her—while Eric sat on the ground facing her at an angle so he could see the cerulean blue lake. His profile had changed. Most of the fur was gone and he sported a shaved skull.

"No sudden movements, no loud noises," Sykes said softly. "If there's any trouble Dr. Teitlebaum will know what to do."

"Have you had any trouble with him?"

"No, only his weird howling at night. Dr. Teitlebaum got him a white noise generator and he stopped."

With a slight wave Sykes turned and left. Pratt leaned against a mature oak and watched. Teitlebaum smiled and spoke, too far away for Pratt to hear. Eric gestured and it seemed so natural, so utterly human that Pratt thought a miracle had occurred. But he knew that was impossible. From time to time Eric appeared agitated and Teitlebaum would reach forward and touch him on the head or shoulder.

Teitlebaum looked up and saw Pratt, her face breaking into a big smile. She looked at Eric and pointed over his shoulder. Pratt walked toward the fence. Eric shifted around on his hands and Pratt could see that his arms and biceps were extremely well developed. Blue eyes in the sandblasted young-old face fixed on Pratt.

Eric smiled.

The words popped into Pratt's head as Eric spoke.

"Squeaky toy."

CPSIA information can be obtained
at www.ICGtesting.com
Printed in the USA
BVOW08s1433141216

470805BV00002B/160/P